She fluttered her right hand back down past his eye and along his cheekbone, and when she couldn't delay the moment of truth a moment longer quickly traced her middle finger across his *'I'm told I have kissable'* lips.

They parted just slightly before she could leave them, and breath heated her finger-pads for half a heartbeat.

'So there you go,' Elliott rumbled, then cleared his throat. 'Now you've really seen me. You know how I sound, how I smell and how I feel. That's pretty much all your available senses taken care of.'

'Well,' she began, 'I haven't—'

Stop!

'You haven't what?'

His voice, his breath, seemed impossibly closer, yet he hadn't moved the rest of his body one inch.

'Nothing. Never mind.'

'Were you going to say tasted?'

'No.' The denial sounded false even to her.

'Really?' His soft voice was full of a smile. 'Because it sounded like you were.'

'No. That would be an inappropriate comment to make in the workplace.'

'I agree,' Elliott murmured. 'Then again, that ship sailed when I asked you to touch my face, so what else do I have to lose?'

His lips—the ones she'd gone to so much trouble to avoid touching—pressed lightly onto Laney's, half open, soft and damp and warm, before moulding more snugly against her. Sealing up the gaps.

Elliott Garvey was *kissing* her.

AWAKENED
BY HIS TOUCH

BY
NIKKI LOGAN

Nikki Logan lives next to a string of protected wetlands in Western Australia, with her long-suffering partner and a menagerie of furred, feathered and scaly mates. She studied film and theatre at university, and worked for years in advertising and film distribution before finally settling down in the wildlife industry. Her romance with nature goes way back, and she considers her life charmed, given she works with wildlife by day and writes fiction by night—the perfect way to combine her two loves.

Nikki believes that the passion and risk of falling in love are perfectly mirrored in the danger and beauty of wild places. Every romance she writes contains an element of nature, and if readers catch a waft of rich earth or the spray of wild ocean between the pages she knows her job is done.

For Jackie—protector of all creatures great and small.
(No bees were harmed during the making of this book)

CHAPTER ONE

ELLIOTT GARVEY LEANED on the bleached timber boardwalk like a seasoned stalker, watching the woman frolicking with her dog where the coastal rock slid down into the aquamarine ocean.

It didn't matter that this lookout and the long, sandy path leading to it were public, the map in his hands and the occasional sign wired to the fence lining the gravel track in this remote, picturesque spot reminded him very clearly that the property all around him was upper-case P private. So, technically, was the beach below. In fact, it barely qualified as a beach since—private or not—it was only about twenty metres long. More a cove, really, eroded out of the hard rock either side of it, protected and quiet.

Back home they'd have turned this into a boat-launching area, for sure. It was perfect for it.

Then again, back home they wouldn't have had anything even remotely like this. Where he was from, further north up the coast, the ruling landform was sand, not the stunning limestone rock forms of the Morgan property. The lookout under his feet 'looked out' over the cove about twenty metres away, as it happened, but its intended view was the spectacular Australian coastline beyond it. Rugged and raw and beaten to death by pounding seas in the off season.

But today the sea was flat and gentle.

His eyes dropped again.

Judging by the very determined way the woman was *not* looking up at him, she was either trying very hard to pretend he wasn't there, spoiling her serenity, or she wasn't supposed to be there. A tourist, maybe? That would explain the long cotton dress that she'd hiked up her bare legs instead of the swimsuit a local would have turned up in. And clearly this was a tourist who liked to travel with her dog. The soggy golden retriever bounded around her, barking and celebrating life in a shower of droplets, and the size of the lead bundled in the woman's right hand suggested her dog was a handful most of the time. But right now it just circled her excitedly as she danced.

Danced? More flowed, really. She practically ebbed in time with the soft waves washing onto the beach and retreating again, her feet lightly skipping in the wet sand. The wet bottom of her long summer dress wanted to cling to her legs, but she kept it hiked up, out of the way, as she splashed in and out of the water with her movements. Dipping and twisting and undulating her whole body to music he couldn't hear.

Out of nowhere, a memory surged into his crowded mind. Of him and his mother, the only trip they'd ever taken away from the city when he was about eight. He'd hung his lean little body half out of the open window of the car she'd borrowed from a friend, overwhelmed to be doing something as exciting as leaving the city, hand-surfing on the wind that whipped past. Riding the current, rising and dipping on it with both hands. Dreaming of the places it would take him if only he were light enough to catch its updraft.

Just as that woman was dancing. There was no wind to speak of down below in the protected little cove, but that didn't seem to cause her the slightest trouble as she moved on air currents no one else could feel. Not him. Not the still coastal wildflowers lining the tiny sandy strip. Not the barely interrupted surface of the water.

Just her, her dog and whatever the heck drugs she must be on to put her in such a sublimely happy place.

Elliott used his camera lens to get a surreptitious look at her while pretending to photograph the bigger view. Her long hair was as wet and stringy as the golden retriever's, and not

all that different in colour, and the water from it soaked anywhere it touched: the fabric of her strappy dress where it criss-
crossed her breasts like a bikini top, the golden stretch of her
bare shoulders, her collarbones. It whipped and snapped as she
circled in the retreating water, her head tipped back to worship
the sun, staring right up into it for a moment.

He adjusted the lens just slightly.

The paleness of her skin and the liberal dusting of freckles
across it fitted perfectly with the strawberry blonde hair. Maybe
if she did this less often out in the harsh Western Australian sun
she'd have fewer marks on her skin. But then, maybe if she did
this less often she wouldn't have that smile on her face, either.
Blazing and almost too wide for the pointed shape of her jaw.

He lowered the lens and stepped back, conscious, suddenly,
of his intrusion into her private moment. As he did so, the
weathered timber under his left foot creaked audibly and the
retriever's sharp ears didn't miss it. Its sandy snout pointed
up in his direction immediately, joyous barking suspended,
and it crossed straight to the woman's side. She stopped and
bent to place her free hand reassuringly on the dog's shoulder
but—luckily for Elliott—she didn't follow the direction of its
intent stare.

Not waiting to be busted, he retreated down the lookout
steps and along the path to the gravel track where his luxury
car waited. The only car here, he suddenly realised.

Ah, well, if Little Miss Lives-Life-on-the-Edge liked to take
that skin outside at noon, trespass on private property and stare
directly into the sun, then she was probably illegally camped
around here somewhere, too.

Either way…? Officially none of his business. He was here
to talk the Morgans into taking their company global. Not to
police their perimeter security for them.

He had one more shot at this. One more chance to eclipse
bloody Tony Newton and his questionable success and get the
vacant partnership. Being good—or even great—at your job
was no longer enough. He needed to be *astounding* at what he

did in order to win his spot on the partners' board and cement his future. And Morgan's was the brand to do it. Newton was too busy schmoozing his cashed-up tech and dot-com clients to notice what was right under all their noses—that Morgan's was about so much more than honey. Whether the board realised it or not.

And if they didn't…?

That was okay. That was what they had him for.

'What is a "realiser" exactly, Mr Garvey?' Ellen Morgan asked him politely an hour later, studying his slick business card.

Falling straight into his corporate patter was second nature. 'Realisers are charged with the responsibility of identifying clients with potential and then helping them *realise* that potential.'

'That's a strange sort of job, I'd have thought,' announced Robert Morgan as he marched into the living room with two cups of coffee to match the one his wife already cradled and handed one to Elliott.

'It's a speciality role. A different focus to my colleagues'.'

Ellen didn't quite bristle, but offence tickled at the edges of her words. 'You believe we have unrealised potential here, Mr Garvey? We consider ourselves quite innovative for our industry.'

'Please, call me Elliott,' he repeated, despite knowing it was probably pointless. He wasn't in with them yet. 'You absolutely *are* innovative. You dominate the local market and you're top three nationally—' if they weren't a company like Ashmore Coolidge wouldn't touch them '—and yet there's always room for growth.'

And profit. And acclaim. Particularly acclaim.

'We're honey farmers, Mr Garvey. One of a multitude in the international marketplace. I'm not sure there's room for us overseas.'

As if that was all they were, and as if their operations weren't perched on one of the most stunning and sought-after peninsulas on Western Australia's ten-thousand-kilometre coastline.

But it wasn't the local market that interested him. 'My job is to help you make room.'

'By nudging someone else out?' Ellen frowned.

'By being competitive. And ethical. And visible.' Currently they were only a twofer.

'You think the enormous sun on our packaging fails to stand out on the shelf?'

The new voice was soft, probing, and very much rhetorical… And coming from the doorway.

Elliott turned as Helena Morgan walked into the room. Ellen and Robert's daughter and reputedly the talent behind Morgan's ten-year surge to the top—

His eyes dropped to the sandy, damp golden retriever that galloped in behind her.

—and also the woman from the beach.

Of course she was.

All the rapport he'd built with the parents since arriving suddenly trembled on whether or not Helena Morgan realised he was the one who had been watching her with her wet dress clinging to her body earlier.

If she did he was dead in the water.

But she didn't comment, and she didn't even glance at him as she crossed into the kitchen, trailing elegant fingertips along the benchtop until she reached the extra coffee mug Robert Morgan had left out. For her, presumably. As tactics went, her dismissal was pretty effective.

'I'm not talking about shelf presence,' Elliott said in his best boardroom voice, eager to take back some control. 'I'm talking about market presence.'

'Wilbur!' Ellen Morgan scolded the dog, who had shoved his soggy face between her and her coffee for a pat. He wagged an unremorseful tail. 'Honestly, Laney…'

The woman made a noise halfway between a whistle and a squeak and the dog abandoned its efforts for affection and shot around the sofa and into the kitchen to stand respectfully beside Helena.

Laney.

The nickname suited her. Still feminine, but somehow... earthier.

'Our customers know exactly where to find us,' Laney defended from the kitchen.

'Do new ones?'

She paused—the reboiled kettle in one hand and two fingers of the other hooked over her coffee cup edge—and looked towards him. 'You don't think we do well enough on the ones we have?'

One Morgan parent watched her; the other watched him. And he suddenly got the feeling he was being tested. As if everything hinged on how he managed this interaction.

'All markets change eventually,' he risked.

'And we'll change with it.'

She poured without taking her eyes off him, and his chest tightened just a hint as steam from the boiling water shimmied up past her vulnerable fingers. That was a fast track to the emergency room. But it certainly got his attention.

As it was supposed to.

'But we've never been greedy, Mr Garvey. I see no reason to start being so now.'

Her use of his name gave him the opening he needed as she walked back into the living room with her fresh coffee. 'You have the advantage of me.'

Half challenge, half criticism. And formal, but not out of place; she had a very...*regal*...air about her. The deliberate way she moved. The way she regarded him but didn't quite deign to meet his eyes.

'Apologies, Mr Garvey,' Robert interjected, 'this is our daughter and head apiarist Helena. Laney, this is Mr Elliott Garvey of Ashmore Coolidge.'

She stretched her free hand forward, but not far enough for him to reach easily. Making him come to her. Definite princess move. Then again, the Morgans did hold all the power here. For now. It was a shame he had no choice but to take the two steps needed to close his hand over her small one. And a shame his curiosity wouldn't let him not. Maybe her skin wasn't as soft as it looked.

Though it turned out it was. His fingers slid over the undulating pads of hers until their palms pressed warmly and his skin fairly pulsed at the contact.

'A financier?' she said, holding his hand longer than was appropriate.

'A realiser,' he defended, uncharacteristically sensitive to the difference all of a sudden.

And then—finally—she made formal eye contact. As if his tone had got him some kind of password access. Because he was taller than her—even with those legs that had seemed to go on for ever down at the beach—her looking up at him from closer quarters lifted her thick lashes and gave him a much better look at deep grey irises surrounded by whites of a clarity he never saw in the city.

Or in the mirror.

Healthy, fresh-air-raised eyes. And really very beautiful. Yet still not quite...*there*. As if her mind was elsewhere.

Some crazy part of him resented not being worthy of her full attention when this meeting and what might come out of it meant so much to him. Perhaps cautious uninterest was a power mechanism on the Morgan property.

Effective.

'I studied the proposal you emailed,' she said, stepping back and running the hand that had just held his through her dog's wet coat, as if she was wiping him off.

'And?'

'And it was...very interesting.'

'But you aren't very interest*ed*?' he guessed aloud.

Her smile, when it came, changed her face. And instantly she was that girl down by the beach again. Dancing in the surf. The mouth that was a hint too big for her face meant her smile was like the Cheshire Cat's. Broad and intriguing. Totally honest. Yet hiding everything.

'It sounds terrible when you say it like that.'

'Is there another way to say no?'

'Dozens.' She laughed. 'Or don't you hear it very often?'

Her parents exchanged a momentary glance. Not of concern at their daughter's bluntness, rather more…speculative. She ignored them entirely.

'I'd like to learn more about your new processes,' he risked, appealing to her vanity since their new processes were *her* new processes. 'And perhaps go further into what I have in mind.'

She dismissed it out of hand. 'We don't do tours.'

'You'll barely notice me. I'm particularly good at the chameleon thing—'

Two tiny lines appeared between brows a slightly lighter colour than her still damp hair and he realised that wasn't the way in either.

'And your Ashmore Coolidge health-check is due soon anyway. Two birds, one stone.'

That, *finally*, had an impact. So Laney Morgan was efficient, if nothing else. His firm required biennial business health-checks on their clients to make sure everything was solid. By contract.

'How long? An hour?' she asked.

His snort surprised her.

'A day, at least. Possibly two.'

'We're to put you up on no notice?'

Who knew a pair of tight lips could say so much?

'No. I'll get a room in town…'

'You will not,' Ellen piped up. 'You can have a chalet.'

He and Laney both snapped their faces towards her at the same time.

'Mum…'

'You have accommodation?' That wasn't in their file.

Ellen laughed. 'Nothing flash—just a couple of guest dwellings up in the winter paddock.'

That was the best opening he was going to get. Staying on the property, staying close, was the fastest way to their compliance he could think of. 'If you're sure?'

'Mum!'

Laney's face gave nothing away but her voice was loaded with meaning. Too late. The offer was made. A couple of days might be all he needed to get to know all of the Morgan clan and influence their feelings about taking their operation global.

'Thank you, Ellen, that's very generous.'

Her face gave nothing away, but Helena's displeasure radiated from the more subtle tells in her body—her posture, the acute angle of her neck, as if someone was running fingernails down a chalkboard on some frequency the rest of them couldn't hear. Except her dog couldn't hear it either—he'd flopped down behind the sofa, fast asleep.

'Laney, will you show Elliott up to the end chalet, please?'

That sweet, motherly voice wasn't without its own strength and it brooked no argument.

When Laney straightened she was back to avoiding eye contact again. She smiled with as few muscles as possible, the subtext flashing in neon.

'Sure.'

She made the squeak noise again and her dog leapt to attention. She turned, trailed her hand along the back of the sofa and then around the next one, and reached for the cluster of leather he'd seen in her hand down at the beach from where it now hung over the back of a dining chair. As she bent and fitted it around the crazy, tearaway dog it totally changed demeanour; became attentive and professional. Then she stood and held the handle loosely in her left hand.

And everything fell into place.

The death-defying coffee pour. The standoffish outstretched hand. The lack of hard eye contact.

Laney Morgan wasn't a princess or judgmental—at least she wasn't *only* those things.

Laney Morgan—whom he'd seen dancing so joyously on the beach, who had taken a family honey business and built it into one of the most successful in the country, and who had just served him his own genitals on a plate—couldn't see.

CHAPTER TWO

'YOU'RE BLIND,' ELLIOTT GARVEY murmured from Laney's right, the moment they were outside.

'You're staring.'

'I wasn't,' he defended after a brief pause, his voice saturated with unease.

'I could feel it.' And then, at the subtle catch in his breath. '*Practically* feel it, Mr Garvey. Not literally.' Though he certainly wouldn't be the first to expect her to have some kind of vision-impaired ESP.

He cleared his throat. 'You hide it well.'

Wilbur protested her sudden halt with a huff of doggie breath.

'I don't *hide* it at all.'

'Right, no…sorry. Poor choice of words.'

Confusion pumped from him and she got the sense that he was a man who very rarely let himself get flustered. It was tempting to play him, just a little, but her mother had raised her never to exploit the discomfiture of others. Because if *she* expected to be taken at face value how could she do less for anyone else?

Even intruding corporate types from the city.

She adjusted her trajectory at Wilbur's slight left tug and passed through the first gate beside her dog. 'I've had twenty-five years to perfect things, Mr Garvey. Plus the direction of your breathing gave you away.'

'Elliott.'

Then he fell silent again and she wondered if he was looking around at their farm…or at her still? Scrutiny never had sat lightly on her.

'He's very focussed. Wilbur, was it?'

Okay, neither of the above. He'd managed to zero in on her favourite talking point.

'Captain Furry-Pants to his friends.' She smiled. 'When the harness is on, he's on. When it comes off he's just a regular dog. Making up for lost time by being extra goofy. Getting it out of his system.'

They walked on to the steady reassurance of the sound of gravel crunching under eight feet.

'Your property is beautiful. This peninsula is extraordinary.'

'Thank you.'

'Have you ever lived anywhere else?'

'Why would I? It's perfect here. The wildlife. The space.'

His lagging steps pulled him further behind. 'The beaches…'

There was more than just tension in his voice. There was apology in the way he cleared his throat.She quarter-turned her head back towards him as she continued onward and the penny dropped.

Wilbur's quiet growls down by the water… 'That was you?'

'I was using the lookout. I didn't realise it overlooked a private beach. I'm sorry.'

Had he watched her wading? Dancing? It took a lot to make her feel vulnerable these days. Not that she was going to let him know that.

She tossed her hair back. 'You got a first-hand demonstration of Wilbur in off-harness mode, then.'

His crunching footsteps resumed. 'Yeah, he was having a ball.'

'He loves to swim.'

Awesome—she was like a radio stuck on Channel Wilbur. Time for some effort. 'So you must have drawn the short straw, being sent by your firm so far from the city?'

'Not at all. I chose to come. Morgan's isn't on anyone else's radar.'

That got her attention. 'You make it sound like a competition.'

'It is. It's the best part of the job. Finding raw talent, developing it.'

Realising it. She stepped with Wilbur around an obstacle and then smelled it as she passed. A cowpat. Behind her, Garvey grunted. Presumably, he hadn't been so lucky. She didn't stop and he caught up straight away.

'Did you miss it?'

'Just.'

He didn't sound irked. If anything, that was amusement warming his voice. Her lips twisted. 'Sorry, we have a couple of milk cows that free range.'

Silence reigned for the next minute or two and, again, she had to assume he was looking around at the farm, its outbuildings and condition. Critically? Morgan's had modern facilities to go with its spectacular coastal location but being judged had never sat comfortably on her. The smell of tiny wildflowers kicked up from underfoot.

'So if it's a competitive process, and we're not on anyone else's radar, does that mean no one else at your firm believes we have potential?'

He took his time answering. Something she appreciated. He wasn't a man to rush to fill a silence.

'It means they lack vision. And they're not paying attention.'

Okay, for a city boy he definitely had a great voice. Intelligent and measured and just the right amount of gravel. It was only when she gave him another mental tick that she realised she'd started a list.

'But you are?'

'I've been tracking your progress a long time—' His voice shifted upwards a semi-tone. 'Are those tyres?'

The rapid subject-change threw her, but he had to mean the chalets that they were approaching.

'Dad had one of his recycling frenzies a couple of years ago and made a couple up for family and friends—' *and inconvenient visitors from the city* '—when they visit. Tyres and rammed earth on the outside but pretty flash on the inside. Bed, open fire and privacy.' For them as much as their guests. 'And what I'm reliably informed are some pretty spectacular ocean views.'

Tension eased out of him on a satisfied sigh. 'You're not wrong. One hundred and eighty degrees.'

She stopped at the door to the chalet on the end, used the doorframe to orientate herself and pointed left. 'Manufacturing is over that way, beach is down that track, and the first of the bee yards is up behind this hill. You should probably take a bit of time to settle in. Can you find your way back to your car for your things?'

Idiot, she chided herself. He could probably see it from here. There was nothing between them and the Morgan's car park but open paddock. What was wrong with her? Maybe her brain cells were drunk on whatever that was coming off him.

'Yep. I'm good. Do I need to be somewhere at a particular time?'

'Are you allergic to bees?'

'Only one way to find out.'

The man faced life head-on. Her favourite direction. 'Well, if you feel like living dangerously, come on up the hill in twenty minutes. I'll be checking the bees.'

Soonest started, soonest done. She turned and thrust the chalet key at him and warm fingers brushed hers as he took it.

'Do I need protective gear?' he murmured.

'Not unless you plan on plunging your hands into the hives. This first community is pretty chill.' Which wasn't true of all their bees, but definitely true of her favourites. 'But maybe wear sunglasses.'

'Okay. Thanks, Laney.'

His voice lifted with him as he stepped up into the unlocked chalet but there was an unidentifiable something else in his tone. Sorrow? Why would he be sad? He was getting his way. She thought about protesting his presumption in using her nickname but then remembered what he'd probably seen down on the beach. Niceties, after that, seemed rather pointless. Although it did still have the rather useful value of contrasting with her own formality.

'You're welcome, *Mr Garvey*.'

With a flick of her wrist Wilbur full-circled and walked her down the hill and back through the gate, leaving the subtle dismissal lingering in the air behind her. As soon as she turned him left, towards one of the closest bee yards, Wilbur realised where they were going and he lengthened his strides, excited. He loved the beach first and the bees second. Because when she was elbow-deep in bees he was free to romp around the yards as much as he wanted.

Laney was always pleasantly breathless when she crested the hill to the A-series hives, and, as she always did, she stalled at the top and turned to survey the property. The landscape of her imagination. It was branded into her brain in a way that didn't need the verification of sight—the layout, the view as it had been described to her over the years. Three generations of buildings where all their manufacturing and processing was done, the endless ocean beyond that.

She had no way of knowing how like the real thing her mixed-sense impression of it was, but ultimately it didn't matter what it really looked like. In her mind it was magnificent. And she had the smells and the sounds and the pristinely fresh air to back it up.

So when Elliott Garvey complimented the Morgan property she knew it was genuine. They'd had enough approaches from city folk wanting to buy in to know that it was one of the better-looking properties in the district. But that was not why her family loved it. At least it wasn't *only* why they loved it. They loved it because it was fertile and well-positioned, in a coastal agricultural district, and undulating and overflowing with wildflowers, and because it backed on two sides onto nature reserves packed with Marri and Jarrah trees which meant their bees had a massive foraging range and their honey had a distinctive geo-flavour that was popular with customers.

And because it was home. The most important of all. Where she'd lived since her parents had first brought her home from the hospital, swaddled in a hand-loomed blanket.

That was the potential they all believed in. Regardless of what else Call-Me-Elliott Garvey saw in Morgan's.

What was the protocol in this kind of situation? Should he stomp his feet on the thick grassed turf so that she could hear him coming? Cough? Announce himself?

In the end Wilbur took matters into his own paws and came bounding over, collar tags jangling, alerting Helena to Elliott's presence as effectively as a herald. The dog was mostly dry now, and had traded damp dog smell for fresh grass smell, and he responded immediately to Wilbur's eager-eyed entreaty with a solid wrestle and coat-rub.

'Hey, there, Captain Furry-Pants.' Well, they were kind of friends now, right? And Wilbur's haunches *were* particularly furry. 'Still got energy left?'

'Boundless,' Laney said without looking around, her attention very much on what she was doing at one of dozens of belly-height boxes.

She'd thrown a long-sleeved shirt over her summer dress but that was it for the protective wear he'd imagined they would wear on a busy apiary. One for the 'risks' column in his report. A handful of bees busied themselves in the air around her but their orbit was relaxed. A steady stream of others took off for the fields behind them and made way for the ones returning.

It was as busy as any of the airports he'd passed through in his time. And there'd been many.

He slid his sunglasses on and felt, again, a pang at Laney's earlier kindness: a woman who had no use of her eyes taking the trouble to watch out for his.

'Can I approach?'

'Sure. Watch your feet in case any bees are on the grass.'

His focus shifted from the airborne bees to the possibility of stealth bees underfoot. There were one or two. 'Are they sick?'

Her laugh caused a whisper of a ripple in the steady hum coming off the bees. Like a tiny living echo. 'They're just resting. Or moisture-seeking.'

'How do you not step on them?'

'I slide rather than tread,' she said, without taking her focus off what she was doing. 'Kind of a rollerblading motion. It gives them a chance to take off.'

He stepped up closer. 'You've rollerbladed?'

'Of course.'

As if it was such a given.

'That's probably close enough,' she confirmed as he moved just behind her shoulder. 'And if I say run, do it. Straight back downhill to the carriage.'

He studied her face for any indication that she was kidding. There was nothing. 'Is that my safety induction?'

'Sure is. It's a fairly simple rule. Don't touch and don't stick around if things get active.'

And leave a blind woman undefended while bees swarmed? Not going to happen. But they could argue that out after they were both safe.

Her fingers dusted over the surface of the open hive, over the thronging mass itself, but the bees didn't seem to mind. Some hunkered down under her touch, others massed onto the back of her hand and crawled off the other side, or just held on for the free ride. None seemed perturbed.

'What are you doing, exactly?' he asked.

'Just checking them.'

'For…?'

'For hive beetle.'

'What's your process?'

He held his most recent breath. Would she hear the subtext clearly? *How can you do that, blind?*

But if she did, she let it go with a gracious smile. Just as well, because he had a feeling that a lot of his questions were going to start that way.

'The bees are kind of…fluid. They move under touch. But the beetles are wedged in hard. A bit like pushing your fingers through barley in search of a pinhead.'

There was a truckload of bees swarming over the hive and Laney's hands, but something about the totally unconcerned way she interacted with them—and her own sketchy safety gear—gave him the confidence to lean in as she pulled a frame out of several racked in the hive. It was thick with bees and honeycomb and—sure enough—the odd tiny black beetle.

Which she cut mercilessly in half with her thumbnail as her fingers found them.

'Pest?'

'Plague.' She shook her head. 'But we have it better here on the peninsula. And want to keep it that way.'

Her bare fingers forked methodically through the thick clumps of bees.

'How are you not a mass of stings?'

'My fingers are my eyes, so I can't work with gloves. Besides, this hive isn't aggressive—they'll only react to immediate threat.'

'And your hands aren't a threat?'

'I guess not.'

Understandable, perhaps. Her long fingers practically caressed them, en masse, each touch a stroke. It was almost seductive.

Or maybe that was just him. He'd always been turned on by competence.

'Hear that note?' She made a sound that was perfectly pitched against the one coming from the bees. 'That's Happy Bee sound.'

'As opposed to…?'

'Angry Bee sound. We're Losing Patience sound. We're Excited sound. They're very expressive.'

'You really love them.'

'I'd hope so. They're my life's work.'

Realising was his life's work, but did he love it? Did his face light up like hers when he talked about his latest conquest? Or did he just value it because he had a talent for it, and he liked being good at things. A lot. Getting from his boss the validation he'd never had as a kid.

Laney gave the bees a farewell puff of smoke from the mini bellows sitting off to one side and then slid the frame back into its housing, her fingertips guiding its way. They spidered across to the middle frame and he grew fixated on their elegant length. Their neat, trim, unvarnished nails.

She lifted another frame. 'This feels heavy. A good yield.'

It was thick with neatly packed honeycomb, waxed over to seal it all in. He mentioned that.

'The frames closest to the centre are often the fullest,' she explained. 'Because they focus their effort around the brood frame, where the Queen and all her young are.'

It occurred to him that he should probably be taking notes— that was what a professional would have been doing. A professional who wasn't being dazzled by a pretty woman, that was.

'Seriously? The most valuable members of the community in one spot, together? That seems like bad planning on their part.'

'It's not like a corporation, where the members of the board aren't allowed to take the same flight.' She laughed. 'There's no safer place than the middle of a heavily fortified hive. Surrounded by your family.'

'In theory...'

In his world, things hadn't operated quite that way.

'If something does happen to the Queen or the young they just work double-time making a new queen or repopulating. Colonies bounce back quickly.'

Not all that different from Ashmore Coolidge. As critical as their senior staff were, if someone defected the company recovered very quickly and all sign of that person sank without a trace. A fact all the staff were graphically reminded of from time to time to keep them in line.

'So the bees work themselves to death, supporting the royal family?'

'Supporting *their* family. They're all of royal descent.' She clicked the frame back into position. 'Isn't that what we all do, ultimately? Even humans?'

'Not everyone. I support myself.'

She turned and faced him and he felt as pinned as if she could see him. 'Are you rich?'

She wasn't asking to be snoopy, so he couldn't be offended. 'I'm comfortable.'

'Do you keep all the money you make for Ashmore Coolidge?'

No. But she knew that, so he didn't bother answering.

'Your firm gets the bulk of the money you generate for them and that goes to...who? The partners?'

In simple terms. 'They work hard, too.'

'But they already get a salary, right? So they get their own reward for their work, and also most of yours?'

'We have shareholders, too.'

Why the hell was he so defensive around her? And about this. Ashmore Coolidge's corporate structure was the same as every other glass and chrome tower in the city.

'A bunch of strangers who've done *none* of the work?' She held up a hand and dozens of bees skittled over it. 'You're working yourself into the ground supporting other people's families, Mr Garvey. How is that smarter than what these guys do?'

He stared at the busy colony in the hive. Utterly lost for words at the simple truth of her observation.

'Everything they do, they do for the betterment of their own family.' Her murmurs soothed the insects below her fingers. 'And their lives may be short, but they're comfortable. And simply focussed. Every bee has a job, and as long as they fulfil their potential then the hive thrives.' She stopped and turned to him. 'They're *realisers*—just like you.'

Off in the distance Wilbur lurched from side to side on his back in the long grass, enjoying the king of all butt-scratches.

Utterly without dignity, but completely happy. As simple as the world she'd just described.

Elliott frowned. He got a lot of validation from being in Ashmore Coolidge's top five. Success in their business was measured in dollars, yet he'd never stopped to consider exactly how that money flowed. Always away from him, even if he got to keep a pretty generous part of it. Which was just a clue as to how much more went to their shareholders. Nameless, faceless rich people.

'I send money to my mother—'

The moment the words were out he wanted to drag them back in, bound and gagged. Could he be any more ridiculous? Laney Morgan wasn't interested in his dysfunctional family.

He was barely interested in it.

A woman with a Waltons family lifestyle would never understand what it had been like growing up with no money, no prospects and no one to tell him it was perfectly okay to crave more. Leaving him feeling ashamed when he did.

But a smile broke across her face, radiant and golden, and a fist clenched somewhere deep in his chest.

'That's a good start. We'll make a bee of you yet.'

He fell to silence and watched Laney beetle-busting. Fast, methodical. Deadly. Inexplicably, he found it utterly arresting.

'I'm sorry,' she murmured eventually.

'For what?'

'For generating that silence. I didn't mean to be dismissive of your work.'

Think fast, Garvey. It's what you're paid for. 'I was thinking about a world in which people only acted for family benefit and whether it could work in real terms.' Better than admitting he was transfixed by her.

'You think not?'

'I question whether that kind of limited focus is sustainable. Outside of an apiary.'

She gave the bees one last puff of smoke and then refitted the lid with her fingers. 'Limited?'

'You've grown Morgan's significantly over the past ten years. Why?'

'To make better use of the winter months. To exploit more of the by-products that were going to waste. To discover more.'

'Yet you're not interested in continuing that growth?'

Time he stopped being hypnotised by this woman and her extraordinary talents and got back in the game, here.

Her sigh said she was aware of it too. 'We don't need to. We're doing really well as is.'

'You're doing really well for a family of four and a smallish staff.' Or so the Morgan's file said. Then again, that same file had totally neglected to mention Laney's blindness.

'That's all we are.'

'So your growth is limited by your ambition. And your ambition—' *or perhaps lack of it* '—is determined by your needs.'

Those long fingers that had done such a fine job of soothing the bees fisted down by her sides. 'Morgan's would never have come to your attention if we lacked ambition, Mr Garvey.'

Elliott. But he wasn't going to ask her again. He wasn't much on begging.

'Yet it is limited. You've expanded as much as you want to.'

'You say that like it's a bad thing. This is our business—surely how hard or otherwise we pursue it is also up to us?'

'But you have so much more potential.'

'Why would we fight for a market share we don't need or want? Surely that's the very definition of sustainable? Not just taking for taking's sake.'

He stared. She was as alien to him as her bees. 'It's not *taking*, Laney, it's *earning*.'

'I earn the good sleep I have every night. I earn the pleasure my job brings to me and to the people we work with. I earn the feeling of the sun on my face and the little surge of endorphins that hearing Happy Bees gives me. I am already quite rewarded enough for my work.'

'But you could have so much more.'

Her shoulders rose and fell a few times in silence. 'You mean I could *be* so much more?'

It was the frostiest she'd been with him since walking into the living room earlier. 'Look, you are extraordinary. What you've achieved in the past decade despite your—'

She lifted one eyebrow.

Crap.

'Disability? It's okay to say it.'

Which meant it absolutely wasn't.

'Despite the *added complexities* of your vision loss,' he amended carefully. 'I can only imagine what you'd be capable of on the world stage with Ashmore Coolidge's resources behind you.'

'I have no interest in being on stage, Mr Garvey. I like my life exactly as it is.'

'That's because you have no experience outside of it.'

'So I lack ambition and now I'm also naïve? Is this how you generally win clients over to your point of view?'

'Okay. I'm getting off track. What I'm asking for is an open mind. Let me discover all the aspects of your business and pitch you some of the ideas I have for its growth. Let's at least hash it out so that we can both say that we've listened.'

'And you think one overnight stay and a tour of our operation is going to achieve that?'

'No, I absolutely don't. This is going to be a work in progress. I'd like to make multiple visits and do some more research in between. I'd like the opportunity to change your mind.'

She shrugged, but a hint of colour flamed up around the collar of her shirt. Had the thought of him returning angered her or—his stomach tightened a hint—had it interested her?

'It's your time to waste.'

'Is that a yes?'

'It's not my decision to make. I'll talk to my parents tonight. We'll let you know tomorrow.'

CHAPTER THREE

WHY WAS IT that everyone thought they knew what she wanted better than she did?

Bad enough fielding her mother's constant thoughts on why she should get out more and meet people and her father's endless determination that not a single opportunity in life be denied her. Only her brother treated her with the loving disdain of someone you'd shared a womb with.

Now even total strangers were offering their heavily loaded opinions.

She'd met Elliott Garvey's type before. Motivated by money. She couldn't quite bring herself to suggest it was *greed*, because she'd seen no evidence of excess on his part, but then again she'd only known him for an hour or two.

Though it definitely felt longer.

Particularly the time out by the hives. She'd been distracted the whole time, feeling his heat reaching out to her, deciding he was standing too close to both her and the hives but then having his voice position proving her wrong. Unless he occupied more space than the average person? Maybe he was a large man?

He hadn't sounded particularly puffed after his hike up the hill. Or while they'd power-walked to the carriage. There was no way of knowing without touching him. Or asking outright.

Excuse me, Mr Garvey, are you overweight?

He'd been just as direct with her, asking about her vision, so maybe he was the kind of man you *could* ask that of? Except she wasn't the kind of woman who could ever ask it. Not without it sounding—and feeling—judgemental. And, as a lifelong recipient of the judgement of others, she was the last person to intentionally do it to another.

Nope. Elliott Garvey was a puzzle she would have to piece together incrementally. Subtly, or her mother would start pressing the paper for wedding invitations. But she couldn't take too long or he'd be gone back to his corporate world, because she felt certain that her father wouldn't agree to a series of visits. He'd only agreed to this one to be compliant with their financial management requirements.

Which didn't mean she wouldn't enjoy the next twenty-four hours. As much as she hated to admit it, he smelled really good. Most men in their district let the surf provide their hygiene and they either wore Eau de Farm or they bathed in fifty-per-cent-off cologne before driving into town to try and pick up. Elliott Garvey just had a tangy hint of…something…coming off him. And he was smart, too, which made his deep tones all the easier to listen to. Nothing worse than a phone sex voice on a man who had nothing of interest to say.

Not that she necessarily agreed with what he had to say, but he was astute and respectful, and he'd been about as tactful questioning her about her sight as anyone she'd ever met. Those first awkward moments notwithstanding.

'So you'd be happy to show him around, Laney?' her father repeated as they laid the table in their timber and glass home for dinner that evening.

Spending a bit more time in Elliott Garvey's company wasn't going to be an excruciating hardship. He was offering her his commercial expertise for free and she'd be happy to see the Morgan's range reflected through the filter of that expertise. Maybe there'd be a quiet thing or two she could implement here on the farm. Without taking them global. There was still plenty of scope for improvement without worrying about world domination.

And then there was the whole enjoying the sound and smell of him…

'Sure.'

She reached over one of the timber chairs and flattened her palm on the table, then placed the fork at her thumb and the knife at her widespread little finger. 'It's only one more day.'

'Actually, I was thinking of agreeing to his request,' her father said.

The chair-leg grunted on the timber floor as she stumbled against it. 'To let him come back again?'

'I'd like to hear the man out.'

'Surely it couldn't take more than a day to give him a courtesy listen?'

'Not if he's to see the full range of our operations first hand. Too much of it is seasonal.'

Spring and summer were all about honey-harvesting, but the remaining six months of the year they concentrated on other areas of their operation. They lived and worked through winter on the back of the honey harvest. Just like the bees did.

'How many times?'

'That's up to him,' her father suggested. 'It's business as usual for us.'

'Easy for you to say—you're not tasked with babysitting.'

'You're the best one to talk turkey with the man, Laney. Most of what we now do are your initiatives.'

'They're *our* initiatives, Dad. The whole family discussed and agreed.'

Well, she'd discussed and her parents had agreed. Owen had just shrugged.

'But you created them.'

'Someone else created them. I just suggested we adopt them.'

'Stop playing down your strengths,' he grumbled. As usual.

'Would you rather I took credit for the work of others?' she battled. As usual.

Frustration oozed from his tone. 'I'd rather you took some credit for yourself from time to time. Who knows? If you impress him enough there might be a job in it for you.'

'I have a job here.'

'A better job.'

The presumption that her job wasn't already about the best occupation a person could hope for really rankled. 'Why would they hire me, Dad? Not a lot of call for apiarists in the city.'

'Why *wouldn't* they hire you? You're as smart and capable as anyone else. More so.'

'How about because I know nothing about their industry?'

'He's trained to recognise raw talent. He'd be crazy not to take you on.'

Laney got the tiniest thrill at the thought of being *taken on* in any way by Elliott Garvey, but she fought it. 'You don't just hire someone because they seem generally capable, Dad.'

'You're as worthy as anyone of your chance.'

Dread pooled thick and low. *Oh, here we go...* 'Dad, promise me you won't do the whole Laney-sell job.'

As he was so very wont to do. Over and over during her childhood, much to her dismay. But the thought of him humiliating her like that with Elliott Garvey... *Ugh.*

'I'll promise no such thing. I'm proud of my daughter and her achievements and not too shy to admit it.'

'He's here to study our operations, not—'

'I liked him,' her mother piped up, apropos of pretty much nothing, as she placed a heavy dish on the table with a punctuating clunk. Chicken stew, from the delicious aroma. All organic, like the rest of their farm. 'He's handsome.'

Her father grunted. 'Don't change the subject, Ellen.'

'You think everyone's handsome, Mum.' Laney lowered her voice instinctively as she and her father helped ferry clean plates to the table, even though she'd heard Elliott Garvey's expensive tyres on the driveway gravel about twenty minutes earlier. 'Besides, what do looks have to do with a person's integrity or goodness?'

'I can't comment on those until I've shared a meal with the man. So can we please just do that before setting our minds in any particular direction?'

'You'll have to invite him first, and he goes home tomorrow afternoon.' So there went the dinner plan. Conveniently.

'I *have* invited him. That's his setting you just laid.'

She straightened immediately. No. She'd only set the table for the usual four. 'Where's Owen?'

'Chasing some surfer tourist,' his father muttered.

At twenty-five she might still be a work in progress, but her twin had pretty much stopped emotional development at eighteen. *Whatever* was Owen's perpetual outlook. If he was around to give one and not off surfing the latest hot break.

'He's taking her for a pizza, Robert. He had his Saturday night shirt on.'

Oh, well...look out, Surfer Girl, then. If her brother had bothered with a clean shirt he was definitely on the make. Girls and surfing were about the only things Owen took seriously.

'And you didn't think to just let us enjoy a quiet dinner without him?' Laney muttered.

'Elliott has nothing in that chalet, Helena.'

Uh-oh— *Helena*. Reason had always been her friend in the face of *mother voice*. 'The chalets are practically five-star, and I'm sure he has a full wallet.' *And an expense account*. 'He could have easily taken himself for a restaurant meal.'

'When we can offer a home-cooked one instead?'

'He went out anyway. He might as well have eaten in Mitchell's Cliff.' In fact she'd been sure that was what he was doing as the crunch of his tyres on the driveway had diminished.

'I'm less concerned with what he does than with what *we* do. Extending Morgan courtesy to our guest.'

Laney opened her mouth to protest further but then snapped it shut again as feet sounded on the mat outside. An uncontrollable dismay that she hadn't so much as combed her windswept hair washed over her.

But too late now.

'He's coming,' her father announced moments later.

Elliott had clearly paused in the doorway and was greeting a dozing Wilbur, which meant his disturbed *man scent* had time to waft ahead. Wow, he smelled amazing. The same base tones as before, yet different somehow. Spicier. Cleaner.

Tastier.

Heat burbled up under her shirt at the thought, but it was true. Whatever he was wearing was tickling the same senses as the stew still simmering in its own heat on the table.

'Thank you for the invitation, Mr and Mrs Morgan—'

'Ellen and Robert, please, Elliott.'

He stepped up right next to her. 'I nicked out to pick this up. Couldn't come empty-handed.'

Another waft of deliciousness hit her as a bottle clacked against the timber at the centre of the big table.

'Oh, lovely. That's a terrific local winery—Helena's favourite.'

'Really? I didn't know.'

His voice was one-tenth croak, subtle enough that maybe she only heard it because he was standing so close. But he wasn't looking at her, she could tell. Plus, she wouldn't be looking at him if their situations were reversed. On pain of death.

Her mother laughed. 'How could you know?'

Was he worried that she might read something into that? Laney spoke immediately to put the ridiculous idea out of the question. 'You're either a man of excellent taste or Natty Marshall did a real sell-job on you at the cellar.'

'She was pretty slick,' he admitted.

'Sit down, Elliott.' Her mother mothered. 'You look very nice.'

The reassuring way she volunteered that opinion made Laney wonder whether he was worrying at the edges of his shirt or something.

'He's changed into a light blue Saturday night shirt, Laney.'

Oh, no...

'Mum likes to scene-set for me,' she explained, mortified, and then mumbled, 'sorry.'

'Blue shirt, jeans, and I combed my hair,' he added, amusement rich in his low voice.

Was that a statement about *her* wild locks? Her hand went immediately to them.

Her mother continued to be oblivious. 'Sit, too, Laney.'

She did, moving to the left of her chair just as he moved to the right of his. They collided in the middle. She jerked back, scalded.

'Sorry,' he murmured. 'Ladies first.'

'We'll be standing all night if we wait for one of those,' she quipped, still recovering from the jolt of whatever the heck that was coming off him, and then she slid into her seat, buying a moment of recovery time as he moved in next to her.

So that was her question answered. She'd felt the strength of his torso against hers. He was solid, but definitely not over-weight. Not as youthfully hard as her twin, but not soft either. Just right.

Which pretty much made her Goldilocks, snuggling down into the sensation.

The necessity to converse was forestalled by the business of filling plates with stew and side plates with thickly sliced bread and butter.

'Home-made bread?' Elliott asked. Such a charmer. So incredibly transparent.

'Organically grown and milled locally and fresh out of my oven.'

'It's still warm.'

The reverence in his voice surprised a chuckle out of Laney. 'Are ovens not hot in the city?'

An awkward silence fell over the whole table. She didn't need to see her mother's face to know it would be laden with disapproval.

But chivalry was clearly alive and well. 'Bread starts out hot, yes,' he admitted. 'But it's not usually hot by the time it gets to the consumer. This is my first truly home-made loaf.'

The fact that he needed to compensate for her bluntness at all made her twitchy. And just a little bit ashamed. Plus it made her wonder what kind of city upbringing he'd had never to have had fresh-baked bread before. 'Well, wait until you taste the butter, then. Mum churns it herself.'

And bless her if her mother didn't join her daughter in the age-old act of making good. 'Well, I push the button on the machine and then refrigerate the results.'

'You guys seem pretty self-sufficient here...'

And off they went. Comfortably reclining in a topic she knew her parents could talk about underwater—organic farming and self-sustainability. Long enough to give her time to compose herself against the heat still coming off the man to her left as they all tucked into the chicken.

Okay, so he was a radiator. She could live with that. And enough of a city boy to never have had home-baked bread. That just meant they came from different worlds. Different upbringings. She'd met people from outside of the Leeuwin Peninsula before. There was no reason to be wound up quite this tight.

She slid her hand along the tablecloth until her fingertips felt the ring of cool that was the base of the glass of wine her father had poured from the bottle Elliott had contributed. She took a healthy swallow and sighed inwardly at the kiss of gentle Merlot against her tongue.

'Still as good as you remember?' Elliott murmured near her left ear. Swirling more man scent her way.

Okay, this was getting ridiculous. Time to focus. 'Always. We have hives at their vineyard. I like to think that's why it's so good.'

'This wine was fertilised by Morgan's bees?'

'Well, no.' Much as she'd love to say it had been. 'Grape pollen is wind-borne. But we provide the bees to fertilise their off-season cropping. So the bees help create the soil that make their wines so great.'

'Do they pay?'

Back to money. *Sigh*. 'No. They get a higher grape yield and we get the resulting honey. It's a win-win.'

He was silent for a moment, before deciding, 'Clever.'

The rush of his approval annoyed her. It shouldn't make her so tingly. 'Just standard bee business.'

'So tell me about your focus on organic methods,' he said to the table generally. 'That must limit where you can place hives or who you can partner with?'

'Not so much these days,' her father grunted. 'Organics is very *now*.'

'Yet you've been doing it for three decades. You must have been amongst the first?'

'Out of necessity. But it turned out to be the best thing we could have done.'

'Necessity?'

Every cell in Laney's body tightened. This wasn't the first time the topic had come up with strangers, but this was the first time she'd felt uncomfortable about its approaching. The awkward silence was on the Morgan side of the table, and the longer it went on the more awkward it was going to become.

'My eyes,' she blurted. 'My vision loss was a result of the pesticides we were using on the farm. Once we realised how dangerous they were, environmentally, we changed to organic farming.'

Her father cleared his throat. 'And by *we* she means her mother and I. Laney and Owen weren't even born yet.'

She was always sure to say 'we'. Her parents took enough blame for her blindness without her adding to it.

'None of us really knew what they were doing to our bodies,' her father went on, 'let alone to our unborn children.'

Well, one of them, anyway. Owen seemed to have got away with nothing worse than a teenager's attention span.

'Have we made you uncomfortable, Mr Garvey?' her mother said after moments of silence. 'Helena said we should have just sent you to town for a meal…'

Heat rushed up Laney's cheeks as his chair creaked slightly. It wasn't hard to imagine *Oh, really?* in the voice that washed over her like warm milk.

'No. I'm just thinking about how many worse ways the

chemical damage might have manifested itself. How lucky you were.'

Again the silence. But this time it wasn't awkward. Surprised was the closest word for the half-caught breath that filled the hush. Was he being intensely dismissive of her loss—and her parents'—or did he actually get it?

And possibly *her*.

Warmth swelled up in her chest, which tightened suddenly. 'Most people wouldn't consider it luck,' she breathed. 'But as it happens I agree with you.'

'And, as threatening as it must have been for you at the time, the decision sealed Morgan's fate. Put you well ahead of everyone else in organics today. It was smart.'

'It was a life-changer in more ways than one,' her mother cut in.

Silence again. Laney filled it with the first thing that entered her mind. 'I gather we'll be seeing you again, Elliott?'

Elliott. The very name tingled as it crossed her tongue.

'Really?' His voiced shifted towards her father. 'You're happy to have me back?'

Robert Morgan was predictably gruff. He always was when he dwelled on the bad old days. 'Yes. I would like to hear what you have to say.'

It didn't take a blind person to catch his leaning on the word 'I'.

'And what about you, Laney? You'll be doing all the escorting.'

'Free advice is my favourite kind. I'll be soaking it up.' But just in case he thought he was on a winner, she added, 'And weighing it up very carefully.'

Approval radiated outwards. Or was it pleasure? Either way she felt it. It soaked under her skin and did a bang-up job of warming her from the inside out as he spoke gruffly.

'That's all I ask.'

Three hours later they walked together back towards the chalet, an unharnessed Wilbur galloping in expanding arcs around them, her hand gently resting on Elliott's forearm. Not entirely necessary, in truth, because she walked this trail often enough en route to the hilltop hives. But she just knew walking beside him would be the one time that a rock would miraculously appear on the trail, and going head-over-tail really wasn't how she wanted him remembering her.

'It's a beautiful night,' he murmured.

'Clear.' *Ugh, such verbal brilliance. Not.*

'How can you tell?'

'The cicadas don't chirp when it's overcast, and I can't smell moisture in the air.'

'Right.'

She chuckled. 'Plus it may be autumn, but it's still summery enough that the odds are on my side.'

He stopped, gently leading her to a halt too. 'Listen, Laney' he said, low and somewhat urgent. 'I don't want every conversation we have to be laden with my reticence to ask you about your vision loss. I want to focus on your processes.'

Was that his way of saying he didn't want to look like an idiot in front of her any more than she did in front of him? Her breath tightened a tiny bit more.

'Why don't you just ask me now? Get it out of the way.'

'Is that okay?'

'I'll let you know if it's too personal.' She set off again, close to his side, keeping contact between their arms but not being formally guided.

He considered his first question for a moment. 'Can you see at all?'

'No.'

'It's just black?'

'It just…isn't.'

Except for when she looked at the sun. Then she got a hazy kind of glow in the midst of all that nothing. But she wasn't even sure she wasn't making that up in response to the warmth on her face. Because she sometimes got a glow with strong emotion too.

'It's like…' How to explain it in a way that was meaningful? 'Imagine if you realised one day that all other human beings had a tail like Wilbur's but you didn't. You'd know what a tail was, and where it went and what its function was, but you just couldn't conceive of what it would be like—or feel like—to have one. The extra weight. The impact on your balance. The modifications you'd need to allow for it. Useful, sure, but not something you can't get by without. That's vision for me.'

'It hasn't held you back at all.'

'Is that a question or a statement?'

'I can see that for myself. You are more accomplished than many sighted people. You don't consider it a disability?'

'A bat isn't disabled when it goes about its business. It just manages its environment differently.'

Silence.

'Are you glaring or thinking?'

'I'm nodding. I agree with you. But there must be things you flat-out can't do?'

'Dad made sure I could try anything I wanted—' and more than a few things she hadn't particularly wanted '—so, no, there's not much that I can't do at all. But there's a lot of things I can't do with any purpose or point. So I generally don't bother.'

'Like what?'

'I can drive a vehicle—but I can't drive it safely or to a destination so why would I, other than as a party trick? I can take a photograph with a camera, but I can't look at it. I can write longhand, but I really don't need to. That kind of thing.'

'Do you know what colours are?'

'I know what their purpose is. And I know how they're different in nature. And that they're meaningful for sighted people. But, no, I can't create colour in my head.'

'Because you've never seen it.'

'Because I don't think visually.'

'At all?'

'When I was younger Dad opened up the farm to city kids from the Blind Institute to come and have farm stays. As a way of helping me meet more children like myself. One of them had nothing mechanically wrong with her eyes—her blindness was caused by a tumour in her visual cortex and that meant she couldn't process what her eyes were showing her perfectly well. But the tumour also meant she couldn't think in images or conceptualise something she felt. She really was completely blind.'

'And that's not you?'

'My blindness is in my retinas, so my brain creates things that might be like images. I just don't rely on them.' She wondered if his pause was accommodating a frown. 'Think of it like this… Mum said you're quite handsome. But I can't imagine what that means without further information because I have no visual frame of reference. I don't conceive of people in terms of the differences in their features, although I obviously understand they *have* different features.'

'How do you differentiate?'

'Pretty much as you'd imagine. Smell, the sound of someone's walk, tangible physical features like the feel of someone's hand. And I have a bit of a thing for voices.'

'How do you perceive me?'

Awkwardness swilled around her at his rumbled question, but she'd given him permission to ask and so she owed him her honesty. 'Your strides are longer than most when you're walking alone.' Though, with her, he took pains to shorten them. 'And you smell—' *amazing* '—distinctive.'

That laugh was like honey squeezing out of a comb.

'Good distinctive or bad distinctive?'

She pulled up as he slowed and reached out to brush the side of her hand on the rough clay wall of the chalet for orientation. 'Good distinctive. Whatever you wear is…nice.'

In the way that her favourite Merlot was just 'nice'.

'You don't do the whole hands-on-face thing? To distinguish between physical features?'

'Do you feel up someone you've just met? It's quite personal. Eventually I might do that if I'm close to someone, just to know, but ultimately all that does for me is create a mind shape, address a little curiosity. I don't rely on it.'

'And people you care about?'

Did he think you couldn't love someone without seeing them?

She pressed her fingers to her chest. 'I feel them in here. And I get a surge of…it's not vision, exactly, but it's a kind of *intensity*, and I experience it in the void where my vision would be when I think about my parents or Owen or Wilbur. And the bees. Their happy hum causes it.'

And the sun, when she stared into it. Which was often, since her retinas couldn't be any more damaged.

'That sometimes happens spontaneously when I'm with someone, so I guess I could tell people apart by the intensity of that surge. But mostly I tell people apart by their actions, their intentions. That's what matters to me.'

'You looked me right in the eye after we shook hands.'

'Only after you spoke. I used the position of your hand and your voice to estimate where your eyes would be. And the moment either one of us moved it wouldn't have worked until I recalibrated. I don't have super powers, Elliott.'

His next silence had a whole different tone to it. He was absorbing.

'You've been very generous with your information, considering what an intrusion my questions are. But it felt important for me to understand. Thank you, Laney.'

'It's no more an intrusion than me asking you what it's like being tall.'

'How do you—? The angle of my voice?'

'And the size of your hand when I shook it. Unless you have freakishly large hands for the rest of your body?'

'No. My hands are pretty much in proportion to the rest of me.'

Cough.

Not awkward at all…

Wilbur snuffling in the distance and the chirpy evening cicadas were the only sounds around them. The only ones Elliott would hear, anyway.

'I'm tall because my father was a basketball player,' he volunteered suddenly. 'It means I spend my days looking at the bald spots of smaller men and trying very hard not to look down the cleavages of well-built women. My growth spurt at thirteen meant I made the school basketball team, and that was exclusively responsible for turning my high school years from horror to hero. It taught me discipline and focus, sharpened my competitiveness and gave me a physical outlet.' He took a breath. 'Without that I'm not sure what kind of a man I might have grown into.'

His words carried the slightest echo of discomfort, as if they were not things he was particularly accustomed to sharing. And she got the sense that he'd just given her a pretty fair trade.

She palmed the packed earth wall of the chalet and opened her mouth to say *Well, this is you*, but as she did so she stepped onto a fallen gum nut loosed by the wildlife foraging in the towering eucalypts above and her ankle began to roll. Her left fingernails bit into the chalet's rammed earth and her right clenched the fabric of Elliott's light jacket, but neither did much to stop her leg buckling.

The strong arm that slid around her waist and pulled her upright against his body was infinitely more effective at stopping her descent.

'Are you okay?' he breathed against her hair.

Other than humiliated? And way too comfortable in his strong hold. 'Occupational hazard' she said, when she really should have been thanking him. 'Happens all the time.'

He released her back onto two feet and waited a heartbeat longer as she tested her ankle for compliance. It held.

'I'm sorry, Laney. Guess I don't have Wilbur's years of training as a guide.'

Guilt saturated the voice that had been so warm just moments before. And that seemed an ungrateful sort of thanks for his catching her before she sprawled onto the ground at his feet.

'It wasn't you. My bottom and hip are peppered with bruises where I hit the dirt. Regularly.'

Talking about body parts suddenly felt like the most personal conversation she'd ever had, and it planted an image firmly between them that seemed uncomfortably provocative.

She released his jacket from between her clenched fingers. 'Thank you for those basketball-player reflexes.'

'You're welcome,' he breathed, and his smile seemed richer in the silence of evening. 'Are you okay to get yourself back?'

She whistled for Wilbur, who bounded to her side from out of the night, and then forked two fingers to touch his furry rump in lieu of a harness. 'Yep. I'm good. I walk these paths every day.'

Not that you'd know it by the wobble in her gait.

Then she set off, turning for the house, and Wilbur kept careful pace next to her, making it easy to keep up her finger contact with his coat. But she wasn't entirely ready to say good-night yet, although staying was out of the question. Something in her burned to leave him with a better impression of her than her being sprawled, inelegant and grasping, in his arms.

So she turned and smiled and threw him what she hoped was a witty quip back over her shoulder.

'Night. Sorry about the possums!'

CHAPTER FOUR

IT WASN'T THE possums that had kept him up half the night, though they'd certainly been having a ball, springing across his chalet's roof in a full-on game of midnight marsupial chasey. *Kiss* chasey, judging by some of the sounds he'd heard immediately afterwards.

Because if it *had* been the possums he would have been able to fall asleep when they'd finally moved on to foraging in the trees surrounding the chalets for the evening, instead of lying there thinking about the gentle brush of Laney's fingers on his arm, the press of her whole body against his when he'd caught her. The cadence of her laugh.

Her amazing resilience in the face of adversity.

Except that Laney genuinely didn't see it as adversity. She understood that she experienced the world differently from the rest of her family, her friends, but she was pretty happy with those experiences. The world was just as much her oyster as his.

More so, perhaps, because she was so open to experience.

And right about then his mind had flashed him back to watching her dance, wet and bedraggled and beautiful, down at the cove. Then to an imagined visual of her perfect skin marred by small bruises from falling. And then just her perfect skin, and the all-consuming question of whether that dusting of freckles might continue beyond the hem of her dress.

And any hope of sleep had rattled out of the chalet to join the possums.

Pervert.

As if he'd never seen a pretty woman before. Or held one.

Did it even count as holding if you were the only thing stopping someone from falling unceremoniously on their arse? It was more community service than come-on, right?

Elliott shook off the early-morning tiredness and wiped his loafers on the Morgans' mat. But he only had one foot done before the door opened and Laney stood there, resplendent in white overalls straight off the set of *Ghostbusters*.

Except he couldn't remember Murray or Ackroyd ever looking this good in theirs.

'I feel underdressed,' he commented.

Laney's smile was the perfect accessory. 'You won't miss out. I have a pair for you, too.'

'I take it today's bees aren't as friendly?'

'We're doing a run to check the migrating hives. I prefer the farmers to see us taking it seriously. Preserve the mystery.'

'We?'

'Hey, mate.'

Only a brother would shove past a blind woman in a doorway with quite so little regard. That was what gave him away. That and the fact he was basically a short-haired male version of Laney.

A stupid part of Elliott bristled at seeing Laney treated with such casual indifference, though she barely noticed.

'You must be Owen.' Elliott gripped the proffered palm in his, introducing himself and swallowing back the disappointment that today wasn't going to be all about him and Laney. 'Many hands make light work?'

'Owen and I work together on the remote hives,' she said. 'We're checking two off-sites today.'

If there had been any question that the intimate truce of last night was going to continue today, he'd just had his answer. Laney Morgan was all about business this morning.

'We're going to take the back gate out of our property so you'll get to see more of Morgan land. Come on.'

She stepped past him and brought a white stick out from

behind her leg. The first time he'd seen her with one. The first time he'd actually *thought* of her as blind. And instantly he understood why she didn't use it more often.

'No Wilbur today?'

She swept the stick ahead of her as though it were a natural part of her body, pausing only to slap the folded overalls and hood she'd been clutching towards him.

'Captain Furry-Pants has the day off. I think three guides would be excessive.'

Owen was already in the front of the Morgans' branded utility.

'So what will we be doing today?'

His question paused her just before she turned and felt her way up onto the tray of the truck, and she waited as he clambered up behind her. Once they were both on board, safely wedged between large, empty hives, she knocked twice on the window of the cab and Owen hit the accelerator. Hard.

They lurched up to speed.

'Today we're checking for beetle and propolis. We do these hives once a month.'

'Propo what?'

'Bee spit. They produce it to patch up any tiny holes in their hive and keep bacteria out. Humans use it for everything from treating burns to conditioning stringed instruments. Every one of our hives has a single propolis frame in it and the bees will totally cover it a couple of times in a year. We're exchanging those frames today.'

Bee spit. The potential for new markets was greater than he'd imagined. And as long as those obscure markets were buying, Morgan's was selling.

Man, they were *so* the right client for him.

They rumbled through the back roads of the property between fields full of bright, fragrant wildflowers and then skirted the edges of dense, tall forest.

'National Park,' Laney said when he queried. 'Between it

and our own lands, it means our bees have a massive tract to forage in and we can leave hives right on our perimeter.'

The ute hit a dip in the road, sending Helena crashing across his lap. A man could get used to this catching and steadying thing. She slid to sit at right angles instead, bracing her feet and her back on the hives packed either side of them. The move meant she wouldn't lurch into him again—a loss—but it meant her long legs bridged his.

Surprise benefit.

'You really couldn't get a more idyllic location—' he started, over the sound of the motor.

'Thank you. That's what I think.'

He'd been about to add ...*for your business,* but is that what she'd meant? Or did she just love and value the property because it was home? She couldn't see its beauty, so what was it, exactly, that she loved about it?

'Someone knew what they were doing when they started farming here.'

'My great-grandfather—though Morgan's was mostly a dairy operation then. Mum and Dad focussed on the apiary side of things when they went organic.'

When their daughter was born sightless.

He filled the rest of the journey with questions about yields and methods and percentile measures and she spoke as comfortably about numbers as she did about bee husbandry. There wasn't a single question she couldn't answer.

'You're being amazingly open today.'

'Given how amazingly closed I was yesterday?'

Well...yeah. Before their big discussion under the half-moon. 'Yesterday I felt sure you were going to send me packing.'

'I see no harm in helping you understand our business. Besides, I'm under instructions from Dad to be civil.'

Oh. Right. 'Not my natural charm, then?'

The ute lurched again and her hand went out automatically and grabbed the first solid thing she could find. His knee. She released it immediately.

'I tend to distrust charming men, actually. I haven't always had the best experiences with smooth talkers.'

'Why's that?' This had nothing to do with business but he was easily as interested in her answer as in anything else they'd yet discussed.

'Most people don't accept my vision as easily as—' She stopped, crunched her face in a frown and then changed direction.

Had she been about to say *as easily as you*? He struggled against the desire to smile so she wouldn't hear any trace of smugness in his voice.

'People tend to want to either rescue me or show me off. As if dating a blind girl somehow improves their status. Neither of which I appreciate, particularly.'

'You don't think they're asking you out for more…traditional reasons?'

'A high-maintenance blind girl? I don't think so.'

Pfff. 'You're the least high-maintenance person I've ever met.'

'They don't know that when they start sniffing around.'

Okay, whatever had happened to her in the past was clearly still a touchy point. 'Maybe they just want to get to know you? Maybe they're just attracted for regular reasons?'

'Knocked off their feet by my beauty?'

Given she'd never seen a sarcastic facial expression in her life, the one she flashed him now had to be innate. And it was a corker. 'You may not prioritise the visual, Laney, but I can tell you for certain that the rest of the world does.'

'Then that's a bonus for them. Poster child for the vision-impaired and passable to behold.'

'Laney, you're more than passable. You have amazing bone structure.'

The compliment hung out there in space, awkward and impossible to undo. She opted to ride through it as though it was any other conversation. 'Actually, I've heard that before.'

'From a man?' *Wow*—that thought bothered him more than was comfortable.

'From the friend who tattooed eyeliner on me.'

That stopped him flat. He stared at her. At the subtle shaded highlighting around her lashes. 'Your friend tattooed you?'

The eyes in question crinkled with her laugh. 'Kelly was training to be a beautician. She needed subjects to work on. She knew I didn't bother with make-up but she said if I only did one thing, ever, to my face it should be that. So we went for it.'

'Kelly was right. You have beautiful eyes.' Eyes that didn't meet his nearly often enough for his liking. He'd work on that. Make a point of touching her and speaking at the same time. 'But what happened to not thinking in visual terms?'

'I'm still a woman, Elliott. And as you pointed out the rest of the planet is so very visual. I saw no reason to go out of my way to look bad.'

Her hands twitched as if they wanted to go to her hair or face or something. It was very typically female. Very human. And really, really endearing.

'Laney, there's not… There's very little chance that what I'm about to say won't sound like a cheesy come-on, but I want to say it because you are nothing if not stoically honest about everything. I think you deserve the same in return.'

For a woman with limited eye expression, the rest of her face certainly managed to convey her nerves just then. 'Okay…'

'Those lightly made-up eyes, in that totally un-made-up face, are pretty much perfect. I give you my word, as a man, on that.'

Her lips parted in surprise.

'Healthy, natural and young, with eyes straight off a billboard. That's what I see.'

She frowned. 'A what?'

He blinked. 'A billboard?'

'Yeah.'

'It's a giant advertising poster.' He knew she knew about those because she'd commented about her brother's bedroom walls, which were still plastered with posters of grunge bands from his youth. 'As big as the side of a house, mounted on free-ways and the sides of high-rises.' And suddenly he realised how it was that she'd never encountered a billboard before. It wasn't just because she was blind. 'Have you ever been to the city, Laney?'

'I went when I was little, for a lot of tests. But, no. Not since then.'

'Have you been off the Leeuwin Peninsula? Out of the district?'

'Not for very long.'

And suddenly those eyes that saw nothing revealed so much more. The subtle change in their shape, the flick away from him. And he realised that after everything she had been pre-pared to talk about he'd just hit something that she wasn't.

Her homing instinct.

He filed it away for later. 'Anyway…that's a billboard. They tend to plaster beautiful models or hot cars all over them. Some-times together.'

'And you think I have a billboard face?'

Eyes, technically, but… 'Yes, definitely.'

The left corner of her mouth lifted just slightly. As if she wouldn't allow herself to be pleased about that but a tiny bit had leaked through anyway.

'Do *you*, Elliott?'

Should he be excited that she was curious about him or wor-ried about what the truth might lead to? It crossed his mind to exaggerate—not lie outright but just…embellish. But that felt dishonest and entirely without purpose. 'No. Not me. I'm okay, but nothing poster-worthy.'

'Mum's liberal with the word "handsome", so I really don't know how to imagine you.'

'You want me to describe myself?'

She frowned. 'Yes. For what it's worth.'

'I… Well, you know I'm tall. Six-three, to be exact. I have dark hair—'

'What kind of dark?'

Right. Dark was effectively a colour. Okay, this was trickier than he'd imagined. Not that he'd imagined in a million years he'd be having this conversation.

'Dark like night.' As lame as that sounded… 'And my eyes are the same colour as that cove where I saw you swimming.'

However she perceived *that*.

She smiled, settled back against the empty hives behind her. 'What else?'

Jeez, this wasn't easy. 'Hang on…' He pulled his phone out and got online.

'What are you doing?'

'I have a corporate photo on our website. I'm going to that.'

'You don't know what you look like?'

'I can't describe myself unless I see me.' He clicked a few more times. 'Okay… So… Hair like night, eyes like your ocean… I have a wide forehead, if not for the bit of hair that flops down over it, fairly dominant brows, but not out of control. Hmmm…apparently I have "Jules Vernian" sideburns.' Then, under his breath, 'Which will be gone by morning.'

Her laugh warmed him straight through.

'Ears?'

'Two.' He grinned for himself more than for her. 'Pretty level, regular size, no real lobe.'

'I'm sure that means something to those who study such things.'

'I hate to imagine. My nose is pretty straight, but there's a slight bump in it where I took a ball to the face back in school. My lips are… Well, I was once told they're "kissable"—whatever that means. There's two of them, too—roughly the colour of…fire, maybe? Though they're not being put to much use in this corporate picture. I look like I've never learned to smile.'

Corporate him looked pretty grim, come to think of it.

'I have more stubble on my face today than in this picture because I'm relaxed, and my beard tends to want to grow further down my neck than I'd like. It's a constant pain.' He clicked his phone to darkness. 'So that's me in a nutshell.'

Her lopsided smile evened out on the right and then broke into a fully fledged, fully glorious thing. 'I'm glad you're relaxed with us.'

So was he. She had no idea how rare a thing that was.

'Want to know what that looks like in my head…?' she offered.

Yes, desperately. 'No. I hate bad news.'

'Heathcliff painted by Picasso.'

His laugh was immediate and genuine. 'That's how you're imagining me?'

'Right now, yes.'

'How do you know how Picasso paints?'

'I told you, Mum likes to scene-set. She has an amazing descriptive vocabulary.'

'And Heathcliff?'

'I'm a big reader.'

'Well…I'll take Picasso's Heathcliff. Happily.'

Her voice turned two shades breathier. 'Want to know how I was imagining you before?'

Something told him he didn't. Yet something else whispered that the next words out of her mouth would be amongst the most important of his life. And his subconscious had never let him down yet.

'Go ahead.'

She tipped her head to the sky and stared into the sun, eyes wide open. Straight into it—just as she had that day on the beach. His immediate urge was to leap across and shield her eyes from the damaging rays. But something in her motion told him she'd been doing this for a long time. And that it was special to her.

She tipped her head back down, towards him. 'When I do that, I get a "ghost". Right up-front, where my vision should be.' Her hand waved in a small arc just above her head. 'That's what the specialists call it. My parents would call it a glow.'

'And you see it?'

Her head shook. 'I *experience* it. It's as much a feeling as a visual thing, and it lasts about thirty seconds. I'm not always sure it's even real or whether it's just my imagination filling in blanks. Because I get it for different people, too.'

He struggled hard not to clear his suddenly thick throat. 'You experience me as a…ghost?'

'Yours is dense.'

'Right…'

Her laugh whipped away on the wind as they sped along between the coast and the trees. 'Not literally. They have frequencies and yours is kind of…thick. Rich. Masculine. Which is stupid, given I have two men in the family.'

One or either of them should be hideously uncomfortable right about now, but he found it hard to be anything other than intrigued. And grateful. 'You make me sound positively mysterious. I think I prefer the ghost to the Picasso.'

'Me, too.'

They rumbled onwards in silence and Elliott looked out at the terrain whizzing past them on the private roads—primarily as an excuse not to look at Laney. Just because she couldn't see him do it there was no excuse to stare.

It occurred to him that Laney Morgan 'saw' things more clearly without ever actually seeing them than he ever had with his twenty-twenty vision. She was all about people's qualities, their goodness and their truth. And he should be worried as all hell about that. Worried that she was going to get to the truth of who he really was: the man beneath the corporate suit, the guy without his desk. Because on his worst days Elliott doubted there was much of a man there at all beneath the trappings of his corporate lifestyle, and that maybe his mother had been right in never pushing him to be more. Maybe she'd seen early what he was too cocky and ambitious to admit.

That there might not be much more of a man to be had.

It would certainly explain the hollow emptiness.

And his blazing desperation to fill it with *stuff*.

Owen pulled the ute to a halt by the barest of clearings in the bush on the side of the road, next to a blue steel gate.

'We're here,' she breathed. 'The Davidson property.'

'It's certainly not as impressive as Morgan's entry.'

'This is the back gate. Their four-year-old is allergic, so the hives are on the farthest corner of their farm.'

Owen pulled through and then closed the gate behind them before driving in low gear up a barely discernible track. He stopped at the top, in a croft of trees, near to two dozen white hives. Elliott pushed to his feet and guided Laney to the back edge of the ute before jumping down ahead of her.

Assisting her seemed the right thing to do, though he knew in his heart she'd probably been jumping down off the back of this truck since she was a kid. She sat on the back edge of the ute and felt for his shoulders as he stepped up between her legs and braced her gently around the waist. Then he lifted as she slid.

Helping her might be appropriate, but there was nothing appropriate about his reaction to her body's slide down his, coming so soon on the tail of yesterday's grope disguised as a rescue. Even through his own clothes his skin immediately questioned what she was wearing below the flimsy safety overalls. A tank top, maybe? Shorts? Didn't feel like much. Instead, as his hands bunched in the light waxy material, all he could feel was heat.

Laney's heat. His own.

She settled more certainly on her feet and tipped her head up on a murmur. 'Thank you.'

'You're welcome.'

And then it happened. Their proximity and the direction of his voice meant she was able to lock those deep grey eyes directly on his and even though his mind knew they were sightless, his heart felt sure that her soul was seeing him.

Right down into his own.

It was as inconceivable as the idea that she saw him as a ghost glow, yet utterly unshakeable.

She *was* seeing him on some level. Whether she knew it or not.

'Suit up, Elliott,' Owen said, slamming his door and moving straight to the side of the ute to unlash the empty hive boxes. 'Heaps to do.'

A pretty flush ran up Laney's jaw and she stepped back. 'Ignore him—everybody does. You're here observing.'

The glance Owen cast his sister was as brief as it was wounded.

'I don't mind helping out. A bit of labour will be good for me,' said Elliott.

'I don't want to be responsible for callousing up those hands.' The colour doubled as she realised what her casual comment was an admission of. 'But it's up to you.'

She turned and walked towards her brother, her knuckles lightly grazing the dirtied edge of the ute, keeping her orientated, and Owen loaded her up with equipment.

Elliott had to bite his tongue. Her brother treated her as if she was as capable as he was—and that was no doubt true—but deep down inside he couldn't shake the feeling that Helena Morgan was someone to be cherished, protected. Spoiled like a princess. He'd thought she was regal in those first moments yesterday and the sense hadn't left him. It was in her carriage. And her confidence. And the way she commanded any space she was in.

And he'd never in his life wanted so badly to cherish someone.

Nor known for certain how unwelcome that would be.

CHAPTER FIVE

IT WAS A full month before Elliott returned to the farm. A few short weeks for Laney to get her headspace and her perspective—and her tranquil existence—back in order.

Nowhere near long enough, judging by the little random rushes of anticipation as the weekend approached. The whole weekend, this time—not just the second half of Saturday and the first half of Sunday. Her mum had told her that Elliott was driving down mid-afternoon Friday, to get ahead of the weekend exodus down south.

She knew his car the moment it began travelling the long drive up to the house. With any other vehicle she'd hear the engine first and the tyre-crunch second. Whatever Elliott drove was close to silent running. Which meant it was expensive. Morgan's generated enough profit that her family could have expensive cars to match their architect-designed house perched high on the bluff, too, if they cared about that sort of thing. But this was a working property, where vehicles were function before form, and nothing here ran silently.

So she knew he was here, and knew he was probably settling in to his chalet—when had it become *his* chalet?—until dinner, and she was determined not to make a big deal of his arrival. Because it wasn't. He was just a visitor.

Despite what the ghost glow urged.

It had come back with a vengeance the moment she'd heard Elliott was returning—so strongly she wondered how she hadn't noticed it diminishing.

Ridiculous.

And just like that she decided to head into town for the evening. She wasn't about to sit through another meal unable to focus on anything but Elliott Garvey. And she wasn't about to indulge her body's insane anticipation, either. It would just have to wait.

She reached for her phone.

'Owen,' she said as soon as her brother answered her call. 'I changed my mind about dinner. How soon can we leave?'

Within the half-hour she was comfortably installed at the Liar's Saloon in Mitchell's Cliff, surrounded by Owen's mates and talking with the younger sister of her best friend. At least, *she* was talking; Kelly's sister seemed to be thoroughly distracted. Only about half of her answers were actually in synch with the conversation.

Laney sighed, giving up. 'So which one is it?'

'Huh?' Kristal asked, still not really attending.

'Which of my brother's mates are you all breathless for?'

Kristal's voice rose a half-octave in a half-croak, half-squeak protest. *'Laney!'*

'Sorry.' She leaned in closer and *faux*-whispered. 'Travis or Richard?'

'What makes you think it's not Owen?'

'Because Owen's *Owen*. He's not distraction-worthy.' And he had no real interests beyond the ocean.

'You say that because he's your brother.'

'I say that because he's a dufus.'

Kristal laughed, overly loud, confirming Laney's worst fears. *Owen.* The man-boy who couldn't keep a girlfriend for five minutes. 'Don't fall for Owen, Kristal. Fall for Travis. He's lovely.'

And Travis was the only one close to Kristal's age.

'I dated him in high school.'

'Oh. What about Rick, then?'

'Meh.'

'What about anyone else in this pub?'

'I don't want anyone else. I want O—'

Kristal's inward gasp was the first giveaway as the opening vowel of her brother's name morphed into a breathy, 'Oh, hello…'

The certain footfalls through the noisy pub were the second.

And Kristal's urgently whispered, 'Incoming!' as a waft of instantly recognisable cologne brushed towards them was final confirmation.

Elliott.

'Owen, good to see you,' that deep voice murmured.

Her brother's chair shifted and palm slapped palm.

'Welcome back, mate,' Owen said, before doing fast introductions around the table. Kristal—typically—gushed and giggled and seemed to forget all about her great infatuation of moments before in the face of a better, more interesting and even less suitable option.

Elliott pulled a chair up next to her with exaggerated movements. 'Laney.'

'Welcome back to the Peninsula. I have a big weekend planned for you.'

'I'm glad to hear it. How have you been?'

'Great. And you?' Every word was a mask for what she really wanted to say. And do. More than anything she wanted to reach out and brush her fingertips across his smooth ones again. In lieu of hello.

'Passable. Busy singing Morgan's praises to the senior partners.'

Oh, joy. 'You *have* remembered that nothing is a done deal, right?'

'Definitely. But in my experience optimism is generally rewarded.'

Laney could practically feel Kristal's speculation, and it must have been just as obvious outwardly because Elliott turned his voice away slightly.

'Kristal, is it? How do you know Laney?'

Once it would have angered her to have every conversation linked back to her. But she recognised it for the strategy it was, reconfirming Elliott as a kind man as well as good, subtly telling Kristal he wasn't interested. Pity Kristal was anything but subtle.

The heavy scent of gardenia wafted off the younger woman's skin as she tossed back her hair. Trademark move. 'Through my sister. They're best friends.'

'Kristal's sister is Kelly,' Laney murmured.

'Ah, the beautician.'

'Ex-beautician.' Kristal was sulky. 'Now shacked up with a farmer in Ireland.'

'You must miss her.'

The slight change in the timbre of his voice told Laney that Elliott was speaking to her. 'We both do.'

'But thank goodness for webcams, hey?' Kristal cut in, bright and overly loud, but in the absence of any kind of response from Elliott her conversation dried right up.

'Kelly did the full backpacking around Europe extravaganza a couple of years ago,' Laney said, mostly for something to say, 'and met Garth in a pub in County Kerry. I always knew I'd lose her to love.'

His chuckle flirted with the fine hairs on her skin. 'You didn't go with her?'

'Backpacking in Europe? Does that seem the sort of thing I might do?'

'I don't see why not.'

'Because she's *blind*,' Kristal pointed out helpfully. In a half-whisper. As if it was some kind of secret. Or maybe a reminder for Elliott.

Actually, Laney wouldn't put that past her. Kristal cheated at board games, too.

He ignored her. 'That doesn't stop you doing anything at home. Why would it be different overseas?'

'I had a business to run.' And it wouldn't have been fair on Kelly, who'd saved her whole working life for the opportunity. And because Laney liked to be independent—which she could be, at home. 'Besides, we get foreign tourists by the busload. Why would I need to leave?'

'Because there's a whole world to discover. People. Places.'

The implication irked. 'Better places? Better people?'

'Different. New. You're missing so much.'

'Surely wherever I went I'd be missing a lot? I might as well stay home and miss it.'

Disbelief puffed from his lips.

'Excuse me,' Kristal announced somewhat sulkily. 'I'm going to talk to Owen.'

Neither of them acknowledged her departure.

'That's quite a theory,' Elliott murmured.

'Feel free to disagree.'

'It seems impolitic to argue with—'

'A blind girl?'

'With the woman I'm relying on to keep an open mind this weekend.'

Oh. Back to business. Of course. 'I'll be sure to trade on that as fully as I can, then.'

'You should.' A smile enriched his words. 'It won't last for ever.'

'Have *you* travelled overseas?'

'Of course.'

As if it was automatically such a given. 'Why?'

'To see the world. To get a better understanding of my place in it.'

'How old were you?'

Maybe on someone else his pause would simply have been swallowed by the pub music. But to her it practically pulsed.

'I first went overseas when I was seventeen.'

'Seriously? Can you even get a passport before you're of age?'

'With parental consent.'

'And your mother let you go?'

'Eventually. It took me a year of campaigning. But I wore her down.'

'You wanted to go at sixteen?'

'I wanted to go at *thirteen*, but the law said I had to wait until I was sixteen.'

'Why so young?'

As always, he gave his answer actual thought. Laney filled the silence soaking up his scent.

'Because it was all there waiting for me.'

'And you couldn't wait for *it*?'

'I convinced myself I'd be missing something. And the only thing stopping me seeing it was my mother.'

'Could she not afford it?'

'She never travelled.'

Something in his tone tightened her chest. 'That's not actually a crime, Elliott.'

'My mother was free to make her own choices. I was trapped, unable to choose until I was sixteen. I hated that.'

'Having to wait?'

'Having to ask. Being reliant on someone who was never going to take me out of the state, let alone the country.'

'You never went anywhere as a kid?'

'We went on a grand total of one family holiday in my whole life. I drove further getting here to you.'

Getting to you. She forced the little thrill of those words down. He meant Morgan's. Of course he did. But still...

'So you headed off to see the world. How did you pay for it?'

'I'd been working after school in a fast food place since I was fourteen, I saved up enough for the first leg of my journey as soon as I left school.'

'To where?'

'Cheapest flight out of Perth was to Bali. You'd be amazed at how many people go to the trouble of travelling to another country and then don't want to engage with the locals. I ran errands for xenophobic Westerners for a few months before hopping over to Vietnam, then Thailand and India. Picking up whatever work I could get, always living local. Living cheap.

Exploiting whatever opportunities I could find as I went along. Country-hopping.'

'How did you manage the languages? The politics in some of those areas? As a kid?'

'I didn't always, but I got by. By the time I hit India I had a system and I was of age. Bars, hotels and restaurants were perfect for short-term work, because you could sneak at least one decent meal a day while getting paid. I kept a low profile and always kept moving.'

'You didn't want to stop?'

'*No.*' Passion leaked out of him as a groan. 'I'd been stopped my whole life. I just wanted to move.'

She shuffled around towards him. 'Then why did you come home?'

When she said 'home' it was with a respectful breath. But she got the sense that to Elliott it was more of a dirty word.

He accepted a drink from the waiter who had delivered it to their cluster of seats and then dropped his voice down for her hearing only.

'I grew up. Got tired of my own pace. And I realised that I could get the same spirit of…*conquering*…from finding small businesses and growing them. Selling for a profit. Eventually, that led to a buy-sell pattern that was as nomadic as my travelling but more profitable, and Ashmore Coolidge took me on as an intern. And the rest is history.'

What he saw as nomadism she saw as reluctance to commit. Not that it had made him any less money that way. 'No more travel?'

'For business, yes. And the odd holiday back to Bali, where it all started.'

'We're very different people,' she murmured.

The only part of his wanderlust that she could relate to was the frustration towards a parent. She'd felt it her whole life, but attached to her over-eager father, whereas Elliott's had been with his apparently under-achieving mother.

'Not so different. You wouldn't have grown Morgan's the way you have if you didn't have a pioneering spirit.'

'I grew it to secure our financial base. I wasn't looking to revolutionise the industry.'

'Yet you have in some ways.'

'What ways?'

'The apitoxin side of your business. Treating rheumatism and Parkinson's. That's pretty unusual. The surf wax.'

Hmm. Someone had been reading up.

'Apitoxin is not revolutionary. I started with bee venom in response to the Davidsons' allergic son—to help desensitise him so that they can stay on the land they love.'

And once she'd discovered that harvesting the venom didn't have to kill the bees, she'd realised it was a perfect by-product of what they did every day, anyway.

'And we produce near one of Australia's best surf regions. Of course we were going to make a speciality board wax. But I still didn't invent the idea.'

'There's nothing that Morgan's is doing that's totally unique? What about your facial recognition work?'

Really? Was he going to keep badgering until she confessed to being the Steve Jobs of bees? 'It's *the bees* that are amazing. And the software engineers. Not me.'

'It was your proposal.' But something in her expression must have finally dawned on him. 'Why don't you want to be amazing, Laney?'

Frustration hissed out of her. 'Because I'm not. I'm just me. Anything I do is out of curiosity or the desire to strengthen our brand. I'm not curing cancer or splitting atoms.'

'Not yet…'

Ugh..! 'Why does everyone try to make me more than I am? I just work with bees. They are my business and I try to be smart about business. But that's it.'

'Laney—'

'We have a whole weekend ahead of us, and I'm not going

to show you anything of interest if you don't let this go. Your visit is about Morgan's—not about me.'

'Okay, take it easy. I'll drop the subject. But at some point you're going to have to accept what everyone else knows—that you *are* Morgan's.'

You are *Morgan's*.

She wasn't. She didn't want to be. She was *a* Morgan and that was it. Morgan's was a family, a plural, a heritage and a way of life. It was the genetic memory and the learning of everyone who'd ever had anything to do with their bees, going right back as far as their founder, her great-grandfather, and that first Queen he'd hived up as a hobby.

She and Morgan's were as symbiotic as queens and their colonies: one couldn't exist without the other. But, as reverent as they were while the Queen lived, ultimately when she was lost the colony just made a new one. They kept the hive strong.

It wasn't personal with bees.

So why was Elliott trying to personalise this? Why was he trying to hang Morgan's success around her neck, all millstone-ish? And why was he working his way up to making Morgan's continued success contingent somehow on her...what had he called it...?

Her pioneering spirit.

As if that was a prerequisite for something to come.

'Good morning.'

Wilbur slowed her to a halt halfway to the chalet. 'Morning, Elliott. Sleep well?'

'I slept brilliantly. May I?'

How did she know what he was asking? Yet she did. 'Sure.'

She unclipped her harness and gave Elliott the moment he'd asked for with Captain Furry-Pants. Released, Wilbur knew he was allowed to enjoy it. Just be a dog. The two of them enjoyed a mutual rough-house until they naturally parted, all done.

She buckled up the harness again and Wilbur sat at attention by her leg. 'No possums this time?'

'Nothing I didn't sleep through.'

Bully for him. She'd slept as badly as those possums. 'Have you had breakfast?'

'I've had coffee. Close enough.'

'That might work for you in the city, but here a coffee doesn't fuel you until morning tea. You'd better have a reasonable lunch.'

'Yes, ma'am.'

She tipped her head. 'I don't want to have to carry you if you faint.'

His chuckle carried them across the paddock. 'So what's the plan for this morning?'

'I thought I'd show you where we make the queens and the Royal Jelly. Two more of our sidelines.'

'You *make* the queens?'

'Well, the bees do it. We just give them a nudge.'

Elliott followed Laney and Wilbur between fences and along the crunch of a gravel path towards the plant sector. Inside, a pair of workers chatted to each other over the *whirr-whirr* of the centrifuge harvester as they worked. It was exactly per the videos Elliott had watched for research. But over in the corner progress was more silent and studied. And that was where Laney was leading him.

If she'd walked him off a cliff he'd have considered following.

Which went to show how desperate he'd become in his hunt for the meaning of life.

'Hi, Laney.' Two voices piped up at the same time.

Laney introduced them and then launched into presentation mode.

'So, when the Queen is ready to step down, she creates special cells and her attendants know to pack them with super-nutritious jelly instead of honey.' She ran her long fingers along the work her staff were doing until she found the enlarged cells. 'It's the exclusive diet of Royal Jelly which produces a fertile virgin queen instead of an infertile worker bee. Hence the name.'

The way she said it—with such a *ta-da!* in her voice… It made him wish he hadn't already done so much reading up. That way her passion could infect him for real. 'So you place artificial cells in the hive and the attendants just fill it? No questions asked?'

She passed him a row of artificial queen cups to examine. 'Bees aren't good with the big picture. And this is the most important moment in their bee career. Thousands of bees will be born and die without ever facing such responsibility.'

Jeez—if he'd waited for opportunities to come to him he'd have withered and died right there in his tiny alley-facing office.

'So a new queen hatches and the hive is happy ever after?'

Her laugh was overly loud even in the busy plant. 'No, multiple virgin queens emerge and fight to the death until only the strongest is left standing.'

Okay, that hadn't been in any of his pre-reading. 'That's very…Machiavellian.'

'Once the victor emerges she has a couple of days to gather her strength and then she mates with as many drones from unrelated hives as she can in a day in a special yard we set up.'

'Bloodied and hepped up on battle frenzy? I'm amazed she gets any takers at all.'

'The drones are highly motivated. Every egg a queen will ever produce in her lifetime comes from that single blazing day of sexual excess.'

'When I come back I want to be a drone,' he said. 'Sounds like they have it best.'

'Sure. If you don't mind getting your genitals torn out for your troubles.'

His, *'Sorry…?'* was more of a choke.

'When the drone yard is littered with disembowelled corpses she flies back to her starter hive and then lays for the rest of her months-long life.'

Lucky she couldn't see his gape.

'I thought you were this gentle, sweet farm girl. I take it all back. You are as ruthless as they come, Helena Morgan.'

She didn't look the slightest bit put out—if anything she looked pleased. 'Surely that's a compliment, coming from you? Besides, if you don't like that then maybe we shouldn't show you how Royal Jelly is produced.'

'What could possibly top pimping, disembowelment, sanctioned orgies and virgins fighting to the death?'

One of Laney's staff busied himself melting the wax seal on the rest of the queen cells with a heat lamp and then scooped out the Royal Jelly onto the edge of a collection container, plucked a tiny grub out and squashed it on the table.

Laney's face was comically grave. 'Bee-o-cide.'

For some reason that shocked him more than anything else she'd done or said. In his mind Laney was as peace-and-love as any hippy, so bee-slaughter didn't sit comfortably. 'But you go to so much trouble to save the other bees?'

'Has it only just dawned on you that we're farmers, Elliott? These ones would have fought to the death anyway. We just pre-pick the survivor.'

'So you play God?'

'They're essentially clones. The ethics get a little murky. Besides, the grubs are tiny when they're swamped in Royal Jelly. Virtually insentient.'

'Wow.' He shook his surprise free. 'Here I was, feeling sorry for the worker bees who slave away keeping the voracious Queen and her royal young in riches, but I think they might actually have the best of the lot. They spend their days seeing the world, scooping up nectar in the warm sunshine, stretching their wings.'

Her pretty face tightened. 'I thought you would have identified more with the Queen.'

'Why?'

'Entombed in your office cell. Growing large on gathered riches. Fighting for supremacy against your colleagues until you run the show and then working yourself to death until you either create your own replacement or someone knocks you off.'

That dismal view of Ashmore Coolidge really wasn't all that far off reality. On its worst days. 'You make my job sound a lot more exciting than it is. I just sit in an office and try to be smart.'

'Bees have a system. It's worked for them for a very long time. We don't mess with it—we just work with it. And we birth a heck of a lot more bees than we kill.'

And this *was* a farm, after all. Primary production. They did the dirty work so the rest of the country could eat. Had he really expected it to include no death at all just because it was bees and not beef?

He watched the process a few times over and got a sense of how fast the two employees could work, how many queens could be created in a day, and how much Royal Jelly was harvested. Then he multiplied that by the number of hives their production report said were in play at any one time and the number of times a year that this process happened to the same hive.

'That's a lot of jelly in a year.' At a small fortune per kilo. Sticky gold. 'What do you do with all the Queens?'

His unease about Laney's straight-faced acceptance of bee-o-cide couldn't outlast his curiosity. His mind buzzed with thoughts of global expansion potential and operational ramifications. An increasing number of northern hemisphere countries were losing entire apiaries as their winters worsened. Southern hemisphere breeders could ship them new hives, ready to go in spring and keep their agriculture alive.

The possibilities, the income—and Ashmore Coolidge's commission—were endless.

'Come on—show me the honey extraction.'

CHAPTER SIX

LANEY HAD BEEN right about breakfast. He should have eaten before starting. It wasn't even noon yet and he was flagging already.

'I blame it on the country air,' he grumbled when she queried his increasing quietness.

'You're standing in a shed full of energy.'

'I can't eat the honey your staff have gone to so much trouble to extract.'

'No. But you can eat honey that *you've* gone to trouble to extract. Come on. I'll show you our smallest sideline.'

Two sun-bleached girls—one brunette, one Nordic-looking—sat with a plastic crate of fresh honeycomb between them, squeezing the honey out by hand.

'Here,' Laney said, nudging an empty stool with her foot. She pulled another over from the corner and sat it next to his.

The Nordic girl handed him a chunk of whole messy honeycomb, complete with the odd bee carcass.

'Have you ever milked a cow?' Laney asked.

Of course he hadn't. That would have required a normal childhood visit to a farm. But she couldn't see his pointed look so he was forced to reconsider his sarcasm.

'No.'

'Okay, then. Um…have you ever caught a fish?'

'Yes.' That he *had* done. He and Danny on *Misfit*. Though, to be fair, their boat trips were more about talking and drinking than any concerted effort at catching a fish.

'Okay, so harvesting honey manually is the same kind of slow, steady action as when you're running a fishing line. Squeeze, release. Squeeze, release.' She demonstrated on thin air.

He glanced at the girl next to him, got a sense of the action and then tried it. A chunk of his honeycomb immediately came away and fell into the collection container—wax and all—with a dull thud.

'Too hard.' Laney laughed and bent to retrieve it before squeezing its honey free herself. 'Squeeze…release…' she repeated, and then leaned half over him to place her hands around his. 'Here, like this…'

Her strong fingers closed gently around his which, in turn, closed much less gently around the honeycomb. Instantly he got a sense of how light his touch had to be.

'Squeeze…' She did so and it was steady and gentle, yet oddly firm at the same time. 'And release…'

Releasing came with a slight twist of her wrists that somehow compelled the honey out of the comb while keeping the waxy parts more or less in hand. She repeated both motions again, brushing more fully against him on the 'squeeze' and then retreating slightly on the 'release'.

The action definitely reminded him of something, but it sure as heck wasn't fishing. And he sure as heck shouldn't be thinking about it now. But with Laney this close, all clean and warm and stretched across him as she was, it was hard to think of anything else.

'You do this manually?' He forced words from his lips just as she was doing with the honey from the honeycomb. Just to return some normality to this highly charged moment. 'Why?'

'It's good training for new staff, but there's also a small market for naturally harvested honey. Wax, dead bees and all. We sell it as Morgan's Naturále.'

Au naturále was not something he should be thinking about right now any more than the sensual squeeze and release action of Laney's hands coiled so intimately around his. He concentrated on the action, on the accumulating pool of raw honey in the container between his legs, and very much *not* on the earthy woman by his side.

She released his hands and sat back, leaving hers dripping over the collection container while he continued.

Eventually Laney spoke. 'Stasia?'

The girl to his right peered into his bucket and then said in accented English, 'Not bad.'

Stasia tapped another tub with her foot and Elliott tossed the remaining ball of waxy mush in with hers. His hands were honey-coated, like sticky, sweet gloves. Stasia took his container and upended his honey into her own as Laney stood. Elliott automatically turned for the sinks that they'd used before the little demonstration.

'No.' Laney caught him with a gentle body-block, given her hands were as honey-coated as his. Her block meant she brushed into him much harder than she already had. 'That's the whole point.'

'Then how do I get it off?'

'Like this.'

She lifted her hand and moved her lips close to where a rivulet of dark honey ran down her wrist. As he watched her tongue came out and caught it, tracing it back up her wrist to its source. His body responded immediately.

Are you freaking kidding me?

'It's the best bit,' she purred. 'You wanted some energy.'

Ah, no... Energy was not going to be a problem now. His bloodstream was suddenly awash with adrenaline and a dozen hormones designed to get—and hold—his attention. But he followed her lead, sucking the honey off his own fingers one by one, watching her do the same to hers. The warm, sweet goo stuck to his lips—and to hers—exactly as his gaze was bonded to Laney. He fully exploited the opportunity to watch her without her knowing.

He closed his mouth around his own finger as she did the same with hers, the real sweetness merging with the imagined sweetness of what her lips were doing as they made steady work of the honey.

If he timed it just right it was almost as if their two mouths were meeting each other through the sticky goodness. His imagination just about exploded over how amazing that might be.

'Nice, huh?' Stasia said from behind him, reminding him that the two of them weren't *actually* alone in a dark place, kissing the heck out of each other.

'Yeah.' He stumbled back a half-step, breaking Laney's spell. Hopefully she'd chalk that deep husk in his voice to honey appreciation.

'It's jarrah,' Laney said. 'From the state forest bees. Nothing quite like it.' Her ponytail tilted. 'Have you had enough?'

Nope. Nowhere near. 'Just about.'

He finished the stickiest bits off and then joined Laney at the wash-trough to scrub the rest free. His body cried out at the wasted opportunity. And he'd never taste honey again without remembering the past few minutes.

And Laney.

'So now what?' he asked, when he was sure his voice would hold.

'I wondered if you'd like to see more of the property? To understand its scope?'

Her simple suggestion was saturated with pride. And of course he did. But he would have said yes to just about anything that would have meant more time with Laney.

'That sounds like a bigger job than Wilbur will be up for.'

'Oh, definitely. I only take him up there occasionally. Both of us lack the stamina required.'

He'd beg to differ. Every part of her screamed endurance.

'If you don't mind driving we can take one of the Morgan's utes. I'll pack us a lunch.'

More time alone with Laney. More time to learn about the business—and about her—and food for his hollow stomach into the bargain. It was just a pity she couldn't pack something to fill his empty soul.

'Sounds great.'

'Okay. Let's head back to the house and you can pick up the ute while I throw together something to eat.'

Throw together.

As if this was just a casual thing. As if her heart wasn't doing the whole *Riverdance* thing on her diaphragm.

The ute slowed to a rumbly idle and Elliott turned to her. 'Now where?'

'Is there nothing in front of us but ocean?'

'From here to the horizon.'

'Okay, turn right along the coast track.'

'How far?'

'Until you see dense trees to the north.'

'And to the south?'

'The south is a little sketchy—as you discovered the first day you were here.' The day he'd watched her dancing and being a fool with Wilbur, wading in the water with her skirt hiked up to her hips—all of the above—without realising he was partly on Morgan land.

They turned north onto the coast track and Laney lowered her window to enjoy the closeness of the sea. It filled the ute's cabin with the smell of ocean and the slight dampness of salty spray.

'You love the ocean?' Elliott asked.

'I love the coast, generally.'

'Well, you certainly picked the right place to grow up, then. It's beautiful.'

She didn't need to agree aloud. Her sigh said it for her.

'How do you experience it?' he risked. 'The coast.'

'I can smell the vastness of the ocean on the air. And the sounds coming off the land are more...muted than the ones from the sea. So, to me, the coast is all about space and open air and beauty and deep, fresh breaths.'

She heard the moment he clicked his teeth closed on whatever he'd been about to say.

'What? Go ahead and ask.'

'It wasn't a question,' he said. 'I just… It saddens me that you'll never see it. So you can see how right you are.'

Don't feel sorry for me…

'Have you ever heard a bee quack?'

As subject-changers went, that was pretty solid. Though hardly subtle.

But she was rewarded with one of Elliott's warm laughs. 'Can't say I have.'

'It's more of a battle cry, really. The first virgin queen to hatch out *toots* to taunt the yet-to-be-born queens and they *quack* back at her from inside their cells, calling her on her challenge and begging to be let out so they can fight her.'

'Uh-huh…'

'But they're not actually making a sound—they're communicating with vibrations. We just hear it as sound because we lack the sensory perception to feel it as vibration.'

'A vibratory Morse code?'

'Yeah. But it doesn't make the experience any less real for us because we hear it as sound. It's just a different way of perceiving the same thing. I'm no more deprived by not seeing something than the bees are by not hearing their own toots. We both still experience it.'

'Wouldn't you like someone to experience the world your way sometimes?'

No one had ever asked her that before. They were usually more concerned about *her* sharing *their* experiences. 'Can any of us ever truly share our own perceptions? I've had other blind kids here and even we didn't experience things the same way.'

'Maybe not.'

'My joys and disappointments are as relative as yours. I get more pleasure from the ocean than just about anything else. I get the least pleasure from thinking about the day I'll need to let Captain Furry-Pants go. And there are a thousand differentials in between.'

'Really? Your dog more than your family?'

'Any of them will break my heart, of course, but Wilbur… He has meant freedom and trust—' *and love* '—for me for so long. I know that's going to be a really, really bad day.'

Vulnerability saturated her voice and she wondered what he'd do with it.

'I get it, you know. Why you get tired of people focussing on your blindness.'

'Actually, that's not it. Not exclusively anyway. I just…'

'Just what?'

'*Ugh.* This whole conversation is harder because of what you do.'

'Realising?'

'It's your job to look at things in terms of their potential.'

'You don't want me looking at your potential?'

'No.' *Because that means you're not looking at me.* 'Because people are more than just the sum of their achievements.'

'Yeah. But I'm not paid to assess how nice people are. I'm trained to look at what they've done and what they still could do.'

Right. She did somehow manage to keep forgetting that. This was *work* for him. 'So what happens to the businesses you work with that aren't realising their potential? Or that have none?'

'I cut them free. Find something with more return on the investment of my time.'

The implication tugged at her heart hard enough to hurt. 'Does that go for people, too?'

His silence was filled with a frown.

She tried a different approach. 'Tell me… Do you have any ordinary friends?'

'Depends what you mean by "ordinary".'

'Do you have any friends who aren't high achievers, or leaders in their field, or go-getters like you?'

'No. But the world I live in tends to be filled with high achievers. We all move at the same pace.'

Just like the bees. All one frequency. And someone new to the hive had to match it or get out of the way.

'Do you not have a single person in your life who is just a regular person? With no great ambitions or plans? Someone who just lives the life they are presented with?'

Elliott's snort was immediate. 'You just described my mother.'

'Really? Yet you ended up so different?'

'Thank you.'

Discomfort dribbled like cool water down her spine. But she held her judgement.

He heard it, anyway, in her silence.

'My childhood was not like yours, Laney.'

Not if he'd left the country at the first opportunity, no. 'Was it bad?'

'It wasn't *hell,* but we struggled for everything we had. We existed, with our noses just poking up above the poverty line. And that seemed sufficient for my mother.'

'But it wasn't enough for you?'

'No. It was not. Not when I could see what others had. I always fought to be better. Brighter. More secure.'

'She didn't share your ambition?'

'She did not.'

Anyone else probably wouldn't have heard his quiet words as he turned them out through the far window. But Laney did. Of course she did. She heard the individual pitch differences between two bees—she wasn't going to have any trouble with gravelly tones less than a foot away from her, no matter how whispered.

'I'm sorry.'

'Don't be. I rose above it—got out.'

'No. I meant I'm sorry that you don't have a good relationship with your mother. Mothers are important.'

Silence.

'It's not a bad relationship,' he defended, finally. 'We're just very different. I think I inherited more of my father's traits.'

'Maybe that made things harder for your mother? That you were like him?'

'Don't go imagining that there was a great "love lost" story there, Laney. He was a one-night stand in the village at a Youth Championships meet. There was no great romance.'

'She was an athlete?' Somehow that didn't fit with the passive woman he'd described.

'Gymnast. Until me. Then she just threw it all in.'

Having a kid would do that to a woman's sporting career... But there was real pain beneath all that judgement, so she holstered that opinion, too.

'How old was she?'

'Sixteen.'

'Wow. The Garvey family all like to strike out young, then?'

The surprise in his voice was palpable. 'She still lives in the house we were assigned when I was born. She bought it in a state buy-back scheme. How is that striking out?'

Oh… A state housing kid. Suddenly that enormous chip on his shoulder took a more defined shape. 'On her own, with a tiny baby and no father… That's just as courageous as you jetting off to Bali.'

More so, maybe.

The ute wheels rattled on the gravel track. Eventually she accepted that he wasn't going to reply.

'Elliott?'

'I'm processing.'

Not happily, by the sound of it. She felt for his forearm where it rested on the gearstick and laid her hand there. But his sigh didn't sound much relieved. If anything it sounded irritated. Tension saturated his tone.

'Do you know how small I feel for giving an earful of *wahh* about my crappy childhood to a woman who was blind all of hers?'

'My childhood was pretty much great,' she said. 'Yours wasn't. It's okay to comment on that.'

A half-breathed *mmm* was her only answer. And something about it gave her the courage to go beyond what was probably polite.

'Do you love her?'

No answer. But his silence didn't feel like a no. On the contrary.

So she amended. 'Does she love you?'

'As much as she can, given I ruined her life.'

Empathy washed through her in a torrent. 'She told you that?'

'She didn't have to. No way she'd have struggled like we did if I hadn't been part of the picture. She was a world champion. Destined for big things.'

The ghost glow high in her consciousness changed shape then, added depth and complexity. Resembled much more a wounded little boy than a confident man.

He cleared his throat. 'Anyway, enough of my bleating. Do I just keep following this track?'

She knew enough about her brother and father to know when to let something lie. 'Have you hit the crossroad yet?'

'Nope.'

Every instinct wanted to reach out and curl her fingers around his. To lend him her strength. But something told her it wouldn't be welcomed. 'Stop driving like such a nanna. We don't have all day.'

His grudging chuckle fuelled a little boost in speed and they started moving along more steadily. When he slowed the ute again a few minutes later she directed him left.

'Where does this lead?'

'Another lookout. Dad proposed to Mum up here.'

'Really? Are you sure you want to show me somewhere so…personal?'

Why? Did he not want to encourage anything personal between them? 'It's not personal for me. I wasn't even born yet. When Mum brings you here I'll start worrying.'

'I should be so lucky.'

'Flirt.' She smiled.

'Cynic.'

'Just pull over anywhere,' she instructed. He did, and killed the engine. 'Now, remember, don't let me walk off the cliff or something. I don't come here that often.'

'Jeez, Laney. No pressure.'

It felt good to laugh again after the tension of the past few minutes. 'I just don't want you to forget that you're my Wilbur this afternoon.'

'What happened to wanting equality?'

'I want to live, more.'

She got out as he did, but stayed close to the ute until he came around to her side and placed her hand gently on his bent arm. She took a few tentative steps forward.

'There's a few loose rocks…'

'I'm really only concerned about the big drop that ends in a splash.' Or a *splat,* probably, if the tide was out. 'The rest is just normal to me.'

He led her forward a short way, then stopped. 'This is about as far as I am comfortable taking you.'

Sweet how nervous he was about this. 'What do you see?'

'More view. More ocean. It's still lovely.'

'Turn around.'

He shuffled them both around so the water was to their back. 'Now what do you see?'

'Wow. *Everything.* It's higher than I realised here. The forest to our left, all green and dense, Mitchell's Cliff in the very far distance, and the highway. Both are Toytown-tiny. And I can even see your homestead and all the honey-harvesting plant in between. Your house looks like it's practically overhanging the ocean from here. No wonder your view is so awesome.'

'Dad says you can see the entirety of the Morgan land from here. That's why he brought Mum here to propose—so she could see what she was getting into the bargain.'

'Did he think she needed a sweetener?'

The truth wasn't quite so romantic. 'No. He wanted her to be clear that she was taking on the life as well as the man. He needed her to know that he wasn't going to change after marriage and that this was where they'd live for ever.'

And their children, and their children's children…

'Did it work?'

'She said that one moment brought it all into crashing focus for her. Morgan's was his life. And so she had to make it hers too. It was all or nothing.'

'But she said yes.'

The tiniest glow filled her, thinking about the love her parents shared. 'Of course. They were perfect for each other.'

'Happily ever after, then?'

'Like all good stories.'

Elliott turned them both back to the ute. 'So, you said something about a basket…?'

'Told you you'd be starving. Even with the honey snack.'

'Stop gloating and start producing.'

Together they unloaded the hastily packed hamper.

Laney turned her back to the stiff breeze coming off the ocean and curled her legs under her. Its every buffet on her back was enhancing her perception of the kind of day it was out on the ocean. Consequently her hair whipped around her face wildly at times.

'You okay there?'

'I figured you might as well get to enjoy the view since it's wasted on me.' Her view was probably of the ute.

'It just got even better, then.'

'Flatterer.' Her laugh was half-snort. 'Totally working, by the way.'

'This is some spread.' He chuckled opposite her. 'Cheese, pickled onions, ham, and more of your mother's bread.'

It occurred to her to tease him for describing for her what was in the picnic that she'd packed herself, but then she realised that the warm sensation under her ribs was because he'd bothered. 'And honey on that bread for dessert.'

'Good choice.'

'Not too rural for you?'

'I had everything but the honey in the gardens of a French

church once and called it exotic. I'd be a hypocrite to call it anything else here, with ocean and sky all around us.'

They busied themselves loading ingredients onto thick wedges of bread. Laney had a few moments of self-conscious-ness, fumbling with the food in front of Elliott, but he didn't comment and he didn't rush in to help her out so she just fin-ished her fumbling and got stuck in to the important job of fill-ing her gnawing stomach.

'So, is your dad still involved with basketball?'

'No idea. I don't know who he is.'

She paused with her sandwich halfway to her mouth. No fa-ther and no relationship with his mother. What a lonely child-hood. 'Oh…'

His voice shrugged. 'You don't miss what you never had.'

Wasn't that exactly what she'd been trying to tell him about her vision? 'You mean that?'

'When I was little I used to make up complicated fantasies of this famous sportsman coming back for me. Taking me away to be part of his exciting, dynamic life. But the reality is he was just a guy who played basketball well and slept with my mother once. He doesn't even know I exist. But I guess I needed the fantasy to hang on to, so he served his purpose.'

The lie resonated through his thick voice. He cared. He cared a lot.

'Well, that's making *my* dad look pretty golden, hey?' she breathed.

'Your father *is* golden. Astute, driven, family-orientated, committed. What's not to love?'

'I do love him, of course. But I didn't always want to.'

'What do you mean?'

'All that commitment and drive? It can be hard when you're a kid and he's focussing it all on you.'

Fiercely.

All the public services he'd challenged and the concessions he'd pressured the district council into for the only blind person in town. All the letters he'd written. All the calls to his local representative. Making sure that his daughter was not denied one single opportunity in life.

Meaning she'd got a heck of a lot more than the average kid as a result.

'He obviously feels he has a lot to make up to you for.'

'And has done so—many times over. But no kid wants to be the centre of attention like that.'

'Especially not you.'

'Meaning?'

'Meaning I'm starting to understand your reticence to own your achievements.'

'I'm not reluctant, Elliott, I'm just a realist. If I thought for a moment that—'

'Don't move, Laney!'

The urgency in his voice completely stole her attention. Was the cliff-face crumbling? Had a snake appeared from the grass?

'What?'

'Bee.'

The seriousness with which he announced the single word was almost comic. 'Where?'

'On your fringe.'

'Don't kill it.'

He puffed his offence out. 'I'm not going to *kill* it. And—PS—you're hardly in a position to lecture *me* about bee-o-cide.'

She sat, carefully motionless. 'This is a fully grown, fully functioning bee. Where is it now?'

'Just clinging there.'

'It's probably exhausted from fighting the gusts. I'll let it recover out of the wind and then point it towards home.'

She leaned forward slightly and felt her way along the remnants of their meal for the honey. It took two seconds to get a fingertip full of instant bee fuel. 'Left or right?'

'On your left, about five centimetres above your eye.' He *whoah*ed her as she slowly slid her finger up past her ear. 'Right there.'

And then she just…sat there… Feeling absolutely nothing and hearing absolutely nothing except the wind buffeting against her body, but hoping the bee would make its way to the unexpected energy source. Hoping she hadn't disturbed it into flying off, leaving her sitting here looking like a complete idiot.

Though surely he'd tell her.

Surely.

Opening herself up to ridicule was not something that came naturally to her.

'It's feeding.' Amazement saturated Elliott's voice.

She made sure not to move during her little laugh. 'You are *such* a city kid.'

'I'll be sure to return the sentiment when you're in the city and you're experiencing something for the first time.'

Thank goodness for the bee or she'd have jerked her head in his direction—sight or no sight. 'Is that an invitation?'

Silence…

Awkward silence.

'It was an assumption. That you'll be up there one day on business.'

Survival instinct forced her to keep it light. 'Are you tired of country runs already? Wanting us to come to you?'

'Not at all. I enjoy the thinking time on the way down and back. But I guess I can't imagine you *never* visiting the city.' He cleared his throat. 'And I assumed I'd see you if you did. You know—for lunch or something.'

'Maybe you would. I don't really know anyone else up there.' Why would she? 'So I'd probably have no reason to go.'

'You truly aren't curious at all?'

'Not really. What does the city have that I can't get here? Things that I could enjoy,' she added before he could start peppering her with a long list of things she couldn't see.

'I don't know…elephants?'

The unexpectedness of that stirred a chuckle out of her. 'There are elephants roaming wild in the city?'

'There's a zoo across the river from Ashmore Coolidge's

offices full of animals you'd never get down here. And concerts… You could go to a concert.'

'We have one of the state's biggest vineyard concert venues in the next district. They have multiple events every season.'

'You could go to the races…'

'Where do you think all those horses qualify for their city races?'

'Okay, what about the university? You could visit the facial recognition team. I'm sure they'd love to show you their progress in person.'

'Ooh…' That could be quite interesting. *Wait…* When had this stopped being hypothetical and started being something she was actually thinking about? 'Or I could just email them.'

'Just admit it, Laney. You won't know what's interesting until you find yourself being interested by it. Who knows? You might share my passion for parasailing or something equally random.'

She shifted her other hand to support the elbow holding up the finger that was feeding the bee. She wished it would eat faster so she could feel a tiny bit less dopey.

'You parasail?'

'Yeah. I co-own a speedboat with a mate of mine and we go out whenever we can, take turns going up. Why?' His voice grew keen. 'Is that something that interests you?'

If it involved flying, it sure did. 'Maybe.'

'Have you ever done any water sports?'

'Owen taught me to surf a little bit.'

'Were you any good?'

'Not really, but I liked the sensation of just…floating on the swell. Being supported by the waves. I've always wondered if flying would be the same.'

Speaking of flight… In the silence between her words and his answer, she heard the bee give a test buzz of its wings.

'I'll take you parasailing,' he offered.

'Down here?'

'No… On my boat. If we do it then you need to come up to the city.'

Need to. Which meant he wanted her to. 'Why can't you just motor down the coast?'

'I work for Ashmore Coolidge, Laney, not for you. If you want to come out with me on *my* boat on *my* weekend off then you need to come up to *my* turf.'

Firm. Uncompromising. And totally reasonable under the circumstances. Her heart pumped out resentment. She'd fought all her life to get people to treat her like anyone else and now that someone was, was she getting snotty about it? Had she grown up feeling more entitled than she'd realised?

Elliott's challenge hung out there, live and real.

'Okay. Maybe I will,' she said. Never one to back down.

'Good. When?'

Sudden pressure—and something else—fisted in her belly. 'When are you going out next?'

'We were going to try for next weekend. Weather permitting.'

So soon? But she wasn't about to admit how much that freaked her out. 'Okay. Next weekend, then.'

Yikes…

'How about I collect you from the train Saturday morning and drive you back down here Saturday night? Or you could stay over.'

Owen had once described the flashing lights of an ambulance that had passed and she saw them now, vivid in her imagination. She definitely heard them.

Or you could stay over.

You know, just like that…

She ignored that part of his comment completely. Very grown-up of her. 'I'm sure you've got better things to do with your Saturday night than chauffeur me around.'

'Not really. Plus then I can finish up my review of your facilities and we'll have something to decide.'

'Um…okay, then?'

'Is that a question or a statement?'

What was she doing? She was twenty-five years old, for cry-ing out loud. Why was she letting him get to her like this? She wanted to flick her hair back defiantly but didn't out of respect for the bee. Instead she just sat up straighter.

'It's a statement. Yes. I'll take the train up next Saturday.'

'Great. I'll schedule it in.'

Elliott's carefully moderated tone was pretty slick, but she'd been mining people's voices for subtext her whole life. She could hear enthusiasm under all the nonchalance. The ques-tion was, was he pleased she was coming out on his boat next week or was he just pleased he'd got his way?

Yeah, well, good luck with that. Hopefully, his super cor-porate training had prepared him for disappointment. Because squiring her around the city wasn't going to change her mind one bit about taking Morgan's global.

The tiny buzz past her ear was her only evidence that the bee had finished its pitstop and headed off back towards its hive.

'At last!' she groaned, lowering her aching arm and slipping her still honeyed finger between her lips.

'You have honey in your hair.'

And before she could do much more than wince about how undignified that particular image was the slight rattle of the food containers on the picnic blanket told her that Elliott had braced a hand amongst them so that his other hand could brush against her forehead gently, plucking the offending lock away from her skin.

He lingered in that position, his knuckles gently brushing against her forehead. 'Want me to pour some water on it?'

'No. I'll have a shower when we get home. Wash it out.'

Obviously. Heck—you'd think she'd never been touched by a man before.

A few slight tugs on her hair told her he was removing the worst of it, but then he let his knuckles brush the rest of her hair back away from her face.

'Your eyes look very blue up here,' he murmured. All close and breathy.

All the better not to see you with. 'What do they usually look like?'

'Grey. Bottomless.'

Even shrugging felt almost beyond her as his knuckles curled and turned into fingers instead. Blue, grey… It was meaningless at the best of times, and this definitely wasn't her brain at its best. It was completely fixated on Elliott's fingers as they brushed—as light and soft as they had been for such a short moment the first time he'd come here—down her jaw.

'Stay still…'

He took her clean fingers in his, raised them to his face, and placed them gently on his own cheek.

'Knock yourself out,' he breathed. Low, intimate. Just a hint of gravel.

Every part of her tightened up. She didn't move her hand a single millimetre. But she didn't take it off, either.

'When I said learning someone's face was something very personal I didn't mean just for you.'

'I know. But I'm hoping since I just played with your hair I've broken the ice sufficiently.'

'Sufficiently for what?'

'That you might be comfortable enough, now, to let your fingers see what I look like.'

'Why?'

'Because I'd like you to know.'

'Why?'

His puff of breath tickled her wrist. 'I have no idea.'

The raw, confused honesty of that disarmed her enough to spread the fingers of her right hand slightly and spider them gently up his face. The rasp of a half-day's stubble teased her sensitive pads and resonated deep down inside her. Incentive enough to move away from the strong angles of his jawline across towards his nose. She kept her trajectory upward so that she bypassed his lips.

Pure survival instinct.

Nose: pretty much where you'd expect to find it, and with the slight kink he'd told her about. Strong wide brow with eyebrows a heck of a lot tamer than her father's.

'Did you cut your hair?'

'No. Why?'

'You said your hair fell down over your brow.'

His fingers came up to guide hers further upward, to where his hair sat neatly corralled against the buffeting winds.

'Is that…?' She frowned at the very thought. 'Is that bee wax?'

'It's a hard styling wax. Commercial.'

She hadn't pegged him for a manscaper. 'Styling wax doesn't get any manlier just because you put the word "hard" in front of it.'

'Surely Owen and his mates use product in their hair before a big night out?'

Her fingers paused on his forehead and she wondered that he'd consider a few hours with her on the farm as worthy of grooming. 'We'd be lucky if they *combed* their hair before a big night out.'

'Why are you frowning?'

'Just thinking of a potential market. Hair wax.'

The shift of facial muscles under her fingers suggested he was smiling, but his voice confirmed it. 'Can't keep a good businesswoman down.'

She raised her other hand and put both sets of fingers to work exploring the texture of his hair, rubbing the waxy residue between her thumb and forefinger. Getting a sense of it.

'Interesting.'

'My hair or my face?'

Right. His face… That was what she was supposed to be doing. Not playing with his thick hair.

She fluttered her right hand back down past his eye and along his cheekbone, and then—when she couldn't delay the moment of truth a moment longer—quickly traced her middle fingers across his *'I'm told I have kissable'* lips. They parted just slightly before she could leave them and breath heated her finger-pads for half a heartbeat.

'So there you go,' Elliott rumbled, then cleared his throat. 'Now you've really seen me.'

A nervous smile broke free. 'And played with your hair for longer than is polite. Though what do you mean, *really* seen you?'

'You know how I sound, how I smell and how I feel. That's pretty much all your available senses taken care of.'

'Well,' she began, 'I haven't—'

Stop!

At the very, *very* last moment her brain kicked into gear and slammed her throat shut on what had been about to come tumbling out.

I haven't tasted you yet.

She was thinking about her four senses. That was all. But there was no way she could even joke about it without it sounding like the lamest come-on ever. Not after she'd just had her fingers in his hair, all over his mouth. Not after she'd spent a relaxed afternoon testing out the waters of flirtation and had had the honey equivalent of foreplay down in the extraction sheds.

'You haven't what?'

His voice, his breath, seemed impossibly closer, yet he hadn't moved the rest of his body one inch.

'Nothing. Never mind.'

'Were you going to say *tasted*?'

'No.' The denial sounded false even to her. And it came way too fast.

'Really?' His soft voice was full of smile. 'Because it sounded like you were.'

'No. That would be an inappropriate comment to make in the workplace.'

Yes. Work. Good.

'Luckily, we're on our lunch break.'

She clung to her only salvation. 'It's still inappropriate.'

'I agree,' Elliott murmured. 'Then again, that ship sailed when I asked you to touch my face, so what else do I have to lose?'

Her brain was dallying dangerously over his 'touch my face' and so it missed the meaning in his words until it was too late.

His lips—the ones she'd gone to so much trouble to avoid touching—pressed lightly onto Laney's—half open, soft and damp and warm—before moulding more snugly against her. Sealing up the gaps. It took her a moment to acclimatise to the feeling of someone else's breath on her lips and he took full advantage of her frozen surprise to open further and gently swipe the tip of his tongue over her hyper-sensitive and suddenly oxygen-deprived lips.

Elliott Garvey was *kissing* her.

Not that it was her first kiss, but it had certainly been long enough between drinks that she'd virtually forgotten what it felt like to have a man's mouth on hers. How it felt and how it smelled and—her whole body just about melted—how he *tasted*. Her senses were flooded with the lime spritzer they'd just been drinking, and fine cheese, and a whole under-palate of *oh, my freaking goodness!*

Elliott Garvey was kissing *her*.

Instinct made her stretch her neck to fit against him better just as he might have pulled back—before she could think better of it, before she could let him go. She lapped at the heavy weight of his bottom lip, adding her breath to his and letting her tongue slip against his teeth. His hand speared in amongst her thick hair and curled warm and strong around her skull.

They tangled like that for moments—exploring, testing—his tongue gently asking and hers honestly answering. Sighing against the smoothness of his hot flesh. Deciding it wasn't enough.

Elliott pulled back the moment she opened to him, his voice thick-breathed and guttural on her name. Cool coastal air rushed into the vacuum caused by his rapidly withdrawn kiss.

'Your eyes are closed,' he breathed.

Another instinctive adaptation, apparently, because she hadn't meant to close them. She concentrated on opening them now. And on staring exactly where his should be as if that would help her somehow read his expression—to back up the Morse code of his rapid thumb-pulse against her scalp—so she could know what he was thinking. Whether stopping was what he'd wanted to do. Whether he'd been as engaged and excited by that kiss as she had.

Whether she'd just made a massive arse of herself.

'Wow.' Not only could she not trust herself to say more, she had no idea in the world what the right thing to say was.

But it seemed he did. 'Laney, I'm sorry.'

The cool rush of air was suddenly a bucket of cold salty water. 'For kissing me?'

'I didn't mean for it to go that far.'

Okay... 'How far did you mean it to go?' And exactly how much thought had he given it?

Breath hissed out of him and he moved further back still. 'Not that far. I was curious. I'd been wanting to do that all day. And I shouldn't have.'

'Why not?'

'Because you're *you*, Laney.'

Confusion stabbed fast and low in her belly. 'Because I'm a client? Because I'm blind?'

'Because you don't kiss strange men every other day.'

Well, that was as good as a slap across the face. Was her limited experience so very tangible? She'd been completely lost in *his* kiss. 'Whereas you kiss strange women regularly?'

'Yeah, actually. If you really want me to answer that.'

No, thanks.

'You're not a stranger.'

'I'm not far off it.'

'*You* kissed *me*,' she pointed out, and then cringed at the defensive edge to her words.

His voice gentled. 'I'm not sorry I kissed you, Laney. I'm just sorry it got as heavy as it did so fast.'

Surely that was like expecting the ocean to apologise for eroding the bluff. 'Oh, really? What *is* the right time to get hot and heavy, in your vast experience?'

'After one date, at least.'

It burned her that his voice could be tinged with humour. She guessed he *was* more used to casual kissing than she was. He sure recovered faster.

'You have a very robust ego if you think I'm going to be going on a date with you.'

'You have to. You promised.'

'Parasailing is not a date. It's a...' What was it, exactly? It was a man asking a woman to go out on his boat. Known in normal circles as *a date*.

If an eyebrow lifting could make a sound, Elliott's somehow made it. She could *see* his twitch as clearly as if her eyes worked. That was how tangible his arrogance was.

Her chin lifted. 'It's an arrangement.'

'Right—okay, then.'

'So there will be no kissing after it.'

'Understood.'

'Just like there shouldn't have been any today.'

'I concur.'

She sat back more fully on her haunches and that was when she realised exactly how far forward she'd leaned to half-consume his tongue. Mortified heat flushed in a hot wave up her neck.

'Right, then.' But the hint of a sound drifted over the ocean to her ears. 'Are you...*laughing*?'

'Of course I'm laughing. This is crazy.'

'Why is it crazy?'

'Because *of course* parasailing is a date, and *of course* I'm going to kiss you afterwards. I just wanted to give you some time to get used to the idea instead of mauling you when you can't run away without plunging to your death.'

A totally foreign kind of light-headedness washed over her. How bad could she have been if he wanted to kiss her again?

And how was she going to endure seven days before it happened, now that she knew how good he tasted.

'I didn't kiss you because I felt obligated, Elliott,' she confessed. 'I really wanted to know what it would be like.'

'My robust ego is very happy to hear it.'

And then there didn't seem much more to be said about it. Elliott Garvey wasn't like those other men—man-boys, really—that she'd dated. He wasn't pitying her or objectifying her or out for any kind of social kudos. He just wanted to kiss her.

Simple as that.

'You're smiling.'

Yeah, she was. She was happy. But she wasn't about to let him know that. 'It's an awkward smile. I don't know what to do now.'

'You don't have to do anything. Just enjoy the sun.'

Really? The sun was shining? Impossible to see it past the honking great *glow* that was Elliott in her awareness. He pulsed, thick and strong, right at the front of her brain.

Silence descended—as uncomfortable and un-ignorable as Elliott seemed to think it *wasn't*.

Until he broke it.

'More cheese?'

Stupid how he busied himself refilling her plate to disguise the tremor in hands Laney couldn't even see, but the simple chore helped him to focus and regroup. That and a decent whack of deep breathing.

Kissing had not been on his radar for this afternoon, though the residual tension in his body following the honey-sucking incident was very happy that it had eventuated. The only thing he'd been expecting—planning—was to get to know Laney better. To address some question marks. He just hadn't realised that *What does she taste like?* was one of his questions.

Though now that he had an answer he could see how very clearly it had been. Since the whole dancing on the beach thing, if he was honest.

He blew out a silent fortifying breath.

He'd had to use all his corporate skills to gather his scattered wits and reassemble them so that he could speak with even the slightest wit after his lips had touched hers. He'd kissed a lot of women—countless—but they didn't usually render him mute the way her soft, tentative exploration had.

Maybe that was it. Maybe he was just used to kisses being more forthright. Kisses usually came sure and easy, because he gravitated towards women who were guaranteed to be interested. Women who were into money. Women who were into him.

Who knew that all this time he should have been kissing women who *weren't* into him?

Though the idea that Laney Morgan might not be into him bordered on the edge of alarming. Which was disturbing in itself.

And he didn't *do* disturbing. No more than he did *need*. In fact he didn't do anything in which the outcome wasn't reasonably assured. Even in business he did his due diligence and only went after the sure-thing clients. Life was just safer that way.

He'd assumed a small outfit like Morgan's would jump at the chance for some guided development into the global sphere, and he didn't understand Laney's reticence any more than he understood what she did to him.

Correction: he understood very well *what* she did to him, but he didn't understand why. Or how. She wasn't even trying. Yet with no apparent effort on her part she'd captivated him as surely as any of the bees in her hives. They thought they were free to come and go, too. But they weren't—not really.

It was kind of insidious now that he thought about it.

Still…knowledge was power. There was no reason he shouldn't continue to explore whatever this was between them now that he knew how Laney worked. And how well *innocent* and *passionate* worked on *him*, particularly.

Two things he hadn't been for a really long time. If he ever had.

He tried to trace the emptiness inside him back to a time

when it had never existed but failed. It was something he'd carried around with him always. When he was younger he'd used it to keep all his adolescent angst in, then later he filled it with his relentless globetrotting adventures, and now it was a handy repository for all his corporate ambition.

He'd once been stupid enough to do his own packing when moving apartment, and he knew exactly how many newspapers he'd balled up to pack into the empty spaces around his many belongings. They did the job, but ultimately they ended up in the recycling.

Laney was just balled newspaper. This fascination he had for her—the fullness he felt when he was with her—it was all just incredibly attractive, stimulating, emotional stuffing. It took the edge off the gnawing hollow, but it wouldn't take much to send it tumbling back out onto the floor.

It wouldn't last. Nothing ever did, in his experience. The one favour his mother had done for him was to instil in him, early on, an acceptance of the disappointments of life. It took a lot to crush him these days, because he didn't let himself count on anything.

Or anyone.

The void was so much a part of him it was impossible to imagine being the man he was without it. Or to imagine what other people kept in theirs. It was tempting to ask Laney, because surely the most fulfilled woman he'd ever known would have to have the answer.

Or maybe he could mine the answer for himself if he just spent more time with her. Really got under her skin.

His whole body high-fived that notion. Even if it was ultimately doomed.

Even if it did nothing more than highlight how big his void had become while he was ignoring it.

Really, what were the chances he *wouldn't* support any plan that ended in him spending more time with Laney Morgan?

CHAPTER SEVEN

LUCKY SHE WAS a country girl, so being dropped at Mitchell's Cliff train station at five a.m. by her father hadn't felt too unusual. Well, the time hadn't felt odd. Being on a train alone for the first time ever kind of did, but she hunkered down in her comfortable seat, squeezed her earbuds in and cranked up her audiobook for the ninety-minute journey north to the big smoke, doing her best not to think about how out of her comfort zone she was.

Alone on a train without Wilbur, whose last city-guiding experience had been thirteen years ago.

But wasn't that the point? Parasailing wasn't exactly in her comfort zone either, but she was super-keen to try that. So why would being on a train freak her out? All around her passengers commuted to the city—some every morning and evening for work—and they managed.

So would she.

She had her stick. She'd be fine.

Yet as she rested her hand lightly on the forearm of the train security guard ninety minutes later, as he led her towards the exit, she was super-glad that Elliott would be meeting her on the platform. Because although she knew that she would be able to ask her way to the taxi rank and a driver who would get her easily to Elliott's house, there was something extra comforting about knowing he'd be waiting right there for her.

Comforting and welcoming.

And not just because he was Elliott.

'Uneventful journey, Laney?'

His deep voice sounded from directly behind her as the security guard released her on the city platform. Her small thanks were totally lost in the ambient noise on the platform, much higher than she was used to, and all the different smells practically assaulting her nostrils with their diversity. Even the underfoot vibrations caused by so many trains coming in and out of the station made her feel less certain of any step she took.

It made her wonder what city folk *did* with all that sensory input.

She was too rattled by the unfamiliarity of the journey and the stimulus here in the station to remember to be rattled by *him*. By what they'd shared just a few short days ago. Or by what he'd effectively promised they would share again today.

That was something to worry about when they got somewhere quiet.

'Elliott. Hi.'

It took him just moments to guide her out of the station to his waiting car, and she broke her own rule by gripping his forearm rather than just resting her own on top of it.

This was a grippy kind of day.

At last she sank into the luxurious comfort of deep leather seats and the expensive seals on the door blocked out the city.

She turned to him and breathed out her relief on an extended greeting—another one—flexing the kinks out of her fingers. Okay, so maybe her grip *was* a bit tight.

'You okay?' Elliott asked.

'New places are always that bit more stressful. I'll be fine now that I'm here.' She fought her subconscious' great desire to say *with you*.

'Have you had breakfast?'

No. Because she'd been too nervous. 'Just coffee.'

'That might work for you in the country, but here a coffee doesn't fuel you until morning tea. Not with what we'll be doing today.'

She was as intrigued by the idea of a day full of activity as she was by the fact he'd remembered her words, almost verbatim, from a full week ago.

'You're going to be towing me behind your speedboat. I don't want to revisit that breakfast at an inopportune moment.'

His chuckle blended perfectly with the purr that was his car ignition. 'We're not going out for a few hours. You'll have plenty of time to digest.'

She'd forgotten that it was not yet seven a.m. 'What will we do until then?'

'I had a chat with the team from VisApis. They're in their lab today and have offered to show us around at nine. So we've got time for something a bit more substantial than just coffee.'

The queasy void in her belly was rapidly closing over just at being back in the familiar warmth of Elliott's company. The glow was fully back in residence, too, and this time it had brought its good friend, tingles. They skittered up and down her limbs.

'Okay. I could definitely eat.'

But just because she *could* eat a full country breakfast didn't mean she wanted to. She still had the niggling concern that she might not take to flight quite as naturally as she secretly dreamed. But organic muesli wasn't too much of a risk and was pretty quickly digested. And she only had a small portion. Elliott had himself a poached egg on a bagel and a gorgeous-smelling coffee, which meant they were easily done in time to drive over to the university and meet with the VisApis crew by nine.

Elliott gave her mother a run for her money as chief scene-setter, describing everything as he drove along the foreshore of the city and followed the river around to one of the established leafy suburbs to its west. Laney was fascinated by his mixed descriptions of the architecture in the suburb, or the odd statues mounted out in the river itself, the portly pelicans roosting on posts along the way, until finally they pulled up at the base of one of the old limestone campus buildings he'd been describing.

'Okay, here we are.'

VisApis's research labs. The place where the studies they undertook at Morgan's had triggered more study on the ability of bees to map the features of human faces.

'The theory is that they use the same ability they use on flowers to discriminate between human faces,' she continued on as Elliott helped her out of his car..

'And you're a favoured flower?'

'They clearly appreciate my extra-gentle handling.'

'So you're in on the ground level with a potentially lucrative discovery?'

She shrugged. 'I just wanted to understand more about the bees.'

'And Edison just wanted to know how to make a lightbulb last longer,' Elliott said, guiding her up a short staircase. 'All innovation begins with a simple question.'

'You're not suggesting the two are even remotely on the same scale?'

'I guess it depends what it leads to in the future. VisApis are claiming their work will revolutionise facial recognition.'

'*Their* work…' she reinforced. 'I'm sure they were glad for the lead study, but I can't imagine they've spared much of a thought for me or the original bunch of bees since.'

'That's why they jumped at the chance to meet you today.'

She hadn't thought about how he might have asked. 'Oh, I hope this isn't awkward,' she said.

'Only one way to find out.'

Ordinarily Elliott wouldn't get quite so hands-on with a client—a woman—but Laney's lack of sight gave him the perfect excuse to touch her. He rested his hand at her lower back and kept the contact up as she negotiated the entry to the building with her cane. It was a greedy pleasure that he felt vaguely ashamed of.

A research assistant greeted them with a smile just inside the entrance.

'Ms Morgan,' the young man practically gushed. 'It's a real pleasure.'

Two extra lines appeared between Laney's brows, but she didn't voice whatever question she'd developed, instead smiling at the man and turning in the direction of his voice to follow him down the hall. Elliott stepped up close behind her so she knew he was still there.

It only took him a few minutes in the lab to understand the reverence, though.

Everywhere he looked computers belonging to the personnel who weren't at work on a Saturday flashed a single word and logo in syncopated order across their dormant screensavers—HELENA. The six letters were stylishly designed along with a close-up illustrated version of one of her eyes. He'd know that grey anywhere.

They'd named their software after her.

'Ms Morgan—at last.' A more senior man in a crisp lab coat introduced himself to her as the project leader.

Laney's soft hair shifted with the tilt of her head. 'Are we late?'

'I'm sorry, no.' The man's laugh boomed. 'I meant it's a pleasure to meet you after all this time. Those of us who have been working on Helena for two years wondered if we'd ever get the pleasure.'

Elliott held his breath. This could end badly.

'You…' Her frown was very definitely real this time. 'You named your project after me?'

Another thing he really liked about her. She didn't waste anyone's time with fake humility.

'To the rest of the world this project is VisApis 439, but we know it affectionately as Helena. And, yes, we named it for you, since it was born out of the research you commissioned.'

Standing this close behind her, Elliott knew the moment she stiffened like an old lock.

'Morgan's commissioned it.'

'But it was *your* experiences that led us to the software breakthrough we'd been chasing for a decade. If not for your experiences we never would have looked at bees.'

For the first and only time he was grateful for Laney's lack of sight. Lord only knew what she'd make of her name splashed across their whole lab. Affectionate or otherwise... And then as he looked around the lab he saw all the evidence of how they'd planned for her visit.

Every chair was pushed in at every computer terminal, every bin had been lifted onto the empty desktops. Every obstacle had been kindly and carefully cleared.

'We're looking forward to learning more about your project,' Elliott broke in, intentionally leaning on the word 'your'. He wanted today to go well—all of it—and this fawning over Laney wasn't the fastest path there.

Fortunately the guy wasn't just engineer-smart. He picked up on Elliott's subtle cue and moved smoothly on to a civilian version of how the software worked and what they were already able to do with it. Elliott used the time well to surreptitiously pull out a chair or two specifically for Laney to negotiate. She did her part by nudging them with her cane and neatly sidestepping them.

It was nearly ninety minutes before they'd seen all the progress the team had made and Laney had answered the many questions the project director had about her observations on bees—and he hers—but finally Elliott gave her his arm to manage the exit.

'I liked them,' she announced, halfway down the steps.

'I'd say the feeling was mutual.'

'They didn't Laney-proof their entire office.'

Any residual guilt he'd felt at littering the office with obstacles evaporated. 'That's important to you?'

'I hate being catered for. I don't expect it and I don't enjoy it.'

Something she'd said once before echoed again. That her father had pushed constantly for others to make allowances for his little girl.

'I like that my sight is the least interesting part of the process for them.'

Two thoughts collided then. First that their choice of name

for the software suggested that wasn't at all true, and second—strong and dominant—that he didn't want Laney heaping gratitude on any man other than him.

A nicely prehistoric little sentiment.

He'd been going out of his way to treat her just like anyone else. He'd been suppressing his own masculine instincts to rescue her every five minutes. It rankled that the white coats had earned her respect so easily—and so quickly—when she seemed to give respect away so sparingly.

Right behind that he realised how important her good opinion was to him.

And right behind *that* he realised that he was still sixteen emotionally.

Come on, Garvey. Man up.

He forced the conversation back on track. 'What did you think of their progress?'

'I think it's exciting. And amazing. I look forward to when it's finished.'

'How do you feel about them naming it after you?'

'Their choice, I guess.'

'It's not an honour?'

'It'll be good for Morgan's to be associated with the research,' she hedged.

Morgan's again. Never Laney. A big part of him wanted her to know that was *her name* emblazoned across their lab. Hers, not her family's. But that wouldn't be helpful to his cause.

'Well, thanks for indulging the detour,' he said, settling her back into the passenger seat. 'It really helped me to understand the project. And the potential.'

'I'd have thought this sort of thing was too random to reliably count as potential.'

'The specifics, maybe. But research could be a good sideline for Morgan's. You can only accommodate so many bees in labs, and Morgan's can offer researchers the kind of sample sizes they need to get verifiable results. Tens of thousands.

Maybe there are other partnerships like this one you can form in the future.'

Tiny creases appeared between her brows.

'That worries you?'

'I just like the…the organic nature of our business. No pun intended.'

'You get less joy out of things that are planned?'

'Maybe.'

'Are you looking forward to today?'

Her head turned to him, though it didn't need to. 'Parasailing? Yes, very much.'

'We planned that.'

'Yeah, but can you imagine how much more exciting it would have been if you'd said to me up at the bluff, "*Come on, Laney, whack on this harness. We're jumping from the cliff right now*".'

'But then you'd miss out on all the anticipation. The buildup.'

'Build-up matters?'

'Laney… Build-up is the best bit.' His car purred to life at the press of a button. 'Didn't you have to plan things out growing up?'

She didn't answer and a lightbulb flashed on above his head, bright and obvious.

That's exactly why she prefers spontaneity, moron.

He paused just before clicking his seatbelt into place and leaned over her before he thought better of it. She stiffened slightly with surprise, but didn't push him away when he brushed his lips over hers.

'What was that for?'

The warm caress of her breath on his lips teased them to life even more. 'I was being spontaneous.'

'By kissing me?'

'You were probably expecting it at the end of the day.'

'I wasn't— I'm not *expecting* anything.'

But that wasn't anger flushing red over her shirt collar. She liked it. Either the kiss or the exhilaration. Didn't much matter which. He was just pleased to have finally unravelled a bit more of the mysterious Ms Morgan.

'Well, you can expect an awesome afternoon on the water. Next stop the Indian Ocean.'

CHAPTER EIGHT

'Seriously, dude. A blind chick?'

Elliott threw Danny his most withering stare. 'She's not a "chick", Dan. She's a woman.'

Danny flicked his gaze to where Laney sat, firm-knuckled around *Misfit*'s gunnel, her white shirt blown back tight against her torso. Showcasing every curve. Elliott instantly felt protective of those curves, because she couldn't see them to know how uncovered they were by either her one-piece swimsuit or the translucent shirt. It felt vaguely wrong to be appreciating them.

'She sure is.' Danny grinned. 'A *blind* woman.'

'So?'

'So that's not your usual type.'

'That's the least of the ways Helena Morgan is not my type, Danny.' He kept his voice low, just in case the laws of physics suddenly decided to change direction and carry their words to her extra-perceptive ears. 'What's your point?'

'My point is what are you doing? Is this serious? Is it casual? Is it work?'

'What does it matter?'

'It matters, mate. If this is work then why is she here, out riding with us? And if this is casual then you might have picked the wrong girl to hit.'

'She's blind, Dan, not impaired.' The vehemence of his own voice surprised him. 'She's as capable as any other woman of dealing with something short term.'

'And that's what this is? A bit of short-term something?'

No. It wasn't as seedy as Danny made it sound. He'd thought he knew, but he was starting to doubt his own mind. 'It's not anything.'

Yet—and only if you didn't count two kisses and the impending promise of more.

'I wanted to get her off the farm. Have a chance to talk with her in a different context.'

Danny glanced back at him from the wheel of *Misfit*. 'Why?'

Good question. 'To see what makes her tick.'

'Why do you need to know that?'

You didn't buy a boat with someone if they weren't a good mate, but that wasn't something he was prepared to answer honestly to himself, let alone his best friend. 'Because this job hangs on getting her co-operation.'

Ugh, when had he become such a good liar?

'Ah, so it *is* work. Are Ashmore Coolidge cool with you sleeping with your clients?'

'I'm not sleeping with her. And the firm trusts me to use my best judgement.'

'In other words they're cool with you sleeping with a client if it leads to revenue?'

'I'm *not* sleeping with her.'

'Right.'

'Damn it, Danny—'

'Hey, I'm just trying to work out if I should bother getting to know her.'

'She wants to try parasailing. That's it.'

'Mmm.'

'Mmm, what?'

'Smacks of dirty pool, Elliott. Getting her high on adrenaline and then hitting her up for whatever it is you want.'

Anger bubbled hard and fast just below the place where he usually kept it contained. 'That's not what I'm doing. She just wants to experience something new.'

Though wasn't he? Could he truly say it hadn't crossed his

mind how good a kiss between them would be right after she landed? Or in the air?

Danny eyeballed him. 'And since when did you become a life coach?'

'Why are you busting my brass about this?'

'There's a blind woman clinging to the front of our boat. That's not usual, man.'

Elliott's eyes narrowed and focussed on Laney's white-knuckled grip on the chrome catch bars that lined the bow. Was that just a secure farm grip...or was she absolutely terrified?

Danny must have read his mind. 'Is she okay out there?'

'She's fine.'

'What if she falls off?'

Irritation warred with concern. 'Last time I checked, blind-ness didn't affect grip.'

'But what if she does?'

'Then she treads water until we circle back and pick her up, like anyone else.'

His friend gaped at him. 'That's harsh, man.'

'She *can't see*, Danny. She's not a two-year-old.'

In one *whump* it all hit him—how tired Laney must be of being treated as if she was a child. Or disabled. When she was the least disabled disabled person he'd ever met. How the two sides of her must come into conflict all the time—the independent woman who didn't want to be treated with kid gloves and the gentle soul who appreciated that everyone truly meant well.

Danny meant well and Elliott wanted to thump him already. 'Just treat her like anyone else. Except maybe ease up on the ogling.'

'She can't see me do it.'

'No, but I can.'

With that, he swung around the boat's windshield and ma-noeuvred his way up to the bow to join Laney. Despite the strong headwinds caused by their speed she either heard his approach or felt his footfalls, because her head tilted towards him just slightly even as her hands tightened even more.

He raised his voice over *Misfit*'s motor. 'Okay, Laney?'

'Loving it.' The wind almost stole her words from him.

He shuffled closer. 'Your knuckles are looking a little pale...'

'I didn't say I wasn't also terrified.'

He slid down next to her and matched her death-grip on the chrome trip rail.

'I think this is the fastest I've ever gone in my life.'

'Really? I thought for sure Owen would have put the pedal to the metal a time or two out on the back roads.'

'Yeah, he has. But I didn't have my head out of the window like Wilbur so it's not the same. And although I've doubled with someone on a horse once it was a shire horse, to take our combined weights, so it didn't get up a whole lot of speed.'

'Want us to slow down?'

'No! This is awesome.'

But her knuckles weren't getting any pinker, and again he realised how many things she must have done in her life *despite* her fear. And right behind that he realised that she wouldn't necessarily have been any more or less afraid even if she could see the water whizzing by at one hundred and thirty kilometres per hour.

She tipped her head back and opened her mouth. 'I love the spray.'

The salt and the speed.

'It stings.'

'*Pfff.* This is nothing.'

Her bees. He chuckled, then raised his voice to be heard. 'No. I guess not.'

'So where are we going in such a hurry?'

'There's a sandbar east of here. We use that as a launch site.'

'You don't lift off from the boat?'

'Not if we have a choice. And not when we're doing tandem. It's easier from terra firma.'

That brought her head around again. 'We're going up together?'

'You think I'm going to send you up alone on your first flight?'

What kind of a man did she think he was?

'Can it hold two?'

His laugh barked out of him. 'We'll find out.'

But she wasn't laughing.

'Yes, Laney. It can hold two. And this isn't optional. You've never parasailed before.'

Her frown didn't ease.

'Who did you think was going to give you instructions?'

'I didn't really think about that. In my head it's all very...'

'Organic?'

'Something like that.'

Misfit lost speed. 'Well, you're about to find out. The sandbar is just ahead of us.'

'When you feel my body move, just move with it. Like we're dancing.'

No. If they were dancing she'd be facing him, respectably, instead of strapped in tight with her back to his big, hard chest. Like upright spooning.

'And as soon as you feel the upward tug if you don't think you can run with me then just lift your legs.'

'And let you do all the work?'

'The boat is doing all the work, really. I'm just keeping us upright.'

Yeah. That was all he was doing. He wasn't giving her the experience of her life. He wasn't keeping her thundering heartbeat in check by his very presence.

He took her again through the basic instructions and then treble-checked the harnesses. Every yank nudged her body closer to his; every buckle-rattle brushed her body with his knuckles. In case she'd forgotten how close together they were standing.

His friend gently revved the boat a way off the sandbar.

'Ready, Laney? Bend forward.'

Right. Because that wasn't suggestive *at all* when you were tucked this close to a man.

But she had no choice as his chest and shoulders bent towards her—

'Now, *run*!'

She did—absolutely determined not to pike out and lift her legs. It took a certain amount of trust to run on unfamiliar terrain, but being strapped to Elliott went a long way to reassuring her that he'd have checked their path for obstacles if for no other reason than his own preservation. His feet ploughed into the sand next to hers—virtually between hers—until the promised yank came, and then another closely after it, and suddenly there was no more sand to plunge her feet into and the harness pulled up taut between her thighs.

And she was running on thin air.

Her stomach didn't lurch, as she'd half expected, and the only clue that they were ascending was the circulation-restricting pressure of the harness and the gentle whoosh of air diagonally down her face.

'Danny's turned on the winch,' he said, and sure enough, the sounds around them changed as they lifted further and further from the ocean. Less boat, more sky.

'How far up will we go?'

'We have two hundred and fifty metres on the winch.'

She knew which hives were a quarter of a kilometre from the house and tried to imagine that in an upward direction. It was tough imagining *high* when you'd never seen it. Or felt it, particularly.

They fell to silence and before too long that was more or less what they had. Even the rumbly engine of *Misfit* and the sounds of the sea were replaced with the sounds of…

'Nothing,' she murmured.

'What?' Elliott leaned in closer to her ear and the comparative warmth of his breath on her cheek was the first time she'd noticed that her skin was so cool. Even though it was a warm autumn day.

'I wasn't expecting it to be so quiet,' she said, and barely needed to raise her voice. 'I thought there'd be whooshing.'

'Danny's slowed the boat to a gentle run.'

'Can you describe what you see?'

He could. He did a great job—not quite as good as her talented mother, but not bad for a rookie, and better again than his descriptions of buildings. He talked about the shape of the land, the winding line of the coast. The island off in the distance to their left. Her brain immediately adjusted and added her version of an island to her imagined vista and she nestled into the deepness of his voice.

The cold nip of the air, the complete ambient silence, the amplified sense of altitude that his words had given her—they all had an effect. She swallowed back the emotion.

'Even the gulls are below us. We're up with the tradewinds. I'll let you know if I see an albatross.'

For some reason the very idea of that hit a place deep down inside her where she'd never looked—a place of longing and loss and what would never be—and tears began to trickle from her eyes. She would never see an albatross hanging on the current. And she sure as heck wouldn't hear it or touch it, so, for her, albatrosses might as well not exist.

'Laney, are you crying?'

'No,' she croaked through thickening tears.

He leaned forward and around as best he could to look at her. 'Don't cry.'

All that did was open the floodgates.

'It's not crying,' she sobbed—though what exactly *was* it? 'It's appreciation. Thank you, Elliott. I might never have had a chance to do this.'

Just above her head he shuffled something and freed up one gloved hand. He used it to stroke some loose damp hair away from her face. 'You're welcome. Just enjoy the view.'

He said that as if he meant every word, and she wondered if he finally *understood* how she worked. Because she *did* have a view—just as real as his. She just didn't see it the way he did.

Their flight—their silence—seemed to go on for eternity. Laney took to wiggling her toes against the cold, and to make sure she had some circulation still happening in legs compromised by the tightness of the harness. She was going to have to run again when they landed, and she didn't want to be the one to send them both plunging face-first into the sandbar.

'So…' he started, still so close behind her. 'How are you feeling about the prospect of more between Morgan's and Ashmore Coolidge?'

'Really? You want to talk about that *now*?'

'Well, we're up here for a while. You want to talk about that kiss instead?'

Ah…no. Not while she was pressed this close to him. She was likely to tip her head back and go for a repeat performance.

'I'm not sure my feelings about growth have changed at all.'

'You still don't trust me?'

His voice was like one of her favourite wines. Full-bodied with things unsaid, but carrying undertones of something more subtle—defensiveness, hurt.

'It's not a question of trust. It's a question of need. I was honest with you when I said I didn't see a need for Morgan's to grow. Why would that have changed just because I've shown you a few things?'

'The research?'

'I can see merit in that but I don't think giving access to a few researchers is the level of growth Ashmore Coolidge is thinking of, somehow.'

'No. You're right. We have our sights set much higher.'

And by 'we' he meant 'he'.

'I don't want you to be disappointed, Elliott. That you've wasted so much time.'

'It's not a waste, Laney. I've met you.'

Her heart lurched, but it was easy to blame it on the sudden dip of the parachute. Far below Danny must have given *Misfit* a burst of speed, because they lifted again almost immediately.

'And I've met your parents and completed Morgan's biennial health check.'

Of course. 'Did we pass?'

'What do you think?'

'I think that means you've seen everything we needed to show you.'

I think that means it's time for you to go.

But Elliott going was not something Laney was prepared to acknowledge just now. 'Well, then, that's a conversation for tomorrow. Between all of us.'

Because she was no more willing to speak for Morgan's than she was to accept praise for all of its achievements. Morgan's was a family brand and this would be a family decision.

'Does that mean you're staying in the city tonight? I got the spare room ready in case.'

'I think that would be hard to explain to my parents.' *Oh, you coward.* 'But I thought…to save you driving back down on Sunday…'

'You want me to stay over on the farm tonight?'

His question—practically pressed into her flesh like Braille by the rumbling of his chest so close behind her—was full of speculation and promise. And her mind was suddenly filled with thoughts she shouldn't be having.

Of a late-night visit to the chalet on the end.

Of whether he'd open the door before she knocked.

Of whether his bed could fit two.

Not a question she'd ever imagined herself asking about the Morgan chalets. But instinct was a demanding mistress, and right now it was demanding she did not expose herself to any more risk than flying two hundred and fifty metres above a shark-infested ocean.

What did she want, exactly?

'I don't want to waste any more of your time if our answer is going to be no.'

And suddenly the prospect of him actually leaving ballooned large in her consciousness. These might be the last hours she'd have with him. Her fingers curled more tightly around the harness. As though it was his hand.

'I told you,' he murmured. 'It hasn't been a waste.'

Slowly, subtly, she felt the tug on the harness change direction.

'Are you ready for it to be over?'

She gasped. Could he read her mind?

'Danny's taking us back,' he breathed down on her.

Oh. No, she wasn't ready—but what possible excuse could she give him for staying up here for ever? Other than wanting it so? 'He probably wants his turn.'

'You've got him pegged already.'

The tug of descent against their straps was subtle but undeniable. Time to go back to the real world.

'What do you do up here when you're on your own?'

'Think...' His heart hammered against her back. 'Breathe, mostly. The rest of the world is a long way away from here.'

Elliott concentrated on the descent, freeing Laney to concentrate on him, and on the feel of his strong thighs below hers as she practically sat in his lap thanks to the orientation of the harnesses. He smelled salty, the sun's heat simmered in his thick wetsuit as she leaned back into him, and his mumured instructions to Danny—who couldn't possibly hear them—rumbled in his chest.

Misfit's engine got louder and louder and then Elliott tensed and bent to her ear. 'Ready, Laney? Straighten your legs and don't go to the ground. Just start running when you feel the sand. Stay upright.'

She pushed her pelvis forward to force her legs into a downward position and immediately missed the comfort and security of Elliott's body curled around hers. But landing safely pushed those thoughts from her head and she set her legs moving the moment she felt his begin to run.

And then there was sand.

And then there was *a lot* of sand.

Her legs, deprived for so long of natural blood flow, and

taken by surprise by its sudden return, instantly turned to a blaze of pins and needles and gave way completely the moment they were faced with actual gravity.

Her tumble meant she snarled Elliott's legs and he tumbled, too, and the two of them were tugged along the sand for some distance by the still buoyant sail.

Finally it dumped them in a tangle of limbs, harnesses and cords before settling to the sandbar.

'*Oof*—' Elliott's sudden weight across her pushed the air from her lungs and ejected the mouthful of sand she'd ended up with.

'Are you okay?'

Close and breathy. And urgent. And very masculine, pressing down on top of her.

She struggled against the singing of her skin. And the creativity of her imagination. 'Are you asking about my dignity?'

The chuckle rumbled from his body into hers. 'I'm asking about your bones and internal organs.'

She surveyed them all briefly as he untangled more of the harness. Everything seemed to move as it should. 'All intact, I think. Unlike my pride.'

He paused. 'Well, don't worry. This isn't my finest moment either.'

'At least I'm not witness to your humiliation.'

'No, but bloody Danny is. I won't hear the end of it.'

Sure enough, unbridled laughter drifted towards them on the lap of waves coming from the boat. He levered his weight off her and pushed to his feet, then reached down and took her hand. She was upright in a moment.

'Send me up with him, then, and let's see how *he* does, landing with a potato sack strapped to his chest.'

'No chance.'

The vehemence in his voice took her by surprise. Standing this close to him, it wasn't hard to orientate her face up to his.

'Was I actually dangerous?' Had she put Elliott at risk?

'No. I wouldn't leave you alone with him for fifteen seconds, let alone fifteen minutes.'

'Why not? Isn't he your friend?'

Methodical hands brushed the sand off the rest of her—methodical, yet somehow not…indifferent. And still super-warm.

'Yes, and I know him too well to trust him with you. I could barely trust myself. Why are you smiling?'

Because she liked knowing that their flight had been challenging for him too. 'I doubt it would have been the same with Danny. He's smaller than you. It would have been a totally different fit.'

A hint of a choke coloured his voice. 'You could tell that from shaking his hand?'

'He went out of his way to press against me when he helped me onto the boat. I just extrapolated outwards. Am I wrong?'

'No,' he breathed. 'You never are.'

They stood there, still partly bound together though the parachute no longer tethered them in a tangled mess. The masculine scent of him swilled around her despite the gentle ocean breeze, stealing the air from her lungs. And all she could think about was kissing him.

This was exactly the right moment for it, and he'd virtually warned her that it would be coming.

Her lips parted.

'So, was it everything you hoped for?'

'Wh…What?' Disappointment surged through her at conversation instead of kissing.

'The flight.'

'Oh. Yes, definitely. You're very lucky you get to do this regularly.'

He plucked a strand of windblown hair from her face and the echo of his touch tingled against her skin. Okay, so he was working his way up to a kiss.

'Not too regularly. I don't want it to ever stop feeling special.'

She licked her salt-coated lips and teased him. 'Oh, that's right. *The build-up is the best bit.*'

'You don't believe me?'

'On the contrary.' Right now she found it totally believable. He shuffled in the sand. 'Put your arms out, Laney.'

Deep and low. And typically demanding. But she complied because she wanted nothing more this very moment than to wrap her arms around all his heat. She gave them an extra hint of width to accommodate his big body. And then she held her breath.

Nothing happened, and then…canvas and buckles clanked in a big pile into her outstretched arms.

'Hang on to this and I'll guide you back to the boat.'

Disappointment surged in where tingles had been only moments before as she curled her arms around the tangle of harness to stop it from falling straight through onto the sandbar.

Seriously? No snatched moment like in the car earlier? No taking advantage of post-flight euphoria? Just…back on the boat? But she wasn't about to beg, and she sure wasn't going to let him see her disappointment. She averted her eyes and concentrated on taking as good care of the harness as the harness had taken of her.

But instead of holding out his forearm for her to take, Elliott curled his fingers through hers in a good old-fashioned handhold and led her towards the splash of the surf.

'The water's clear,' he murmured. 'And the boat is a ten-metre wade out. When we get there I'll pull you up.'

They passed Danny midway, coming in for his turn, and Laney threw him a big smile of gratitude for piloting the boat for her amazing experience. She hoped he was too absorbed in himself to examine the smile too closely, in case it looked as hollow as it felt.

She shouldn't care.

She certainly shouldn't let one absent kiss suck all the joy from her otherwise amazing afternoon. She'd taken her first speedboat trip. She'd *flown*, for crying out loud—hovered two hundred and fifty metres above the world like one of her bees on the breeze. That already made this day exceptional.

A kiss would have been wasted on it, really.

Elliott let go of her hand and placed it on *Misfit*'s hull and Laney felt the dip and slap of the boat as he hauled himself up into it. A moment later he relieved her of her harness and a moment after that he was back, both hands strong and sure in hers as he pulled her up to safety, her feet walking up the hull of the boat and then over the edge. She slid down the length of his body until cool deck pressed into her feet.

Totally wasted...

Yep. She'd just keep telling herself that.

CHAPTER NINE

AMAZING HOW EXHAUSTED she felt, given she'd pretty much done nothing but sit—or hang in space—all day. Must be the sea air. Elliott had taken his time giving his friend a good run on the parasail and she'd snuggled down in the boat's comfortable leather seats and enjoyed the sea air.

As she'd slid down the length of Elliott reboarding *Misfit* she'd realised his wetsuit hung, unzipped, from his hips—which had given her a startling but not entirely unwelcome flesh memory of broad shoulders, firm chest and belly, and the strong arms that had hauled her up out of the water onto the boat. And that was how she 'saw' him now. As a sensory memory of heat and salt and smell and soft skin over firm muscle.

Who needed vision?

'You still awake?'

She turned towards the honey tones of his voice in his comfortable Audi. 'Yes.'

'Your eyes were closed.'

Her smile was as lazy as his voice. 'Takes energy, keeping them open.'

'Have I worn you out?'

'Just about. It's a good feeling.'

'Why do you have your eyelids open at all?' he asked. 'Generally speaking.'

'The natural resting place for eyelids is half closed, and that seems to creep sighted people out, so when I was little Mum just trained me to open them up, regardless.'

'For the comfort of others?'

For her survival. 'My entire childhood was a push-pull between my mother wanting to help me fit in and my father ensuring I never could.'

Whoops… Had she said that out loud? Clearly she was more tired than she'd realised. Certainly she hadn't meant it to sound so bitter.

'My mother was the very definition of "don't rock the boat",' he said. 'That's not exactly what you want in a parent either. A little fight is a good thing.'

'A little, maybe.'

'You came out okay.'

'Chalk it up to my mother's moderating influence.'

'Something else to be grateful to her for, then. I get to look into your eyes when we speak.'

'Even though I'm not in there?'

His pause went on for moments. 'Laney, just because you can't see me doesn't mean I can't see you.' He cleared his throat. 'At least I try to.'

'Really?'

'Do you imagine your eyes don't carry intelligence? Meaning? Or that they're not a window to who you are?'

'Honestly, I don't know what to imagine. I have no idea what someone would see in someone else's eyes, sighted or otherwise. Aren't they just…eyes?'

'Oh, no. Not at all.'

'What do eyes do that's so interesting?'

'They sparkle. They challenge. They contradict. They lie. They reveal. They pretty much show what someone is feeling regardless of what they are saying.'

That sounded awful. 'How do you keep a secret?'

'Some people don't.'

'So the whole "window to your soul" thing is actually true? I thought it was just a pithy saying.'

'Depends on whether there's much of a soul to be seen.'

Flat. Almost lifeless. Was he thinking about someone in particular?

'It's different, though, right? Knowing I can't see you back?'

'It's different, yes. But not worse necessarily.'

She turned fully towards him, as if the change of angle would help her pick up more of the vibes he unintentionally gave off. 'You think it's better that I can't see you?'

'If you're asking me whether I'd prefer to be able to make actual eye contact with you, yeah, of course I would. I'd love to be able to look in your eyes and have you *see* me. Read me. Know me. But too much eye contact is confrontational for most people. Sometimes you want to really look at a person but you can't because it's socially inappropriate.'

'And you can look all you want at me?'

'Your eyes are busy doing a lot of interesting other stuff when they're not seeing,' he murmured. 'And they tell me a lot more about you than you necessarily do.'

She turned her face back to the oncoming road, screening him from the very organs that they'd been discussing. She wasn't sure how she felt about him being able to *see* her quite that much. It felt like an unfair advantage.

'Why would my body use my eyes without my consent?'

'Why does a blind woman use any of the facial expressions you use? Expressions you've never seen or learned. Clearly some things are just innate. Joy and anger and unhappiness—'

She frowned again.

'—and consternation. Yep, you use that one a lot. I think the rest of us grow up learning how to disguise our expressions more than anything, so yours—when you have them—flash in neon.'

'Neon?'

'Bright light.'

'Not literally, I assume?'

His chuckle warmed her through.

'No, not literally. But they're very…honest. Do you want a real world example?'

Yes. Yes, she did.

'Today, on the sandbar, you were disappointed I didn't kiss you.'

She shot upright in her seat and only then realised how comfortable she'd become in it. 'I was not!'

'Yeah, you were. I could tell.'

'No, you couldn't.'

'You worked hard to school your features, but your eyes screamed disappointment.'

Oh, and didn't he sound pleased with himself about that?

'They did not…' But it wasn't very convincing, even to her own ears.

'I wanted to kiss you,' he murmured.

Air was sucked into her lungs. 'Why didn't you?'

'Because of something Danny said. It made it feel not right.'

Danny, who hadn't had a single meaningful thing to say all day? 'Danny told you not to kiss me?'

'Danny told me not to take advantage of you. In the afterglow of the flight. And it got me thinking. When I kiss you again I want you to be one hundred per cent present and clearheaded. Not all dosed up with adrenaline.'

When. Not *if.*

She folded her arms across her chest. 'You're assuming a lot. I'm not sure I want to kiss you again.'

'Yeah, you do.' His voice was rich with a smile.

Yeah. She did. She dropped her head and cursed under her breath. 'How do any of you have any privacy?'

'We spend a lot of time not looking at each other, I guess—'

No doubt.

'And not being entirely honest with each other.'

'Clearly a survival strategy I need to work on.' Though how exactly did one begin to train eyes that had gone rogue not to give away her deepest secrets? And who knew she'd still find anything in life yet to be perfected?

'Don't joke, Laney. Your honesty is a strength, not a weakness.'

'It's a vulnerability.'

'You don't want to be vulnerable?'

'I don't care for being exposed.'

The concept hung out there, thick and real.

'Fair enough. How about this? Whenever I'm reading your face I'll let you know. So we'll be equal.'

'So I'll at least know if my privacy is being breached?'

'Come on, Laney. It's not like you don't read the slight tone-shifts in my voice or the temperature-changes in my skin.'

She laughed at the thought.

'I give you my word, as a gentleman, that I will be honest with you about what I'm thinking and seeing when I look at you. If you'll extend me the same courtesy about reading me.'

'I'm always honest with you.'

'You don't lie. That's not necessarily the same thing.'

His words sank in. He had a point. She *did* read people—read Elliott—in a dozen ways he probably wasn't aware of, so was it really any different from him reading whatever messages her eyes were apparently giving off?

Honesty wasn't really all that much to ask for. Or to expect. She took a deep breath. 'Okay. Can we start right now?'

'Sure.' Though he'd never sounded less sure.

'I feel like you're working up to kissing me now, and I...'

Ugh, honesty wasn't much fun.

'And you don't want that?'

'No.'

Hurt tinged his words like a barely perceptible harmonic. 'Can I ask why?'

She took a deep breath. 'Because I've decided to take matters into my own hands. Kiss you. Tonight, at the chalet. And I've kind of talked myself into how that's going to go.'

The hurt morphed into a tightness. 'And how *is* it going to go?'

She lifted her chin. 'Really well.'

Maybe eyes did a lot more than he'd said, because she was pretty sure she could feel his boring heat into her very soul.

'Far be it from me to ruin a good plan.'

* * *

Laney checked in with her parents so they knew she was back and then begged off to go and have a much needed shower. To wash the salt from her skin and hair. To make herself beautiful. Not that she knew what that was or, until today, why anyone would bother.

But now she got it.

This was why they bothered. This gorgeous anticipation.

She wanted Elliott to open that chalet door and see her standing there looking pretty. Better than pretty, really. But short of inviting her mother in here and explaining what she was up to that wasn't going to happen. And if she trusted Owen with the task she couldn't guarantee what she'd end up looking like. So she'd just have to work with what she had. Kelly had used her as test dummy enough times that she left a small make-up kit in her bedroom perpetually, the contents personalised to her, and she hunted it down now and quickly fingered her way through it, opening lids and testing the contents. Isolating the bits she recognised.

Mascara. Lip-gloss. Loose powder. All past their best-by date, probably.

Not much she could do wrong with any of them if she was careful. Even so, it took her an eternity to apply them, and she was conscious the whole time of Elliott sitting in his chalet, wondering if she'd forgotten. Or just chickened out.

She almost did. Twice. But determination had never been her weak point, so she ran her brush through her hair one last time and whistled for Wilbur. He came running in from the other room, all toasty and sleepy from the fire, a disbelieving little yowl in his voice when she produced his harness.

'We won't be outside for long,' she promised. 'Then you'll be warm again.'

And so would she. Extremely warm. Fingers crossed.

The audacity of what she was about to do hit her then. A clandestine meeting with a man. A man from the city. A man she might not see again after this weekend.

But then wasn't that part of the attraction? And the excitement? And she was twenty-five years old. It was time.

'Hey…' She poked her head around Owen's bedroom door. The rustling told her he was pushing to his feet. 'What do you need?'

'Nothing. Just…is my face okay?'

Ugh… How ridiculous.

Confusion coloured his response. 'Compared to who?'

'No. I mean, does it look okay? Nothing out of place?'

'Is that—?'

'Forget it.'

'No…wait. Are you wearing *make-up*?'

'Is it or isn't it applied correctly?'

'Is.' Typical Owen shorthand. 'Did you do it yourself?'

'Yes.' Why else would she be humiliating herself like this?

'Why?'

'Thanks, O.'

'Wait—!'

But no way was she going to explain a thing to her twin brother.

Wilbur hurried her more than usual through the still garden and she barely had to tell him where they were going. As if it was such a given. Within minutes her knuckles were on the glossy wood of Elliott's door.

'Hey,' he breathed as warm air spilled out onto her. 'I thought maybe you'd changed your mind.'

'Sorry, I was—' *obsessing like a teenager over something that probably doesn't matter* '—caught up.'

'Your parents?'

'No, they've gone to bed.'

'Come on in. It's cold.'

Wilbur didn't wait to be asked twice and Elliott chuckled as he scrambled in, claws clattering on the timber floors.

'Watch yourself,' Elliott muttered as he helped her up the steps. 'There are candles…well, pretty much everywhere.'

'Where did you get candles?' Though what she really wanted to ask was why.

'I found a packet of tealights in the bottom drawer. For power outages, presumably.'

'And you thought I'd enjoy them?' she teased.

'I thought I'd enjoy looking at you in candlelight.'

'Well, that seems to be a waste of perfectly good make-up, then.'

He stopped so suddenly she walked right into him. 'You put make-up on?'

'You can't tell?'

His heat increased marginally as he stepped closer. 'Is that strawberry lip-gloss?'

Really? He had to ask? The scent of it was pulsing off her.

'Some kind of berry.' Her tongue dashed across her lips without being asked. 'It's very sweet.'

Elliott's voice dropped to a half-growl. 'I'll bet.'

In the silence Wilbur harrumphed and found himself a comfortable spot to flop down.

'So, where are all these candles?'

'Just avoid anything above elbow-height; that should do it.'

'That's not all that helpful.'

His low chuckle tickled the hairs on her whole body. 'Okay, how about we just sit on the sofa.'

Sofas were generally candle-free. 'Okay.'

'Anything you need I'll bring to you. This is a full service date.'

'Is it a date?'

'I consider this a continuation of the first date, so…yeah.'

'Okay.'

Wow. She was rocking the vocab tonight.

'Wine?'

Her, 'Yes, please!' was almost unseemly in its haste. But when Elliott pressed a glass stem into her hand and she lifted it to her lips she discovered the rather dramatic downside to flavoured lip-gloss. 'Ugh, this wine is *not* enhanced by berry flavour.'

'Hang on,' he said. 'I'll get you something to take it off with.'

She felt the coffee table to her left and placed her glass down as he pushed out of his seat. But then his hands were at her shoulders, gently pressing her back into the sofa, and his lips were close against hers.

'I seem to be out of make-up wipes,' he murmured.

Did such a thing even exist? Her voice was mostly a chuckle. 'Shame...'

Hot lips pressed down onto hers, sliding against the gloss and roaming over her mouth. She arched up out of the sofa to meet them more fully. Hazy heat swelled up and dazzled her senses as Elliott kissed her, mouthing her the way she'd wanted so desperately on the sandbar—tasting and exploring and teasing—torturing her tongue with his. His arms slid around behind her and kept her hard up against him.

It was like the parasailing again, but her position was reversed. She sighed into his mouth.

But then he relaxed her into the sofa-back and lifted his head. 'There—that's sorted it.'

For a moment she was too disorientated to speak, but she forced her wits back into line as she straightened in her seat. Back upright like a regular person. 'Are you now wearing it?'

His laugh was mostly snort. 'My sleeve is'

'You're worse than Owen.' Her wine returned magically into her hand. 'So that's the kissing over with, then?'

Boo.

'It really wasn't my plan to maul you the moment you walked in the door...' He sounded genuinely confused.

'But you couldn't resist?'

'Opportunity presented itself.' He leaned into the sofa more fully but his voice didn't leave her for a moment. He stayed close. 'And what kind of a host would I be to leave you without assistance? But I haven't forgotten what you said, so I give you my word the next kiss is entirely up to you.'

If it was up to her then she'd like to resume kissing right now, actually. But social niceties made that impossible.

Her breath shuddered in quietly. 'So I just wanted to say thank you, again, for today. Parasailing was amazing.'

'I agree. It's going to be hard to go back to solo lifts.'

'You're so lucky you get to do that whenever you want.'

'Whenever work lets me.'

'You work weekends?'

'I'm working *this* weekend.'

Work. That was like a bucket of cold lip-gloss. 'Oh.'

'Tomorrow, I mean. Not today—definitely not now. But, yes, that's the sad truth about the lifestyle. You spend so much time funding it you can't always be free to enjoy it.'

'Guess that's the difference between your job and mine. I live my love every day.'

'If I wanted to do that I'd have to become a parasailing instructor.'

'Would that be so bad? You're very good at it.'

He gave that his usual thought. 'I'm pretty sure Ashmore Coolidge wouldn't let me go without a fight. And I'd have to move out of my penthouse. And I don't know how long I could go before I would feel like I was under-achieving. You know?'

Back to the *realising.* 'Isn't doing what you love fulfilling your potential?'

'Not if it's not making you decent money.'

'What about being happy?'

'I'll be happy when I'm retired.'

'No, you won't. You'll be appalled at how much time you have and how much money you might otherwise be making with that time.'

His chuckle warmed her even more than his closeness. 'Yeah, probably.'

Conversation dropped off and Laney fought her natural inclination to flinch when soft fingers lifted a lock of her hair and draped it back, away from her face.

'I can see the make-up now,' he murmured.

Yeah, she'd bet he could. He was leaning close enough. 'Did I do it right?'

'I can barely tell it's there. Which is probably the point.' The sofa-back shifted as he did. 'You always look good. Natural.'

'Thank you.'

'So tell me about this kiss you're imagining. Do you have make-up on in it?'

'When I imagine it, it's all about sensation. Not really how good we look while doing it.'

His smile warmed the conversation. 'Describe the sensations.'

Discomfort washed through her. 'Um…'

He helped. 'Is it fast or slow?'

Yeah, this would be easier. 'Slow.'

'Why?'

'So it will last.'

His small grunt said *good reason*.

'What else?'

'You're standing. So I have to stretch up to you.' And press her body against his—but she wasn't going to share that part.

'Sounds like a lot of work on your part.'

'I don't mind. It's worth it.'

He liberated the wine glass from her and it clanked on the coffee table. Then strong arms pulled her to her feet and he stepped in close. She had to tilt her head to avoid her nose pressing into his chest.

'A good kiss, then?' he murmured.

'Yep. Just right.'

Gentle hands lifted hers up and linked them behind his neck. Her body pressed against his, just as it had in her mind. Warm and soft met hot and hard. His hands slid around onto her hips.

'And what's *just right* to you, Goldilocks?' Ragged breath totally betrayed his interest, no matter how casual the hold of his arms.

Speech was almost impossible past the tight press of her chest. 'Lazy. Explorative.'

'Who controls it?' This breathed right against her lips.

'Me, at first.' She took a long, slow breath. 'But then you.'

He immediately suspended his descent. Froze there. Waiting. 'Then it's your move, Laney.'

Yeah.

Only real kisses weren't quite as easy as fantasy ones. Every breath pulled in her chest, like Wilbur against his harness when he wanted to be released. But Elliott's patient silence and oh-so-warm body encouraged her, and she feathered her fingertips up his jaw to rest on his cheek, then pushed up onto her toes to make contact. It didn't matter that they'd already kissed—that had been *him* kissing her.

This was *her*…

Initiating a kiss for the first time.

Her lips fluttered as they met his—half missing his mouth, but all the more exciting for landing so squarely on his full bottom lip by mistake. She loved that bottom lip, though her experience of it was somewhat limited. She hoped to get to know it a whole lot more. A hint of stubble below it scraped her own hyper-sensitive flesh and Elliott's arms tightened around her, slid up to entwine them and trap her within his embrace.

The security of his hold gave her courage a boost, and she pressed her kiss more firmly against his receptive mouth, lapping gently at his closed lips until they gave her the access she wanted.

Elliott bound her closer—into a space she hadn't even realised could exist—and tangled her tongue with his, challenging her to yield. Fighting for control was fun, but ceding to his experience was a pleasure, and she whimpered as he took over the exploration, roaming and tasting and tormenting with his talented mouth.

It was just as she'd imagined. Yet so much more.

'And then what happens?' he ground out as he rose for breath.

She tipped her spinning head.

'In your perfect kiss, Laney? What comes next?'

'I don't know. I haven't let myself think beyond that.'

She felt his immediate tension everywhere. It pressed against her. The subtle tightening of his muscles even as they loosened—just as subtly—their hold on her.

'You haven't let yourself or you don't know what comes next?' His hold loosened even further at her silence. 'Have you ever slept with anyone, Laney?'

Her mind spiralled in a slow circle, making thinking difficult. 'Wilbur.'

'Not counting your dog.' He chuckled.

Then, no. 'Why? Does that make a difference?'

He released her that little bit further. 'Yeah, it does. Of course it does.'

'I'm twenty-five, Elliott. It has to happen eventually.'

She really wanted it to happen eventually. Actually, she kind of wanted it to happen now. While her body was still on board with that plan.

Those lips that had just tortured hers so perfectly shaped new words. Final words.

'But not tonight.'

She placed one foot behind her to steady herself as her stretch shrank backwards. Away from Elliott.

Here it comes...

Confusion stained her pretty face. 'You're not attracted to me?'

'Laney...'

'That's a genuine question, Elliott.'

Yeah. She wasn't the fishing for compliments type. 'It's not about attraction, Laney. It's about appropriateness.'

Half the extra colour birthed by their kisses drained from her face. 'What?'

His stomach fisted hard, deep in his body. 'Sleeping with you would be...'

'Inappropriate?'

Just do it, man. It was always going to end like this. Of course it was.

'Unethical.'

That word—that sentiment—had her taking a second step back. The coffee table hit her calves. But she stabilised and straightened. 'Isn't that something you should have thought about before all the kissing started?'

'Look, Laney. There's a big difference between kissing someone and taking their virginity.'

One meant something. The other meant *everything.* And he didn't do *everything.*

Her arms crept around her torso. 'So if I wasn't a virgin we'd be having sex right now?'

Would they? Would his galloping confusion be any less if he was not her first? Or would his conscience still have raised its unwelcome head.

He sighed and turned partly away. 'No. There's still a difference.'

And his brain had been trying to get his attention as he'd paced up and down in the little chalet, waiting for her to arrive, but his body had kept overruling it. Because he wanted to be able to want her. So badly.

'Who's going to know?'

'I'll know, Laney. That's not the kind of man I am.'

'Really? The kind of man that would lead a woman on and then drop her cold?'

He couldn't say he didn't deserve that. Except he discovered he couldn't say anything at all.

'Why not have someone else assigned to Morgan's?' she suggested finally. 'Nothing inappropriate then.'

And he'd have jumped on that if it were the only thing stopping him. If it weren't for the raging tightness deep in his chest. But she was handing him the perfect out and he was coward enough to take it.

'Because you're my case.'

'Sure—normally. But under the circumstances…'

'No one else wants you, Laney. I'm the one pushing Morgan's at executive level.'

Speaking of pushing…something was driving him hard. Pushing Laney back. Pushing her away as determinedly as he'd dragged her towards him only minutes before.

'But if they agree we have potential? Wouldn't someone else run with that?'

Everything he'd worked for over so many years suddenly felt unstable—unreliable and totally out of his control—and that big, gaping void inside him seemed to loom large and hollow.

'I don't want someone else running with it. Morgan's is my client. *My* opportunity.'

She sagged down onto the coffee table and the rest of her colour abandoned her. 'Opportunity for what?'

Surely she'd understand… This was Laney. She was amazing. If anyone could understand him, what drove him—

'I've been gunning for partner for two years, Laney. And Morgan's is going to get me there. I'm not about to pass that opportunity off to someone else, even for—'

He caught himself, but the sentiment hung out there, all miserable and unmissable. *Even for a blind woman.*

Her fingers curled on the table-edge just as they had on his boat.

'For me?'

Hurting her hurt him. It was like an open wound in his body. But something stopped him from going to her. Some ancient fear. Some inherent…*lack*. When all he wanted to do was trust someone with the truth.

Trust Laney with the big void inside him.

'I see. So the kissing? The parasailing?'

'I wanted to get to know you, Laney. I still do. I really wasn't thinking about what would happen next.'

'You've filled the place with *candles*. And you had a couple of hours to think about it…'

He opened his mouth to defend the undefendable. So he just closed it again.

Her spine forced her upright, rigid and erect. 'Your career means more to you than an opportunity to take things further with me?'

No. That wasn't it at all. But lying was easier than trying to untangle the truth when the truth was so deeply woven into his flesh. 'My career *is* important to me,' he hedged.

She pressed her palms to her cheeks, as if that could mask the dread now there.

'Laney, don't look like that.'

'There is no way this could have worked,' she whispered. 'We're such different people…'

'No, we're not. But the timing is all off.'

Her head came up. 'How is time going to change anything?'

'Circumstances could change.'

Misery thickened her voice and deadened her eyes. 'I told you Morgan's isn't interested.'

'You haven't heard my proposal yet.'

'I don't really need to, Elliott. We're just not interested.'

'Wait until you see the numbers.'

'Like that's all that matters.' But then her face lifted. 'If Morgan's was not an Ashmore Coolidge client any more…could we keep seeing each other?'

'You'd *fire* us?'

'I can get anyone to do our financial management.'

The implication being she couldn't find just anyone to make her feel the way he did. His heart hammered dangerously faster.

'Just so we could be together?'

And there it was.

The great imbalance in their respective feelings and attitudes made manifest in that one little word.

Just.

Laney would have done almost anything to give them a chance to explore this thing between them more. Elliott would do virtually nothing.

She shot back to her feet. Angry enough to stir. 'So, a one-night stand, then?'

Not that she had any intention of doing anything of the sort.

Anger hissed out of him. 'I told you. It's—'

'Unethical. I know. But that's a relationship. I'm talking about a one-off thing. No strings attached.' She waved her hands wildly around her. 'What happens in the chalet stays in the chalet.'

'Laney—'

'Come on, Elliott. Throw a girl a bone. I want to get it out of the way.'

'Laney… You're angry.'

Fury boiled from down deep inside. 'Yeah, I'm angry! You started the whole touchy-feely thing. You with your interesting conversation and gorgeous smell and gentle touch. Why even start it if you knew you couldn't do anything with what happened?'

'Because I didn't think anything *would* happen. I thought it was safe.'

Her snort startled a collar-jangle out of Wilbur. 'To mess with a blind girl?'

'To get to know you. To have you get to know me. To enjoy it.'

Natural justice ran strong in her. She couldn't really stand here and criticise him for not thinking it though when she'd totally failed to do so. She was just so caught up in him.

'Why bother?' Except it hit her then. Exactly why he'd bothered. 'Or did you think it would improve your chances of us saying yes if we'd all come to like you?'

She couldn't bring herself to say *I*. She could barely manage 'like'. Because somewhere this weekend she'd gone flying past 'like' as surely as if she was back in that parasailing harness.

What she felt for Elliott Garvey had stopped being 'like' a half-dozen conversations ago.

Not that it mattered now. Except to name exactly what it was she could never show him.

'At first, maybe. It's good business to build a good working relationship with clients.'

'Do you have dinner with all your clients? Drink wine and share stories?'

'Yeah. Pretty much.'

'Do you kiss them all too? Take them up into the sky and press your body against them?'

Who knew? Maybe he did…

'That's not why I took you parasailing.'

'Then why did you? You called it a date.'

He sighed. 'That's what it felt like.'

'So why do it?'

'Because you wanted to. And because I—'

'Because you what?'

'Because I wanted you to get off this farm. I wanted you to try something new and see that it wasn't so earth-shattering.'

Something cold sliced in under her diaphragm. And the hole it left sucked every bit of joy out of the day they'd just shared. Breakfast, the research lab, the flight, the kissing.

Yet earth-shattering was exactly what it had been.

'You thought one train trip to the city and an afternoon boating was going to make me change my mind about taking Morgan's global? How much of a hick do you think I am?'

'Be honest, Laney. Your horizons are bounded by ocean, trees and a small town. It doesn't hurt to stretch them a little.'

Offence blazed large and real in her chest. 'I was just spending time with you. I didn't realise I was signing up for a self-improvement class.'

Though now she could clearly see what today had really all been about. And what that meant Elliott thought of her.

Nice girl. Smart and business savvy. Good kisser. *Charmingly provincial.*

'You think that taking me to the big smoke and spoiling me

with experiences, getting me to trust you, was going to change my mind? I'm not that shallow, Elliott.'

Though it looked as if maybe he was. Disappointment leaked in with all the hurt.

'No, you're not. But you are—above all else—unfailingly sensible and loyal to Morgan's. I was counting on you wanting the best for them. Regardless of your own fears.'

She reeled back as if he truly had slapped her clean across the face. 'Is that what you think? That I'm afraid?'

He took both her hands in his, gave them a little shake. 'You shouldn't be. You are amazing. You can do anything.'

Snatching them back caused a suck of breath from him. Seriously—he was *still* campaigning? 'Just because I can doesn't mean I should!'

She turned and fumbled with her hands for the nearest grabbable surface, but only encountered a tealight full of molten wax. It spilled as she upended the tiny candle in her haste and she stumbled away from the pain. But of course it only went with her.

Life in a nutshell, really.

'Laney, let me—'

'No!'

Her bark drew Wilbur to her side and he leaned against her leg, where she could more easily reach the handle on his harness. She grabbed it like the lifeline it was. Hardening wax and all.

'I thought you understood me.' *I thought you liked me.* 'But you're just like all the others. Humouring me.'

Using me.

She thought back on how she'd been with him. How vulnerable she'd let herself be.

'This was a mistake.' Emotion thrummed through her voice. 'Something between you and me could never have worked.'

No matter how good the kisses were. Or how he made her laugh. Or how attracted she was to his brain. *Damn it.*

'Laney, let me walk you back to the house.'

'I'm fine. I have Wilbur.' There was one male in her life, at least, who accepted her for who she was and was always there for her. Unfailingly.

'Will I see you tomorrow?' he risked.

She threw her arm out and found the doorframe before feeling her way down to the handle. 'Where else am I going to go with such diminished horizons?'

'Come on, Laney—'

She swung the door open, tiredly, and stepped down off the step. 'Leave it, Elliott. Let's just get back to the real reason for your presence.' For every single thing he'd done here. 'Back to business.'

'I don't want to leave it like this.'

'Well, too bad. It's not your call. I'm a bit over doing what other people want of me. Now I'm doing what I want. And what I want is to end this conversation and get the hell out of your cabin.'

And his life.

She nudged Wilbur on with more force than he deserved and he shot forward in apology. Guilt immediately washed through her.

'Sorry, pup,' she whispered as he led her back through the silent paddock towards the house. Towards privacy. Towards her long, lonely future.

As if being physically blind weren't difficult enough... Now she could add social blindness to her list of challenges.

How could she not have realised which way the wind was blowing? Elliott had made it perfectly clear how important his work was to him and how fully he was backing his proposal. But she'd looked right past the obvious the moment a man came along who appeared to understand her.

Pretended to, perhaps?

Yet for all his corporate gloss, charming words and plain yummy smell, Elliott Garvey was just like all those other men she'd dated. In it for number one. And feeling disappointed and disillusioned was painful enough without also feeling like the blindest blind woman ever to have stumbled on the earth.

Although there was one benefit to having no vision—it made no difference to how fast you could move while tears streamed down your face.

CHAPTER TEN

WHAT A MORON. He really couldn't have messed things up any better.

Any worse.

Elliott moved quietly behind Laney as she showed him the final remaining area of Morgan's operations. Her movements were as dull as her expression. As carefully distant. Closed to any further discussion outside of the necessary.

Utterly closed to him.

And why wouldn't she be? Everything she'd said last night was right. He shouldn't have started anything with her without knowing where and how it was going to end. He didn't do un-evaluated risk. He did strategic risk. Carefully measured risk.

He absolutely didn't do head-swimming, mind-addling, re-solve-defying risk.

Because this was how it ended.

Enjoying Laney's company was an indulgence, and kissing her had turned out to be a luxury he couldn't afford. But it was because of his personal values—not his corporate ones. Ash-more Coolidge was an old-school boys' club. They wouldn't have given a toss about one of their team sleeping with a client if it meant closing the deal. Actually, in truth, they would have had *a lot* to say behind closed doors—especially with a client as young and attractive *and blind* as Laney—but none of it would have been negative. Unless it had lost the deal, of course.

And he wasn't about to lose the deal. He was a realiser. Not a loser. Without his professional success, what did he have?

Just him, his nice apartment, and the big vacant place inside him.

Laney finally wrestled free the front base cover on one of the hives in the stack they were looking at. Her fingers dusted over the front of it.

'When the slide is in this position—' she lowered it '—access to the hive is uninterrupted. But when I raise it—' she did so '—the bees have to go through the collection plate to get inside.'

'It's tight,' he said, really just so that he could gauge her reaction to him. So that she had to engage with him and not just deliver some kind of professional monologue.

'That's how we harvest the pollen. They have to drop the biggest bundles in order to get through with the rest. Then we sell it to the commercial food industry.'

Her eyes were utterly lifeless. And that was when he realised just how full of life they usually were—if you took the time to look for it.

'They don't sound too happy.'

'They don't like change.'

'Or having to work doubly hard to bring in their quota?'

She turned. Finding criticism where he'd intended none, judging by her unhappy expression.

'I would have thought that was right up your alley? Maximising their output. No wasted potential.'

Yeah, it was. But it wasn't like *her*. So there had to be a good reason. 'Is pollen lucrative?'

Her frustrated sigh was telling. 'Yeah. It is.'

Like everything bee-related except maybe honey.

'But that's not why you do it?'

'I do it because we can freeze it and feed it back to the hive during winter to sustain them. It means fewer deaths in winter.'

Death in winter. That was about the most perfect opening he was going to get to talk about his expansion ideas. But that freckle-kissed face was not open to ideas. Not right now.

Maybe never. Not to him.

'That makes more sense.'

Because Laney just wasn't about the money. Or the market. She was all about the bees. Bees and family. And maybe those two things were one in her mind.

'I'm glad. I would hate to be doing something you didn't understand.'

Wow. Sarcasm really didn't sit well on those lips. 'Laney—'

'So anyway,' she bustled on. 'That's it. Bees in here, pollen catches there, and we empty it twice a day for a week and then they get two months off.'

Now she sounded just like the disaffected tour guide she was trying to be. All her passion gone.

And he missed the other Laney horribly. This one made her business sound like…a business. Regular Laney made it sound like her life.

But at the end of the day it was the business that he was here to talk about. Not her. Not her great love for what she did or how fascinating the various aspects of the apiary were. His job required him to stay focussed.

On getting Morgan's signed up. On getting his promotion.

'What time are we meeting your parents?' he asked, forcing himself back on track. Just as the debacle that had been last night had.

'Lunchtime.'

Noon. That was still a couple of hours away. What the hell were they going to *not* talk about for that long?

'So what's next?'

She turned to face him. 'That's it, actually. You've seen everything. I've got to get on with doing my job, so you'll have to entertain yourself until our meeting.'

Right. 'You need any help?'

'I'd say yes if I thought you could do much.'

The barb glanced off his corporate-thickened hide, but the fact she'd fired it off at all really bothered him. It was symptomatic of how much he'd hurt her last night. And he was not going to leave things like that.

'Laney. I'm really, really sorry about last night. You were right. I shouldn't have indulged myself in getting to know you better. It was unfair of me.'

She kept her face averted so he couldn't even read her accidental expressions. Only her silence.

'I should have known better,' he went on. 'And been stronger.'

She turned, straightened. 'What's the matter, Elliott? Trying to ingratiate yourself before the meeting?'

His head reeled back. Actually, it hadn't occurred to him that last night might go against him in his presentation. Because that wasn't Laney. She loved Morgan's too much to let something personal get in the way of its success.

But there was no way she'd believe him if he told her that. 'I am trying to make good, Laney. But not because of the meeting. Just because I've hurt you. And I'm sorry.'

'Don't be. I appreciate knowing where you stand. And what you think of me.'

'I think highly of you.'

Her hands balled on her hips. 'You think I'm too afraid to step off this property.'

Every moment they spent on her deficiencies distracted him from his own.

'You have good reason to be—'

'I am not afraid!' she urged. 'And I don't need your patronising concern. I stay because I love it here. I love what I do and the way I do it. This is my home.'

This wasn't making things better. 'Okay, Laney…'

'And I don't need you to humour me, either, Elliott.' She stepped closer. 'I get it, you know. I may be inexperienced romantically, but I'm a big girl. I know what this is. You're interested. I can tell. But you're interested in your career more. That's just how it is.'

Before he could reply she barrelled onwards.

'I'm not angry that things didn't work out between us last night. I'm angry because it's revealed a barrier between us much more fundamental than geography. We have different values. Despite the chemistry. Despite everything. And all the good fit in the world can't change a person's values.'

Did she mean *his* values? As if hers weren't half the problem?

'So this isn't anger at you, Elliott. It's disappointment. And resentment that something so fundamental is in my way. And anger at myself for not being more alert for the possibility. I was just enjoying you so much.' She shuddered in a big breath and when she spoke again all the vulnerable momentum of her last words was gone. 'That's all this is. And there is nothing you can do or say to undo that. Is there?'

Sure there was. He could say, *Hey Laney...screw everything I've worked towards for years, and screw the big, freaking terrifying void inside me. Let's just see where this leads.* But he wouldn't. Because he couldn't just throw away everything he'd worked at his whole adult life. Not to address someone else's fear.

He'd walked away from that once before—left his only family rather than diminish his life down to his mother's level. And that sacrifice would be totally meaningless if he didn't keep chasing his dream.

Success challenged him and drove him. And it defined him. Without that, who the hell was he?

And it was the only thing that kept him from collapsing back into that big void inside.

'If things were different—'

'But they're not. Let's get real about that. I'm a bee farmer from the country. You're a corporate realiser from the city. And ne'er the twain shall meet.'

And there it was. Their almost-relationship fully nutshelled. She was right—it didn't matter how much either of them wanted things to be different; they were what they were.

'I'll see you at the meeting,' he murmured after a long silence.

'Yeah. You will.'

But after that…? Whether or not Morgan's went ahead with expansion, chances were good he wouldn't be seeing Laney again. Not if he wanted to be fair to her. Because the two of them couldn't spend time together and not feel this thing they had. And it was impossible to feel it and not want to act on it.

Like he did right now.

He just wanted to pull her into his hold and rest his chin on her head and promise her that everything was going to be okay.

But he couldn't, because that would be lying.

Nothing about this was okay.

And so all he could do was leave her in this place she loved so much, with the bees that were her life, and trust that it could heal the damage he'd done since arriving.

Laney gave it a full sixty seconds after Elliott's steady, heavy footfalls on the turf had diminished to make sure he was really gone. Then she sagged back against the hives and buried her hands in her face.

Not her finest moment.

None of this was Elliott's fault any more than it was hers. They just didn't fit. This must happen to people all over the world every day. Relationships that had a lot going for them but suffered from some fundamental flaw that just…*broke* them.

Not that what they had was a *relationship*, but it had started to feel like one. Hadn't it?

Wilbur shoved his snout against her thigh and she lowered one hand to his damp, cool nose.

'It's okay…' she murmured.

Though she was pretty sure that was what he was trying to tell her.

Yeah, she was all right. None of her feelings were terminal. She wanted to be like everyone else, didn't she? Well, ordinary didn't come much more ordinary than heartbreak. Just another life experience she was coming to late in life.

Her own thought stopped her cold.

Was her heart *broken*?

She peered inwards. Yep, just like the big divot that Owen had put in their ute last year when he was jack-arsing around. Nice and dented but nothing terminal.

Except the deeper ache still bothered her. The fingers of her imagination probed and poked, looking for rifts that she couldn't find, but as they did so pain oozed out from below. As if the dent had damaged something much more delicate deep inside.

Hope. Self-belief. Faith. Haemorrhaging away quietly.

Yep; those were the things that had suffered most last night. That had taken such a knock. The pain of rejection she could learn to live with, but if she let him damage those essential parts of herself she'd never forgive herself.

Or Elliott.

She turned and felt her way along the hives until she reached the ones she knew were in the down phase of pollen collection. Where the bees didn't have a grudge to bear. She lifted the top two boxes off and let her hands rest on the open hive. Bees swarmed up and over her hands in a mix of surprise and curiosity—each of their soft feet a gentle, tiny kiss on her skin—until their collective weight became tangible. She slowly turned her palms up and the mass crawled around, chasing gravity, surrounding her with happy bee sounds and the comforting tickle of all their oscillating wings.

This was what she did. This was what she'd been born for. And who she was.

She had an idyllic life here on the Morgan property—a life she loved, where she was safe and happy, and where her proficiency as an apiarist gave her immense satisfaction. She'd be foolish to brush all that off like so many bees. Some people never had any of those things in their lives, let alone all of them.

So it wasn't going to come with a romantic happy-ever-after...? Three out of four was pretty darned good.

But consigning herself to a life without love didn't sit comfortably, and her gently waving fingers trembled to a bee-laden halt even as her chest squeezed down into a ball.

Love.

Did she love Elliott? Surely that took more time than they'd had?

So what if he was the first man she'd ever met who treated her like a regular person? He made allowances for her sight but he didn't treat her as if she was deficient.

Sure, he was the first man she'd kissed when she had initiated and really *wanted* his kiss. And more.

And, yes, he was the first man she'd ever met whom she truly *saw*. Both as a man and as a glorious, rich glow in the nothing of her visual perception.

And that was what she was going to miss most. Elliott was the only person other than her family that she'd ever had inside her head. Rarefied ground.

She tipped her fingers down towards the hive and gently shook most of the bees free, then turned them over and repeated the exercise. Some clung to her, exactly as she was clinging to a stupid wish that things could be different. But eventually they gave in and dropped off—just as eventually she'd realise the truth.

Elliott Garvey was going to be her 'once upon a time' man.

The man she'd kissed, once.

The man she'd gone parasailing with, once.

The man she'd started to fall in love with, once.

CHAPTER ELEVEN

'So what do you think?'

The whole Morgan clan watched him intently except for Laney, who faced off to one side, looking for all the world as if she was a million miles away. Though Elliott knew by her stillness that she'd been concentrating one hundred per cent during his long spiel.

Wilbur snored over by the crackling fireplace.

'Surely customs issues would make it impossible?'

'Collectively, they're losing hundreds of millions of bees every year as northern winters worsen and lengthen. This is now a priority for their agricultural boards. Customs are prioritising supply from apiaries like yours.'

'Won't it be a problem that we haven't used pesticides?'

'Outweighed by the benefits of your geographic isolation and good disease rankings.'

The whole family fell to silence. He'd given them a lot to think about. A whole new market that could be more lucrative than all their other operations put together. Shipping ready-to-go hives to the northern hemisphere in time for spring to replace their disturbingly depleted local species. Populations that were suffering from ever-worsening northern winters.

He took a breath and focussed on the only silent person in the room.

'Laney? Nothing to say?' Quite the opposite, he suspected. Something about her posture said she was fighting to hold her tongue.

'It's certainly a big market—' she said, still flat.

Even her mother looked around, frowning, at the death in Laney's tone. Then Ellen's perceptive regard came straight to him.

He couldn't return it.

'But I'm sure everyone's getting on the bandwagon.'

'Everyone doesn't have Morgan's spotless organic pedigree.'

'We'd be sending our bees overseas to die.'

Was she serious? 'After a full season of foraging. Just like they would here.'

'They're biologically adapted to do best here.'

'They don't have to do "best"—they just have to do okay. Even okay is better than nothing when you have no other choice.'

'They *belong* here.'

The fervency of her assertion bothered him. It was as if she was talking about something much bigger than bees. *Okay...* 'You're just looking for reasons to say no.'

She sat up straighter. 'I don't like the presumption that our bees are just a product to be packed up and shipped into a biological warzone.'

'You're an apiarist, Laney. Your bees *are* a product, no matter how well you treat them while they're here.'

'What you're describing is a massive undertaking.'

'It's big in scale, sure, but you have the skills.'

'*I* do?'

'Morgan's does. And, yes, you definitely do.'

Her hands twisted in her lap and he realised, too late, that he'd said the wrong thing.

'So this comes down to me?'

He opened his mouth to respond and then discovered he didn't know what to say. So he just looked at Ellen.

'It's a family decision, love,' she ventured.

Laney's lips pressed tighter. 'But let's be realistic, Mum. Are either of you going to want to run this? You guys are gearing up for retirement.'

There was a strange kind of agony in her voice. Controlled panic. Almost palpable. And her parents' silence was another nail in the coffin of his promotion at Ashmore Coolidge. If they weren't going to support this then he was dead in the water.

That vast nothing inside him seemed to swell and loom, almost in celebration. Had it just been waiting for everything to fall in a pile?

Laney turned back in his direction but her gaze overshot him. 'So it does come down to me, then? A massive change in direction, constant overseas travel, mountains of paperwork. All taking me away from what I love doing. Why would I do that?'

'I'll do it,' Owen said quietly.

'Between waves?' Laney snorted and didn't even bother directing it at her brother. 'No, this comes down to me. As it always was going to.'

'Your mother could help with the administration—' her father started.

'Seriously, Dad? She can barely keep up with the admin as it is.'

'You'd be making enough that you could hire someone,' Elliott pointed out.

'Laney, it could set us up—all of us—for life.'

'Aren't we already set up, Dad? What more do we need?'

'You'll need a place of your own,' he said. 'And Owen will. Then your children will, and his. What will you do? Continue to subdivide Morgan land until our descendants are living on quarter-acre blocks?'

'Children? I think we're getting ahead of ourselves a little.' She kept her words firmly averted from Elliott. Even putting them in a thought together hurt her physically. 'A couple of months ago we were thrilled with how the business was going. Now suddenly I'm being short-sighted?'

No one laughed at the poor joke.

'It's the same business, Laney,' Elliott urged. 'You just scale up and add an export arm.'

'My existing arms are kind of full,' she practically shouted back at him.

'I'll do it,' Owen tried again.

Elliott glanced at him where he sat across the room. His gaze was steady in his father's direction. The most serious he'd ever seen him.

'It would be massive, Owen,' Laney tossed back. 'Don't be ridiculous.'

He lifted one eyebrow, but then went back to watching his father. 'I'm not Superwoman over there, I realise,' he said, 'but even Helena would have to learn that side of things—why not me?'

'Because *you* would rather surf than work,' Laney dismissed him.

'Only because what we do here is boring and repetitive.'

'It's not boring!' she defended, turning her anger to him. 'It's streamlined through years of perfection.'

'It's mind-numbing, Laney. Same tasks, over and over. I'd love a chance to do something new. And to travel.'

'Helena, you can do anything you set your mind to,' Robert said, firmly dragging the conversation back to her again.

'I don't want to do it, Dad.'

'You'd be great at it.'

'Why is no one listening to me?' she urged. 'I'm not interested.'

'Take one trip,' Elliott offered. 'Come with me and meet some of the apiarists who are really struggling.'

'Why? So I can add their guilt trip to yours?'

'What guilt trip?'

'"*Come on, Laney, my promotion hinges on this*".' Her excellent impression of him was none too flattering. 'You've made it abundantly clear that you've hitched your star completely to Morgan's. And to me.'

'To you, how?'

'Please… Do you seriously expect me to believe that you

wouldn't use my vision to get a point of difference in the
market?'

Injustice bit low and hard. Was that what she thought of
him? 'I would not.'

'I think you'd use anything at your disposal once you'd built
up a bit of momentum.'

The silence grew thick. 'This isn't about me. It's about Morgan's.'

Laney snorted.

'It's hard for her, Elliott.'

Her mother's words were excruciatingly kind, but all they
did was rile Laney up. 'Not you, too, Mum. I'm just *not interested*!'

'*Why* aren't you interested?' Elliott pushed, without really
understanding why. It just felt really critical. 'When it's such
a great opportunity?'

'I love it here. I don't want to leave. I don't want it to change.'

'It's all she knows,' Ellen piped up, her voice a study in com-
passion but her eyes closely focussed on her daughter.

And suddenly Elliott wondered if Ellen Morgan was quite
as sweet and passive as she seemed. Her words seemed very…
calculated.

'I'm not afraid!' Laney insisted, reading very neatly between the lines.

'No, no. Of course not,' her mother gushed.

But the concept was hanging out there in public now, and—
in a master stroke on her mother's part—it was Laney who'd
put it there.

Her father spoke up again. 'I'm sure a country like the
United States is very accommodating for people with vision
impairment. And if they're not—'

Laney shot to her feet. 'It doesn't matter, because I'm not
going to America.'

'I'll go,' Owen said, waving a lazy arm in the air as if he expected to be completely ignored. Which he pretty much was.

'We'll hire someone,' Robert went on.

Elliott tried not to be buoyed by his use of the future tense.

'Oh, please—you know me.' Laney sighed 'Do you think I'll be happy with the way anyone else does it? I'll end up doing it anyway.'

'Yeah, you will,' Elliott agreed. 'Because you can't help yourself, and because despite yourself you'll want this to be done well. Because that's the kind of person you are, Laney. A perfectionist.'

Owen snorted. 'That's one word for it.'

'Come on, Laney, you're intrigued. Admit it.'

'Because you *want* me to be, Elliott?'

'Because you *are*. I was watching you. You think the idea has merit. So do your parents.'

'Of course you'd say that.'

'Am I wrong?'

Her frown intensified and he knew he was right. She *was* interested.

'Carving the Morgan's logo into Mount Everest for PR has merit, too—doesn't mean we should do it.'

In his periphery, Robert and Ellen's glances ricocheted between him and their daughter like a tennis crowd.

'This is an outstanding opportunity for Morgan's. It will be a mistake not to take it.'

'No, what will be a mistake is to let our financier bully us into doing something that isn't on our radar.'

And by 'financier' she really meant him.

Elliott worked hard to keep his temper out of his voice. 'This is imploring, Laney, not bullying. This will *make* Morgan's. Just look at the figures.'

'Why do you even care? What is it to you? Other than your promotion.'

Good. At least she was prepared to acknowledge there was more at stake here than just his job. Not that she would have any idea of what was really at stake.

A man's soul.

'I hate to see this potential lost.'

'Life is full of disappointments, Elliott. You'll survive.'

She frowned as he crossed to stand right in front of her and took her hands in his. 'Laney. I know this is outside your comfort zone, but everyone in this room believes you can do it. You just have to believe in yourself. Be brave.'

The snatch as she pulled her hands back just about gave him whiplash.

'You assume this is about courage, Elliott. You call yourself a realiser, but what you really are is a *judger*.'

'I've been nothing but supportive of you.'

'You're judging me now. Finding me lacking because I don't want to take the risks you think I should. Well, people are built differently, Elliott, and it doesn't make them less. It just makes them different.'

'This could be massive for Morgan's.'

'Not everyone wants *massive*.'

'Why don't you? Why have you grown Morgan's this far only to stop. Why hold your family back?'

She reared up out of the chair. 'Everything I've done I have done for my family. Don't you dare suggest otherwise.'

'They're not going to do this if you don't support it, Laney. You're the centre of this family. Everyone takes their cues from you.'

Her eyes sparkled magnificently. Dangerously. 'I guess that explains why you've put so much effort into winning *me* over, particularly.'

'Don't, Laney...'

'Why not? You win me over with your attention and your interest and your...your aftershave, and all of it was strategic. I'm the *Queen* of the Morgan's colony, after all.'

'This isn't about me, Laney—'

'This *is* about you, Elliott. You and your inability to accept anyone who isn't as driven as you.'

'Being driven is how people get things in life.'

'No, being driven is how *you* get things in *your* life. There're plenty of us who take a different route.'

He blew air between clenched teeth.

'Admit it, Elliott, you think I'm weak for not wanting this.'

'I don't think you're weak—'

'Despite all your flattering words, deep down you think I lack gumption. And you can't understand that in me any more than you could understand it in your mother. Admit it.'

Tension doubled deep inside. 'I do understand it in you, Laney. Your vision—'

'My vision has nothing to do with this. You're just using that as an excuse to justify it.'

'Justify what?'

'The fact I don't want to chase down every opportunity in life and kill it with a club. Well, guess what? It has nothing to do with my vision, Elliott, it's me—just me. My choice.'

'Laney—'

'And you know what? There are plenty of people just like me—just like your mother—who find their pleasures in simple ways. It doesn't make us faulty.'

Two forked lines appeared beneath Ellen Morgan's down-turned eyebrows.

Elliott's gut clenched harder than his fists. 'This has nothing to do with my mother. This is about you letting your disability stop you from being everything you could be.'

The D-word hung out there, all ugly and un-retractable, in the sudden silence that followed.

'Why do I have to be everything?' she whispered harshly.

'Because you can. Because you shouldn't let anything get in your way.'

'Name me one thing that I could possibly have done that I've not tried in my life.'

There was one obvious answer.

'This,' Elliott said, low and hard. 'And I'd like to understand why.'

'Why...?' she squeaked. 'Maybe because I'm tired of being the poster child for the vision-impaired. I'm tired of the Morgan name coming up on Council minutes all through my childhood as Dad pushed for tactile strips on the main street or audiobook cassettes in the school library or modifications on the school bus to accommodate an assistance dog.'

Robert half croaked in protest and Laney snapped her face towards him.

'I'm sorry, Dad, I know you were trying to make life easier for me, but the world doesn't actually owe me anything. Maybe I didn't need to do every activity under the sun in order to be a full person. Or maybe I could have just found friends in my own time rather than you bussing them down and forcing us together just so we could all stay in denial about how different I was. Maybe it would have been okay for me to *not* try something out, or to just be ordinary at something, or—God forbid—even be bad at something. And maybe that's why I don't want to be railroaded into this. I *know* I could do it but it should be enough for everyone that I *just don't want to*. I want to be here, on the property I love, working with the creatures I love and pursuing the things that interest *me*.'

She turned back to Elliott.

'Not my parents. Not Ashmore Coolidge. Not you.'

Silences didn't really come much thicker.

Laney shuffled in her seat but it did nothing to remove the discomfort of a hard truth finally aired.

'Honey,' her mother said finally, 'you never said.'

Laney flung her hands into the air. 'When is the right time to hurt your father? To throw your family's effort back in their face?'

Now, apparently.

'I love you both to death, but why isn't the person I am enough for anyone? Why do I always have to be…*more*?'

'Seriously, Laney?' Owen piped up. 'You're going to complain because you've had too many opportunities in life? When I'm sitting here trying to put my hand up for this one and the only person who *isn't* completely disregarding that is the person who barely knows me.'

She turned towards her brother. And she knew both her

parents would be doing so too. 'You never put your hand up for things.'

'Why would I bother? Opportunities automatically go to you.'

'That's not true.'

'It's absolutely true, Laney. We were born at the same time but you got all the Royal Jelly in life. And you thrived. I turned out just a plain old worker.'

She sagged back into her chair.

'Why didn't you say?'

'Why didn't you ever tell Dad how you were feeling?'

Point taken.

What she wouldn't give right now to be able to look into her brother's eyes.

'You actually want to do this?' she whispered.

'I think I do.'

'But what about your surfing?'

'I love to surf, but I'm never going to be a pro. And fiddling with hives isn't enough for me. I'd like to do more. I *could* do more. And I'd really love to travel. There's a whole world out there, waiting to be seen.'

She snorted. 'You sound like Elliott.'

'I'll take that as a compliment. I think there's a lot I could learn from him. And you'd be a hypocrite to judge me for wanting to follow my own path.'

She soaked that in, then turned back towards Elliott. 'This wouldn't obligate us?'

'Phase one is fact-finding and relationship-building only. All decisions will come back here.'

'Could Owen do it?'

'With my help. I'll be there with him.'

Another excellent reason for her to say no. Travelling in close confines with Elliott and not being able to touch him? *Ugh,* imagine…

'How long would you be gone?' Robert asked, his voice still wounded.

'A couple of months. To get around to all the big suppliers personally and see the impact of winter on their spring.'

'Months? But we're going to need Owen to close out the season.'

'You mean *you* are,' Elliott said quietly. 'To be your eyes. And your driver. And your assistant.'

Her stomach rolled. Both at the ugliness of Elliott's statement and at its stark truth. He'd watched their operations closely enough to know exactly who did what. And for whom.

Oh, God...

Her chin sagged to her chest and mortification washed in around the realisation. She was as guilty of making presumptions about her brother's life as the world was about hers. Every time she brushed off an idea of his...every time she thought he was sweet for voicing an opinion. Owen didn't lack the grey matter to do more at Morgan's, he just wasn't engaged here. That was why he'd put his energies into other things, like surfing and girls. Because he'd trained himself not to care.

Because of her.

And he could learn a lot about business from Elliott. Things he'd probably never learn from his sister. Things that would give Owen the same kind of reward as the bees gave her.

The kind of reward he'd been forgoing all this time so that she could enjoy her life.

Tears stung dangerously at the back of her useless eyes.

'It's okay, Laney—' Owen started, genuinely aggrieved at her distress.

She shot a hand up to stop him. Because, no... It very definitely *wasn't* okay. Being blind was no excuse for what she'd failed to recognise. And she wasn't about to allow him to put himself second for her again.

A couple of months...

About the same time she'd known Elliott, and she'd managed to fall half in love with him in that time. Would a few months without him be enough to fall safely *out* of love again? At least she wouldn't have to deal with him every weekend.

She turned back towards her brother without consulting her parents. She knew them well enough to know what their silence meant.

She sighed.

'You're going to need a suit.'

'Are you okay?'

Elliott followed her outside when she took her leave from the awful family meeting. Awful, but probably necessary.

'I'm a horrible person.' She shuddered. No wonder Elliott didn't want her. Why would he?

His voice softened. 'No, you're not. Families are…complicated. Sometimes you have to step out of it to see it clearly.'

'I've hurt them all.'

'They'll live. Maybe today was just a day for saying overdue things.'

Mostly by her.

'I'm sorry if I set you up for that with my comments,' he murmured.

'It was the truth. And he wouldn't have his chance without your intervention.' Because she and her parents would still be dismissing Owen.

'What will you do while he's gone?' he asked.

'Hire someone in to help, maybe. Something we should have done years ago.'

'Why didn't you?'

Yeah…excellent question.

Her throat tightened. 'As long as Owen was a bit of a flunkie and helping me kept him positively occupied I got to hide behind the happy image of brother and sister working together. Contributing to the family together. And I got to overlook the hard truth.'

'Which was…?'

'That as long as it was my brother helping then I didn't have to feel disabled.'

'That's not the truth, Laney.'

'It's absolutely true. I let Owen believe that the only value he added to Morgan's was the one he brought to me. *I* did that, Elliott.' No wonder he was so desperate to stretch his wings. He was probably desperate for a bit of self-worth. 'I hadn't realised how self-absorbed I am.'

'You're not.'

'You said it yourself. I'm the Queen of my family.'

She heard the sag of his body in his voice. 'Laney…'

But, no… Being blind was no excuse for some of the things she'd been overlooking.

'It's a good proposal,' she admitted, desperate for a new subject. 'Congratulations.'

'This was never a contest.'

Wasn't it? From day one it had been a challenge to see who would outplay the other.

'You can still be involved,' he went on. 'As much as you want. Or as little.'

The latter was added with such reluctance. And shades of disdain. She lifted her head. 'Why are you pushing me so hard, Elliott?'

'Because you have so much more in you.'

More. Always *more*.

'What if I don't want to be more?'

What if she just wanted to be *her*.

'I don't believe that.'

'You mean you don't want to believe it.' She sighed. 'What happened to you to make you so intolerant of the choices of others?'

'Nothing happened. That's the point. Not one thing happened in my life unless I made it happen. Unless I went out and chased it down. Like you should.'

'I don't want to. I don't need to. I'm happy with my life exactly like it is.'

Well, mostly anyway. She wouldn't mind having a do-over with Owen. And a bit of love for a good man in the mix.

'I don't *need* to either, Laney.'

'Are you sure? Because it seems to me that someone who spends so much time sucking the guts out of life must have an awfully big space to fill inside. And all the cars and speedboats and penthouses and promotions and busyness will pad all that nothing out, but never really fill it.'

'You think I'm missing something?' he said, after the longest silence they'd ever shared.

Echoed in his voice it sounded more terrible than she'd meant it to. But why stop now with the revelations.

'Can I be honest?'

'Are you ever anything but?' he snorted.

'I think you have your priorities all messed up. I think you walked away from your only family because it was easier than addressing whatever it was going on inside you.'

'Based on the twenty seconds I've spent talking about my mother?'

'She made some hard choices, Elliott. She gave up her career to keep you and raise you.'

'She taught me to be afraid, Laney.'

'How?'

'Through example. She never encouraged me. She never believed in me. Just like you and your brother.'

The accusation stung. Because she could now see what her family's under-estimation had done to Owen's self-confidence. But the guilt only fired her up more.

'You beat your head against a brick wall trying to change her, and now you want to change me, too.'

'I don't want to change you.'

'You may not *want* to, Elliott, but I think you *have* to. Because me being happy and fulfilled exactly the way I am only highlights how empty you are.'

'Really? That's what you think?' His voice had chilled several degrees.

'I'm starting to.'

'And why exactly should it matter to me what you do? We're not a couple. We're barely even friends.'

A dull ache spread through her thorax. 'That's what I'd like to know. What is it to you?'

'I guess nothing,' he said, after an eternity, his voice rich with sorrow. 'I just wanted to help you.'

Poor little blind girl.

'I'm not your project, Elliott. I'm just asking you to respect my choices. To respect me.'

When he spoke again, his voice was hard. 'I don't think I can, Laney.'

Her gasp cracked the still air. She stared at him through her unseeing eyes. He couldn't bring himself to *respect* her?

'You're hiding out here in this paradise, Laney. A place and existence that's customised for you, that's as streamlined and predictable as the lives of your bees. And you've convinced yourself that you're happy that way because you don't know any different.'

'Any *better*, you mean?'

Could he be any more patronising?

A cold certainty washed over her. 'Is that why you stopped things between us last night? Because you can't be with someone you don't respect?'

His voice dropped. 'It's a pretty fundamental thing.'

Hurt clenched in her stomach. Yeah, it was. And pretty immutable, too.

She sagged back against the side of the house, struggling to breathe normally. All this time she'd just wanted to be accepted for who she was, but Elliott found it impossible to like that Laney.

Not much she could do about that.

'Well…' What the hell did you say in this situation? 'Good call, then. That would have been much more painful to discover if we'd got any more involved.'

You know—if I'd fallen in love with you or something…

She dropped her eyes in case he read the silent irony in them, unguarded. A silent minute ticked by.

'So, I guess I won't see you until I get back from the trip,' he finally ventured, thick and low. 'I'll keep you informed—'

'No need. I'm sure Owen will be in touch regularly.'

Don't call me.

Despite his itchy feet, she felt sure that Owen would start missing his family about two minutes after leaving them. And, really, she'd get over Elliott much more quickly if he wasn't at the front of her consciousness, all glowing and present.

'Laney—'

She straightened and thrust out her hand. 'Goodbye, Elliott. I hope the trip is everything you want it to be.'

She stood there like that—hand outstretched, back straight, chin up—until his warm glove of a hand closed around hers. Firm. Tight.

A true goodbye shake.

And when he spoke his voice was no steadier than his hands. 'Bye, Laney. Take care.'

CHAPTER TWELVE

CRAWLING.

Just like the bees on the frames of the hives she checked multiple times each day, the weeks crawled by until they formed reluctant months.

Doing the hive runs wasn't as much fun with Rick as it was with her brother, but productivity sure was higher when Owen's replacement didn't pepper their every journey with side-trips and errands.

Maybe that had been Owen's way of making a dull job more interesting.

'Is this boring to you, Rick?' she asked between frames. About the job she adored.

'Nope. It's awesome.'

Thank you! 'Awesome because you've only been doing it a few weeks and the novelty hasn't yet worn off?'

'Awesome because it's outside.'

See? Rick got it. He'd scored a great job in a surf shop but then discovered he was basically a till jockey, trapped indoors all day, surrounded by boards and wetsuits and diving gear he could only use on the weekend. So he'd jumped at Owen's offer of filling in for him through autumn.

'And because I get to work with you,' he went on.

Laney fumbled the frame as she slid it back down and a heap of bees launched off with a slight angry-bee tone in their buzz.

Was that an overly appreciative *'work with you'*?

She'd always liked Rick, and considered him the better of

her brother's friends, and they did have a lot in common, but there was no...*whatever*...with Rick. No spark. No intellectual attraction.

And definitely no glow.

The vacant place behind her eyes was still and dark when Rick was around. The light had been extinguished pretty much the day Elliott drove away from the farm for the last time.

'I'm sure I'm not that interesting.' She laughed carefully.

'Yeah, you are. I love watching you work with the bees. How they respond to you.' He closed one hive and moved to the next. 'But mostly I can just be myself around you, without worrying that you're working up to hitting on me.'

The hitch of anxiety in her chest that Rick was suggesting *more* fizzled into flat understanding. How like one of her brother's mates to be so utterly self-absorbed. And how contrary, on her part, that she should feel the stab of his rejection even when she didn't even want his interest. It really didn't help her to be reminded that the only man she'd welcome interest from was on the other side of the planet.

And found her philosophically repugnant.

As always, a deep ache took root low in her belly when she thought about Elliott and the way he'd judged her and found her wanting, and, as always, she forced it deeper, where she didn't have to think about it. Logically, she knew that she'd done her share of judging, too—echoes of the word *empty* came back to her at the most inconvenient moments—but as far as her heart was concerned the damage was all his.

'You should be so lucky,' she joked aloud.

They worked like that—casually chatting, but mostly getting on with the business of managing the hives—until their growling stomachs forced Rick back to the staff rest area for lunch and her back to the house to make a sandwich before her parents got back from the city with Owen in tow.

They'd cut their trip short because they'd had more business than any of them could have imagined fulfilling in their first year of exporting, leaving them all feeling very positive about the potential. But did her brother's enthusiastic reports really need to come so liberally sprinkled with anecdotes about Elliott?

Her brother's voice, but she *heard* Elliott.

Maybe it was just because he was the first person to take Owen seriously. Or because he was so good at what he did. So lateral and so driven. Maybe he was just the first person to give Owen the right mix of support, belief and education. To appreciate his potential.

Now that Elliott had turned his full attention to the *other* Morgan twin, ten weeks' intensive travel had clearly birthed a serious bromance between the two men.

And she could hardly blame Owen. She'd had one herself for a while there.

Fortunately she'd had nearly three months of absolute nothingness to wean herself off Elliott. Not a word directly—only updates channelled through her brother. That kind of total shutdown was as good as a saturated blanket tossed on a grass fire. Total spark-killer. Even the glow had retreated to something that only emerged when she let herself think about him in any way outside of the strictly professional.

Which was never.

So everything she knew about what he'd been up to she heard from her brother or her parents. And once from when she web-searched Elliott in a moment of lapsed self-discipline.

She settled in at her desk with her sandwich—at the computer that had freaked Elliott out so much because it didn't have a monitor—and checked her email for something from Owen. Although of course there'd be nothing from Owen, because he would have been in the air for the past twenty-four hours.

So really this was about Elliott.

Of course it was. It was his name she was secretly hoping to hear her text-reader announce. But, no. Nothing.

She keyed the software to instant sleep and reached for the phone instead.

Time for this to end.

'Welcome to Ashmore Coolidge,' an *über*-professional voice answered.

'Helena Morgan for Elliott Garvey, please.'

The faultless voice stumbled. 'Uh…one moment please.'

It hit her then, blazing and obvious—maybe he'd taken the day off since his international flight had only landed this morning. Assuming he'd flown back with Owen at all. And right after that she realised that she didn't know his home number. Or his address. Ashmore Coolidge was her one and only channel to Elliott.

'This is Roger Coolidge, Ms Morgan.'

Senior partner Roger Coolidge? Surely Elliott didn't get to bump his work *up* the food chain while he was away on business?

She stiffened. 'Mr Coolidge, I'm so sorry to have troubled you—'

'How can I help you, Ms Morgan?'

Time is money. Right. 'I was calling for Elliott. I've just realised he's probably not back in the office until tomorrow.'

'Elliott?' he repeated, as though her use of his Christian name was somehow inappropriate. 'Garvey?'

'I have…um…some questions about the Morgan's proposal.' Total rubbish, but somehow she couldn't imagine Roger Coolidge responding positively to *I just want to hear his voice*.

'The export proposal?'

How many proposals were there? 'I just wanted to see how it was tracking.'

Ugh, such a bad liar.

Office sounds clanked away in the background of Roger Coolidge's silence. 'Ms Morgan, Elliott Garvey is no longer employed at Ashmore Coolidge. I assumed you'd been informed.'

Her stomach dropped away, along with her only lifeline to Elliott. 'What? No…'

'As of several months ago.'

But their proposal… 'Why?'

His voice grew softer. Kinder. 'I'm not really at liberty to say—'

'Elliott Garvey is in possession of a lot of our financial data,' she improvised—badly. 'I would have thought as our financial advisors you would recognise the necessity of my question.'

The kindness evaporated. Utterly. She should have known better than to try and play someone as experienced as Roger Coolidge.

'Ms Morgan... He left of his own accord after we rejected his proposal for Morgan's.'

Rejected?

'He left?' The job and the company he loved? His promotion fast-track? 'Why?'

'We disagreed on some of the...conditions of approval. He was inflexible and opted to leave when we denied the proposal.'

'What conditions?'

'Again, I'm not at liberty to say. You'll need to ask him.'

'How, if he's not our rep any more?'

'My understanding is that he's with one of your personnel in the United States right now, pursuing the proposal privately.'

Those last words were strained.

'Well, I—'

'If you have any questions relating to Ashmore Coolidge's services, or its current work with Morgan's, I'd be happy to have Garvey's replacement contact you personally...'

The rest was a blur of impatient political correctness until Roger Coolidge disentangled them both from the awkwardness of the conversation and hung up.

Laney squeezed the phone hard in her hand.

Gone.

Proposal rejected. Promotion jettisoned.

Yet Elliott hadn't told them before whisking Owen off overseas. What had he done after his proposal was rejected? Taken his bat and ball and decided to play on by himself? To go for the money if he couldn't have the promotion? Show them what a mistake they'd made?

Was he that desperate to succeed? Or was it just ego, frustration and maybe even anger at the lack of vision shown by his superiors—men he was supposed to respect?

Though she knew what a big deal respect was to him.

Unfortunately.

But more pressing… Ashmore Coolidge was the only way she knew of getting in touch with Elliott now that he was back from his travels. And there was something terrifyingly final about not having one single communication channel to someone you loved…

'Knock-knock.'

Rick's deep voice sounded just inside the front door and sent her leaping out of her chair and Wilbur scrabbling to his feet, both of them as guiltily as if he'd caught them up to no good.

'There's a dust plume coming in from the highway,' he announced.

Owen.

It occurred to her suddenly to wonder if he'd have Elliott with him and her heart began thumping in earnest.

'One plume or two?'

And she held her breath.

'Just the one.' He kept on talking over her plunging hopes until he finished up with, 'Is that okay with you?'

'Um…sure.' Whatever she'd just agreed to. If her vacant expression didn't give her away.

'Great. I'll see you tomorrow, then. Say hi to Owen for me.'

And then he was gone, leaving her with just enough time to finish her sandwich and brush the pollen out of her hair, thoroughly distracted, before the return of the prodigal son.

'Lake Erie.'

Her mother had given up describing what was in the photos at image number eighty-seven. Now Laney was lucky if each picture in Owen's excited slideshow even got a descriptor name.

Part of her would have liked to '*see*' Lake Erie. But another part of her—the part that really would have preferred to be doing something more productive with these hours—figured she could pull up a few pictures on the internet and have her mother describe those instead. At a more mutually enjoyable time.

A time when her thoughts weren't so completely filled with thoughts of a different man.

She'd made a total fool of herself, nervously holding her breath as first Owen, then her mother and finally her father had alighted from her dad's wagon. A pathetic part of her had desperately wanted to hear a fourth door-slam.

But there had been no fourth slam.

Owen in full so-tired-he-was-wired mode after his epic flight from the US was just a babbling sequence of stories with barely a breath drawn between them. And every story featured Elliott one way or another.

Elliott did this… Elliott said that… Here's Elliott at the biggest apiary in the States…

Ugh.

'I need to go for a walk.' She cut across her brother's slide-show narration, surprising herself with the intention and pushing to her feet.

'Right now?' her father asked. 'But your brother's only just back.'

She pushed to her feet and felt for her coat before there could be any dissent. Apparently, yes, right now. 'I need some air.'

And she needed—very badly—to extract herself from the Elliott Garvey show.

She felt her way to where Owen sat and kissed the top of his head. His gorgeous surf locks were gone in favour of a much more business-like short haircut. Somehow that made him even more a whole new Owen.

'Good to have you back, O.'

'We need to talk later,' he threatened—and that was really the only word for the sudden seriousness in his voice. Owen—the man who was never serious about anything.

Wilbur groaned as he heaved himself to his feet, and she surprised herself again by signalling him to stay. He sank his old bones back down gratefully. 'I won't go far,' she assured him.

But she was lying, and his slight doggie whine told her he knew it.

Staying close was safe, and safe wasn't what she burned for just now. *Safe* was what Elliott had accused her of being all those weeks ago. Something deep inside her wanted to prove him wrong. Wanted to show him—or maybe just herself—that she could take as many risks as the next person.

As *him*.

She grabbed up her stick as she left the house and all Owen's exciting stories behind and turned left towards the coast track.

What she wouldn't have given for a bigger butt right now.

Laney shifted from one cheek to the other on the rocky track and flexed tired, sore muscles, then tipped her face up to the sun to give her flagging spirits a boost.

Stupid.

She had her phone, but she wasn't about to use it to call for help. In fact she'd turned it off so that no one could ring her, either, and offer to help. That would defeat the entire purpose of her ridiculous trek up to the lookout without Wilbur. The furthest point she could imagine going on foot. Somewhere she'd never been alone before.

Somewhere not entirely safe.

The lookout was a statement, and that statement was not going to be strengthened by a call for the cavalry to rescue her from the stupid stone she'd twisted her ankle on.

But two hours on her butt in the dust and her throbbing joint wasn't easing off any. She'd enjoyed the first hour—had used it to think and to gently test her abused ankle, to stretch out the yank on her tendons, waiting for the *ouch* to ease. But two hours without any improvement and she was starting to question the wisdom of this whole impetuous statement.

All she'd done was prove Elliott right, really.

Still she didn't use her phone. She'd spend the night out here before calling for help. Turned ankles were hardly a new experience for her—she just needed to wait it out. Although she would turn for home just as soon as her leg was up to the challenge. There really was no point in denying reality.

She was *blind*.

And this was *far*.

She tipped her face back and stared straight into the sun, her ears full of the wind buffeting the coast, her perception full of the golden glow of the sun. And she used it to calm her anxious nerves.

'Hey…'

Her ankle protested at her startled lurch. And the sun's glow turned rich and masculine.

Elliott…

'Whatcha doing, Laney?'

'Thinking,' she replied, struggling not to move. Struggling for some dignity. Struggling not to weep at the sound of his voice.

'On the ground?'

'Benches seem to be in short supply out here.'

'Yeah, you're a long way from home,' he murmured, squatting next to her.

'I could say the same thing.'

Why are you here? That was what she wanted to say. And right behind that was an immense gratitude that he was.

'Your phone is off.'

Heat washed up her neck but she lifted her chin anyway. 'I prefer to do my thinking in silence.'

'Are you planning on getting up any time soon?'

'When I'm ready.'

But this man was no fool. His sharp brain was one of the things she loved best about him. The present tense of that thought sucked at her spirits. All her good work of the past two months undone by mere moments back in Elliott's company.

Her feelings for him hadn't changed one little bit.

'Laney, are you hurt?'

Horribly! she wanted to sob. By everything he'd shown her about herself. And about himself. And about the unfairness of life in general.

She waved her left leg loosely. 'My ankle.'

His answer was immediate and infuriating. But she was too distracted by the heaven of his arms around her after all this time, and by his scent pressing so close to her, to protest as he lifted her off the ground. He resettled her more comfortably and her arms crept around his neck.

Where she'd once let herself believe they belonged.

'What are you doing here?' she asked, breathless, as his footfalls crunched.

'Looking for you.'

Ugh…such intensity. How badly did she want to imagine that it had something to do with her and was not because her parents had issued some kind of all-points bulletin?

'Lower your good foot.'

She slid down his body, with the polished gloss of his car at her back, until her strong foot hit the ground. He opened the door with one hand and helped her inside with the other.

'I mean on the peninsula,' she said as soon as he'd closed himself in with her. 'Why are you here?'

Looking for you. Please say it…please say it.

But his voice was guarded. 'I've spent the last ten weeks on the go in the constant company of your brother. My apartment felt pretty big and echoey all of a sudden.'

'And you thought you'd remedy that by driving four hundred kilometres to hang out on one of our windswept cliffs?'

She refused to let his chuckle warm her.

'I thought you'd have gone to the office if you were in need of company,' she tested. 'I'm sure it's full of people working way past their home time.'

'I stopped off to see my mother, but otherwise I headed straight down from the airport.'

Nice hedge. She straightened further as he bypassed confession, but played along. 'How is she?'

'She's good. She—' He stopped as suddenly as if something had caught his eye in the distance. 'We had a good chat.'

What? Could he barely believe his own words?

'About your trip?'

'About a whole bunch of things. Overdue things. Turns out I had my share of unspoken baggage there.'

'You shock me.'

He didn't take offence.

'Did you get it sorted?'

Because mothers mattered.

'Yeah. I think we did. There was a lot I didn't understand.'

'Like what?'

'Like how I came about.'

'Elliott, I could have given you the birds and the bees talk if I'd realised you were lacking...'

'Funny girl. I mean *why*. Turns out Mum was acting out when she was sixteen. Trying to get herself fired from the squad.'

'Why?'

'She was miserable. She hated that life. She hated the pressure she'd been put under her whole childhood. The stress. The intense expectation.'

'So getting pregnant was her solution?'

'Getting pregnant was just the result. She knew fraternisation would get her sent home.'

'So you *made* her life, then? Not ruined it?' His earlier words echoed, clear and pained.

'I changed it. But...' A gentle lightness stole over his deep voice. 'Yeah, not for the worse, as far as she was concerned.'

It was hard to resent a man for his own personal healing. Even one who had hurt you.

'I'm glad for you. Does that help?'

'It explains a lot. Her background too. Now I know why she didn't push me harder. Or at all. She thought she was protecting me from the sort of experience she'd had. Letting me just emerge at my own pace.'

'But you wanted the pressure?'

'I wanted her belief.'

Yeah. Laney could definitely relate to that.

'Let me just call your parents,' he said. 'They are frantic. And Owen's cursing because you've upstaged his glorious return.'

No. Not the Owen who had come back from his travels. That Owen was infinitely more self-assured than the one who had left. But she sighed anyway. 'It seems I haven't really learned anything in the months you were gone.'

Except that wasn't true. She'd learned how to be humble. And that a person couldn't just *wish* feelings away. More was the pity.

'Where were you headed?' he asked after a brief call to her brother. 'Before gravity intruded?'

'The lookout.'

'You weren't far off. I can see it from here. Why so far from home?'

'I can't really explain it… I needed to do it. To prove I could.' Never mind that apparently she couldn't. She shuddered in a calming breath. 'I hate that you were right.'

He could have said something comforting, something patronising. But he didn't. He shifted in his seat, turning his voice more fully on her. 'You want to tell me what's really going on, Laney?'

'I could ask you the same,' she murmured.

'What do you mean?'

Enough of the eggshells, already. 'You lied to us.'

His surprise was more of a stammer. 'About what?'

'About not representing Ashmore Coolidge any longer. About quitting your job in protest when they denied the export proposal.'

Awkward.

'I didn't lie, Laney.'

'Yeah, you did.'

'No, I didn't. I emailed your father with full details when it happened. Did he not tell you?'

She thought back to how injured her father had been after that evening, and how long it had taken the two of them to get back to a cautious happy place where he finally understood the pressure he'd put on his young daughter, with his relentless drive to give her every experience available, and she'd finally accepted that those same experiences had nurtured and drawn out her talents. Made her the woman she now was.

'Guess he forgot.'

Unless he was just too hurt…

'Or he didn't want you to worry about Owen.'

'Why would I worry about Owen?'

'Because there's a big difference between heading Stateside under the auspices of an international finance company and two freelancers cold-calling in a rented RV.'

'There may be things about my brother that I was unaware of, Elliott, but I know Owen well enough to recognise that the latter would have suited him down to the ground.'

'He did really well.'

The proud confirmation of a mentor. And a friend.

'So…what happened with Ashmore Coolidge? Why did you leave?'

'Water under the bridge, Laney. Wouldn't you rather talk about the trip?'

Actually, what she wanted to say was *Why didn't you call me?* But his ex-employers seemed a much safer topic. And one likely to keep him at a distance.

'No. I want to talk about Ashmore Coolidge.'

'They passed on the deal. Ripples from the global financial crisis.'

'You don't seem the type to poach a client.'

'I'm not. I told them when I resigned that I was going to pursue it with your family. Independently.'

'And they were okay with that?' Not the Roger Coolidge she'd spoken to.

'They didn't love it, but they were prepared to be flexible after…'

'After what?'

'Laney, it really doesn't matter.'

'It does to me. If there are good reasons why we shouldn't be proceeding.'

'They aren't related to the feasibility or the figures. And they aren't good reasons.'

'Then what?'

'Look, Laney. I believed in the proposal and I believe in Morgan's. And I really believed in the opportunity. Too much to just let it go.'

'What about your promotion?'

'I walked away.'

For a guy whose dream had been ripped out from under him he sounded pretty…relaxed. 'I want to say I'm sorry about that, but something tells me I shouldn't.'

'I can't say I enjoyed the face-down with my employers, but a couple of months of being freelance has shown me how much I've been missing by tethering myself to a company as conservative as Ashmore Coolidge.'

'Face-down about what?'

Frustration issued tight and tense from his throat. 'A fundamental aspect of their approval.'

Wait. There'd been a moment when they *would* have accepted? And he hadn't jumped at it? 'Come on, Elliott, you know I'm not going to stop asking.'

'Laney, can you just trust me that I did what I thought was in your best interests?'

'"*Your best interests*" Morgan's—or "*Your best interests*" mine?'

'Laney—'

She reached for her phone. 'Maybe I'll just ask Roger, then.'

Strong fingers curled around hers to stop her dialling. '*Roger?* You're on a first-name basis with Coolidge?'

'A lot has changed since you've been gone.'

You know—in the time when you were completely ignoring me.

'I'm amazed he wasn't too ashamed...' he said, under his breath.

'Of what, Elliott?'

Breath hissed out of him like a deflating balloon.

'Ashmore Coolidge made acceptance of my proposal only on certain conditions—' That was the world Roger Coolidge had used, too. '—and certain marketing strategies that I didn't agree with.'

'Carving our logo into Mount Everest?'

'Actually, I thought that had merit,' he quipped.

But his silence only grew more awkward, and she recognised that awkwardness from those first hours when they'd met. 'Wait... Was it to do with me?'

Silence.

'What did they want you to do?'

'You weren't even comfortable with the researchers naming their project after you. I was pretty sure you wouldn't have wanted to be the international face of Morgan's.'

Correct.

'Ashmore Coolidge particularly wanted *your* face,' he nudged.

'Did they imagine a pretty face would open doors with the apiaries?'

His sigh was almost lost in the rasp as he ran his hands over his chin. 'They felt you would open doors on the media circuit.'

And then the penny finally dropped. And rolled right off the edge of the cliff behind them. 'They wanted to trade off my vision?'

'It's not going to happen, Laney.'

'Damn right, it's not! I can't believe they asked.'

'They don't know you.'

'Do they not have any shame?' Heck, and she'd been so polite to Roger Coolidge!

'If they did they'd never do half the things they do.'

But as her umbrage eased off a little the meaning of his words sank in. She twisted back towards him and whispered, 'You quit your job rather than sell me out?'

'I found a line I wouldn't cross. Who knew?'

His laugh was one hundred per cent self-deprecation.

No. He was making light of it, but just…*no.* 'You gave up your dream.'

For *me*.

'It was repugnant, Laney.'

So…what…? Anyone would have done it? Did he expect her to believe that?

'Not to them. They would have quite happily used my blindness to sell a truckload of honey.'

'Don't deify me just yet, Laney. I walked away from that opportunity straight into another one. A better one. I wasn't exactly taking a leap of faith. If we proceed, I stand to make that same truckload.'

'So you're in this for you? You're not a good guy? That's what you want me to believe?'

'I'm a reasonable guy, Laney, but I'm not a saint. There was a time your vision was on the assets side of *my* assessment file. Back at the start.'

Sure, he'd thought about it—but he hadn't done it. Big difference.

'What stopped you?'

'You. I got to know you.'

Her heart clenched before she remembered not to let it. 'I don't need you to run interference for me with Ashmore Coolidge. I would have told them where they could shove that idea.'

His full laugh washed over her like a warm wave. It had been a long time since she'd heard it.

'I know. It wasn't about you. It was about me. Drawing that line.' He cleared his throat. 'I didn't want to be a man who had no line.'

A decency line. And she was it. But not because of *her*; because of him.

'Thank you,' she murmured. 'For whatever reason you did it. You had a lot to lose.'

'I have a lot to gain, too.' He took her hands in his again. 'Laney, it took me a while, but I got there. I understand you don't want to be defined by your vision. The woman who does extraordinary things *despite* her blindness. Or *because* of it. You don't even want to be extraordinary.'

'Wasted potential, I'm sure you'd say.'

'Yeah, I would have—before I met you. Because before then…you were right…I associated potential with achievements. Things. Value. I had no idea that the most important potential is the person that we are.' Breath sighed out of him. 'And you're the most fully realised person that I've ever met, Helena Morgan.'

She swallowed, but couldn't think of one clever thing to say.

'It took me a few weeks away from you to see it clearly. And lots of conversations with your brother—who worships the ground you walk on, by the way. I'm the one that's been dipping out on my potential. In favour of money and status. Glossing over relationships, skipping from country to country, never settling in one place long enough that it became obvious. But I can't stand next to you for more than a few minutes before I start to feel inadequate.'

'You're hardly that.'

Confusion leached out of him. 'I'm not happy. Not like you are. I'm not content in my own company and with my life the way I've built it. I'm rich, and I'm well-travelled, but I don't get up each morning and just…smile.'

'You say that like you have no experience of happiness at all.'

'My mother chose her simple life as an antidote to the first sixteen years of her life. All that pressure. All that expectation from her parents and her coaches since she was five years old. She was happy—genuinely happy—and healing through our simple life. But I couldn't be. I was ambitious and proud, even as a kid, and the absence of her encouragement and support really rankled. I hated myself for finding my own mother so lacking, but that was easier than looking at what was really going on. She had nothing in life yet she seemed so full. And I had nothing in life but was also completely dissatisfied. Completely empty. All that travel, all that accumulation, was to compensate for the great nothing I felt inside.'

'I was angry when I said you were empty—'

'You were *right* when you said it.' He turned her towards him. 'Turns out I'm the real blind one here, and I've been fumbling around in the dark for years, in that same emotional metre-square, avoiding real relationships, avoiding giving myself to anything, thinking that's all there is. And then I met you, and you showed me this whole other world I was missing.' His fingers threaded through hers. 'But I didn't hold on hard enough. You were my guide and I let you go.'

Everything in her shrivelled into an aching ball. Was he saying she was his Wilbur? When he knew full well that Wilbur meant everything to her.

'A whole other world?' she croaked.

'I just wanted to return the favour, Laney. I didn't know that was what I was doing in trying to get you off the farm, but I was trying to give you *my* world.'

'I thought you pitied me.'

'I know.'

'I thought my lack of ambition repelled you.'

His hand tightened around hers. 'I'm so sorry that's how I made you feel.'

'You made me feel impaired. And I'd truly never felt that until then. In all my life.'

The silence then was awful. But she took some solace from the fact that he at least recognised that to have been the cruellest thing he could do to her. So maybe he did know her a little bit, after all.

His forehead leaned gently on hers, and it was more eloquent than anything he could have said just then.

'I have nothing against new things,' she murmured into the silence. 'Or places. I just object to being expected to do them or go to them because I somehow *owe* it to blind people everywhere. I was even a little bit jealous that Owen was off having this great time—*with you*—and having experiences I might never get to have. But the more everyone expected me to do it the less I wanted to. On principle.'

'You don't need to explain. And I don't ever want you putting yourself at risk like today just to show me you can.'

'I think I needed to show *me* I could,' she admitted. 'And so when I couldn't it was confronting'

He drew her into a careful embrace—welcoming, not forcing. So that she could disentangle herself if she wanted. But she didn't want. She'd been missing these arms for months.

'You're not empty, Elliott,' she breathed.

'Not when we're together,' he vowed. 'Empty doesn't feel like this.'

Their combined body heat warmed his scent and it shimmied around them. She nestled more fully into his hold and was warmed through from the inside out.

'Bees do this,' she murmured against his chest. 'The "cuddle death". The workers embrace the retiring Queen, *en masse*, until the combined heat of their vibrating wings means she gently expires.'

And right now, in the warmth of Elliott's hold, she'd have happily ended her days just like this.

'Nice analogy.' He leaned away from her slightly, to murmur against her hair. 'If a little creepy.'

Maybe it was because this was the first time she'd really laughed in months. Or maybe it was because a matching one rattled through his big body and vibrated against her cheek. But whatever the reason it gave her the confidence to be truly vulnerable with him.

'I missed you so much, Elliott.'

'Ditto.'

And then they were kissing again. After such a long hiatus.

His finger under her chin lifted her waiting mouth for the press of his warm lips, the challenge of his tongue, and the comfort of his hot breath mingling with hers. And somehow she knew that he was the last man she would ever kiss.

No matter what happened from here.

He broke away from her gently to start the car and reversed, only to park again.

'What are we doing?' she murmured, twisting back towards him.

'I wanted to look at the view. Morgan's is spread out in front of me.'

'You haven't been gone that long, Elliott. It hasn't changed.'

'I want you to understand that I know exactly what I'm taking on by loving you. The whole Morgan package.'

Her heart plunged to her stomach and then did its best to beat there, awkwardly wedged below her diaphragm. Her breath grew laboured. Excruciatingly so.

Loving you?

'America was agony, Laney, despite your brother's best attempts at being good company. I should have been ecstatic—we were slaying the opposition and signing memoranda of understanding everywhere we went—but the only time my spirits lifted above sea level was when Owen spoke about you. Or gave me news about you from home. Eventually it got so bad he'd intentionally hold back snippets to give me just before we walked into an appointment. So I'd be on my game.'

'We need to talk...' her brother had vowed when she'd left home earlier today. She'd thought he meant about their own relationship, but maybe he was wanting to tell her about Elliott.

Loving you.

But years of protection were hard to walk away from. 'What are you saying?'

'I'm saying I understand what I'm accepting by loving you. All of that land. All of that heritage. I understand what I'm giving up, too, and I want you to believe that I'm ready to do it.

I have nothing of value in the city. Everything I need is right here on this lookout.'

Elation threatened to lift her two feet above his plush leather seats. But still she couldn't trust it. 'What about parasailing?'

Big hands framed her face, stroked the ridges of her cheek-bones. 'Hmm, good point. Okay, you and parasailing are the only things that I love. Conveniently, both of which I can have on the peninsula.'

'You'll go mad sitting on the farm,' she breathed, and it was far more wobbly than she preferred. 'Like Owen.'

'I wouldn't have to sit. I could be like one of your worker bees, flying out, strengthening the business, then returning to the property.' He brushed a lock of hair back from her face. 'Returning to my Queen.'

Well... Could she trust this to be real? 'With a stomach full of nectar?'

'And pollen balls wadded up under my armpits.'

A smile broke through entirely without her permission and she realised that, yes, she could trust this moment. More importantly, she could trust this man.

She wriggled more comfortably into his arms. 'You think you can just swan in and exploit all our hard work to make an easy fortune?'

'You think life with you is going to be easy? Pfff...' He kissed her, fast and hard. 'Besides, I'm not swanning in. I'm buying in. At great expense. I want to be a Morgan's partner, regardless.'

'Regardless of what?'

'Of whether you love me back or not.'

She kept her lashes low in case her traitorous eyes broadcast her thoughts. 'You doubt my feelings?'

'I don't know what to think. You're protecting yourself.'

'Does that surprise you?'

'No, I definitely get it. But I'm not taking anything for granted. Even if it's all too soon between us now, we have years of working together—as partners—to get to know each other fully. Maybe I can make some headway on winning you over.'

As if that ship hadn't sailed weeks ago.

'How?'

'By loving you. And believing in you. And returning to you on the trade winds like the good drone that I am.'

She found his mouth with her fingers and then kissed him long and hard. When she was done she spoke against his lips. 'If you're a drone, that means we only get one night together. And that's not going to be nearly enough.'

'If that's all I get, I'll take it.'

'And what if I want you to have more?'

His arms circled more tightly around her and his thighs pressed flat against hers. 'Then I'm yours. However much— or little—you want.'

'You think I might not want more?'

'I just don't want to make any assumptions.'

No. Because she hadn't given him any reason not to yet. Time for that to change.

'I love you, Elliott. As fast and crazy as that seems. You are the most important person in my life.'

Laney's senses reeled as he plunged his fingers into her hair and his lips half devoured hers.

But then the spinning slowed and he pulled slightly away. 'Wait a minute—do you mean the most important *non-hairy* person in your world?'

Wilbur. 'Is that going to be a problem?'

'Whatever it takes. Just so long as you will always be my Queen.'

EPILOGUE

Four years later

THE HIGH-PITCHED SQUEALS and delirious barking merged together into one of Laney's most favourite sounds as she sat, her hand resting gently on a curve of stones, atop her favourite hill, occasionally visited by bees from her favourite hive.

Best sound ever.

A girl and her dog.

Running and playing and just loving each other so intensely. Even though he wasn't technically her dog to love. Even though he had a serious job to do.

Those kinds of distinctions were meaningless when you were three years old.

All little Ashleigh Morgan Garvey cared about was that her three great loves loved her back: *Mummy,* who gave her the best cuddle death hugs of all time, *Daddy,* who let her sneak into bed with them for three nights straight after every plane trip away, and her *'woof buddy',* who was the most grown-up three-year-old Ashleigh had ever met.

Born the same year as Ashleigh and delivered fully assistance-trained—and festooned in a bow on the day of the ceremony they'd very belatedly got around to organising—Toby had been a wedding gift from her husband, who'd recognised what she'd been unable to admit.

The future.

Laney sipped at the cup of tea in her right hand and patted

the stones by her thigh as she so often did. And—as it so often did—it brought her peace and comfort and an incredible feeling of rightness with the world.

Her beautiful husband—who was away as much as Morgan's needed but at home every other waking minute—had helped her collect every rock. He'd made the jarrah cross and then helped her engrave the letters with her own hands—not perfectly level, not even properly punctuated, but every letter packed with love and devotion. And he'd held her tight and patient in his arms as she'd cried her heart out at the loss of the first great love of her life.

Wilbur.'Toby!'

A split-second warning before fifteen kilograms of puppy-at-heart splashed warm tea all over her hand. And then he was off again. Being a regular dog, because his harness was off. She rested her mug on the ground.

'Hello, Wilbur,' Ashleigh whispered to the stones, slumping down into her mother's lap and tucking her little arms around her.

They sat there like that for priceless, precious moments, and a glow more blazing and complete than any other she'd known filled her consciousness.

'Daddy's coming,' Ashleigh said in hot little breaths under her jaw, as much a scene-setter as her grandmother. 'He's got some papers.'

'Thank you.'

'I love Daddy.'

Laney smiled and rubbed her left thumb on her daughter's cheek. 'Me, too, chicken.'

'What am I missing?' Elliott's deep, sexy voice rumbled as he bent and plucked his daughter from her lap.

Laney leaned back into the strength of his long legs the same way she leaned back into his arms—his chest—in front of the fire in their timber house up near the lookout.

'Just two girls chatting about the men they love.'

'Girl-talk, huh? I guess I should get used to it. I've got a lifetime of it ahead.'

Laney put one hand on her belly and the other brushed again over the smooth stones on Wilbur's grave. Both touches as comforting as each other. 'You never know. This one might be a boy.'

'Not a chance.' Elliott's honey voice rained down on her. 'Our little colony is going to be as female-dominated as a hive. I can feel it.'

'Would you mind?'

'Nope. Not if they're all as clever and strong as you.'

'And if they're not?'

'Then they'll be unique in some other way. And I'll love them just as much. No matter what.'

No matter what.

No expectations, no conditions, no pressure. Just love and support. Just as it should be.

She leaned back into him and let the glow surge, growing and engulfing everyone and everything around them. Elliott, Ashleigh and her unborn sibling, and Wilbur's final resting place. The emotional brightness brought moisture to her sightless eyes, but it was a good kind of damp—the best kind—and she decided that, if nothing else, *that's* what her eyes were good for.

For loving her family.

* * * * *

She stood when the little boy braced himself on the pumpkin. "Definitely his first steps." And then she threw herself into his arms. "Oh, my gosh, Justin. He's walking."

"I know."

And he was excited about that, too. But damn it, Emma felt so good in his arms, pink jacket, funky hat and all. He couldn't help himself and pulled her in tighter for full body contact. Being this close to her had him thinking about long, slow kisses in his bed. There was no question that he started breathing faster, and it wasn't his imagination that Emma was, too. He saw it when she stepped away and couldn't look at him.

"It's getting cold," she said.

Justin hadn't noticed. He was hot all over and wanted to do something about it.

* * *

The Bachelors of Blackwater Lake:
They won't be single for long!

FINDING FAMILY...
AND FOREVER?

BY
TERESA SOUTHWICK

Published in Great Britain 2014
by Mills & Boon, an imprint of Harlequin (UK) Limited,
Eton House, 18-24 Paradise Road, Richmond, Surrey, TW9 1SR

© 2014 Teresa Southwick

ISBN: 978 0 263 91268 5

23-0314

Harlequin (UK) Limited's policy is to use papers that are natural, renewable and recyclable products and made from wood grown in sustainable forests. The logging and manufacturing processes conform to the legal environmental regulations of the country of origin.

Printed and bound in Spain
by Blackprint CPI, Barcelona

Teresa Southwick lives with her husband in Las Vegas, the city that reinvents itself every day. An avid fan of romance novels, she is delighted to be living out her dream of writing for Mills & Boon.

To Susan Mallery, Christine Rimmer,
and Kate Carlisle. You're my plotting family
and so much more. I'm grateful to call you friends.

Chapter One

"**I**'m not looking for a wife."

"Thank you for clarifying, because that's not the box I checked on the nanny application."

Justin Flint, M.D., stared at the young woman sitting across the desk from him, liking the fact that Emma Robbins had a sharp, sassy sense of humor. On the other hand, that didn't change the fact that his comment was out of line.

It was just possible he was trying to discourage her because she was too pretty. He was a Beverly Hills plastic surgeon and had relocated to Blackwater Lake, Montana, to give his almost one-year-old son a normal life. That didn't include being taken in again by a pretty face, but saying so out loud would be too weird.

"I'm sorry." He dragged his fingers through his hair. "This is going to sound egotistical, but women applying for the nanny job have been coming on to me. That's not the qualification I'm looking for in the person who's going to take care of Kyle."

"You're right. That does sound egotistical." She smiled and, if possible, was even more beautiful. "It also makes you a concerned father, which I can respect. But let me assure you, I'm not the least bit interested in anything but a job."

"Good." It *was* good but still took his ego down a peg or two. "Okay. Let's take it from the top. This interview didn't start off very well. My fault entirely. And I *assure* you that normally I behave in a completely professional way with my employees."

"I'd expect nothing less. But I can see why women flirt with you. It just has to be said that I'm not one of them."

If he were still in Beverly Hills, an agency would vet all nanny candidates, but in this small town things were different. Advertisements in the local paper and recommendations from the employees here at Mercy Medical Clinic, in addition to those of the mayor and town council, had generated half a dozen prospects. Unfortunately, the first four had clearly been more interested in batting their eyeslashes and giving him a look at their cleavage.

"All right, then." He browsed through the paperwork. "So, Miss Robbins, you're from California." That was the address she'd listed.

"Yes, Studio City. It's in the San Fernando Valley north of Los Angeles."

"Blackwater Lake is a long way from there."

She smiled. "I can see that."

He knew the Southern California neighborhood and it wasn't far from the entertainment capital of the world. With a face like hers, she could be a starlet and he'd stake his professional reputation on the fact that she'd had no work done. The flawless skin and stunning features were nothing more than excellent genes.

Emma Robbins looked as if she belonged on a movie screen. Long, shiny brown hair streaked with gold fell past her shoulders. Her eyes were brown and framed by thick lashes. But it was her mouth that mesmerized him—full, sculpted lips made for kissing, and he couldn't seem to drag his eyes away from them. *That* thought definitely hadn't been vetted by his common sense.

"So, what brought you to Montana, Miss Robbins?"

"Vacation."

"Have you ever been here before?"

"No."

"What made you decide to come here? As opposed to, say, Hawaii?" He would bet she'd turn heads in a bikini. Although right now she looked like a preppy college girl with a white collar sticking up from the neckline of her navy pullover. Tailored jeans and loafers completed the look. "I'm just trying to get to know you."

Was it his imagination or did she not quite look him in the eyes?

"This will sound corny, but one of my favorite books was set in Montana. I was between jobs and did some research. This town was advertised as the new and unspoiled Vail or Aspen. I wanted to check it out."

"So, what do you think?" he asked.

"Words can't describe how beautiful it is here," she said sincerely.

That didn't answer the question about whether or not she wanted to stay. "I need to be honest with you about my situation."

"I would appreciate that, Dr. Flint." The tone was firm, almost abrasively adamant, hinting that maybe someone hadn't been truthful with her.

Justin could relate. "I brought my current nanny with me from Beverly Hills where my medical practice was."

"Obviously there's a problem or I wouldn't be here."

"If you call hating mountains, a lake, trees and blue sky a problem, then yes."

She laughed. "I have nothing to say to that."

"The issue has more to do with missing her grown children and the fact that one of her daughters is a month away from giving birth to her first grandchild."

"That could distort your perception of the most majestic mountains ever and a lake and sky that are prettier than anything I've ever seen in my life."

He thought so, too. "The thing is, I talked her into staying until either her replacement could be found, or two weeks prebirth. Kyle hasn't known any other caregiver, and the change is going to be disruptive for him."

"How old is he?"

"Ten months."

She glanced at a photograph on his desk. "May I?"

"Please." He handed her the frame.

"He's a cutie. Just like his father." She caught herself, then met his gaze. "I swear that wasn't flirting. What I meant was, he has your eyes, and the shape of his face is all you."

He took the photo back from her and smiled at the baby, pleased she thought Kyle had inherited something good from him. Hopefully his son would have better judgment in people, specifically women people, than his old man.

"He's little and doesn't understand what's going on. I'd like the change to be as easy as possible for him."

"I can understand that." She folded her hands in her lap.

"If I decide to hire you, what assurance can you give me that you'll fulfill your obligation?"

In truth, there wasn't anything. If the sacred vows of marriage didn't stop his wife from ignoring her responsibilities, what could this stranger say to convince him? Kyle's mother had put her own interests over what was best for her son, their son. Since her death, Justin found that buying the best child care possible was the only guarantee he had.

"Dr. Flint—" She leaned toward him, earnest in her defense. "There's nothing I can say to convince you of my sincerity, but I'm well qualified. I have a degree in early childhood development and the references I provided might help ease your mind. A short-term contract would probably be best. If either of us isn't satisfied with the bargain at any time, a suitable notification period should be spelled out. Enough time for either or both of us to make other arrangements."

That seemed fair to him, but he wasn't ready to say so just yet. Instead, he asked, "What about your life in California?"

"I'm not sure what you want to know."

"Do you have family? Friends? A house to be sold or closed up?" Someone special?

Justin found himself most interested in the answer to the question he hadn't asked out loud. She was pretty. He was a guy and couldn't help noticing. She must have a boyfriend and, if not, candidates were probably lined up around the block waiting to apply for the position.

Emma sat back and crossed one slender leg over the other. "I don't have family. On top of being an only child, my father died when I was ten and Mother passed away a little less than a year ago."

"I'm sorry."

"Thank you." Her mouth pulled tight, but it looked like more than grief. "She left me the house, but I have a friend who will take care of it."

He wanted very much to know if the friend was a man, but asking wouldn't be professional. Before he could say more, there was a knock on his office door just before

Ginny Irwin, the clinic nurse, poked her head into the room. "Dr. Flint, your first afternoon appointment is here."

Since she could have relayed that information by intercom, Justin suspected she hiked upstairs to the second floor in order to get a look at the nanny applicant.

"Thanks, Ginny. I'll be right down."

"Okay." She stared curiously at the young woman across the desk from him, then backed out, closing the door behind her.

"All right," he said, "I guess we're finished."

"There's just one more thing I'd like to say." Emma picked up her purse from the floor beside her, then stood.

"What?" he asked.

"I want this job very much. And I'm very good with children."

He would check that out for himself. "All right. I have one more interview."

"Will you let me know one way or the other?"

"Yes." He stood up and felt as if he towered over her, then hated that it made him feel protective. There was something vulnerable and fragile about this woman, but getting sucked into the feeling was a bad idea. "I'll do a thorough background check and personally contact all the references you listed."

"Good. I'd expect nothing less. And I'll do the same for you."

"Oh?"

"It's a live-in position, right?"

"It is. And light housekeeping will also be required. But my primary concern is the well-being of my son. If I get called for an emergency in the middle of the night, trying to find child care could be a problem. I need someone there."

"So if I'll be living under your roof, it would be a good

idea for me to know something about you. That way, everyone feels better." She shrugged then held out her hand. "It was very nice to meet you, Dr. Flint."

Justin wrapped his fingers around hers and felt a sizzle all the way up his arm. That was enough to make him want the next job applicant to actually *be* Mary Poppins. He needed to hire someone right away. His current nanny was very close to leaving him in a real bind when she headed back to the Sunshine State.

So far, Emma Robbins was the most qualified applicant, if her references checked out. That made her the leading candidate. On the downside, he was too aware of her as a woman.

Nothing about that made him feel better.

Emma drove up the hill to Justin Flint's impressive, two-story house. After parking, she took a good look. The place was big and located in the exclusive, custom-home development of Lake View Estates. She took a deep breath and exited the car. The wraparound front porch had a white railing that opened to double front doors with etched glass. Light danced through it and was like a beacon of welcome.

"Homey," she whispered to herself. The warmth was unexpected. Maybe she'd been expecting pretentious from the renowned Beverly Hills plastic surgeon.

She walked up the three stairs and pushed the doorbell, then heard footsteps just on the other side. Bracing herself to face Justin Flint again, she wasn't prepared for the short, plump, fiftyish blonde woman who opened the door.

"I'm Sylvia Foster."

"Emma Robbins," she said, extending her hand.

"My replacement." Blue eyes twinkled good-naturedly. "That's my hope, but I'm happy just to have a second interview." Emma hadn't expected it. The doctor had seemed distant after they'd shaken hands.

"I probably shouldn't tell you this, but he's desperate. I gave him an ultimatum and it wasn't easy. Breaks my heart to leave this baby. But…"

"He told me your first grandchild is due soon."

"A boy," Sylvia revealed, excitement sparkling in her eyes. "I'm so torn. I'll miss Kyle terribly, but my three children are in Southern California, not to mention a sister and brother. My whole family is there."

A little voice chattered unintelligible sounds behind her and she turned. On the gorgeous dark-wood entryway floor was the doctor's son, crawling toward the open door as fast as he could.

The older woman tsked, although there was no scolding in the sound. "Kyle Flint, just where do you think you're going?"

She started to bend and grab him as he scooted by her with every intention of getting outside. Emma squatted on the porch side of the low threshold and looked up at the older woman.

"It took a lot of energy for him to make a break for it. Would it be okay if he comes out just for a minute? A little reward to encourage his sense of exploration?"

"I like the way you think." Sylvia nodded and watched the baby touch the slats separating his protected world from the unknown beyond.

He sat and slapped it a few times before going on all fours again and venturing out. Turning wide eyes, his father's gray eyes, on Emma, he took her measure. Just as the doctor had done.

"Hi, cutie." She let him look, get used to her. Overwhelming him with verbal, visual and tactile stimuli could be disconcerting to the little guy.

After several moments, he crawled outside and over to her, putting a chubby hand on her thigh. Then he boosted himself to a standing position.

"He's pretty steady," she observed. "Is he walking yet?"

"Not quite," Sylvia confirmed. "He's a little hesitant to take that first step."

Emma knew how he felt. She had a family here in Blackwater Lake that she hadn't known about until just before her "mother" died. The woman had confessed to kidnapping Emma as an infant from people who lived in this town. Shock didn't begin to express how she'd felt at hearing the words, and she was still struggling to wrap her head around it all.

This trip to Montana was about her own personal exploration. She'd been in town for three and a half weeks, checked out the diner that her biological parents owned and managed. But she hadn't taken the next step of telling them who she was. Everything would change for them and there'd be no going back. She wasn't sure turning their world upside down all over again was the right thing to do. Observation showed that they'd found some sort of peace, and learning the truth might not be for the best.

The little boy slapped her jeans-clad leg and grinned as he took steps while barely holding on.

"Hey, buddy," she crooned. "You're a handsome little guy."

"A heartbreaker in training, just like his father," Sylvia said.

Emma wondered if Justin warned women away because he didn't want to break hearts. He was a doctor, after all, a healer. Or maybe he really wasn't looking for anyone because he was still grieving the wife he'd lost in a car accident. She'd checked him out on the internet and there was a lot of information on the celebrity plastic surgeon who'd given up fame and fortune due to shock and grief over losing the woman he'd loved.

An expensive silver SUV pulled up in front of the house and parked behind the little compact she'd rented at the airport nearly a hundred miles from Blackwater Lake. So the doctor was in. If this second interview went as she hoped, she'd have her car shipped from California and return the rental. The next few minutes would determine her course of action.

"Daddy's home, Kyle." Sylvia smiled at the baby and clapped her hands.

"Da—" he gurgled.

"Aren't you smart," Emma said.

She stood, gently holding the baby's upper arm to keep him from falling. Bending, she held out her hand to see if he was willing to be picked up by a stranger. He smiled and bounced, holding out his arms.

"Hey, sweetheart," she said, lifting him up and cuddling him against her. "You're a heavy boy."

Justin got out of the car and walked toward them, then up the steps. A man who looked as tired as he did had no right to still be so handsome. His short dark hair was sticking up a little, as if he'd run his fingers through it more than once that day. Piercing gray eyes grew tender when he looked at his son. In that moment he was an open book and it was as if the hidden path to his soul were exposed. He could have been a troll, but the feelings so evident on his face made him nearly irresistible.

"Sorry I'm late," he said, stopping beside Emma. "There was an emergency."

"Everything okay?" she asked, automatically swaying from side to side with the baby in her arms. Kyle had discovered the chain around her neck and the butterfly charm attached to it.

"A little girl had a run-in with broken glass." The doctor's eyes turned dark and intense when he looked at her holding his son.

"Is she okay?"

"I gave her my personal guarantee that when she's wearing her high school cheerleader uniform, no one will ever know she had stitches in her knee when she was eight."

"So you're a hero," Sylvia said.

"I wouldn't say that, but if you're passing out compliments…" He held out his arms. "Hey, buddy. Can I have a hug?"

The baby turned away and buried his face in Emma's shoulder. Not her fault, but not how a father away at work all day wanted to be greeted by the child he clearly adored.

"Hey, sweetie, want to say hi to your dad?" She wouldn't hand the boy over to his father until he was ready, or the doctor insisted.

"That's not like him," Sylvia commented. "Usually he crawls up and into your arms. I think he likes Emma. Seems very comfortable with her. Just my opinion as his primary caregiver, but you should hire her."

"And that judgment has nothing to do with the fact that you're about to leave me in the lurch."

"You're an evil man, Dr. Flint," Sylvia teased. "I don't have *enough* mother's guilt, so you feel the need to pile on more?"

"Would I do that?"

"In a heartbeat," the older woman said good-naturedly.

"Let's go inside." Dr. Flint gave no hint about whether or not he was annoyed.

Emma followed the older woman into a big entryway with a circular table holding a bouquet of fresh flowers. Twin stairways on either side led to the second story. To the left was a large formal dining room with a dark, cherry-

wood table and eight matching chairs. Directly to the right
was the living room with a striped sofa in rust, brown and
beige. Two wing chairs in a floral print with coordinating
colors were arranged in front of a raised-hearth fireplace.

As they walked toward the back of the house, the little
boy wiggled to get down. Emma set him on his tush, making sure he was stable before straightening. He crawled
over to his father and pulled himself up before strong arms
grabbed him and held him close.

"Hey, I missed you today, buddy."

He nuzzled the boy's neck and the child began to giggle. After a few moments, he pushed to get down and his
father complied.

"Why don't you talk to Emma in your office," Sylvia suggested. "I'll take this little man to the kitchen and
feed him."

"That would be great, Syl. Miss Robbins?"

"Lead the way," she said.

She followed him down a hall off the family room into
his office where there was a large, flat-topped desk and
computer. Two chairs sat in front of it and he indicated she
should take one. She did, and looked around as he sat in
the black leather chair behind the desk.

"This is surprisingly homey," Emma said.

"Why surprising?"

In a perfect world, Emma thought, she would have kept
that observation in her head. Since it was out, she had to
explain.

"I did an online search on you."

"So you checked me out." One corner of his mouth
lifted.

"It's not like you weren't warned."

He didn't look at all bothered. "And?"

"You were *the* plastic surgeon to the stars. The go-to

guy for new noses, lips and—" She glanced down at her chest, which suddenly felt woefully inadequate. Then she looked up and saw the amusement in his gaze. "Other things."

"I do more than that."

"So I found out. Doctors Without Borders. Trips to Central America to work on children with cleft palates. Donating your time to Heal the Children."

"The specialty is more than just changing parts of the body a person doesn't like." He leaned forward, resting his elbows on the desk. "Most plastic surgery isn't cosmetic. It involves reconstruction. The adjective *plastic* in front of *surgery* means sculpting."

"Very interesting."

"I correct functional impairment caused by traumatic injuries, infection or disease—cancer or tumors. Sometimes a procedure is done to approximate a normal appearance. Trauma initiates sudden change, which can cause depression, make a person question who they are."

Emma had questioned who she was every day since her mother's deathbed confession about stealing her from another family when she was a baby. Plastic surgery couldn't fix her. There was no procedure that would restore what she or her biological family had lost.

"Is it my imagination, or did you quote all that from Wikipedia because you're the tiniest bit defensive about public perception regarding your field of expertise?"

"No. Maybe." His grin was a little sheepish, a little boyish and a whole lot of sexy. "Sorry. Since moving to Blackwater Lake, I've been reeducating the locals who want Angelina Jolie's lips or George Clooney's chin."

"Really? Men?"

"You'd be surprised."

"For the record, I think what you do is very impressive."

She held up her hand. "Again, not flirting or flattering. Just stating the truth as I see it."

He leaned back in the chair, more relaxed now. "Suddenly I feel like the one being interviewed."

"It was more like adding context to the information on the internet."

"I think that was a diplomatic way of saying that I like to talk about myself." There was laughter in his eyes, making them sparkle. Very different from the gray intensity that reminded her of a storm.

"You said it." She liked that he could make fun of himself.

"Speaking of interviews... Why are you surprised my house is homey?"

Too much to hope he'd been distracted enough not to remember that comment. She took a deep breath. "You made a lot of money doing what you did in Beverly Hills. I just figured your home would be chrome, glass, electronic gizmos, sculptures and art that cost the equivalent of a small country's gross national product."

His mouth pulled tight for a moment. "That was then, this is Montana. I wanted a change."

"Because of losing your wife?" Emma winced as the words came out of her mouth. She could kiss this job goodbye. If she ever faced her biological mother, one of the things she wanted to know was which side of the family to blame for this chronic foot-in-mouth problem. "Sorry. That's none of my business. You're supposed to be asking the questions."

"I am, but you touched on something important. Kyle will never know his mother, and whoever looks after him will be dealing with that issue as he gets older."

"Of course. You'll want to keep her memory alive."

"For my son."

For you, too, she wanted to say, but the sadness in his eyes stopped her. Obviously it hurt to talk about the woman. He'd probably moved here because it was too painful to live in the house and city he'd shared with the wife he loved. He'd run from his own memories but wanted to make sure his son knew about his mother.

She could relate to that. The only mother Emma had ever known wasn't really her mother and she knew next to nothing about her real family. From her perspective, information about a parent was priceless.

She'd brought up the topic but sensed he wanted to change it. "Your son is a charmer."

"He's got me wrapped around his finger." The shadows lifted from his face, leaving a tender expression.

"I can see why. So good-natured." Her cheeks grew warm remembering her own words about the boy being as handsome as the father. It was true, but she still wished to have the comment back.

"He seemed to take to you." Those eyes zeroed in on her and turned darker, more observant. "Something I needed to know. Which is why I wanted to do the second interview here at the house in Kyle's environment."

"I understand."

He nodded. "Your background check didn't turn up anything. I talked to your previous employers, who all said I'd be crazy not to hire you."

"I'm glad to hear that."

"In fact, one woman I talked to said you were personally responsible for her decision to quit her job and be a stay-at-home mother."

Emma remembered. "Carly Carrington. But her choice wasn't because I didn't do my job."

"She was very clear about that. It was about how much

you enjoyed her baby and she was jealous. Unwilling to miss any more of her child's life."

"I lost the position, but her child got the most important thing. Her mom."

"She told me you said that. So my decision all came down to chemistry."

She wasn't worried about bonding with the baby, but it was decidedly inconvenient that she was attracted to the father. Her life was way too complicated to deal with something like that even if he was interested, which clearly he wasn't. She should turn down this job right now, but the fact was, the doctor needed a nanny and she needed a job.

"I get the feeling that you've made up your mind."

He nodded. "I'm told that kids have a highly reactive blarney meter and can spot a phony a mile away. Like I said, Kyle warmed to you really fast."

"I thought so, too. And the feeling is mutual."

"That was obvious, too." He stood and walked around the desk, half sitting on the corner beside her. "So, when can you start?"

"Right away." It probably wouldn't be appropriate or professional to pump her arm in triumph, so she sat demurely with her hands folded in her lap.

"Good." He thought for a moment. "Sylvia is going back to California in two weeks. I'd like you to work with her until she leaves. Transition Kyle."

"He'll feel the change, but it will be more gradual that way," she agreed. "I appreciate this opportunity, Dr.—"

"Call me Justin."

"Okay." It was a strong name and suited him.

"I've had a short-term contract drawn up with the stipulations that we discussed in the first interview." He took a paper from his desk. "Look it over and if you're okay with everything, sign at the bottom, Emma."

It felt as if he was testing the sound of her name on his tongue, and for some reason that started tingles skipping up her spine. But she managed to read the words and signed with the pen he'd handed her.

"Welcome aboard, Emma."

"Thank you."

She wasn't sure that this opportunity was a sign of how to proceed with her own personal predicament, but it bought her time to figure everything out. She was very good at her job and he was lucky to get her, but that didn't ease her conflict. After finding out she wasn't who she'd thought, absolute truth took on a whole new meaning for her. Now she felt guilty for not confessing to Justin why she was really here in Blackwater Lake, but that wasn't an option.

What man in his right mind would hire a nanny whose whole life was a lie?

Chapter Two

Two weeks later, Sylvia was gone and Justin had just spent the first night alone with Emma. Well, not *alone,* he corrected, although it was an interesting and unforeseen way to think about her, especially since he'd never thought about his former nanny that way. Like every other morning, the smell of coffee drifted to him, but this didn't feel like just another day.

He looked in the bathroom mirror, still a little steamy from his morning shower, and applied shaving cream to his cheeks and jaw. An electric razor would be faster, but didn't do as precise a job.

The master suite was downstairs and there were five more bedrooms on the second floor along with a big open playroom area the size of the three-car garage. Emma had the room next to Kyle's with a shared bathroom between them. Sylvia would be missed, but from a father's perspective, the new nanny had been well oriented to his son's routine and she interacted with him naturally. He seemed to like her.

Justin liked her, too, in a way that was potentially problematic.

After shaving and combing his hair, he dressed in jeans and a long-sleeved cotton shirt for work at Mercy Medical Clinic. There were no surgeries scheduled for today, but in the case of an emergency, he had scrubs in the office. When he was ready, he walked upstairs to spend as much time as possible with his son before leaving for the day.

At the top of the stairs he heard Emma's voice and Kyle's chattering. The nursery door was open the way it always was in the morning, so he walked in as he always did. But however much the scene was routine and familiar, everything felt different.

The baby was on the changing table with a clean diaper already in place. Emma had him in an undershirt and was in the process of sliding his arms into a one-piece terry-cloth romper. Her back was to him and she didn't know he was there yet.

"Hey, big boy," she crooned. "Did you have a good sleep?"

The baby was holding an orange-and-yellow plastic toy car and he clapped it against his other hand as he babbled his response.

"I'm so glad to hear it. You look well rested and I didn't hear a peep. I was listening and I'm right there if you need me. Just say, 'Hey, Em, some help here.'"

Justin moved a little farther into the room, but quietly. Not to nanny-cam her, just reluctant to interrupt this quiet, happy scene. He could see her profile and knew she was smiling. His son was grinning back, proudly showing off four top and a matching number of bottom baby teeth.

"So, what's the plan for today, Mr. Kyle? Are you going to help with laundry? Maybe the house cleaning? I know. How about you dust the toys in your basket? That would be a big help." She put a firm hand on his belly to keep him from rolling off as he unexpectedly squirmed toward her. "Not so fast. And just where do you think you're going, mister? It was a good try. Points for that. But we're not quite finished here."

She encircled his chubby leg in her fingers then bent slightly and kissed the bottom of his foot. He started to giggle and there was a smile in her voice when she said, "Are you ticklish?"

This time the smooch on his foot was accompanied by a loud smacking noise and Kyle laughed, a consuming sound that came from deep inside. Emma laughed, too, and repeated the action several more times, eliciting the same happy response.

Justin smiled at their play and would challenge anyone to keep a straight face under the same circumstances. A baby's laughter could enthrall a room full of adults. That was just a given and didn't explain his own feelings about the woman making his son laugh.

Something weird curled and tightened in Justin's gut and made this morning different from every other morning since he'd moved to Blackwater Lake. It was nothing like the other mornings he'd come upstairs to see the nanny caring for his son. But Sylvia was the grandmotherly type and Emma wasn't. That changed everything.

The sweet sound of her amusement mingling with his son's mesmerized him, and her fresh, wholesome beauty made it hard to turn away. In her jeans and soft powder-blue sweater, she was also dressed for work but on her it didn't look like work. Until yesterday, Sylvia had been there to blunt this reaction, and now all he could do was hope it would go away. Unfortunately, if anything, he felt it more sharply now that they were the only two adults in the house.

Speaking of adults, it was time to start acting like the one in charge. He moved close enough for their arms to brush and the smell of her to drift inside him. "Hey, there, you two."

Emma glanced up and smiled. "Good morning."

"Hey, buddy." He leaned down and kissed his son on the forehead. The boy babbled and held out his car. "I see. Did you sleep okay?"

The answer in baby talk sounded very much as if he were carrying on a conversation. Justin knew the chatter was the beginning of speech and his son was right on target developmentally. Absolutely normal. His goal was to maintain the average and ordinary, but the fact that his son would never have a mother already changed the usual domestic dynamic, and that bothered him. His job was all about fixing and there was nothing he could do to make this right for his son.

The child held out his arms to be picked up and Justin said, "Just a minute, buddy. You have to get dressed first."

"My fault," Emma said. "I got sidetracked. He's just too much fun to play with. I don't want you to be late because I didn't stick to the schedule."

"No problem. I'd much rather he's happy. That's the number-one priority."

She nodded then quickly and efficiently grabbed one foot at a time and slid each one into the legs of the outfit. "I'll put clothes on him later, but this is more comfortable for now."

"Sounds practical to me." When she finished, he picked up the baby and hugged him close, loving the smell of fresh-scented soap and little boy. He nuzzled the small neck until the child squealed with laughter. "I'll carry him downstairs."

"Okay. I'll get breakfast going. The coffee is ready."

She stopped in the doorway. "Is there anything special you'd like?"

You.

The thought popped unexpectedly into his mind with such intensity that it startled him. He swallowed once because his mouth was dry, then said, "Surprise me."

"Okay."

Mission accomplished, he thought, before she'd even had a chance to get downstairs. He looked into his son's gray eyes and smiled ruefully. "So, this is the new normal, kid. We just have to get used to it."

And by "we," he meant himself.

He settled the baby on his forearm and carried him downstairs and into the kitchen. There was a steaming mug of coffee sitting on the long, beige-and-black granite beside the pot.

That was something Sylvia had never done for him.

"Thanks," he said, grabbing it with his free hand.

"You're welcome." She glanced up from the bowl of raw eggs she was stirring with a wire whisk. "I'll put Kyle in his high chair."

"That's all right. I've got him and your hands are full."

The chair was set up beside the oak table in the kitchen nook that had a spectacular view of Blackwater Lake below. It was one of the things he liked best about this house. He put his mug down and settled his son, then belted him in before adjusting the tray for comfort. On the table beside it was a plastic dish of dry cereal and he set it in front of the little guy, who eagerly dug in. This was the established routine that he'd learned worked best. Keep Kyle happy so Justin could get breakfast in before work. After he left, Emma would feed him other appropriate nutritional stuff to balance his diet.

Right now she was scrambling eggs in a pan and folded

in sliced mushrooms, tomatoes and grated cheese. There was a blueberry muffin sitting by his plate. Obviously she'd been downstairs already to prepare everything before Kyle was awake.

"You're very organized," he commented. "Did you get up before God to do this?"

She looked over her shoulder and smiled. "Almost. It doesn't take long without interruptions. And this morning your son slept like a baby and made me look good."

"I just want to say that grabbing breakfast on the way to work is never a problem if he needs anything. The schedule is flexible."

"Understood," she said. "But there's always a contingency plan so you shouldn't have to."

"Like this tantalizing muffin on the table?"

"Exactly. I hope you like it."

He lifted the small plate and sniffed. "Smells good."

"I baked them yesterday afternoon while Kyle was napping."

"From scratch?"

"Yes." She used a spatula to lift the eggs onto a plate and brought it to him. "I hope this passes the taste test, too."

He sat beside his son's high chair and cut the muffin in half. Although there was butter on the table, the cakey inside was so moist he didn't think it would need any. The bite he took told him he was right. In silence, he chewed and savored the sweet, moist flavor.

Emma hovered close, waiting. "Okay. I can't stand it. Silence makes me nervous. If you hate it I need to know. I prefer honesty."

"Hate it?" He looked at her. "This is quite possibly the best blueberry muffin I've ever had, and I can't believe you didn't use a mix."

"I wouldn't lie." Her smile slipped and a sort of bruised look slid into her eyes.

Again he thought that something or someone had made the truth very important to her. "I was teasing, Emma. This is so good that if you wanted another career as a pastry chef I'd lose a very good nanny."

"I'm glad you like it." She smiled. "Hopefully, the eggs will hold up to the same scrutiny."

"I'm sure they will." He could already tell by the smell that they'd be delicious.

"Sylvia gave me lots of pointers and I took notes about your preferences. And what Kyle currently likes best. She also made sure I have her cell number and email address in case there are any questions. I'm doing my best to make the transition as seamless as possible."

"Mission accomplished."

So far she was superbly fulfilling all the objectives for which she'd been hired. His son was happy. Her cooking was really good. It wasn't her fault that the changeover could have been more seamless if she looked like Mrs. Doubtfire. If not for his blasted fascination with her, she'd be the perfect nanny.

But he'd learned the hard way that there was no such thing as the perfect woman.

Justin would be home any minute and Emma was carrying Kyle around the kitchen on her hip because it was the time of day when he was too fussy to play independently. He just wanted to be held and nothing would distract him.

"I don't mind telling you that I'm a little nervous about this first dinner on my own with you and your daddy."

Kyle looked at her then rubbed his eyes, a sure sign he was nearly at the end of his rope.

"I know, sweetie. Even after a good long nap, a busy

boy like you is just plain tired." She hugged him a little closer and her heart melted a little more at the way he burrowed against her. "The thing is, my man, your dad hasn't seen you all day and he works pretty hard. All for you, although you should never feel guilty about it. If you could hang in a little longer so he can spend some quality time with you before your bedtime, that would be pretty awesome. Okay?"

He grinned a gooey, wet grin, then babbled two sylla-bles that sounded suspiciously like, "Okay."

Emma glanced around the kitchen and ticked things off the list in her mind. The chicken was in the Crock-Pot, a recipe that included vegetables and potatoes all together. She didn't want to tackle anything too time-consuming and labor-intensive in the final prep stages. With the little guy constantly on the move, it was a scenario with disas-ter written all over it.

The table was set for one adult and the high chair was ready for one baby. While Sylvia was there, they'd all eaten together, but without the older woman's presence Emma was concerned that it would feel too intimate. Justin Flint wasn't her first employer, but he was the only single dad she'd ever worked for and the dynamic was awkward. At least for her.

She found him charming and attractive and under dif-ferent circumstances would probably have flirted, even though she'd sworn off men. Discovering that your fiancé was a cheating weasel tended to make a girl do that. The thing was, she wanted to flirt with Justin, but that was completely unprofessional. It was a constant strain to sup-press the natural inclination.

Every time he was in the room, butterflies swarmed in her stomach. She was clumsy and tongue-tied. As if that wasn't bad enough, she was also a big fat fraud. Even though her mission in Blackwater Lake was delicate and intensely personal, it seemed wrong not to give Justin all that information before he'd made the decision to hire her. She would do her very best for this child and hope Justin wouldn't regret his decision. This job was vital in order to buy her time to decide how to handle her private situation.

The front door opened and closed, telling her that the employer she'd just been thinking about was here. A small twist of anticipation registered before she could shut it down.

She smiled at Kyle. "Your daddy's home."

"Da— Da—" He bounced in her arms and squirmed to get down.

Emma set him on the floor and instantly he got on all fours and crawled out of the kitchen as fast as he could go. She followed, not to intrude on a private father-son moment, but to make sure he made it to the safety of his dad's strong arms. Getting sidetracked on the way by something potentially harmful was always a possibility. She wouldn't let him out of her sight until she knew this house and all its baby hazards like the back of her hand. Assuming, of course, that she was here long enough to know it that well.

"Hey, buddy." In the entryway Justin had set his laptop case on the table, then grabbed up his son for a hug and kiss. "How are you?"

He lifted the baby high over his head in those strong arms she'd just been thinking about. Emma knew Kyle was sturdy and solid and holding him up like that took a lot of strength. Justin made it look easy. And the obvious love he had for his son would soften a heart harder than hers.

He settled the boy on his forearm and smiled at her. "Hi."

Some part of her brain was still functioning and she came up with a brilliant response to his greeting. "Hi."

"Something smells good."

"Chicken, potatoes, vegetables. All in the Crock-Pot." She folded her arms over her chest, an instinctively protective gesture. "It's not fancy but should taste good."

"Best offer I've had all day. I'm starved."

Emma wasn't sure, but she thought he was looking at her mouth when he said that. And there was something compelling and intense in his eyes, but probably that was just her imagination.

"It will be ready as soon as I thicken the juice for a gravy."

"Lead the way. I'll bring this guy."

Emma was more than a little self-conscious as he followed her to the kitchen. She shouldn't be; she was just the nanny. She'd started new jobs before and knew that this wasn't the usual new-job nerves. Doing her best to ignore the feeling, she headed for the Crock-Pot sitting beside the cooktop.

Behind her he said, "There's only one plate on the table."

She finished putting meat and vegetables in small casserole dishes on a warming tray then glanced at him. "I thought you'd like alone time with Kyle."

"And are you planning to eat?"

"Of course."

"When and where?" he persisted.

"Upstairs. In my room."

His eyes narrowed. "Except on her day off, Sylvia had dinner with us every night."

"I know. But…" There was no way to put this into words that he would understand. In her interview, he'd been straightforward about the fact that he wasn't looking for anything other than a nanny. To adequately explain why she wouldn't eat dinner with him, she would have to confess her attraction. Other than throwing herself at him, that was probably the fastest way to lose this job.

Justin was staring at her. "It just feels wrong to me for you to segregate yourself. Too *Upstairs, Downstairs*." He shook his head. "Or like you're an orphan in a Charles Dickens book."

That was ironic. Not only *wasn't* she an orphan, she had more family than she knew what to do with.

He settled Kyle in the high chair then met her gaze. "Emma, I'd like you to have dinner with us."

"Is that an order?"

"Of course not. It just feels..." He shrugged, as if he didn't know how to put it into words either. "I'm trying to maintain as much family atmosphere as possible for Kyle."

"I understand." And she did. "Thank you."

"I'll set another place at the table," he said.

"Okay. Thanks."

She felt pleased yet awkward at the same time. And guilty that this extraordinarily nice man didn't know the whole truth. A few minutes later the two of them were sitting in their respective places at a right angle to each other with Kyle in the middle. Emma cut chicken, cooked carrots and potato into pieces big enough for the baby to pick up with his chubby fingers but small enough so that he wouldn't choke.

Justin filled his own plate and took a bite of meat. "This is as good as it smells."

"I'm glad." She spooned some of everything for herself and tasted a little bit of each, satisfied that it was all right. "It should fill you up."

"A hearty meal for a cold night." He glanced at his son, who was busy with his food, part eating part playing. "Kyle approves, too."

"Do you like chicken salad?"

"Yeah." He met her gaze. "Why?"

"I can make some with the leftovers. A little celery, cucumber. Maybe dill pickle chopped up?"

"Sounds good to me."

She knew from her two weeks of orientation with Sylvia that he sometimes took lunch with him to Mercy Medical Clinic. "I can make a sandwich for you if you'd like. Maybe a piece of fruit and macaroni salad."

"If it's not too much trouble, that would be great."

"I'm happy to do it." Emma was being well paid for her work, but it didn't feel like work because she wanted to please him. That's what bothered her the most.

Justin chewed a carrot then glanced at his son, who had little orange pieces of vegetable all over his face. "Tell me what he did today."

"He was an angel."

"Don't sugarcoat it. What was this scoundrel really up to?"

She smiled. "It's the absolute truth. He's practically perfect. And by that I mean perfectly normal for his age."

"What you're diplomatically telling me is that my son got into everything. Or tried."

"Yes, he did."

"So, how is that perfect?"

"It's exactly what he should be doing. Natural curiosity in a child is completely appropriate. Exploring his environment is his job." She smiled. "And he's really good at it."

"He kept you running?"

She nodded. "It's my job to make his surroundings secure. If I had a chore to do, I set up an area with a safe zone for him. And he loves to help. Folding towels, for instance. Did you know he loves the laundry basket?"

"I didn't." He tousled the boy's downy, light brown hair.

"Way to go, buddy." In answer, Kyle slapped the high-chair tray, splattering food.

"And anything that needed doing in a nonsafe zone waited until he was down for a nap." She sounded like a walking baby textbook, but it was important that he know how his son was being cared for. "He took a long one this afternoon, but now he looks tired to me. I have a feeling he's growing."

"What makes you think so?"

"Look at the way he's eating."

Justin laughed ruefully. "It's really hard to judge how much is actually going in."

"I gave him quite a bit and he's not wearing that much of it," she said, smiling at the grubby boy. "Do you like it, Kyle?" He shook his head but was grinning. "Silly."

"That's my boy."

"He also needs more sleep, which is an indication of a growth spurt."

"Good to know."

There was silence for several moments and to fill it she said, "How was your day?"

"Calm. Routine. On schedule." He wiped his mouth on a napkin. "Mostly surgery follow-up appointments and I'm happy to report all the patients followed doctor's orders and are progressing well. Then there were consultations for elective surgical procedures. Stuff like that."

"Nothing out of the ordinary? No emergencies?"

"No. It's a good day when that happens."

"I'm glad."

Uneventful *was* a good thing. Her life had been just the opposite of that lately. And this dinner was no exception. On the surface it was a peaceful, seemingly normal meal, but she couldn't help feeling as if talking about their respective days blurred the line between employer and employee.

Maybe the mountain air was messing with her mind. Lack of oxygen was doing a number on her head. What felt like thirty seconds ago, she'd broken her engagement to a man she'd learned was a liar and cheat. Now here she was thinking flirty thoughts about the employer who signed her paycheck and praying she didn't forget herself and kiss him goodbye as he went off to work.

The right thing would be to confess to him the whole truth, then offer her resignation, but she couldn't. Not yet. For the time being she had to keep her secret.

Chapter Three

"Our first trip to the grocery store, little man."

Not surprisingly, Emma heard no verbal response from the rear seat where Kyle was happily staring out the window of her midsize SUV. It had arrived from California, and Justin had approved the safety factor. He'd installed the baby's car seat himself, even though all child-related equipment was in her sphere of expertise.

It was kind of endearing how seriously Dr. Flint took his responsibilities as a father. That was another check mark in her employer's "pro" column. Not that she was actively looking for "cons," but it would help. In the few days since she'd become the solo nanny, her attraction to him hadn't subsided.

She drove down Main Street and turned left into the parking lot of the town's biggest market, appropriately named The Grocery Store. There were smaller stores for gourmet olive oil, coffee, health foods and specialty items, but this was where Sylvia had suggested she go for the bulk of the shopping. There weren't too many cars here on this weekday morning and that suited Emma just fine.

She parked and turned off the ignition, then grabbed her purse and the diaper bag before exiting. After rounding the vehicle, she opened the rear passenger door and released the straps on the car seat to lift Kyle out. Propping him on her hip, she walked to the automatic doors with neat rows of shopping carts beside them. She released one then fished the cheerful animal-print seat liner out of the diaper bag and arranged it before lifting the baby in.

"Can't be too careful," she told him. "There are enough germs in the world that I can't protect you from, but this I can do." She smiled at him and he grinned in response.

"You're in a good mood, big guy." His answer was an unintelligible sound that she liked to think of as affirmative.

Pushing the cart, she walked into the store and scanned the layout, preferring to pick up boxed and nonperishable items first. After that, she'd get things like milk and the cream Justin liked in his coffee.

She watched Kyle scratch at a giraffe on the seat cover. "You seem like a naturally cheerful little soul to me. Did you get that disposition from your daddy?"

She walked down the baby-products aisle and grabbed baby wipes and the largest package of disposable diapers, which she set on the very bottom of the cart. After that, she bypassed cleaning products and headed for cereal and canned goods. There was no one around and she chattered away to her little charge as she picked up canned tomatoes for a batch of marinara and some enchilada sauce for a recipe Justin liked.

"So far, your dad seems like a pretty agreeable sort, too. I sure hope so, because if he ever finds out the whole truth, I could be in trouble."

Rounding the corner to turn down the next aisle, Emma was trying to take in everything around her and not paying attention to where she was going. In her peripheral vision she saw another shopper. Just in time to avoid a cart collision, she pulled up short and automatically apologized. Then she got a good look at the woman she'd almost hit and her heart stopped, skipped once then started to pound. There were very few shoppers in this store and of all the people to run in to...

She was face-to-face with Michelle Crawford, her biological mother.

"I'm really sorry," she mumbled. "Not watching where I was going."

"No harm done. You've got pretty good reflexes."

Emma's mind was racing as fast as her heart. Questions without answers rattled around in her head. Should she say something about their connection? In a place as public as a grocery store? Was there a perfect place to drop the bombshell of who she really was? Getting away as fast as possible seemed like the very best idea.

She started to push her cart past the other woman. "Have a nice day."

"Hello, Kyle. How are you?"

Emma looked at the baby, who was staring uncertainly, as if he sensed her tension. "How do you know him?"

"The doctor brings him into the diner when Sylvia has the night off." She looked more closely. "You must be the new nanny."

And so much more. "That's right."

"Welcome to Blackwater Lake. I'm Michelle Crawford."

"Emma Robbins. Nice to meet you."

Emma took the hand the other woman held out, half expecting it would be a conduit to her thoughts. She braced for an aha moment that didn't happen. It would have been too easy. She was simply a stranger, a newcomer to Blackwater Lake.

Finally she pulled herself together and met her mother's gaze. Emma was looking into brown eyes the same shade as her own. The two of them were the same height and their hair was a similar shade of brunette, although silver streaked the other woman's.

"I own the Grizzly Bear Diner. With my husband," she added. Apparently she hadn't seen Emma there. "Actually, Alan and I were co-owners with Harriet Marlow. She met a man on one of those internet dating sites and they had a phone relationship for a while because he's from Phoenix. That went well, so he came all the way to Blackwater Lake to meet her in person. They fell in love and she decided Arizona was a good place to retire. So, my husband and I bought her out. She married him and moved away."

"Wow." At least someone got their happily-ever-after.

"Listen to me. Blathering on. Is that what kids call TMI?"

Too much information. Emma hadn't thought it possible that she could laugh but she did. "No. Finding love is always good information. I guess."

"Sounds like you have a bad story."

"Could be."

So far, Michelle hadn't put her foot in her mouth, so Emma couldn't say she'd inherited the tendency there. However, she did lean toward blathering in certain situations, although the one in progress didn't appear to fall into that category because she wasn't saying much.

"Where are you from, Emma?"

"Southern California."

Should she go with the partial story she'd told Justin? The truth, even half of it, was easiest to keep straight.

But Michelle continued talking and saved her from having to respond. "Montana weather is really different from where you lived. It gets cold here in the mountains. It's

September and already heading in that direction. Are you ready for snow?"

"I guess we'll find out."

"If you need any winter-survival tips, just come over to the diner. Alan and I will be glad to help you out."

"Thanks. I wouldn't want to be a bother." Emma meant that more sincerely than this woman could possibly know.

She waved a hand, dismissing the concern. "It's no bother. You'll find people here in Blackwater Lake are really friendly. Willing to help out their neighbors."

"That's good to know." Also reassuring to learn her biological mother seemed to be a really good person.

Kyle chose that moment to join the conversation. Along with the stream of chatter, he started to wriggle in the cart, trying to pull his legs free and climb out.

"Just where do you think you're going, Mr. Kyle?" She laughed when he held out his arms. "I think that's my cue to get a move on."

"Kids do let you know…"

Emma was just starting to get comfortable, to shake off the urge to run. But Kyle came first and he was obviously getting restless. "It's time to finish up the shopping."

"You're not the only one. I'm due at the diner for the lunch rush. Alan will send out a search party if I'm late."

Because a member of his family had disappeared once? She couldn't imagine what that must have felt like.

"I've got to get this little one home for lunch and a nap."

"He seems like a good baby."

"That's an understatement. He's practically perfect."

Michelle studied her. "You seem really fond of him."

"That's what Dr. Flint pays me for."

"It's more than that." The other woman rested a palm on the handle of her basket… "The way you look at him is something a paycheck can't buy."

Emma shrugged. "I like kids."

"So do I."

"But Kyle is especially easy to like."

"I can see that."

Emma glanced at her watch and saw that it was pushing noon. "I'm sorry to keep you."

"It's all right." But the sad, wistful expression that slid into her eyes as she looked at the baby said something was *not* right. The warm friendliness from moments ago faded.

"Is something wrong?"

"Not really. No," she said firmly, as if she was working hard to make that the truth. "It was nice talking to you, Emma. I hope we'll see you in the diner."

"Maybe."

She watched the other woman walk away and knew this perfect, happy baby had been a reminder of what was taken from her. At first, she'd been bubbly and outgoing, then they started talking about Kyle. That had made her withdraw. Apparently, she'd learned to cope with the loss and had come to terms with it.

Seeing the change convinced Emma that she was right to keep her identity to herself. She was a grown-up now and couldn't give the woman back the baby girl she used to be. Shaking up Michelle Crawford's world all over again just didn't seem like the right thing to do.

Justin walked up his front steps and realized he was whistling. He didn't whistle; he'd never whistled. And it had nothing to do with a radio tune looping in his head because he'd been listening to news on the way home from the clinic. He realized it was a symptom of a condition he hadn't experienced for a long time. It was called happiness.

Part of the reason was seeing his son content. Growing and thriving in this place that couldn't be more different from Beverly Hills. The other part was about the woman who was making sure his son was happy.

Emma Robbins.

Just thinking her name produced an image of her in his mind, and the vision was enough to make his senses quiver with anticipation. If she had a flaw, he couldn't see it. Not only was she easy on the eyes, she took care of Kyle as if he were her own. And she was a great cook. Her inclusion into the household had been seamless.

He jogged up the steps to the front door and unlocked it, then stepped inside. "I'm home."

Justin felt an irrational impulse to add "honey." Maybe it was time for a mental health professional to join the staff at Mercy Medical Clinic. A shrink would have a field day with him. Diagnosis: unreasonable romantic feelings where there weren't any because he was obsessed with having an intensely loving and respectful relationship like the one his parents had enjoyed.

His first marriage had been a failure, which meant he'd already screwed up any chance of following in his mom and dad's footsteps. That wasn't a failure he wanted to repeat, but it was hard to remember why when he looked at Emma's mouth.

"We're in the kitchen," she called out.

"On my way."

Just the sound of her voice, which was two parts silk and one part gravel, made him want to start whistling again. He held back as he walked to his home office and put his laptop on the desk. Then he joined them at the dinner table where Emma sat beside Kyle, who was in the high chair.

"Daddy's home," she said to the boy.

"Da—" He didn't look up, too deep in concentration. With tiny thumb and forefinger he picked up a pea and put it in his mouth.

Emma clapped her hands at the accomplishment. "Good job."

The boy grinned at her praise, and then went after a small piece of cooked carrot.

"I tried to hold off his dinner until you got home," she explained. "But he was just too hungry."

"No problem." The room was filled with tantalizing smells that made him realize Kyle wasn't the only hungry guy in the family. "What's for dinner?"

"Rigatoni and meatballs. Salad. Now that you're here, I'll cook the pasta."

"Sounds good. I'll just visit with this guy while you do that."

Her only response was a smile that did amazing things to her mouth. One glance was like touching a hot stove and he pulled back, turning his attention to the neutral subject of peas and carrots.

Justin put a few on the plastic tray. "Here you go, buddy."

"Da—Da—" After slapping both small hands on the vegetables, Kyle rubbed the mushed goo into his hair and over his face.

Justin laughed and said, "Code green emergency."

Standing at the stove in front of a pot steaming with simmering pasta and another bubbling with marinara and meatballs, Emma glanced over her shoulder. "That means he likes them."

"I'll have to take your word for that because wearing food seems counterproductive to the goal."

"Just wait and see how much he likes my rigatoni and red sauce."

Justin groaned. "Dear God—"

"Prayer is pointless. Straight upstairs to the bath for him. It's why messy meals are at night."

"A good plan."

"I try."

She looked over her shoulder to satisfy herself that all was well before sliding her hands into oven mitts. After lifting the boiling pot of pasta, she poured the contents into a colander in the sink and let it drain.

Five minutes later the two of them were eating salad and Kyle was popping pieces of rigatoni into his mouth and smacking his lips.

"I know what you mean, kid. This is really good, Emma."

"I'm glad you like it."

For the first time, Justin had a chance to study her. There were shadows in her eyes obscuring the sparkle that he'd come to expect.

"Is everything all right?" he asked.

"Yes." She looked up quickly, but her gaze didn't quite meet his. "Why?"

"Just checking." He cut a meatball and forked half into his mouth. After chewing and swallowing, he asked, "What did you guys do today?"

"Grocery shopping." Her mouth pulled tight for a second, then she moved lettuce around her plate without eating any.

He wasn't imagining the tension. "How did that go?"

"Fine."

Obviously she and Kyle were home safe and sound. The household supplies were replenished, all of which indicated a successful shopping experience. But he couldn't shake the feeling that something had happened. Justin wanted to know what, but since it didn't appear to have any connection to his son, he had no right to grill her like raw hamburger. For all he knew, it could be about her love life.

The background check hadn't turned up a significant other, although that didn't mean there wasn't one. He didn't like the idea of Emma being in love, but that had nothing to do with Kyle and everything to do with a feeling he'd had little experience with.

Jealousy. He wasn't proud of it, but there was no denying the truth.

Maybe he'd ask a few questions, after all. "So what did you think of Blackwater Lake's premier grocery store?"

The expression on her face turned wry. "It's the only grocery store. And it seemed fine."

"Kyle wasn't a problem?"

"Not at all." She cut a rigatoni and speared half with her fork but didn't eat it. "How was your day?"

This question had come up every night since she'd taken over from Sylvia, but this time it smacked of changing the subject. There was no subtle way to push harder, so he decided to back off. But he couldn't resist giving her a taste of her own medicine.

"My day was fine," he said.

"I'm glad."

After that, they made small talk while he finished dinner. She ate very little, mostly pushing her food around the plate. When Kyle got grouchy and restless, she jumped at the chance to take him upstairs for a bath.

"I'll clean up the kitchen," he said.

"No, leave it for me."

Emma scooped Kyle out of the high chair and held him against her, oblivious to the red sauce and smashed peas that got all over her shirt. He couldn't help comparing her to the baby's mother, who wouldn't touch her own child if he was less than immaculate.

"You do enough," he insisted. "I don't mind squaring things away here."

She looked as if she wanted to protest but nodded and carried Kyle out of the kitchen and upstairs.

Justin stowed the leftovers, rinsed plates and utensils then scrubbed the pots. The busywork occupied his hands, but his mind raced. He thought about the employees at the clinic, body language and bad mood indicating when someone was dealing with a personal problem. It never occurred to him to get involved, but none of the clinic staff lived under his roof and cared for the child he loved more than anything in the world.

He heard sounds from upstairs—splashing, laughter and baby chatter. There was clinic paperwork to do, but he suddenly felt as if he were on the outside looking in. After drying his hands, he went upstairs and found the two of them in the bathroom where water was draining out of the tub.

Emma covered her front with a thick terry-cloth towel then lifted the baby out of the tub and wrapped him up. She carried him to the nursery then diapered him as quickly as possible. All the red-and-green smears were gone, although she still sported them on her clothes. But Kyle was now a clean boy with neatly combed hair.

"That was quick," Justin said.

"He's tired." With quick efficiency, she put the baby in a small, soft blue one-piece sleeper and picked him up. Then she headed for the glider chair in the corner beside the crib. "It was a busy day. You can see the signs when he's had it and is ready to go to sleep."

"I'll rock him tonight. You take a break."

"That's not necessary—"

"I insist. Kyle had a busy day, which means yours was even more tiring. Just take some time and relax."

She tilted her head and studied him. "Are you sure?"

"Positive."

"Okay." She walked over and started to hand the baby to Justin, but he let out a wail and clung to her, curling against her with his face buried in her neck. "I'm sorry. Do you want to just grab him?"

"No." He moved close and put his hand on the small back. "It's okay, buddy. I know you're tired."

And his son wasn't the only one. That was as good an explanation as any for his own intense reaction to the warmth of Emma's skin, the scent of her that twisted his senses into a knot of need. The only good thing was that it pushed jealousy out of the number-one position.

"Kyle?" Emma crooned softly. "Daddy's here. Don't you want some man time with him?"

As if he understood, the baby lifted his head and held out his arms. Justin took him and said, "That's my guy. We're just going to sit in the glider and have a little chat. I'll tell you a story. I get the feeling that reading would be a bad idea tonight."

"I think you're right about that." Emma headed for the door. "You're sure you don't mind?"

"Yeah, I'm sure. I don't do this enough."

The baby clinging to her was proof. On the one hand, he was glad Kyle had bonded with her so completely. The flip side of that was that Justin didn't have the same connection. It was good to have a reminder that he needed to spend more quality time with his son.

Just before walking out of the room, Emma stopped. "Justin?"

"Hmm?" He sat in the chair and settled the baby to his chest, then met her gaze.

"Would you mind if I borrowed your computer in the office? My laptop is acting squirrelly."

"Of course." He smiled and started the chair gliding back and forth. Almost instantly Kyle relaxed into him. "And, for the record, squirrelly is not an official technological term."

The corners of her full lips turned up. "And there's a good reason for that. I don't speak fluent tech."

"Ah."

"Thanks."

Her words were light and teasing but didn't match the expression on her face. It could only be described as tense, distracted. Before he could study her more, she was gone.

He rubbed his hand over his son's back and moved slowly, lulling him to sleep. "What's going on with your nanny, Kyle? You obviously are attached to her and I'm glad about that, but there's something up with her. The good news is that she's not very good at hiding her feelings."

In a matter of minutes, his baby boy was sound asleep. He waited a little longer, moving gently to make sure before putting him down in the crib. A short time later, that was accomplished without a peep, and Justin covered him with a baby blanket, then softly kissed the tiny forehead.

"I love you, buddy." For a few moments he stood over his son, watching the rhythmic rise and fall of the little chest, savoring the peace of knowing his child was safe and happy.

He picked up the baby monitor and soundlessly left the room, going downstairs. Emma was nowhere in sight and he remembered she was using his home computer. After pouring himself a cup of coffee, he walked down the hall and into his office. Emma's back was to him as she looked at the computer monitor and he moved closer to the desk.

On the screen in big, bold letters was a newspaper headline that read, "KIDNAPPED! BABY GIRL DISAPPEARS. STOLEN FROM A BLACKWATER LAKE FAMILY."

The date on the article was about twenty-eight years before, and Emma was completely engrossed in reading the information. She hadn't heard him approach and never looked up.

This appeared to be a private thing, but Justin didn't give a flying fig if he was overstepping. She had some explaining to do and it was going to happen now.

"Interesting stuff," he said.

She jumped, then pressed her hand to her chest and swiveled the chair around to look at him. "Good gracious. You startled me."

"Startling pretty well describes it. And I'm talking about what you're reading on the computer." The look on her face told him that she was hiding something. "What's going on, Emma?"

"If you want to look for another nanny, I completely understand. And that would probably be best since I lied to you."

Uh-oh. Just a while ago he'd thought that if she had a flaw he couldn't see it. Well, she'd just pointed one out and it was a beaut. What could possibly be so bad that Emma felt she had to keep it from him? If she'd broken the law, it would have turned up in her background check. Her record was spotless yet she'd just admitted she'd been less than honest.

Could a woman as sweet as Emma seemed to be have something in her past that was worse than his own guilty secret? No one knew how he'd really felt about the wife who died and that wasn't information he wanted to share. A problem for another day. Finding a new nanny wasn't what he wanted and he hoped her lie turned out to be a fib about the weight on her driver's license.

But he wasn't whistling now.

Chapter Four

"What lie? I can't imagine you've done anything that bad."

"Justin, I…" Emma didn't know what to say to him, how to soften what had happened to her. Then she figured there was no point in carefully picking words. Saying it straight out was the only way. "I didn't tell you the whole truth when you asked why I picked Blackwater Lake for my vacation."

"So, you didn't read a book set in Montana?"

His expression was serious, but she would swear the question was meant to lighten the mood. It seemed empathetic somehow, as if he understood or at least wanted to. But he couldn't until she explained and then she would have to accept the consequences, whatever they might be.

She realized she was sitting behind his desk and stood, rounding it to stand in front of him. She met his gaze and forced herself not to look away. "I came here to meet my biological parents."

"So your secret is that you were adopted?"

"Not exactly."

He looked at the computer monitor where the newspaper headline from the past screamed out. The incident was years old, but not to her. It was fresh and painful, complicated and confusing.

His eyes moved over the words of the article and the expression in them said he'd skimmed the contents and was making guesses. "What exactly?"

Emma's legs were trembling and she desperately wanted to rest a hip against the desk but wouldn't show weakness. This was the mess she'd made by not being completely up front with him in the beginning. It was honesty time and she'd do that standing up straight.

"I was kidnapped as a baby and raised by the woman who took me."

Shock and anger hardened his face. "And you never knew she wasn't your mother?"

"Not until recently. When she was diagnosed with cancer, the disease progressed very quickly. Just before she died, she confessed the truth and told me where I came from, where to find my biological family. They live here in Blackwater Lake."

He rested a hand on the back of one of the chairs in front of the desk. "How did she explain turning up with a baby? Not being pregnant? Weren't there questions?"

"I don't know. I was a baby." She shrugged. "My dad— the man I thought was my dad—died when I was a kid. She, my mother—" Emma shook her head. "She's not my mother, but it's hard for me to think of her any other way. What she did was wrong—"

"Yeah."

"But I never knew her as anything other than loving and kind. She was Mom to me." Emma looked away for a moment and shook her head. "I was too little to remember anything else. She was a single mom when they met and if my dad knew what she'd done and was complicit in the whole thing, he never did or said anything that made me question my family. I don't know how she explained everything. And at the end she was very weak." She shrugged helplessly. "I didn't know any different. They were my parents. She was my mother and there was never any reason to question it."

Justin dragged his fingers through his hair then met her gaze. "Would you like a glass of wine?"

She'd love one, but she never had alcohol when there was a child in her care. It might be his way of subtly preparing her to be let go. "Unless this is your way of firing me, I'm on the job and I don't drink when I am."

"Emma..." He moved closer and looked down as if he wanted to touch her. It was a disappointment when he didn't.

The yearning to burrow against him for comfort was a different kind of problem and she couldn't deal with it right now. She studied his expression, tried to guess what he was thinking. "Justin, for all you know, I could be making this up."

"But you're not."

"How do you know? I deceived you once."

"Withholding information isn't deception. The personal facts were yours to do with as you saw fit. And the thing is, I'm mostly a good judge of people. I was only really wrong once." There was a grim look in his eyes. "I don't think you're a good enough actress to not be telling the truth about this."

She was relieved that he believed her, but it still didn't mean he wanted to keep her as his son's nanny. "Don't be nice to me. I need to know where I stand."

He ignored that. "Kyle is asleep. One glass of wine won't be a problem if he needs anything. And I'm here."

Yes, he was. She was always aware of him when he was in the house. She shook her head. "I really shouldn't."

"You're shaking. It will help."

Emma looked at her trembling hands and realized he was right. She stuck them in her jeans pockets. "That sounds good. Are you sure you don't mind?"

"Consider it doctor's orders."

He held out his hand and she put hers in it, then let him lead her from the office into the kitchen. She missed the warmth and strength of his touch when he sat her at the table and moved away. But after taking advantage of his trust, this was more consideration than she deserved. While he was busy assembling glasses and opening a bottle, she stared out the window. The patio and rear yard were illuminated by perimeter lights, but darkness and shadows hid the incredible view of the lake and the mountains beyond it.

Emma felt as if she was finally moving out of the shadows that had swirled around her for months. Whatever Justin decided about her employment she would have to live with because the decision to keep this to herself had been hers alone. But for right now it was an enormous relief to talk about everything.

He set a glass of white wine in front of her, then sat down at a right angle. "I hope you like chardonnay."

"Right now you could give me balsamic vinegar and I'm not sure I could taste the difference."

"It must have been a shock to find out what happened to you."

"*Shock* is such a bland word to describe how I felt. It was so surreal, something that happens to other people, not to me."

"The fact is, we're all 'other' people. The news is full of ordinary human beings who have gone through extraordinary things. It's how one copes and moves on that matters. What did your friends say?" he asked.

"I haven't told them."

He was just taking a drink of wine and slowly lowered the glass. "No one knows?"

"My fiancé. And now you."

Again his surprise showed. "Really?"

"Yes. It didn't work out. No need for you to worry that I'll go back to him and leave you without someone to care for Kyle." She saw more questions in his eyes, but didn't feel like getting into it. "If it's all right with you, I'd rather not talk about him."

"Okay." He nodded. "But you didn't tell your other friends about this? Why?"

Emma knew what he was really asking was why she hadn't said anything to people she knew better than him. After sipping her wine, she said, "Mom died shortly after telling me, so there was a funeral to plan and it wasn't something I wanted to bring up then. A decent length of time passed and I didn't know how to start that conversation. It seemed wrong to say, You know my mother who died? She actually wasn't my mother. She stole me from another family."

"Why did she tell you?"

"I guess because confession is good for the soul. She wanted to clear her conscience before she died."

"Why didn't you come to see your biological family sooner?"

"A lot of reasons." Emma drank more wine as she gathered her thoughts, trying to figure out how to make him understand. "I was grieving the woman who'd loved and raised me. A woman I'd loved because she was good to me. Not only that, I had a job. I'd signed a contract and there was a child to take care of. And I was engaged to be married. As the days went by, I figured I'd come to terms with everything and let it go."

"What changed?"

"I found out my fiancé was cheating on me. He was one more trusted person in my life who was lying. I guess it hit a nerve."

"No kidding."

"And I've sworn off men." She almost smiled. "It was more than just being hurt. I'd recently learned my whole life was a lie and to find out he was a two-faced scumbag made me question who I am. I needed to find some truth."

"So you came to Blackwater Lake."

"Yes. My biological parents own the Grizzly Bear Diner."

"Michelle and Alan Crawford." He nodded slowly as the information sank in. "So you've met your family."

Emma chose her words carefully. "I've seen them."

"They must have been over the moon to find out their missing daughter is alive and well."

"I don't know how they'd feel about that."

His eyes narrowed. "You haven't told them?"

"Until today, I hadn't even talked to them." She took a deep breath. "I ran into Michelle Crawford at the grocery store."

"So that's why you've been preoccupied." Justin's gray eyes darkened with questions. "How did it go?"

"She's very nice. Friendly. And she'd looked sad when Kyle chattered nonstop in his sweet baby way. The encounter shook me. I couldn't get it out of my mind. I needed to see the newspaper accounts of the kidnapping again."

"But she still doesn't know?" When Emma shook her head, he said, "I'm sure you had your reasons for not telling them who you are."

"It's complicated."

"No kidding." His tone was wry.

"My mother told me where they are and how to find them." She took a big drink from her glass. "When I got here, the Grizzly Bear Diner was my first stop. Michelle and Alan were there and I watched them interacting with the customers and each other. They're—" She struggled to figure out how to say they seemed like two people who were content and working at something they enjoyed. It was hard to express, when one picture was worth a thousand words. "They seemed okay. I didn't want to change that."

"And you think finding out their daughter is alive would be a bad thing?"

"What happened to them was bad."

"Can't argue with you there." But his eyes narrowed. "Still, you said nothing?"

"There's probably no way for you to understand, but I just couldn't."

"So why didn't you go back to California?"

There was the burning question, and she didn't have an answer. "I couldn't do that, either."

"But you needed a job while you figure it all out."

It wasn't a question, but she felt he deserved an answer, anyway. "Yes, and you wouldn't have hired me if I'd told you all that."

"We'll never know." He finished the wine in his glass then met her gaze. "I'm going to give you a piece of advice, but keep in mind it's worth what you paid for it."

"Okay." She braced herself.

"My parents had the kind of marriage that everyone wants but so many don't get. They're both gone now, but every day together they taught me what love looks like. Then my son showed me how it feels, what unconditional means. I couldn't begin to imagine losing him. So, for what it's worth, you should tell the Crawfords who you are."

"You don't—"

He held up his hand to stop her. "All I'm saying is that if it were me, I'd want to know."

"That's easy for you to say."

"I know. I'm not walking in your shoes. Or theirs, either. But that's what I think."

It was so easy to stand on the outside looking in and give an opinion. But Emma needed to be sure what the right thing was because once the words were said there was no going back. So the story she should have told him in the beginning was out now and it was time to save them both an awkward conversation.

She stood. "So, I'll just go upstairs and pack my things."

"Why?"

"Because you're going to fire me. It will be uncomfortable for you to say and humiliating for me to hear since I've never been dismissed from a job before. So, I'll make this easier on both of us and just go quietly."

He put a hand on her arm when she started to move away. "Not so fast."

"But, Justin, I lied to you."

"Everything about your professional background was the absolute truth. There was no lie. It was more about not revealing personal details, which technically you're not obligated to do."

"But you know as well as I do that puts my personal life up in the air and it's not fair to you."

"What I know is that you're terrific with Kyle and I would like you to stay. If that becomes impossible, all I ask is a decent amount of notice so that I can replace you."

The knot in her belly started to unravel. "That's very generous of you."

"Actually, it's selfish."

"You say potato, I say po-tah-to." Emma wanted to argue with him but figured she shouldn't look a gift horse in the mouth. "Thank you."

He waved the words away. "I'm just sorry you had to go through what you did. If I can help in any way, please let me know."

"I appreciate that very much." More than she could even put into words.

So, the truth was out there and it felt good to come clean to Justin. She was relieved that he knew the whole truth.

That was sort of what she was doing to Michelle and Alan Crawford, but it felt different. She was in control of this information. It affected her, too, and everything would change if they knew she was their daughter. Before taking that step, she needed to know more about her family.

"The best way to get acquainted with the Crawfords is to spend time with them."

It was Saturday and Justin had shut off his laptop and stopped working on patient medical records in order to spend time with his son. This was Emma's night off and usually he took Kyle to the Grizzly Bear Diner for dinner. He'd asked Emma to come along and she was less than enthusiastic about the invitation.

He leaned back against the kitchen island and folded his arms over his chest. Studying her anxious expression, he said, "You're scared."

"That's ridiculous." The baby crawled over and pulled himself to a standing position, using her leg for leverage. She lifted him into her arms and automatically hugged him close.

"No one blames you for being scared."

Justin had been mulling over what she'd told him and as

secrets went, hers wasn't that bad. None of it was her fault. He couldn't say the same about his past. All he wanted was to forget that he hadn't been in love with his wife for a long time before she died, and they were planning to get a divorce when she'd been involved in a fatal car accident.

Like Emma's story, this was personal information that had no direct bearing on his job performance. Everyone assumed he was in mourning and it was easier not to correct that impression because he didn't want to talk about that mistake. He would never have wished her dead, but it would be a lie to say he missed her. For reasons he didn't understand, it was very important that Emma not know about all that ugliness. She wouldn't like him very much and he couldn't blame her. Hell, he didn't much like himself.

"Look, Justin—I'm not afraid to see my family." She met his gaze. "Just cautious."

Justin wanted to help resolve the situation. It was a lousy thing for Alan and Michelle, who were good people, but he hated the bruised and betrayed look in Emma's eyes. Also, she was right. Her situation was unstable and a difficult reunion with the family she'd just discovered could send her running back to California.

"Caution is good. Who would know that better than a doctor. The cornerstone of the Hippocratic Oath is to do no harm. Going to their diner on Saturday night when the place is busiest would be a careful first step. They won't even notice you, but that makes it possible to check them out from afar." Justin decided a hint of challenge wouldn't be a bad thing. "What else have you got to do on your night off? You don't have a date."

"How do you know?" There was a saucy, sassy, rebellious expression in her eyes.

"Because you've sworn off men."

Justin realized he was unreasonably pleased about that. He didn't especially like the idea of her dating. She was a beautiful woman and men would notice. *He'd* noticed and couldn't seem to stop. There wasn't anything he could do to prevent her from seeing another man. She was under no obligation to tell him what she did in her free time.

"You remembered," she said.

"Yeah."

"Too much information." Her expression was charmingly sheepish. "Although true. And you're right. I don't have plans."

That was a relief but also made him feel guilty and he wondered what she did when she wasn't caring for Kyle. Was she meeting people? Making friends? Putting down roots in Blackwater Lake? Part of him hoped so for his son's sake. For himself, he didn't need or want this attraction.

"So you're free." He met her gaze. "Then there's no reason you can't have dinner with Kyle and me. At the diner. What can it hurt?"

"Nothing, I guess."

That still wasn't enthusiastic, but he'd take it as a yes before she changed her mind. He looked at the baby. "Kyle, want to go for a ride?"

The little boy's eyes lit up and he held out his arms to Justin who took him from her. "I'll get his jacket," he told Emma. "Meet you at the front door in five."

"Okay." She started out of the room, then stopped in the doorway and said, "I lied when I said I wasn't scared. I am a little afraid. But it's not a habit. The lying part. Maybe just a little defensive."

"We'll keep that between you and me." The words made her smile and he felt the familiar tug in his gut that was all about wanting to kiss her.

Twenty minutes later, the three of them walked into the Grizzly Bear Diner. It wasn't quite six o'clock and not too crowded yet, so they were seated right away. Violet, one of the servers, brought over a high chair and Emma pulled out a disposable antiseptic wipe from a package in the diaper bag. She started cleaning the straps and tray of the chair.

"No offense," she said to the waitress.

"None taken. The other moms who come in do the same thing." The girl was blonde, blue-eyed and probably in her late teens. She looked at the three of them. "You guys are a really beautiful family."

"Oh, I'm not—" Emma stopped her clarification when the girl hurried away, clearly not listening. She shrugged at Justin. "I'll set the record straight when she comes back."

"She must be new. Don't worry about it. Someone will tell her." He settled Kyle in the chair and strapped him in before hooking on the tray, then sat in the booth across the table from her. "People in Blackwater Lake talk. You've been warned."

Emma slipped off her lightweight jacket. "Understood."

She looked around at the decor. There were framed bear photos on the light yellow walls and the menus reflected the same theme with items called the Mama, Papa and Baby Bear combos. In the front half of the diner there was a counter with red-plastic-covered swivel stools. Michelle and Alan Crawford stood behind it, talking to an older man and woman seated there. Justin watched Emma studying them.

When Kyle slapped his hands on the high-chair tray, she reached into the diaper bag and pulled out a Ziploc baggie with crackers. She smiled at him and brushed the downy hair off his forehead. "Here you go, sweetie."

Justin realized that she was off the clock, so to speak,

but she didn't turn the nurturing off. It was just natural to her and something he found as sexy as it was appealing.

He glanced over his shoulder to where the diner owners stood. "They're a nice-looking couple."

"Who?" Emma looked away from Kyle and met his gaze.

"Your parents."

"This is completely surreal. Shouldn't I feel some connection to them?" There was conflict in her eyes, changing them from warm brown to almost black. "They seem like very nice people, but that's nothing more than an observation. I don't feel anything more than I would for strangers and it seems like I should since their blood is flowing through my veins."

"Sharing DNA doesn't automatically create a bond. It's the whole nature versus nurture thing. Only time can develop a relationship." Or show a guy that there isn't one, he thought, remembering how his own feelings for Kristina Bradley-Flint sputtered and died until he felt nothing but critical of the woman he'd married. "Kyle and I usually stop to chat with them when we come in. They're very friendly."

"That's how Michelle knew Kyle. When I ran into her at the grocery store," Emma reminded him.

He nodded. "They have three sons. None of them live here in Blackwater Lake."

"I have brothers?" There was shock and surprise in her voice.

"Yes. All very successful in their respective careers, according to the proud parents."

"I never thought about having siblings."

"By all accounts, Michelle and Alan did a great job raising their kids. That means after losing their youngest child and going through a parent's worst nightmare, they had the strength of character to pull it together for the sake of the children. Who all turned out to be good, productive men," he finished gently.

"What's your point?" There was an edge to her voice and she blinked. "Wow. That was abrasive. But in my own defense, this is my night off. No offense."

"None taken." He wanted to reach across the table and squeeze her hand, but, as he'd told her, everyone talked. "My point is that you come from good people."

"Like you said—that's DNA. But they didn't raise me."

Justin grabbed the menus tucked behind the salt-and-pepper holder next to the half wall separating them from the booth on the other side. He handed one to her. "What's *your* point?"

"I'm not sure. But it never crossed my mind that I might have siblings and I don't know why."

"Because you didn't know any different. You were raised an only child."

"And that's her fault."

"Who?"

"My mom—Ruth—the woman who stole me from them." She pressed her lips together, frustrated with distinguishing who was who in this bizarre scenario. Her expression changed from moment to moment, reflecting her contradictory emotions. "I loved her. She was my mother. She was also the worst kind of liar. I was raised by a woman who did the most despicable thing and lived a lie, forced me to live a lie all my life." Her eyes were bleak and anger wrapped around the words. "What does that make me?"

"An innocent victim."

"Children learn what they live. Maybe that made it easier for me not to tell the whole truth."

"The deception isn't yours to be responsible for." Justin didn't have the right words to reassure her, but every part of him rejected what she'd just said. "But I can tell you one thing."

"What?" She turned troubled eyes to his.

"Whatever else she did wrong, the way she raised you wasn't part of it. You're an honest woman."

"How do you know?"

"I could tell that keeping this to yourself took a personal toll. I can also say that you're a good and loving woman."

"How can you be sure of that?"

"The way you are with Kyle."

She glanced at the counter where the diner owners stood, then absently opened the menu on the dark-wood table between them. "She stole from me, too. It would have been nice to have big brothers."

"Why?" He handed Kyle another cracker, which the boy eagerly took.

"When someone was mean to me, they could have beat him up." She watched the little boy crumble the cracker then use both hands to sweep the pieces off the tray.

"By someone, I assume you mean the two-faced scumbag?"

"Yeah." As he'd hoped, she smiled. "I was really in a bad place after my mother confessed then died. He and I were having problems and I thought we should take a break."

"Sounds reasonable."

"It didn't last long, at least for me. I was lonely." She caught the corner of her lip between her teeth. "So I stopped by his apartment and as it turned out, *he* wasn't lonely at all."

"Another woman."

"Yeah. And I found out she wasn't the only one. He'd

been seeing other women the whole time we were engaged."

"Two-faced scumbag is too good for him." Justin hated
the idea of anyone hurting her and the words came out
before he could stop them. "*I* could beat him up for you."

"Really? And what about those surgeon's hands?" Her
eyes brightened for a moment, then the expression faded.
"Another big brother?"

"Sort of."

Justin could handle feeling like a big brother a whole
lot better than what he was feeling now, which was more
like a jealous boyfriend. That was all kinds of trouble. He
supposed it was a plus that Emma had sworn off men. As
much as he wanted to kiss her, acting on it would be the
fastest way to chase her off.

So, he had to rein in his hormones, but that was easier
said than done.

Chapter Five

"Seriously, Emma, if there's something else you need to do on your afternoon off, I can handle buying winter clothes for Kyle."

"It's your afternoon off, too." She looked at him with the baby in his arms and couldn't help smiling.

Three days after dinner at the diner, Emma, Kyle and Justin were ready to walk out the door and drive to the nearest mall, which wasn't all that close. Time was flying and September was ending and would soon give way to October. As Michelle had told her, the weather quickly turned cold in Montana. Several days before, there had been a light dusting of snow and Justin asked if she would help him buy winter clothes for the baby, since their respective afternoons off were the same.

This was the first time he'd asked her for a favor, and the only reason she'd even considered turning him down was because of how appealing it was to spend time with him.

"Call me crazy," she said, "but when you mentioned shopping, I could swear you looked like a man who'd rather take a sharp stick in the eye than step foot in a mall."

"I didn't think it showed."

"Oh, please." She couldn't help laughing. "Show me a guy who actually wants to shop and there's a better than even chance that he's gay."

"So given my aversion to shopping, I passed the test."

In so many ways, she thought, her heart beating just a little too fast. Fortunately, she didn't say that out loud.

"Well, I like to shop. Especially for Kyle's clothes," she said, brushing her palm over the boy's chubby cheek. "And the best part is it's *your* money."

"There's no one I'd rather spend it on." He looked at his son and there was a mother lode of tenderness softening the masculine angles of his handsome face. "What do you say, Kyle? Should we go bye-bye?"

The little boy pointed a chubby finger at the front door and jabbered, "Ba."

"I think we have a yes vote," Emma said.

"Okay, then, let's get this over with." He grinned. "What I meant to say was, let's get this show on the road."

The three of them left the house through the downstairs laundry room, which had a connecting door to the garage. Justin hit the automatic opener and the door went up, letting in the sunshine. He settled his son in the car seat of his SUV and she set the diaper bag on the rear passenger floor before getting in the front. Justin slid in behind the wheel, started the car and backed out of the driveway.

Truthfully, Emma would rather spend her afternoon off with Justin and Kyle than have time to herself. She had acquaintances in Blackwater Lake, but friendship took a while and putting in time and effort could be pointless. Her future was uncertain; she didn't know how long she would stay.

Six weeks had passed since Justin hired her and so far her crush on him showed no sign of letting up. But he'd made it clear that his feelings were more in the big-brother camp. She still didn't know whether or not to tell the Crawfords she was their daughter and had been so busy with her job, she hadn't had time to make a decision on the issue. Probably she was procrastinating, but for now she put it on the back burner.

Justin drove around the lake and headed out of town, where he guided the SUV onto the highway. Emma glanced into the rear seat and smiled.

"He's asleep already," she said. It had been her idea to leave the house around nap time to make sure the baby was rested for shopping. "How far is it to the mall?"

"About forty-five minutes."

"Good."

"Really?" He glanced at her, one eyebrow raised. "Most women would be euphoric if shopping was in their backyard."

"I'm not most women."

"Tell me something I don't know."

His voice sounded a little raspy and wrapped in male appreciation, although a quick glance didn't confirm. There was a muscle jumping in his jaw, but dark aviator sunglasses hid the expression in his eyes. Did he just pay her a compliment? Her own feelings being so close to the tipping point, she decided it was best not to go there.

"Don't get me wrong," she said. "I have nothing against shopping. And this is my afternoon off, but I still have my nanny hat on."

"It looks good on you." He glanced over for a moment, but his expression was still impossible to read.

Again she heard huskiness in his tone, but chalked it up to altitude and cold air. That was safer.

"My point is, and I do have one," she persisted, "Kyle

will get in his nap. As we discussed. That means this expedition will go smoothly. Our little angel—"

The words sank in and she stopped, appalled that she'd said that to the man who'd made it clear the first time they met that he didn't want to be a we, us or our. "I meant to say *your* little angel. That wasn't flirting, I swear. It's just that I'm attached to him. In a professional way. Really, Justin, that was an unprofessional thing for me to say and you shouldn't be concerned that—"

"Take a breath." He slid her a brief look and the corners of his mouth curved up. "Don't worry about it. I'm glad you care about him."

"I do, but—"

"No buts. I have an idea. You're off and I'm off. For the rest of the day we'll just be friends shopping together."

The tension in Justin's voice had disappeared, leaving behind a teasing and carefree mood. So, for today, she was making a conscious and deliberate choice to relax and have fun.

The problem was, it would be easy to cross the invisible line into personal territory and that was a no-no. There was a risk to letting go of traditional boss-employee roles and sliding into something more casual. But to say that out loud would lead to a place too delicate to navigate without revealing her simmering feelings.

"Okay," she said. "Friends for the afternoon."

Forty-five minutes later, when Justin drove into the mall parking lot, she couldn't believe they were already here. She'd had so much friendly fun talking with him, the time had flown.

As she'd done every few minutes, she glanced in the backseat. "He's still asleep. Maybe I can get him out without waking him and he can have a little more rest."

"Okay." He drove the outer perimeter mall road until

seeing the store he wanted, then turned left into an aisle and guided the car between the white lines of a parking space. "Here we are."

"Here" was a big warehouse of a store that specialized in all-weather outdoor gear for the whole family. She'd been told by mom acquaintances in Kyle's weekly play group that it had the best selection of warm clothes for a child his age.

Emma got out of the car as quietly as possible and waited while Justin removed the stroller from the back and unfolded it. When all was ready, he nodded, giving her the go-ahead. "Here goes nothing." She opened the rear passenger door and gently released the car seat's restraint closure before lifting the baby out and setting him in the stroller. He squirmed some but didn't wake up and she quickly belted him in and snuggled a blanket around him.

Standing on tiptoe, she whispered in Justin's ear, "I can't believe he's still asleep."

"You've got the magic touch."

The husky tone sent shivers dancing over her skin that had nothing to do with winter and everything to do with heat. It was one of those forbidden feelings that came without warning and were happening more frequently.

"There's no telling how long we've got, so let's roll," she said quickly.

"You're the expert."

While Justin pushed the stroller, she quickly moved across the pedestrian crosswalk and into the store, trying to forget how good he smelled and how easy it would have been to lean into him. Inside, there was a lot to distract her. The warehouse had racks of jackets and snow pants, recessed cubbyholes stacked with sweaters and thermal shirts and long underwear.

Knit hats and gloves were everywhere. Overhead signs

directed them to the infant and toddler section, where Kyle's size was located. The sheer volume of choice was overwhelming. They were standing between racks of tiny jackets and heavier clothing appropriate for really brutal cold weather.

Bewildered, Justin looked at her. "Boy, am I glad you've got a master's degree in this stuff."

"Just to keep things real, I never took a class dedicated to the finer points of dressing a baby for winter in Montana. The way I see it, this is all about common sense." She headed for the jackets.

"Wait." Justin stood with his hands on the stroller but didn't push it. "We should look at snowsuits."

"I don't think he'll need that."

"Really?" He slid his sunglasses to the top of his head. "People in Blackwater Lake tell me the temperature can drop to below freezing."

"But Kyle is too little to be out in weather like that."

"What if you have to take him to the doctor or grocery store?"

Emma thought it over. "We go from house to car to building. All heated or protected from the worst cold."

"But what if we build a snowman or have a snowball fight?" Justin persisted.

He was taking paternal protection to a new and endearing place where practicality didn't go. She couldn't help smiling at him. "He's not even walking just yet."

"Almost."

"Be that as it may, I highly doubt that he'll be outside long enough to warrant a snowsuit."

"I don't know." He rubbed the back of his neck and scanned the abundance of warm outerwear. "It seems like he should have it just in case."

"Certainly you can get whatever you want," she said, "but if that's the case, why did you ask me to come along?"

"For an educated opinion. So what do you think? And remember, money is no object."

Her eyes narrowed as she read between the lines of what he'd just said. "You want me to tell you it's okay to buy both."

"Not true." Although the amusement in his eyes hinted that he was busted. "I don't need your permission."

"Of course not. But that doesn't change what you want to hear. You can buy out the whole toddler department, but it won't prove anything about your parenting skills."

"That's not what I'm doing."

"Yes, it is. For the record, let me say—in my expert opinion—you're a fantastic father, Justin. But what you're suggesting is impractical. If you get something that will fit for a couple of years, it will be too big and bulky for him to move easily. If it fits now, he'll outgrow it for next year. That just seems wasteful."

"So what? Call it doing my part for a sluggish economy. I—"

"Excuse me, but I couldn't help overhearing."

Emma turned at the sound of the voice behind her. A saleswoman in her mid- to late-twenties had joined them. Her long brown hair was shot through with red highlights and she smiled pleasantly. Her manner was very professional, although she did let slip one appreciative female glance in Justin's direction. Emma couldn't fault her; he was an exceptionally good-looking man.

Her name tag said Peg. "I couldn't help noticing that you're having a parental difference of opinion."

"Oh, we're not—" Emma rethought what she'd been about to say. "Well, he's the father—"

"Yes, he is. The resemblance is unmistakable."

Justin jumped in. "The thing is, Peg, I know you're in sales and would happily sell us the whole department, but what do you think is best for cold-weather protection for a one-year-old?"

"The baby is too little to spend an extended length of time outside in weather too cold for any sensible human being," Emma interrupted. "Don't you think?"

Peg indulgently smiled at each of them. "This isn't the first time I've had to referee parents."

To his credit, Justin didn't correct her and pull rank. "What do most of them do?"

"After a difference of opinion, when they end up buying more than is really necessary for their child, I'm pretty sure they go home to kiss and make up." She laughed, then studied the sleeping baby. "He's an incredibly beautiful child. Such a combination of you two."

"Thanks." Justin looked amused by the comment and still didn't correct her. "So, we're originally from California. What do you think?"

"He'll need a snowsuit."

"Okay," he said. "Then that's what we'll look at."

"I'll leave you to it," Peg said. "Let me know if you have any more questions."

When the woman was far enough away that she couldn't hear and assume another parental argument, Emma said, "Go ahead. You can say I told you so."

Justin grinned. "Would I do that?"

"You should." She shook her head. "And you should have told her we're not married."

"She would have thought my son was born out of wed-lock."

"So? No one thinks anything about that these days. Or you could have told her the truth. That I'm the nanny."

"Not this afternoon," he reminded her.

"Right." For a few hours they were friends. She looked at the little boy just starting to wake up. He opened his eyes, lifting the thick, dark lashes fanning his pink cheeks. "I'm incredibly flattered that anyone would think a child as beautiful as Kyle was mine. I can't believe it."

"I can." There was a fierce, hungry expression in his eyes before he looked away. "What I mean is that you're so natural with him, no one would guess you're not his mom."

That was a good save and she was grateful. "Thank you for saying that."

The truth was that caring for Kyle came naturally to her because she was genuinely fond of him. She didn't have to work at it.

"That's not flattery," Justin said. "Just a fact. And I'll do whatever I can to make him happy. And he's happy with you as his nanny."

This time there was no huskiness in his voice; any need, real or imagined, had disappeared from his eyes. He was all business. She should have been appreciative of another reminder that she needed to keep her feelings in check or risk them being crushed.

Later, when she went from friend back to nanny, she'd find a way to work up the appropriate level of gratitude. For a little while she'd felt as if she was part of a family, and going back to being the hired help wouldn't be easy after getting a small taste of everything she'd ever wanted.

While Justin and Kyle answered the door, Emma sat on the edge of the sofa in the family room feeling like a bump on a pickle. It was the baby's first birthday. Friends had been invited to the celebration because Justin was an only child and his parents were deceased. There was no extended family.

She wasn't family *or* friend, just the nanny, but he'd

overruled any misgivings and asked her to join them. She wanted to be a part of celebrating this momentous first birthday but felt like an intruder, filling an empty place that wasn't hers to fill. It felt like overstepping, something for which she would be judged in a bad way.

But Justin was the boss. Voices drifted to her and she stood just before the boss walked into the room with his friends.

"I'll do the introductions." Justin put Kyle on the rug and he crawled over to her to be picked up. "Emma Robbins, this is Camille Halliday and her fiancé, Ben McKnight."

She lifted the little boy into her arms, then moved closer and shook hands with both of them. "It's nice to meet you."

"Likewise." Camille studied her. "You're so pretty. Ben, don't you think she looks like that actress? The one who blindsided her superstar husband with a divorce then moved with their daughter to New York?"

Her fiancé hesitated, obviously trying to pick his words carefully. "I don't keep up with celebrity stuff. If it's not a revolutionary new procedure to repair a shattered ankle…" He shrugged.

"Don't pay any attention to my friend the hotel heiress," Justin told her. "You can take the girl out of L.A., but you can't take L.A. out of the girl. That's where Cam and I met."

"Not because I had work done." The other woman looked down at her chest, perfectly displayed in an expensive black knit dress. It also showcased her small baby bump. "This bosom has only recently become impressive and I give credit where credit is due."

"And where would that be?" Emma asked.

"The baby."

"What about me?" Ben's voice was teasing. "I had a role in the process."

"Since this is your baby, you do get some credit. That way you can't complain when it eventually disappears."

"Never happen." The love shining in his eyes left no doubt he was telling the truth. He was holding a gift wrapped in blue paper with red fire trucks covering it. "And this is for the birthday boy."

Emma envied the two, who were clearly in love and starting a family. She smiled at the little boy in her arms, just a bit sad that other people's children might very well be the only ones in her life.

"That's for you, Kyle." She smiled when he stared at the present, then wiggled to be put down.

"What can I get everyone to drink?" Justin asked.

"Beer for me." Ben glanced at his wife.

"Nothing alcoholic or caffeinated. For obvious reasons." Cam absently rubbed her belly. "I miss coffee more than I can say."

"Club soda with lime. Wine for you, Em?"

She knew that was Justin's subtle way of saying he had no problem with it. "That would be nice."

"Okay. I'll be right back. Talk among yourselves."

Since the large family room was adjacent to the kitchen, he could hear every word. But for several moments there weren't any. The three of them watched Kyle trying to figure out how to unwrap his package. When he slapped it several times, Emma knew his patience was fading fast and there would be a loud protest any second.

"Do you mind if I help him a little?" She looked at the couple who were watching, estimating their reaction to the suggestion. "He's getting frustrated. I'll just tear one end a bit to give him the idea."

"Please." Cam smiled tenderly when Emma slid a finger under one of the corners and pulled loose enough paper for the baby to grab and rip to his heart's content. "Ben told me it would take SEAL Team Six to extract that box from all the tape I put on."

"Don't be too disappointed if he has more fun with the paper than with what's inside." She observed as the child happily ripped paper away, leaving the wide ribbon and three-dimensional red bow still attached. "At this age it's the simple things that entertain them. Sticks, rocks, empty boxes."

Eventually a box emerged with the picture of a block set, complete with figures of doctor and nurse. It was age appropriate for safety, but clearly Kyle was more interested in happily tearing wrapping paper to shreds.

Ben sighed. "I think we have a lot to learn."

"You'll do fine." Justin walked over with a tray holding their drinks. "Cam and I actually met at a fund-raiser for a children's hospital in Los Angeles."

"That's right." Camille took the glass of club soda he handed her. "It was one of those galas where the rich and famous give away gobs of money in exchange for positive public opinion and tax write-offs."

"Sometimes they have a passion for the cause," Justin reminded her.

"Mostly not." Cam gave him a pointed look. "And I know this because I went to a lot of them for atonement. It took time and money to make people forget or at least forgive my teenage transgressions."

Emma finally realized who she was. "You're *that* hotel heiress."

The other woman sighed. "Guilty."

"The only thing you're guilty of is being a teenager. We've all been young and stupid." Justin set the tray on the coffee table and grabbed his beer. "Why don't you sit?"

"Are you saying I'm old?"

"I'm saying you're pregnant."

The couple took seats side by side on the full-size sofa and Justin sat on the shorter one at a right angle to them. The only place for Emma was beside him and when she put herself there, their thighs brushed. His gaze jumped to hers for a charged moment then they both quickly looked away. Camille's shrewd expression said she hadn't missed the exchange and the jury was still out on whether or not she approved.

Justin cleared his throat. "I actually have Cam to thank for the fact that I'm here in Blackwater Lake."

Emma felt like gulping the white wine he'd given her but forced herself to sip. "Oh?"

He nodded. "She's been in town since January."

"I drew the short family straw and was given the assignment of turning a profit at Blackwater Lake Lodge. At first I thought I'd been exiled to a foreign country and the employees treated me like an alien." She smiled at her fiancé. "Everything changed when I met Ben."

"His specialty is orthopedics, so she had inside information on the medical position that opened up at the clinic and passed the information on to me," Justin explained. "I just had to wait until the building project to expand Mercy Medical Clinic was complete, then I got the job. Now Ben and I work together."

"Speaking of expansion," the other man said. "Cam and I aren't the only ones working on a family. My brother, Alex, and his fiancée, Ellie, are expecting a baby just a couple months after us."

"A toast to the McKnights." Justin held up his long-neck bottle and they all touched their glasses.

Cam leaned back and rested a hand on her baby bump. "What brought you to Blackwater Lake, Emma?"

She should have expected the question but hadn't. She wasn't prepared. "Wow. Where to start."

Justin had not only kept her secret, he'd supported her during this confusing time. But if she told anyone else, the news could get out in a way she couldn't control.

She glanced at Kyle, for once wishing he would have an immediate need for a dirty-diaper change. But he was happily enthralled with unraveling his ribbon.

"Emma came here on vacation." Justin's expression said he had her back. "Hawaii's loss is Montana's gain."

She was disturbed and relieved in equal parts. He'd covered for her but she'd never considered that confiding in him would compromise his honesty. Still, she couldn't help liking him a whole lot more for the gallant gesture.

"That's true," she agreed. "I'd wanted to visit Montana and settled on Blackwater Lake."

"She liked it so much, she decided to stay." Justin took a drink from his beer. "It was my good fortune she did. Sylvia was leaving with or without a replacement and Emma is great with Kyle. Not to mention a seriously good cook."

"Really?" Cam shifted on the sofa, trying to get comfortable.

"Absolutely. And it's the little things she does," he continued.

"The way to a man's heart is through his stomach." Ben grinned when his friend choked as he was taking a drink.

"If that were true," Cam said, giving her fiancé a look, "you wouldn't be the father of this baby. I run a hotel and cooking isn't part of my skills set." She met Justin's gaze. "So tell me about the little things she does."

Justin thought for a moment. "Take Kyle's birthday. The menu tonight is all about his favorites. Macaroni and cheese. Green beans."

"I made a chicken dish, too, for the adults," Emma said. "Sounds yummy."

"It is." Justin rested his forearms on his knees. "She

made the birthday cake from scratch, too. And baked a little one just for him."

Emma picked it up from there. "He can eat it, play with it, wear it or throw it on the floor. This is his day to be the man, in his one-year-old way."

"Who's cleaning up?" Ben wanted to know.

"Me," she said. "The parameters are broad, but I draw the line at smearing cake on the windows."

"Aw." Cam's expression went all gooey. "I'd never have thought of that."

"A kid is only one once."

"That does it." Cam looked at Ben. "When Delaney is born, I'm stealing Emma for our nanny."

"Is that a girl name?" Justin grinned.

"Yes," the parents-to-be said together.

Then Cam smiled and added, "When our children grow up, maybe they'll fall in love and Kyle will propose. I'd love that because we could pick our little girl's in-laws."

"You're such a romantic," Justin teased. "Were you always that way or is it pregnancy hormones?"

"Some of both. And don't think you distracted me." She looked at Emma. "Will you consider a job offer?"

"Never say never. But it would have to be pretty spectacular." She smiled as Kyle held her leg and pulled himself to a standing position. "This little guy has stolen my heart."

She loved him; it was as simple as that. Her feelings for Justin were far more complicated. There was always the acute attraction, but more than that was his loyalty and sense of honor. She was incredibly grateful to him for compromising his truthfulness in order to protect her secret. That suddenly made it more urgent to figure out her personal situation.

She owed it to Justin to settle her life so that he could settle his.

Chapter Six

Justin couldn't believe that Halloween was only two weeks away. "I'm really glad you talked me into coming to the pumpkin patch."

"I didn't talk you into anything," Emma retorted. "It was merely a suggestion and you seized the moment to start Flint-family traditions. And rightly so."

It was a clear but chilly night as Justin pushed Kyle's stroller on the dirt path past the bales of hay and displays of ghosts, witches and zombies. It was all set up in a field just a couple streets over from Main, where, in about six weeks, there would be Christmas trees.

"Well, someone was talked into something." He snapped his fingers. "Oh, right, that was me talking you into coming along with us."

He wasn't sure why it was any more important than helping him shop for a jacket or being part of his son's first birthday celebration, but it was. So he made sure she was here.

"Make fun if you feel better." Her chin lifted a notch and just made her look cuter with her cream-colored, pom-

pom-topped knit hat. Her hands were shoved into the pockets of a puffy pink jacket as they walked past a fun house and its weird chain-rattling sounds, thumps and screams.

"I'm not making fun. Just giving credit where credit is due." He glanced at her, and his fingers tingled with the urge to run them through all that shiny brown hair tumbling down from underneath her hat.

"It really wasn't a creditworthy situation," she protested. "Halloween is coming and I saw a flyer at the grocery store. Every kid should have a pumpkin and make a project of carving it. Never too early to start traditions."

"I couldn't agree more. The thing is, I get busy with work, and stuff like this could slide under my radar if not for you."

The path was crowded with people; there was excitement in the air. Children were chasing each other and some had their faces painted with pumpkins, bats or scarecrows. Adults followed their kids, called out to slow them down if they got too far ahead.

Justin wanted Kyle to be a part of this but wasn't good at being aware when it was going on. He wasn't sexist, but events like face painting and haunted houses fell into the female sphere of expertise. Since he got so easily wrapped up in a demanding job, Emma was necessary for balance in his son's life.

He was a single father raising a child alone.

He glanced at her and the overhead spotlights showed her frown. It was an ongoing struggle to keep her from seeing that he wanted her more every day. Maybe that leaked out in what he'd just said. If not for her...

"What's wrong?" he asked.

"Nothing."

"Then why are you making that face?"

She met his gaze, her expression wiped clean of any emotion. "What face?"

"The one you were making before going deliberately blank."

He studied the smooth skin on her forehead where the frown had been and the realization came out of the blue as it so often did. She was so beautiful that sometimes it was like a punch to the gut. And he couldn't let her know.

"Look, Emma, I know faces. It's my job. So come clean. What's bothering you? If I did something…"

"No. Gosh, no, Justin." Their shoulders brushed and for a moment she put her hand on his arm. "It's not about you. I was just remembering my mother bringing me to pick out a pumpkin. Every year, I think, until I went to college."

He figured she meant the woman who'd kidnapped her. "Not a good memory?"

"Just the opposite. It was wonderful." The frown was back. "But because I had them with her, Michelle and Alan didn't have them with their daughter."

Justin wondered if she realized she was talking about herself in the third person. She was still conflicted about her loyalty to the woman she loved, the same one who'd done a horrible thing and hurt a lot of people, including Emma. And because Emma made Kyle's life practically perfect, Justin sometimes forgot that she had an agenda that wasn't necessarily compatible with his.

He stopped the stroller and put a hand on her arm. Troubled brown eyes held his own. "I'm going to tell you three things that you probably already know. But it never hurts to hear them out loud."

"Okay." It looked as if she was bracing herself.

"Number one—what happened isn't your fault. Next— it officially sucks what happened to you. Finally, and most important, you don't need to figure things out tonight."

The corners of her mouth curved up just a fraction, but as the words sank in she smiled and it was beautiful to see. Like a sunny day after a storm.

"You're right." She nodded emphatically. "Now who should get credit where credit is due?"

"Shucks, ma'am—"

She laughed and shook her head at the silliness. "If Beverly Hills could only see you now."

Before she could finish the thought, Kyle let out a wail at the same time he was doing his best Houdini imitation, trying to get free of the stroller belt holding him in. When his efforts didn't work, the verbal complaints escalated to a pitch that would make a dog cringe.

"Better get moving," he said.

"I'm with you."

Justin pushed forward, but the little boy didn't let up and the protest got louder, which hadn't seemed possible. He started leaning to the side, trying to get out.

"He's so over the stroller," Emma said. "I think he needs a break."

They stopped beside several huge crates filled with pumpkins for sale. "This seems like a good place."

"I agree." Emma unbelted the little boy and lifted him out, but he didn't want to be held, either. He whined and tried to wiggle out of her hold.

Justin wouldn't complain if she was holding him. Her arms were a place he'd imagined being too many times to count, but he had a completely different perspective on the issue.

Emma looked at him, the corner of her full bottom lip caught between her teeth. "Okay, don't do a father freak-out about where I'm about to put him. There's grass here. I'm just going to set him on the ground, give him a little space."

"I'm trying to decide whether or not I resent the freak-out remark," he teased. "Which one of us used antiseptic wipes on a perfectly clean high chair at the Grizzly Bear Diner? Just saying…"

"The diner is a public restaurant. Different children sit in those chairs with runny noses and heaven knows what other germs. You don't know that it was perfectly clean," she said as if that explained everything.

Without another word, she set Kyle on the grass and he looked happy as could be. Immediately he crawled over to the cardboard crate and put a hand on it, for leverage to stand up.

"Okay," Justin said, "we might as well pick out a pumpkin now. How do you know if it's a good one?"

"Didn't you ever do this with your parents?"

"Yeah. But it was a long time ago."

She sighed as if he were dull as dirt. "It's all about shape. And remember, a face is getting carved out of this." She grabbed a plump, round one. "Faces are your business, Doctor. What would you do with this one?"

He studied it for a few moments, then touched the widest part of the curve. "First I'd use my scalpel here and here for defined cheekbones."

Emma nodded her approval. "I can see that. If we use a carrot for a nose?"

"I think that's more a snowman thing, but let's go with it." He walked from one side to the other, pretending to assess. "I'd take a potato peeler to that pointy thing and try to soften the tip."

"Harsh." Emma laughed, then picked up another one that was narrower, elongated. "And what about this one?"

He glanced at Kyle, who was bouncing even though barely touching the box for balance. His little boy was essentially standing on his own. Good man.

Then he looked back at the pumpkin. "This guy needs a chin. The forehead is a little high, but we can distract from that by drawing focus here." He indicated the bottom. "Every guy wants a granite jaw."

"Every guy?" She looked at him as if assessing his chin. "I don't think I'd change a thing if I were you."

In his head Justin knew she was teasing, but the rest of his body went tight and hard at the compliment. Obviously he cared too much what she thought when she looked at him. And she must have seen something on his face, because her smile slipped and she quickly looked away.

"What do you think about this one, Kyle?" she asked, plucking a pumpkin from the pile and putting it on the ground.

The little boy gurgled as he removed his small hand from the crate and took one step, then another without holding on to anything. He stood on his own, a little unsteadily, beside the big, orange pumpkin.

"Did you see what I saw?" Her voice was calm, but Emma's eyes were bright with excitement that had nothing to do with her job.

Justin knew that because it felt as if that same thrill was on his own face. "I think he just took his first steps. What do you think?"

She stood when the little boy braced himself on the pumpkin. "Definitely his first steps." And then she threw herself into his arms. "Oh, my gosh, Justin. He's walking."

"I know."

And he was excited about that, too. But damn it, Emma felt so good in his arms, pink jacket, funky hat and all. He couldn't help himself and pulled her in tighter for full body contact. Being this close to her had him thinking about long, slow kisses in his bed. There was no question that he started breathing faster and it wasn't his imagination that Emma was, too. He saw it when she stepped away and couldn't look at him.

"It's getting cold," she said.

Justin hadn't noticed. He was hot all over and wanted to do something about it.

"We need to get Kyle home."

"Yeah." His house wasn't the neutral territory it had once been, Justin realized. Emma had made it a home.

Damn this gray area where he was living. He wanted her more than he'd ever wanted a woman in his life. But she was his employee and clearly very fond of his son. Just a while ago he'd reminded himself that she had other concerns in her life beyond her job.

She was really good at being a nanny and he'd been lucky to find her in this small town. He hated the thought of her leaving, hated that Kyle would be affected by the change. But she *was* an employee.

She could be replaced.

The morning after the pumpkin patch Emma was tired because she hadn't slept well. Almost kissing your boss who didn't want to be kissed tended to keep a nanny up most of the night. Although, if she was honest, he *had* pulled her closer when she hugged him. His breathing had quickened, too, and what did she do with that information?

Nothing if she wanted to keep her job.

And today her job was about Kyle's play group at Blackwater Lake Early Childhood Learning Center. It was located on Main, just down the street from the Grizzly Bear Diner, nestled between Tanya's Treasures and Potter's Ice-Cream Parlor. The class was technically Mommy and Me, but Emma figured the fact she wasn't his biological mother didn't matter.

She pulled the car into the rear lot utilized by customers of all businesses that faced Main Street. Her gaze automatically went to the diner where *her* biological parents worked and managed their business. It weighed heavily on her that she still hadn't made up her mind what to do, and being sleep deprived didn't help. As Justin said, she didn't have to decide today and gave herself permission to table the issue until she wasn't so tired.

Maybe there would be a sign from the universe when the time was right. Or she had to face the fact that a fear she didn't understand was standing in her way.

"Here we are, big guy." Emma turned off the ignition, then exited the car. She smiled at the memory of this little heartbreaker-in-training always gravitating to little Danielle Potter, a beautiful child who was also a year old. "Maybe your little friend will be here today."

"Ga—"

She opened the passenger door and grinned at him. "I'll take that as a 'Wow, I hope so.'"

After getting him out of the car seat, she reached for the diaper bag and slid the strap over her shoulder. "And you get to show off today, mister. You're the man. Taking your first steps is a very big deal."

A first kiss from Justin would have been a big deal, too, but not in a good way.

"You're getting heavier every day, pal." She moved through the parking lot toward the center's backdoor. "It's a good thing you're starting to walk. Your daddy doesn't have a problem lifting you because he's strong."

Emma shivered at the thought, but chalked it up to the cloudy gray sky and chilly wind that blew from the north.

"Da—"

"Yes, Da." She kissed his cheek. "You are too cute. Go easy on Danielle. I like her and her mom."

After opening the door, Emma moved past the office

and storeroom to the big open play area where a quick glance told her the majority of moms and babies were already gathered. She stopped at the cubbies on the wall and removed Kyle's jacket then stored it along with the diaper bag.

A few moments later, she took the last empty spot in the play circle and sat cross-legged on the floor with Kyle in her lap. Maggie and Danielle were to her left.

There was no teacher for this particular class; it was about moms and babies socializing and the children learning to share. The toys were blocks, simple four-to-six-piece wooden puzzles and shapes to introduce basics and increase major muscle development. She'd been to a few sessions and was getting to know the mothers, who seemed to be accepting her.

"Hi, everyone," she said, glancing around. There was a chorus of greetings in response. "How are you, Maggie?"

"Good. Look, Danielle—Kyle is here." She dropped a kiss on the top of her daughter's head. "What's up, Emma?"

"Not much," she lied.

"You look tired."

"Maybe a little." Wow, was this woman perceptive.

Maggie was a pretty brunette, petite and fragile-looking, but looks could be deceiving. She was a widow; her husband had been a soldier and died in Afghanistan several months before his daughter was born. It took a lot of strength to get through that alone and run a business, too. And she always seemed cheerful, although her beautiful brown eyes held a soul-deep sadness.

The sadness disappeared when a gleam stole into those eyes. "So, taking this little guy to the pumpkin patch last night wore you out?"

The only way she could know that was if she'd been there. "I didn't see you."

"I saw *you*." The teasing tone implied she'd seen more than that.

"Me, too." Lindsay Griffin watched her ten-month-old son crawl toward the toys in the center of the group. A blue-eyed redhead wearing square black glasses, she had the eager look of feminine curiosity. "What's it like to live with hunky Dr. Flint?"

Emma felt her cheeks burn as she realized at least two of these women had seen her hugging Justin. Why hadn't she noticed them?

Duh. She'd been a little preoccupied trying to ignore the fact that he'd held her just a little too long. After that, she was concerned with doing damage control. Trying not to get fired after letting her emotions get out of control had been her priority. But apparently there was still more damage control to do.

She glanced around the circle. Half the moms closest to her waited impatiently for her answer. The other half were too far away to hear and were chatting among themselves.

"I'm not living with Justin. He hired me to care for Kyle."

Maggie held her daughter's hands as the little girl in her pink flowered dress and white tights stood. "Correct me if I'm wrong, but the two of you occupy space under the same roof, no?"

"Yes."

"Then you're living with him," Lindsay said, like a trial lawyer who got something out of a hostile witness. "How is it?"

"A job," she answered carefully.

"So you are attracted," the redhead persisted.

"I didn't say that, either." She helped Kyle stand, then let his hands rest on her palms so he had the illusion of holding on.

"Do you have a boyfriend?" Plump, blonde Rachel Evans hugged her look-alike, curly-haired daughter, Casey.

"No." Emma saw no point in adding that she'd been engaged and it didn't go well.

"So there's nothing standing in your way if you decided to go with the attraction," Lindsay chimed in.

Maybe she *should* share a few details to throw them off the scent. Evidence that she had no interest in anything serious. "I was engaged in California but he was cheating on me."

"Jerk." Lindsay turned up her nose.

"Actually, that's too good for him. He's a scumbag weasel dog," Emma clarified and they laughed.

"I'm sensing that you're not in the mood for love." Maggie looked as if she understood not wanting to go there.

"Exactly." Emma nodded for emphasis. "Especially with my employer. Very unprofessional."

"Let me get this straight." Lindsay pushed her glasses up more firmly on her nose when her little guy knocked them off center. "You live in the same house and care for his son. There's cooking and light housekeeping involved."

"That's right."

"What do you get out of it?"

"A paycheck," she answered dryly.

"Of course, but—" Lindsay tucked a strand of red hair behind her ear. "Isn't it a lot like being married without the fringe benefits?"

"No. He's my boss and pays me very generously to take care of this beautiful little boy." She watched Kyle and Danielle crawl to the center of the circle and pick up blocks, then hold them out to each other.

Emma looked past Maggie and met the redhead's gaze. "Even if I were interested, he's not. He's a grieving widower and may never want another relationship."

"Good point." The sad look was back in Maggie's eyes and she nodded her understanding. Better than anyone here she knew how much love and loss hurt.

"I've heard that a man who's been married once is more likely to take the plunge again," Lindsay said.

"I don't get the impression that Justin is open to that." Emma remembered her first interview when he came right out and said he wasn't looking for a wife. However, sharing that information wasn't something she would do. "It's just a job."

"That's not what it looked like in the pumpkin patch last night." Lindsay stared over the top of her glasses.

"Kyle took his first steps. That was exciting." She was telling most of the truth.

"It looked awfully personal." Lindsay's expression indicated she expected all the details. "It seems to me—"

"All right, give Emma a break," Maggie interrupted good-naturedly. "Let's change the subject. Is Ryder still waking up every night? He could be teething."

Thank God the conversation shifted from her, and Emma sent Maggie a grateful look. The subject had changed but Emma couldn't stop thinking about it. Hugging Justin was a fringe benefit that she'd be better off without because the memory of it was driving her crazy.

She loved Kyle so much and leaving him would be very hard. But falling for his father would make the current situation even worse. It was frustrating because she'd done her best to put distance between them. Then she promptly forgot all of that and threw herself into his arms in the excitement of a baby's first steps. If he hadn't hugged her back, she'd just be embarrassed. Now she was all kinds of confused.

The rest of the playtime hour flew by and before she knew it, the session was over. The moms said goodbye and picked up their babies to leave. But Kyle and Danielle were still happily playing on the floor.

Maggie stood and smiled. "They're so sweet together, aren't they?"

"I know what you mean. They do seem to have a special bond."

"I hate to break this up, but I'm pretty sure the learning center will need the space for the toddlers in the next class."

Emma laughed. "These two would get mowed down by the bigger kids."

"That could ruin their whole day." Maggie looked at her watch. "It's almost noon. Why don't we take them to get something to eat?"

"You're not working today?"

"After lunch. I drop Danielle off at my mom's before going to the ice-cream parlor. I'll need to get something into both of us before that."

"If you're sure, I'd love to." Emma liked this woman a lot and felt they could be friends if she stayed. And if she didn't, that would be one more thing to regret. But, again, not today. "Where?"

Maggie tapped her lip. "You know the Grizzly Bear Diner is only a couple doors up, so we can walk. We don't have to load the kids into car seats to get somewhere and the food is good. Any objections?"

More than you could possibly know, Emma thought before saying, "Let's do it."

Chapter Seven

Emma walked into the Grizzly Bear Diner and automatically looked at the counter where Michelle and Alan Crawford spent a lot of time talking to the regulars. They weren't there, probably because there were no customers occupying the swivel chairs. It was just after the breakfast crowd and before the lunch rush, which meant the owners might not be here and she was sort of hoping she didn't have to see them. She wasn't ready yet.

Wendy, the thirtysomething hostess, showed them to a booth before bringing over two high chairs. With Kyle in one arm resting on her hip, she dropped the diaper bag on the booth bench seat and pulled out an antiseptic wipe. Then she proceeded to wash the plastic high chair tray and laughed when she saw Maggie doing the same thing.

Emma said to the hostess, "This isn't about not trusting you to clean off every last microbe. It's the only way to be sure."

"I'm not judging," Wendy answered, clearly not insulted. "It's a mom thing. What can I get you?"

"Coffee?" She looked at the other woman, who nodded.

"Coming right up. Your server will be with you shortly."

"Thanks."

"A mom thing," Maggie commented thoughtfully, settling Danielle in the chair. She fastened the strap and arranged the tray so it was snug but not too tight. When she looked up there was a gleam in her eyes. "She's new in town. Otherwise she would know you're the hunky doctor's nanny."

"Actually, not *his* nanny. I take care of Kyle."

"Whatever." Maggie waved her hand in dismissal. "You're an awesome nanny or she wouldn't have mistaken you for Kyle's mom. You take good care of him."

"It's what I'm paid to do."

"Technically. But there's an obvious emotional connection, too."

"I have a connection with all the children I'm responsible for."

"Okay. I won't push the issue," Maggie said. "But it's there for all the world to see."

Emma settled the little boy in his chair and gave him a cracker to keep him busy. He immediately handed it to the baby girl in the chair right next to his. The two of them were side by side at the end of the booth.

"Is that the sweetest thing?" Maggie's expression turned tender. "He's going to leave a trail of broken hearts behind him when he grows up and I just hope he spares my daughter."

"They'll be good buddies." Emma didn't think she would be around to see it, though. "That's so much better than anything romantic."

"No kidding." The other woman's dark eyes filled with a wistful sorrow when she looked at Danielle. "Never falling in love means a lot less crying."

"Yeah. That's sort of my motto." Emma's heart twisted

as she looked at the young woman across the table from her and realized she'd been through so much worse. "I'm so sorry about your husband."

"You know about Danny." It wasn't a question.

"I brought Kyle into the shop for frozen yogurt and talked to Diane and Norm Schurr. They told me about him."

"My regulars. Older couple who keep fit and come in for a treat once a week," Maggie said. "I think they just want to check up on me."

"Nice couple." They had the love, respect and years together that most people yearned for. "We started chatting and, just so you know, I did tell them I'm not Kyle's mother."

"Honesty is the best policy."

Mostly, Emma thought. She glanced past Maggie to the diner counter, but still didn't see either Michelle or Alan. Her stomach knotted and she did her best to hide it.

"Diane pointed out the picture hanging on the wall behind the cash register of you and your husband, taken the day Potter's Ice-Cream Parlor opened."

Maggie smiled, a faraway expression in her eyes. "He loved ice cream and there wasn't anything like it in Blackwater Lake. So, when we were looking to start a business, that's what we did. He was here at the grand opening and had about six months left until getting out of the army." She handed Danielle a cracker and the corners of her mouth turned up when the little girl gave it to Kyle. "Danny was so excited about becoming a father."

As words of comfort went through Emma's mind, she immediately dismissed each one. She met the other woman's gaze.

"I'm sure you've heard all the platitudes. He's her guardian angel. Watching over both of you from heaven. He's in a better place." She shook her head in frustration, remembering how it was after her mother died. "People mean well and are just trying to console. But, Maggie, it officially sucks that you were robbed of a life with him and your daughter is going to grow up without knowing her father."

"Thank you for that." Maggie looked genuinely amused. "I'm so tired of people feeling sorry for me. I hate that the whole town thinks of me as 'the widow.'"

"So, you're ready to move on?"

"It's not something you get ready for. I had a baby. Under the circumstances you just do it."

Emma looked at the two little ones happily chattering in a language only a one-year-old could understand. The father of this little boy was a widower. "You and Justin both understand how it feels to lose a spouse. Maybe—"

Maggie held up a hand. "Don't go there. I'm doing great without yucky love stuff messing everything up."

"Don't hold back. Tell me how you really feel."

The other woman laughed. "And I'll tell you something else. I like you, Emma Robbins."

"The feeling is mutual."

But Emma experienced a surge of relief that her friend wasn't interested in Justin. Jealousy wasn't a very good foundation for friendship. And friendship wasn't something she'd anticipated when making the decision to stay in town a little longer. Not that she was isolating herself on the English moors like a gothic heroine from a Charlotte Brontë novel. But the longer she was here, the more regrets she would have about leaving people behind when she was gone.

"Good." Maggie leaned forward, a conspiratorial gesture. "Because I'd like to talk to you. There's something I've been thinking about."

"Oh?"

"The crafts store next to Potter's parlor just closed its doors forever. The owners are moving to Texas to be near their daughter. I'm thinking about leasing the space."

"To expand the ice-cream business?"

"Expanding, yes, but it's not a lateral move, more of a branching out and complementing what I'm already doing." Maggie gave her daughter a sippy cup of water and the child eagerly grabbed it.

Emma did the same for Kyle. "I need a little more information if you want feedback. No pun intended."

She kept an eye on the diner behind her friend. The owners had just come out from the back and were involved in a conversation behind the counter.

"I'm thinking of adding food to the menu," Maggie said. "Sandwiches, maybe quiche. Soup and salad. Healthy choices."

"Something fast but nutritious," Emma guessed.

"Exactly. But I don't want to poach business from the diner. Michelle and Alan Crawford are friends."

Just then Wendy brought two cups and saucers and poured coffee in them from the pot she carried. "The menus are right there on the table when you're ready to order. Do you need cream?"

Both women nodded and she left again.

Emma picked up where her friend had left off. "I'd think both businesses are different. This is a sit-down-and-order place. More leisurely. You're talking about order, pick up and go, for people in a hurry."

"Exactly."

"I'd talk to the Caldwells." Technically she was a Caldwell, too, and she felt a sort of weird protectiveness for the people she barely knew.

"I planned to. But first I'm going to run it by Brady."

"Who?"

"My brother. Brady O'Keefe. He's the one in the family with business flair." Maggie was obviously proud of him. "He has an internet conglomerate that he runs remotely from his house. It's a really big house."

"Wow. He sounds like a very impressive guy."

"Hmm." Maggie tapped her lip, a speculative look in her eyes. "Speaking of setting people up…"

"Who was talking about setups?" Emma tried to look innocent.

"You. My brother is a bachelor. Never been married."

"And, to quote you, never falling in love means a lot less crying. God knows I've done enough."

"So that's how it is. Bad experience?"

"Like I said during the group, lying weasel dog." Emma figured she'd dodged a bullet there. "I've sworn off men."

"Okay. I understand. But if you ever want to talk—"

"No." Partly she just didn't want to reveal her stupidity, but mostly it was because Michelle was headed this way with an order pad in hand.

She stopped at the end of the table and looked at the children. "Hi, Danielle. Maggie, she's getting so big."

"Just turned one," the proud mother said. "Same age as Kyle."

"It's good to see you again, Emma. You, too, Mr. Kyle." She smiled at the babies. "Are these two little ones having their first date?"

"No," the two women said together with vehemence.

"Okay, then." Michelle laughed. "I am so sorry it took me such a long time to get over here."

"No problem. Emma and I have just been getting better acquainted."

"You're so sweet. We're short a waitress today. She had the flu and no one wants to be around that, including Alan and me. We told her to stay home and get better."

She glanced sympathetically at each of them. "But you must be starved."

"Don't worry about it." Emma had lost her appetite the moment Maggie suggested the diner. "The kids are happy. If they weren't, the crying would hit a decibel level that could be heard in the next county and you'd have begged us to leave."

"No," the other woman said teasingly. "That's not the best way to keep customers coming back."

"I guess not."

"So, what can I get you?"

Emma didn't need to look at the menu. "When Justin and I were here—"

"What?" Maggie stared at her. "This is news. You were here on a date?"

"It wasn't a date. We just had dinner—"

"Michelle, did you see this dinner?" Maggie was on a mission.

"I did."

"And?" The other woman studied the diner owner, then glanced at Emma. A curious expression slid into her eyes.

"It looked friendly enough." A diplomatic answer. "But not too friendly."

"Thank you," Emma said.

"I just noticed something." Maggie looked back and forth between them. Comparing. "Your eyes are almost exactly the same color."

Emma was just starting to relax, but now her heart jumped. "Really?"

"Yes. And the shape of your faces is very similar."

"You don't say?" The older woman looked more closely at Emma. "I consider that a compliment. You are so pretty and if Justin Flint doesn't see it, then he's not as smart as a doctor should be."

"Thank you again. I think." Emma wished she needed a menu. Maybe she could hide behind it. "You're short-handed. We should order. I think Kyle would like the Bear Cub combo. He loves macaroni and cheese. And just a Mama Bear burger for me."

"I'll have the same," Maggie said.

"Coming right up. And I'll bring a warm-up for those coffees."

When she was gone, Emma felt as if she could breathe again, trying to tell herself that this was no big deal. How many times had she been out with a friend and someone commented that they looked like sisters? That they must be related. What had just happened was the same thing, but she couldn't make herself believe the lie.

They *were* related.

Should she feel something for the woman? Her mother? The truth was, they were strangers. But how long before someone else noticed the resemblance and there was no way to blow it off?

Maybe this was the sign she'd been waiting for.

Justin watched Emma all through dinner, trying to figure out if she was upset or tired. Or both. She'd gone through the evening ritual of telling him about Kyle's day socializing and lunch at the Grizzly Bear Diner. Mentioning the restaurant her parents owned had made her mouth pull tight. If he had to put money on it, he'd bet something happened at lunch.

If he was smart, he'd mind his own business, but apparently he wasn't that bright, after all. He just couldn't stand the haunted look in her eyes.

After Kyle was tucked into his crib and sound asleep, it was her habit to putter in the kitchen. Before she went to her room, she got things ready for the Flints' morning rush. Everything was put together for breakfast except the food, and often she made a lunch for him to take to work. After turning off his computer in the office, that's where he found her now.

"Emma?"

She turned away from measuring grounds into a coffeemaker filter. "Hi. Is there something you need?"

You. The surge of yearning was startling in its intensity, but he was almost sure he didn't say that out loud. She looked so beautiful, so fragile and unhappy that he pushed his own feelings aside. More than he wanted her, he wanted to chase away whatever was troubling her.

"No," he said. "I don't need anything." He moved closer and leaned back against the island, sliding his fingers into the pockets of his jeans. A reminder to keep them to himself. "Do you want to talk about anything?"

Her gaze snapped to his and her hand froze. "Why would you think that? Did I do something wrong?"

"No, of course not. It's just you're not your usual perky self."

Justin had learned to watch his wife, read her mood, interpret when things were going her way and when to stay out of her way. He was pretty good at reading women, and mostly Emma had been easygoing—sweet, funny and sassy, which was why this pensive quality concerned him so much.

"What's bothering you?" he asked.

"It's not something that will affect my ability to care for Kyle. I'll handle it. Don't worry. It's not your responsibility. You're my boss."

"And your friend. At least I thought we were." They were something and it was a bad idea to define exactly what. Friends was the simplest label. "It might help to talk out whatever is going on."

She stared at him for several moments before the tension in her body eased with a slight nod. "Something happened at the diner today."

"Okay." He folded his arms over his chest. "Since there was no breaking news on the local TV station, you're going to have to give me a tiny bit more."

She thought for a moment, then said, "It's going to sound stupid when I say it out loud."

"I promise not to point and laugh."

"That doesn't make me feel better, but I sense you're not going to back off." She sighed. "Okay, here goes. Maggie Potter noticed that Michelle and I have some of the same physical characteristics. Face shape. Eye color."

"She said you look alike?"

"Not quite that direct. Just that there's a resemblance."

"She's your mother. If someone looks for it—"

"That's what bothers me," she said. "Maggie doesn't know. It was just an observation."

"Tell your mother the truth," he suggested.

"It's not that simple. They might hate me. What if they think I'm like the woman who took me?"

"Why would they?"

"I don't know," she said helplessly. "Maybe because my whole life is a lie."

"No, it's not."

"It feels that way. My fiancé cheated on me and I didn't know. That relationship was a lie. And my mother let me believe she gave birth to me when, in fact, she took me away from another woman." Her brown eyes were dark with the conflict raging inside her. "I can't bring myself to tell Michelle the truth, so doesn't that make me a product of my environment? A liar, too?"

"No." He rejected that categorically. "The woman who kidnapped you did a bad thing and we'll never know what desperation drove her to do it. But she didn't raise you to be a deceitful person. If that were the case, you wouldn't have told me the truth after I hired you. None of this is your fault."

"Not the situation, but I'm certainly responsible for what's going on now. And I was wrong. It is affecting my work performance."

"No, it's not." His son was happy and healthy. His household ran like a well-oiled machine. She did her job superbly. She wasn't to blame for the fact that he couldn't stop thinking about her in his bed.

"Don't you see? If I was doing my job well, you'd never have known there was something bothering me. I'm normally a better nanny than this." Her eyes filled with what looked like pity directed at him. "You ought to have someone stronger, someone better. Especially after losing your wife."

"Don't," he snapped.

"What?"

Justin was sick of holding this inside and couldn't do it anymore. "Don't pity me. I don't deserve it."

"I'm not. I don't feel sorry for you. It's just—"

"Nothing. Don't say it," he pleaded.

"I have to." Her small smile was sad around the edges. "You lost the love of your life. A lot of people would have been immobilized by something like that, but you weren't. You moved forward. You relocated to Blackwater Lake, a place where her memory wouldn't get you down."

"I came here so Kyle could have a normal, well-balanced life."

"Where he wouldn't miss his mother as much because people didn't know her," she protested.

"Unfortunately, my past followed me."

"What do you mean?"

"People knew my story and treated me like the lonely widower—" He dragged his fingers through his hair. "I can't stand it anymore. I can't stand living the lie."

"You're scaring me, Justin." She folded her arms across her waist. "What are you talking about?"

"I didn't love my wife. I wouldn't have wished her dead because no matter her flaws, she was Kyle's mother. Whatever she was, he needed her in his life and her being gone will always make him wonder what might have been. But when she died, we were separated. I'd asked her for a divorce. We both knew there was nothing between us anymore."

She looked surprised but not disapproving. "No one knows this?"

"At first I didn't want to talk about it. I wanted to forget and thought it would blow over, but somehow my previous life has become mysterious and intriguing. It was just easier to let them go on believing than to confess the truth. What could it hurt? She's gone." He didn't see anything in Emma's expression that hinted at her despising him. That was a plus. "After she was involved in that fatal car accident, it was the first and only time I was grateful that she'd ignored her child."

"She turned her back on her baby?"

"All the time. Even when he wasn't feeling well. Heaven forbid she'd miss a social thing. She'd still go to formal events, turning him over to me or the nanny. She walked out without looking back." The memory made him angry all over again. "It drove me nuts how she could do that. Finally I realized that I didn't much like the woman I married."

Understanding dawned in Emma's eyes. "You were grateful she ignored Kyle because he wasn't in the car with her when she had the accident."

"Yes." He met her gaze because now that he was finally coming clean it was important that she fully understood how low he could go. "So, you're not the only one living a lie. I'm not the man everyone thinks."

"That's your private past and no one's business but yours. You're a good man. Never doubt that."

He wasn't so sure. "It's hard not to."

"Oh, Justin—" She moved close and put her arms around him. "I've never seen someone who needs a hug more than you do right now."

He had every intention of pushing her away. He really did. But the nearness of her body, the exquisite feel of her soft curves pressed against him were too much temptation after weeks of denying himself. Last night in the pumpkin patch when they'd held each other was never far from his mind. The feminine weight of her in his arms haunted his dreams and he wasn't completely convinced that right this moment wasn't another dream.

So he held her close for several moments and sighed, a ragged shuddering sound, because touching her overwhelmed his willpower.

"Emma—" Her name was a sigh on his lips as he cupped her cheek in his hand and lowered his mouth to hers.

A moan of acceptance caught in her throat and the sound set his blood on fire. His brain shut down as his senses kicked into overdrive. He kissed her slowly, thoroughly, concentrating on the feel of her full lips, the cadence of her quickened breathing, the silky hair that tickled his fingers.

He wanted more. The idea of carrying her to his room had far too much appeal and he ached to do just that. But some part of his sensation-drugged brain managed to sputter to life and convey the message that this wasn't a good idea.

"Emma—" Justin pulled back, breathing hard. "I'm sorry. That was out of line."

She met his gaze, her own breathing unsteady, her eyes full of wonder. "It was just a kiss."

"That's where you're wrong." He cupped her face in both hands now, unable to stop touching her. "I want more than just a kiss and we should stop right now."

Her voice was husky, her expression full of sass and searing need when she said, "Maybe we shouldn't."

Chapter Eight

"One of us has to be strong." The words were right, but there was no conviction in Justin's voice. "Do we really want to take this step?"

Emma couldn't speak for him, but *she* desperately wanted to. When he'd confessed to not being in love with the wife he'd lost, her reservations had disappeared. Or it could be the way he'd kissed her had chased away her will to resist. Either way, she couldn't rally the enthusiasm to be the strong one here.

"Emma…" He brushed his thumb gently over her cheek as his eyes searched hers. "You're so sweet—"

His hesitation took the air out of her brazen balloon. She'd jumped to a conclusion and it was wrong. He didn't want her and, dear God, this was humiliating on so many levels.

She stepped away from him, incapable of thinking rationally when he was touching her. That much was obvious because apparently she'd been under the impression that if she let him know how she felt, he would want her, too.

"This was obviously a mistake. I'll just be going. Good

night, Justin." She turned, prepared to head upstairs as fast as possible.

He put a hand on her arm. "Wait—"

Without looking at him, she shook her head. "You're right. We have to be strong—"

"No."

She heard the grinding need in his frustrated tone and gratefully turned into his arms, then slid her own around his waist. "I thought I was the only one who felt this way. I thought—"

"You'd be wrong." He kissed her mouth softly, a peck and a promise. "I felt something the first time I saw you. When you came to my office at the clinic."

"Really?"

He nodded. "I had an idea in my head of the nanny I was looking for and you're not it. Except that you're a natural with my son."

"Oh? What was your vision?"

"Old. Gray. Plump. A wart on the end of your nose would have been an excellent qualification."

"And you hired me, anyway."

"Your work history and recommendations were impeccable." He shrugged. "And I was so sure the attraction would go away. Wow, was I wrong about that."

He wasn't the only one, she thought. "I know exactly what you mean."

"Emma?"

She left her hands at his waist and looked up at him. "What?"

"I'm taking you to bed now."

"Yes." She picked up the baby monitor beside her on the counter then slid her free hand into his.

Justin took her through the family room to the hall that led to the first-floor master bedroom. It was a suite, really, large and masculine, decorated in shades of brown, beige and black. The furniture was pine and so right for this house with its spectacular views of tree-covered mountains.

Obviously Emma had seen it, what with putting away laundry and replacing towels in the attached bath. But she'd never *seen* it from the perspective of being in the big, soft king-size bed with Justin. She'd fought so hard against this, but apparently it was true what they said about the wanting being bigger than both of them. The present was clear as a bell, but the future wasn't. She refused to think about that right now and set the baby monitor on one of the nightstands by the bed, then turned to Justin.

Light from the hall trickled over his face as they stood beside the high mattress. Gray eyes stormy and intense, he reached for the hem of her sweater and lifted it up and off. She slowly unbuttoned his shirt, then spread it wide, sliding the cotton from his broad shoulders.

With their gazes locked, she reached behind her back to unhook her bra, letting it fall to the carpet at their feet on the growing pile of discarded clothing. Justin's breath caught as he slowly reached out and gently took her left breast in his hand, rubbing the tip with his thumb.

"I honestly can't believe how beautiful you are," he whispered reverently.

"You make me feel that way." Her heartbeat went wild as he caressed her bare, sensitive skin. Tingles two-stepped up and down her arms.

Without looking away, he reached for the buckle on his belt and unfastened it before flicking open the button on his jeans. After toeing off his shoes, he slid the zipper south and pushed off pants and briefs.

Emma removed her own sneakers and skimmed off everything until she was naked, too. Along with their clothes, it felt as if all pretense and secrets had been stripped away. They were simply a woman and a man who wanted each other. There were no barriers between them; this intimacy was honest.

Justin pulled her into his arms, skin to skin. He kissed her tenderly and left her needing so much more. But when he looked into her eyes, he put into words exactly what she'd been feeling.

"This is the first thing that feels real to me in a very long time."

"I know what you mean."

He let her go long enough to toss throw pillows aside and drag the comforter down, leaving the sheets bare. Then he took her in his arms again and held her tight against him while lowering them together onto the thick mattress.

His mouth took hers slowly, thoroughly, and when her lips parted, his tongue slid inside to explore the interior with just as much attention. On their sides facing each other, they nibbled and nipped, quick drugging kisses as his hand skimmed the curve of her waist. Moving first up to the side of her breast, his fingers stroked and touched until she could hardly stand the pressure building inside her. Then he slid his hand over her belly and lower, fingers hovering, teasing while her tension surged.

Emma drifted on a sea of sensation, each wave cresting until the next, larger swell took her breath away again. She let her hands roam freely, restless strokes up to his broad shoulders and down over the wide contour of his chest. When her palm brushed his nipple, he hissed out a sharp sound of arousal.

Each moment was like a bright fluffy cloud pushed by the wind across the sky before she could absorb the magnificence. She wanted to hold on to everything, keep each second close to her heart forever.

Then rational thought vanished completely as he touched a finger to the place at the juncture of her thighs where nerve endings came together. The sensation had her gasping against his lips and nearly brought her up off the mattress. Justin was panting with fractured breaths as he reached into the nightstand.

"What?"

"Condom—"

She nodded, unable to say anything else, grateful that he'd thought about it because she hadn't. In seconds he'd ripped open the package and put on the protection. She rolled to her back as he levered himself over her, gently urging her legs wide with his knee. Then he braced on his forearms and slowly nudged inside, letting her grow accustomed to the feel of him, the thickness.

Emma turned her face into the masculine swell of his biceps and breathed in the tantalizing spicy scent of his skin. He moved inside her, stoking the knot of tension tighter and tighter until she came apart in a glorious explosion. He held her tenderly, kissed her forehead, cheek and hair, as pleasure rippled through her. When she could finally think again, she lifted her hips, urging him on until he went still and groaned out his own release.

"Oh, God, Emma. Not yet—" He buried his face in her neck.

She held him for a long time, something scratching at her thoughts, warning not to let go.

Not yet.

Finally, Justin rolled away and without a word got out of bed. Dimly she was aware of a light switching on, but she didn't open her eyes.

In the darkness of burned-out passion, Emma could feel unease creeping in. Then the mattress dipped and Justin pulled her against his side. But she felt the difference, a distance, a reluctance. There was tension in his arms now where before he hadn't been able to hold her close enough.

She'd managed to turn off her head because touching and being touched had felt too good to stop. It was two people doing what they wanted in all the right ways. Now all the ways it was wrong couldn't be silenced. Just enough time had passed for the magnitude of what they'd done to penetrate the afterglow of lovemaking. Rules and regrets came rushing in.

"Justin, I'm sorry—"

"I'm not," he said fiercely. "It's just—"

She knew. "It can't happen again. I'm the nanny and you're my employer."

"If that was all, I would just fire you." There was anger and frustration in his voice. The words implied he had different reasons for backing off.

"Maybe you *should* let me go." She'd find another job. Something to get by until she resolved her situation.

"It's not that simple." He rolled onto his side toward her. "I just don't want you to get the wrong idea."

"About what?" She pulled the sheet up more snugly, as if it could protect her from what was coming.

"We want different things. You're looking for family and mine is already complete. I have Kyle and he's all I want. I have no intention of ever marrying again. Nothing has changed for me."

Hearing that he hadn't liked his wife very much had freed her to make love with him, but the pain of what he'd gone through locked her out now. His words from the first job interview came back to her.

I'm not looking for a wife.

The thing was, he was right to say that. She wanted honesty and he'd been that way right from the beginning. Besides, her life was too complicated already. If they pulled back now, this was nothing more than momentary weakness. No harm, no foul.

"I understand, Justin. And you're absolutely right. We'll forget this ever happened."

"Okay," he answered with genuine regret. "That would be best."

There was a snuffling sound from the baby monitor followed by a whimper. Bless that baby boy who spared her from having to say more.

"I need to check on Kyle."

From now on, she would keep busy with the baby and try not to wonder how she was going to keep the promise she'd just made to his father.

Forget this ever happened? Fat chance.

"You had sex."

Justin had no idea how Camille Halliday knew, but he didn't plan to comment on her declaration. Instead, he pointed at her pregnant tummy and made a declaration of his own. "Someone certainly did."

"Yes, but I'm in a relationship. And you didn't deny it."

He looked around the hallway to make sure no one in the clinic had heard what she said. "Do you enjoy being outrageous?"

The question was a deflection, mostly because he didn't want to ask how she'd guessed. The guilt was probably there in his eyes; he was the scumbag boss. Creating a hostile work environment. Although what they did felt anything but hostile. Maybe he should start a new reality show about sleazy employers who slept with the staff. Except she'd been so warm and willing in his arms.

"I used to enjoy being outrageous when I was young and a mixed-up kid." Cam settled her hands on her pregnant belly. "Now I've reformed and have a kid of my own on the way. And, I say again, you didn't deny having sex."

Another deflection was needed since she was calling him out. "What are you doing here?"

"I had a doctor's appointment. The baby and I are in very good health and all is progressing normally, Adam says."

Adam Stone was Mercy Medical Clinic's family practice physician and took care of the pregnant patients. Justin liked and respected him.

"So if you've seen Adam, how come you're still here?" Bugging me, he wanted to add.

"I'm waiting for Ben. He's taking me out to lunch."

"So where is he?"

Justin could really use some help here, because he didn't particularly want to talk about Emma. They'd said everything there was to say in his bed last night, just before she'd gone upstairs to the baby. This morning she'd made an effort at normal and so had he, but tension was on the menu right along with his omelet.

"My gorgeous fiancé is with a patient. What are you doing right now?"

He slid his hands into the pockets of his white lab coat. "I'm on my way to the break room for lunch."

"Good. I'll keep you company." She put her arm through his and tugged him down the hall, past patient rooms to the last door on the left.

Inside, there was a refrigerator, stainless-steel sink and cupboards. A card table and four folding chairs dominated the center of the room. At one time this area was used for storage as well as a place for employees to take a break. But since the clinic expansion, there was a much larger room designated for storing supplies and equipment.

Camille looked around, an odd expression in her pretty blue eyes.

"What?"

"It just now hit me. This sure is different from your Beverly Hills office."

"I know."

"Do you miss it? Do you ever regret moving here?" she asked.

"No," he said instantly.

"Take your time. Think about it."

"I don't have to. The longer I live here in Blackwater Lake, the more convinced I am that moving from Beverly Hills was the right decision. Blackwater is a close-knit community made up of down-to-earth people. It's the ideal place for Kyle to grow up."

"So, you have doubts," she teased.

"Right." He grinned, then opened the refrigerator and took out the brown bag Emma had packed his lunch in.

A vision of her in his bed, silky brown hair spread over his pillow, was like a sucker punch to the gut. It had been one of the best nights of his life. And the worst. Any doubts he had weren't about what they'd done but were directed at himself. He'd let down his guard and couldn't take back having sex with her. His punishment was that he continued to want her even though he couldn't have her.

He sat in one of the chairs and pulled out the chicken sandwich but suddenly wasn't hungry, at least not for food.

Camille tapped her lip, studying him. "You've got that look again."

"What look would that be?" he asked with as much innocence as he could, what with the guilt he was carrying.

"You had sex. With Emma."

He was just lifting half the sandwich to his mouth and

froze. A couple seconds later and he'd have taken a bite, probably choked on it.

"Seriously, Cam. You think I'm that low?" He was, but she didn't know it for a fact.

"I think you're that attracted to your nanny. And who could blame you?" She took a bottle of water from the fridge and sat at a right angle to him. "She's beautiful, Justin. Inside and out. Kyle adores her."

"She's good with him," he agreed.

"And you." She tucked a strand of blond hair behind her ear then folded her hands around the plastic bottle. "You look different. More relaxed, or something."

"Or something."

He sure didn't feel in control. If anything, he was even more tense. Having Emma was even better than he'd imagined and his imagination was pretty good.

"Oh, for Pete's sake." Cam's voice was full of friendly frustration. "Are you afraid I'll spread stories around town?"

"It never crossed my mind," he said truthfully. "But why do you want to know?"

"Female curiosity. And a sincere hope for you to be happy."

"That's sweet." If he'd had a sister, he would want her to be just like Camille Halliday. Funny, abrasive, straightforward and sympathetic.

"All right, then. Just admit it. This is me. I've been victimized by gossip and rumors for as long as I can remember. Do you really think I'd spread around something so personal, something you shared with me privately? As a friend?"

"No." The truth was, he could use someone to talk to. "That's one lucky kid you've got there. You're going to be a great mom."

She smiled with pleasure. "How do you know?"

"Because that child won't be able to get away with anything. You're very discerning." He took a big bite of chicken salad on wheat. It was every bit as good as Emma always made it. The thought of her made his body grow tight with need and a hunger that had nothing to do with food.

"It was actually just a guess, but now you've pretty much confirmed that you had sex with Emma."

"Just out of curiosity, how did you know it was her?"

"She's living under your roof. You haven't been seeing anyone else or I'd have heard about it. And I saw the way you looked at her when Ben and I were there for Kyle's birthday." She shrugged. "Easy."

"Hmm." He took another bite of his sandwich.

"So why don't you look happier?"

"It's not going to happen again."

"Yes, it is," she insisted.

"No."

"Why not?" Her eyes narrowed. "She's not trying to pull a fast one, is she?"

"No way." Justin was surprised by how quickly and aggressively he defended Emma. "You're too cynical."

"With good reason." She twisted the top off her water bottle. "But if you two have the hots for each other, I don't understand how you can back off."

"We're in agreement about it." He couldn't speak for Emma, but it was the hardest damn thing he'd ever done. "There's baggage. On both sides."

He looked at the other half of his sandwich, cut like a triangle. Such a little gesture that kept it from being ordinary. Probably didn't take any more time, but was just one more thing that Em did for him. Unlike Kristina. The woman he'd been stupid enough to marry had only ever thought of herself.

"You met my wife," he said to Cam. "You know the marriage was an unqualified disaster."

She nodded. "I was always surprised that you married someone so shallow and self-centered. You're such a good man and she didn't deserve you."

"I fell hard and fast for who I thought she was." He shrugged. "I didn't know she was putting on an act."

"She'd made up her mind that she wanted to be married to a renowned Beverly Hills plastic surgeon and pulled out all the stops to get him."

"If you knew, why didn't you warn me?"

"A—you wouldn't have believed me. And B—I didn't know you very well back then. I'm sorry."

"You didn't force me to propose."

She took a sip of water. "But you got a perfect little boy out of it. And you have to think about him."

"He's all I am thinking about. The worst thing I could do is burden Kyle with another mistake. My bad judgment is the best reason not to get serious again."

"Well, I'm a good judge of character and in my humble opinion Emma is the real deal."

"But what if you're wrong? What if she's not?" He dragged his fingers through his hair. "I won't take another chance, and it would be really wrong to lead her on when I have no intention of getting serious."

"But, Justin—"

He held up a hand. "Not going to happen, Cam."

"Okay. You're wrong to deny yourself happiness, but I think you'll get over it in time, with someone willing to be patient with you." She smiled at the pun. "But I'll get off your back for right now."

"Thank you."

"So, that witch of a wife is your baggage. What about Emma? What's hers?"

Justin couldn't tell her that. Emma had confided in him and he wouldn't betray her trust. The question was how to get the message to this sharp, curious woman without letting anything slip. "Cam, it's not for me to—"

"Dr. Flint?"

He looked at the doorway where the nurse stood. "Hi, Ginny. What's up?"

"You have an emergency walk-in. Alan Crawford, from the Grizzly Bear Diner. A grease burn. Room one."

He nodded. "I'll be right there."

"Michelle, his wife, is with him and she's filling out paperwork."

"Okay." The nurse disappeared and he looked at Cam. "Gotta go."

"Of course. I hope it's not too serious."

"Me, too."

"But if there's anything good about this, it's that he's got you for his doctor." Cam smiled her encouragement. "Bye, Justin."

Speaking of Emma's baggage, he was on his way to see them.

Chapter Nine

Justin headed down the hall toward room one where Emma's father waited. If the man had walked himself into the clinic, chances were good the injury wasn't too serious. Hopefully, that was the case because the last thing she needed was more conflict.

He stopped at the closed door and took the chart from the plastic holder on the wall. Voices, one male the other female, drifted to him as he flipped through the pages and scanned Mr. Crawford's medical history. Adam Stone's notes indicated he had regular physicals and was a generally healthy man who exercised and took care of himself.

He knocked once on the door and heard a deep voice say, "Come in."

Alan was sitting on the exam table, a wet white towel draped over his left forearm. He was wearing a short-sleeved green-collared shirt with an embroidered grizzly bear on the left front. His worn blue jeans showed dark splotches that could be oil, but it didn't appear that any clothing had adhered to the wound.

"Hi, Justin."

"Alan. I'd shake your hand and ask how you are, but rumor has it there was an accident."

"Hot grease." Michelle's chin quivered as she stood beside her husband, worry evident in her eyes.

A feature that she'd passed on to Emma. No wonder Maggie had noticed the resemblance. He was surprised he hadn't seen it before. Probably because he hadn't been looking for it. Now he saw the similarity in the curve of her cheek, lip and brow lines, the shape of the forehead. And their eyes were the same warm shade of brown shot with specks of gold. She was still a very attractive woman and in twenty-five or thirty years this is what Emma would look like.

"Justin?" Alan's voice was a mixture of pain-laced tension with a dash of teasing. "Should I be worried?"

"Sorry, Alan." Justin pushed all thoughts aside and focused his concentration on the patient. "Let's take a look and see what we've got."

After sliding on a pair of disposable gloves, Justin lifted the towel to look at the wound. The area from just above the wrist almost to the elbow was bright red. So far there was no blistering and he gently touched the area. The patient hissed out a breath.

"Sorry." Justin met the other man's gaze. "Believe it or not, pain is a good sign."

"Oh?" Beads of perspiration popped out on the other man's forehead. "Obviously I'm still breathing, but on every other level it just plain sucks."

"Pain is an indicator that it's a second-degree burn and only two layers of skin are affected. No pain would mean that it's third-degree trauma and all layers of skin destroyed. That type of injury can't heal without surgical intervention and recovery is more than twice as long. Scarring is usually severe."

"So I'm lucky." He smiled at his wife, who nodded.

"I'll need to reevaluate this in a couple of days to make sure, but all signs point to you being very fortunate."

"If it turns out to be more severe," Michelle asked, "what's involved in surgery?"

"I'd need to debride the burn—that means remove the dead skin. Then apply a graft."

"From Alan's skin?" she asked.

"That's right. We take it from the buttocks or inner thigh, somewhere it's not noticeable. Then it's applied to the open wound as a covering and held in place by a dressing and a few stitches. All of that is done under general anesthesia because, honestly, it's a painful procedure. But that's worst-case scenario. We're not there yet. And I don't think surgery will be necessary if the burn is taken care of now."

"Then I guess pain *is* good."

"It's annoying," Justin agreed. "But always a good idea to pay attention."

"In the meantime, what's the treatment?" Alan asked.

"Skin is the largest organ in the body and the first line of defense when there's an injury. But infection is a major risk with injuries like this. Many medications are hard to use with burns. Some cause pain. Others are effective only against a narrow range of bacteria." Justin met his gaze. "So, I'm going to clean it up with Betadine, then apply a coating of silver sulfadiazine cream. It doesn't initiate pain and should knock down most bacteria. It lets the body devote all energy to healing instead of depleting reserves to fight infection."

Alan nodded at his wife. "Probably a good thing you bullied me into coming to the clinic."

"I'd say so." She looked at Justin. "He kept insisting ice water and lavender were just what the doctor ordered."

"And she demanded to know if I'd bought a medical degree online," her husband teased.

Justin laughed. "The internet is full of information, but not all of it is accurate. When in doubt consult a health care professional."

"We're lucky to have you in Blackwater Lake, Doc."

"It's a great place to live and I'm happy to be a part of this community and Mercy Medical Clinic." He took a prescription pad from his lab coat pocket and started to write on it. "This is the cream and I want you to put it on twice a day. Keep the affected area covered with nonstick pads and gauze to hold it there. I've given you several refills, and if you need more just have the pharmacy call for an authorization."

Michelle took the paper from him and put it in her purse. "Thank you, Justin."

"For now, I'll clean and dress the wound."

"That's going to hurt, right, Doc?" Alan glanced at his wife.

Justin nodded sympathetically. "I believe in telling the truth. It will smart, but I'll be quick."

Michelle looked at her husband with the same concerned expression that Emma sometimes wore. "I'll stay if you want."

"She can't stand to see someone she loves in pain," Alan explained. "With our boys there were always stitches, scrapes and even a broken bone once."

"I felt like the world's worst mother when Alan held their hand through the treatment." She sighed. "We both agreed that was probably better than me passing out or getting sick in front of them."

"You're an amazing mother," her husband defended. "And we're a team. What I did was easy. You kept the rest of the family calm and on a steady course. That was hard."

Justin could see their family dynamic at work. It's how they'd gotten through the trauma of their daughter's abduction. The divorce rate was very high in situations like that, but Emma's parents beat the odds. She came from strong and resilient roots. He just wished he could make her see that deep character she'd inherited would get her through.

"So, you're going to be in the waiting room, honey?"

Michelle nodded. "If he passes out, you know where to find me, Justin."

"I'll be fine." Alan leaned over and kissed her quickly. "Don't worry."

"Yeah, that'll happen." She opened the door and stepped out, then closed it behind her.

"I thought she'd never leave."

"Excuse me?" Justin stared at him.

"Look, Doc, you get the hard part done, then we'll talk. There's something I want to ask you."

Justin didn't get the feeling it was about anything serious. In spite of the no-doubt-painful burn he'd suffered, Alan Crawford was excited and had clearly wanted his wife out of the room for some reason.

After retrieving a basin from the cupboard above the sink, Justin handed it to the patient. "Hold your arm over that. I'm going to disinfect the wound."

"Okay. I'm bracing myself."

Justin worked quickly to wash the burned area. Then he took the sterile pad and smeared it with silver sulfadiazine cream, placing the compress over the affected area before winding white gauze around the arm to hold the covering in place.

"That wasn't too bad, Doc."

"Good. A tip for changing the dressing. It's easier on you if the cream goes on the pad first."

"I'll pass that information onto my wife."

"If necessary, try over-the-counter medications for pain. But if that doesn't help, call me and I can prescribe something to make you comfortable."

"Will do."

"Okay," Justin said. "So, what did you want to ask?"

"I'm having a birthday party for Michelle." He grinned. "She's turning fifty-five. I didn't get my act together when she was fifty and she won't be expecting this until the next milestone at sixty. So I think I can pull off a surprise with this one."

"Sounds reasonable." Justin wasn't sure why he was sharing this.

"I want you to come."

"Me?" He slid his hands into his lab coat pockets. "Why?"

"She likes you." He shrugged. "Go figure."

"Thanks, I think."

"Seriously, the invitation is for the whole clinic staff and I'd be grateful if you could extend it to everyone for me. That way, Michelle won't catch on. It will be tricky enough to have it at the house without her getting suspicious, but I'll figure out something."

Justin folded his arms over his chest. "I don't know what to say."

"Say you'll be there. And bring someone. Michelle would call it your plus one, and if you don't have anyone with you, it's pretty much a sure thing that she'll fix you up. So if you know what's good for you..."

"I don't really know anyone to ask." Emma popped into his mind, but that probably wasn't a good idea.

"I'm sure there are a lot of ladies in Blackwater Lake who would like to change that. But if you want my advice, you should invite that pretty nanny of yours." He held up his good hand to stop a protest. "I saw you two at dinner in the diner. Seemed like you were getting along fine."

They had been, Justin remembered. But that was before he'd taken her to bed. "I don't know…"

"Call it a job perk for her. She's with the baby all day and sure seems to love what she does, but I'm sure she'd enjoy an evening out. Michelle sure did when we had four little ones."

Justin saw the dark look in his patient's eyes for just a moment and knew what he was thinking. "I know about your daughter being taken. I don't mean to pry—"

"I know. The thing is, sometimes I need to talk about her." Alan sighed, his good hand fisted on his thigh. "In our hearts we never moved on from the baby we lost, but for the sake of our sons, we couldn't stand still."

"That took a lot of courage."

The man shook his head. "It was all we could do. The cops told us there was probably no chance that she was still alive, but we think about her every day and hold out hope that she'll come home. There are stories on the news with happy endings. It happens."

"That's true," Justin said. He could feel this man's emotional pain and was deeply tempted to tell him the truth. But it wasn't his truth to tell.

Alan met his gaze. "Closure is something of a cliché, but only people who go through what we did can understand why it's precious. We'd just like to know what happened to our baby girl."

Justin simply nodded. There was nothing he could say that wouldn't betray Emma's confidence.

The other man blew out a long breath, then slid off the exam table. "Michelle and I really like you. I hope you'll come to the party. Bring Emma and Kyle, too. We think the world of that little guy."

He is my *world,* Justin thought. Just as Emma would have been for her parents. This party might be just the thing to put her mind at ease. All he had to do was figure out how to convince her to go.

"Knock, knock."

With a very sleepy Kyle in her arms, Emma stood just outside Justin's office and rapped lightly on the door frame. The baby tried to imitate her and slapped at the molding. He was growing so fast, getting big and heavy. He was all little boy in his footie pajamas and ready for bed.

His father smiled. "Come in. The door is always open."

"Literally," she teased. "Seriously, you never close your door. And this little boy can get pretty loud and rambunctious." She hugged the baby and nuzzled his neck until he laughed.

"It seems like the paperwork never ends. There are charts to update and procedures to study. I like to plan and be prepared before a surgery."

"Patients like that in a doctor."

He laughed. "But I always want Kyle to feel he can come in if he wants. For any reason."

"Even if it's to take this new walking thing out for a spin?" She set the boy down on his feet and steadied him before letting go. "I told him it was time for bed and he made a break for it. I grabbed him up just outside your door."

"Were you coming to say good-night, pal?" As the boy rounded the corner of the desk, Justin picked him up and held him close for a moment.

The sight of the strong man holding his child and the love shining in those intense gray eyes never failed to trip up Emma's heart. Justin Flint was capable of such deep emotion, and any woman fortunate enough to win his affection would be extraordinarily lucky. She knew he wasn't willing to take a chance now, but maybe someday a woman would come along to chase away enough of the bad memories for him to try again. Emma also knew she wasn't that woman.

The sex had been amazing and if he were a less principled man it would have happened again. She ached from wanting him, but he was too ethical and honest to promise what he couldn't give. The morning after had been awkward, but they'd both pretended to ignore what happened and the uneasiness passed. He was friendly, a little reserved, but that was to be expected. Emma was doing her best to follow his lead. He would never know her feelings for him had grown stronger.

Justin was talking quietly to the toddler, who was doing his level best to get at the computer, paperwork and other office paraphernalia that were too tempting to a little boy.

He looked at her. "I'm not sure whether or not to be proud that he doesn't give up."

"Repeat this ten times. Determination is a good quality in an adult."

"Meaning, not so much in a one-year-old."

"You got it. Also keep in mind that this stage doesn't last forever. He'll learn what's okay and what's not."

Kyle almost got his little hands on the stapler, and Justin stood up so everything was out of reach. "And that's something not okay. I shudder to think what staples would do if he swallowed them."

"It's my job to make sure that doesn't happen," she said.

No one could take better care of him than her, Emma realized. That wasn't ego talking. It wasn't about the job. It was love, pure and simple.

When Kyle couldn't get to what he was after, he let out a loud wail and began to rub his eyes. Then he leaned to-

ward her and tried to wriggle out of his father's arms. Good
luck with that, she thought. The man had that devastating
combination of strength and tenderness that would have
women throwing their panties at him if he were a rock star.

Kyle cried again and she moved closer to take him,
trying to ignore the sparking sensation when her hands
brushed Justin's.

"Okay, kiddo. I know you're tired. Time to go night-
night." The toddler's nose was running and she fished a
tissue from her jeans pocket to wipe it. Then she turned
so Kyle could see his father. "Tell Daddy good-night."

Because she was facing away from him, Justin couldn't
see the yearning she knew would be in her eyes. But she
could feel the warmth from his body when he moved in
behind her and kissed his son's forehead.

"Sleep tight, pal."

Maybe it was wishful thinking, but she would swear
he was breathing just a little unsteadily and his voice was
this side of smoky. Whether or not that impression was fu-
eled by imagination, her body responded and liquid heat
poured through her. When Kyle was in his crib, she could
stay upstairs. All things considered, she was better off
with a flight of stairs between them.

When father and son had said their good-nights, she
started for the door, grateful to get some distance.

"Emma?"

She half turned toward him. "Yes?"

"When Kyle is settled for the night, would you mind
coming back down? There's something I'd like to talk to
you about."

"Of course."

He looked serious and she wondered if this was where
he gave notice that the situation wasn't working for him.
Her stomach dropped at the thought of leaving Kyle. And

Justin. She wasn't sure which one of them she would miss more and knew they were a package deal.

She walked up the stairs and Kyle seemed to get heavier in her arms as he relaxed into sleep. Normally she rocked him in the glider for a few minutes, but he was practically out now. Pressing her lips to his forehead, she decided he didn't feel too warm, but the runny nose and cranky disposition were out of character for him. She hoped he wasn't getting sick.

Emma put him on his back in the crib and covered him with a light blanket. "Good night, little man. Sleep well."

She turned on the night-light, picked up the baby monitor and tiptoed from the nursery and down the stairs. Prepared to meet Justin in his office, she was surprised to see him sitting in the family room. She wasn't sure what to make of that, figuring he'd wanted to discuss her continued employment, and the office was best for that kind of conversation.

She walked over to the sofa and set the monitor on the coffee table without sitting down. "So what did you want to talk about?"

"I saw Alan Crawford today at the clinic."

Several things raced through her mind. Did Alan know something about her? Or was he at Mercy Medical Clinic because of a health issue? It surprised her that she felt anxious about a man she barely knew.

"Is he all right?" she finally asked.

Justin nodded. "An accident at the diner. He'll be fine."

She wanted to fire questions at him, the way she'd done with her mother's doctor after the breast cancer recurred. But she didn't have the same relationship with her biological father. And how messed up was that?

"I know I can't ask you for details on his condition because of privacy issues. That would put you in an awkward position."

Justin nodded. "But you could ask him yourself."

"I can't do that." She shook her head. "No way can I march up to the counter at the diner and say, 'So you saw the doctor. Care to share?'"

"You don't have to go to the diner," he said mysteriously.

"What do you mean?"

"Alan is having a surprise fifty-fifth birthday party for his wife."

It was noteworthy that he didn't say the get-together was for her mother. Emma appreciated his sensitivity. "That's really sweet of him, but I'm not sure what that has to do with me."

"I was invited and he suggested you come along."

"Why?" Did this mean he wasn't terminating her employment? Suddenly, sitting down seemed like an awesome idea, so she did. She was at a right angle to him on the full-size sofa.

"He said you probably needed a night out and remembered that Michelle appreciated it when they had four small kids."

"Four? But there are three… Oh," she said when his meaning sank in.

"Yeah." He rested his elbows on his knees.

"Why did he ask you?"

"Actually, he invited the whole staff at the clinic. To put a finer point on it, he asked me to invite the staff because he couldn't figure out how to do it without spilling the secret to his wife. I got the feeling he's pretty much inviting most of Blackwater Lake. He said the diner is closing down for the evening so their staff can attend, but the gathering will be at their home."

"I see." No, she didn't. "It's really nice of him to think of me, but it's probably not a good idea."

"For whom?" His question was direct and challenging.

Instead of answering him immediately, she made a lateral move. "Who's going to take care of Kyle? I can't leave him."

"Alan said we should bring him. Other people are bringing their kids along." He straightened and leaned back against the sofa. "This would be a good opportunity for you to get to know your family."

"You're probably right about that," she agreed. "But I'm not sure about telling them who I am. It doesn't seem right to put them through all that emotional upheaval when they seem okay."

Part of her actually believed that. The other part figured fear was holding her back. Fear of rejection followed by having to move on with her life. Moving on might mean leaving town and she was selfish enough to want this time with Justin to go on just a little longer.

"You need to know something, Emma." He blew out a long breath. "It might appear that they're okay, but I still saw the pain in Alan's eyes. He told me they went forward for the sake of their sons. People have to move on when something bad happens."

"You didn't," she pointed out, not sure why the words tumbled out of her mouth.

His eyes darkened, but his voice was calm when he answered. "My situation was different. I moved on emotionally before my wife died. Not wanting to make another mistake isn't the same as living in the past."

Maybe not, but that distinction didn't make much difference to the present. It was just wrong that a man so capable of great love would be alone by choice. The realization made her angry at the woman who'd done this to him.

"I'm sorry. It's none of my business." Although that didn't keep her from having an opinion.

"Don't worry about it." He met her gaze and something hot slid into his before he said, "The thing is, I have another reason for wanting you there."

"Oh?"

"Alan warned me that if I'm alone, his wife will do her best to fix me up with someone at the party."

"I see." She couldn't help smiling now. "So, this is all about you."

"Of course."

"You're not worried that we might be the focus of town hearsay, grist for the gossip mill if we're seen at a big party together?"

"Nope? You?" Again he was issuing a challenge.

She decided not to share the fact that because they lived under the same roof they were already rumor central with the moms at Kyle's play group. Emma figured that was a pretty good sampling of what was being said all over Blackwater Lake.

It was clear that for his own reasons he wanted her to go with him to this gathering. And when he'd first asked, she'd had every intention of turning him down, even though it was a very good opportunity to interact with her parents, not to mention her brothers. Oddly enough, it was the matchmaking thing her father had probably said in jest that changed her mind.

For the record, jealousy was a powerful motivator.

"All right, Justin. You've made your point. I'll go with you to the party."

Chapter Ten

The next morning, the party several weeks away was the last thing on Emma's mind.

After talking with Justin, she'd gone upstairs when Kyle whimpered in his sleep. He'd been up every couple of hours during the night with a stuffy nose until finally she'd sat in the chair with him in her arms. He was fitful but did get some sleep, and rest was the best thing for a cold. It was morning now, but she was still in the glider chair, moving back and forth with the baby in her arms.

She kissed his forehead, partly to assess his body temperature, but mostly because she needed him to know she cared. "I don't like it when you're not feeling well, sweetheart."

Justin walked into the nursery as he did every morning, freshly showered and shaved. He looked like a Hollywood heartthrob, while she resembled a back-to-nature reality show contestant who'd been on the island too long. She shouldn't care; it wasn't part of her job to be camera ready. Since she couldn't quite control the feeling, she acknowledged the flaw and let it go for now.

"Hi." She kept her voice soft and low.

His forehead creased with worry. "What's wrong?"

There was no point in asking how he knew that. The humidifier was going and this wasn't how the morning usually started.

"I had a bad feeling when I put Kyle to bed last night." Then she'd gone back downstairs and Justin had convinced her to attend the Crawfords' party. Her issues seemed so small when this little guy was sick.

"Why? What was up last night?"

"He was a little sniffly. More tired and cranky than usual." She lifted her shoulders in a shrug. It was hard to put that instinctive sensation into words. She *knew* this child so well and cared so deeply about him, she was tuned in to his needs. "Just a feeling. I didn't want to be right, but he has a cold."

"Did he sleep through the night?" Justin asked.

She shook her head. "About every hour he woke up crying. Finally, about four I just held him."

"Oh, Emma—" He dragged his fingers through his hair. "I didn't hear a thing. You should have gotten me up."

"I would have if there was something you could have done. But there was no point in both of us being tired. And you have to work today."

"Does he have a fever?"

"It's about a hundred. I've been giving him fluids and checking his diaper. It's wet, so he's well hydrated."

Justin started pacing. "I think Adam should take a look at him."

"I'm pretty sure it's just a virus." She looked at the baby when he whimpered in his sleep. "Unless something changes and his temperature spikes, it might be better to treat him at home rather than expose him to more germs at the clinic."

"I have connections there." He stopped in front of her and looked down, concern darkening his eyes. "He won't have to sit in the waiting room."

Emma nodded. "If that's what you want, I'll bring him in today."

"I'll call Adam. Kyle will be the first patient in and out before normal working hours start."

"Okay."

Justin used his cell to call the family practice doctor, who agreed to meet them before the clinic opened its doors. When he put the phone back on the case at his belt, she stood up and handed him the baby.

"I'll throw some clothes on."

Emma went to her room and dressed in jeans, sweater and boots. She ran a brush through her hair and sighed at the dark circles under her eyes.

"You should see the other guy," she said to her reflection.

Less than five minutes later she joined Justin in the nursery where Kyle was awake and fussy. She put fresh supplies in the diaper bag and looked at the sippy cup on the table beside the glider chair.

"I'll refill that and get him ready to go."

Justin stood and gave her the baby. "Let me do the cup."

"Okay. Half water, half ginger ale." She saw his disapproving look and said, "Now isn't the time to worry about nutrition. He likes it and will drink. The most important thing is making sure he's hydrated."

"You're not a pediatrician."

"Neither are you."

"But I am a doctor." Annoyance chased away the worry in his eyes for just a moment.

"But your specialty isn't babies. I've cared for a lot of little ones. They're not just small adults."

"I know that."

She blew out a long breath. "Look, we can stand here and argue about what he should drink or get him to someone you trust to tell us."

He nodded curtly. "I'll meet you downstairs."

"I can drive him to the clinic. Then you'll have your car there and won't have to bring us home."

"I'll drive." He walked out of the room before she could say anything else and that was just as well.

She put the fussy baby on the changing table and he rubbed his nose and eyes. The frustrated whimpering broke her heart.

"I know, sweetheart. I wish I could make you all better, but it just takes time."

She felt guilty for snapping at Justin. In spite of the one mistake that had landed the two of them in his bed, she and her boss got along really well. He was easygoing and a devoted father. Today he was a worried one and the tension made him short-tempered. She'd been up most of the night and was tired, which made for a volatile mix.

About twenty minutes later she and Justin were in exam room one at the clinic and Adam Stone was taking a look at the boy. Emma had met him at Kyle's one-year checkup and liked him very much. He was tall, dark and handsome, but on him it wasn't a cliché. Married to Blackwater Lake girl Jill Beck, he was a stepfather to her son, and the two had a baby of their own on the way. More important, he was a nice man and easy to talk to.

"His temp is just under a hundred," Adam said.

Justin was standing by the examination table trying to comfort his son, who was wearing nothing but a diaper. "He might need an antibiotic."

The other doctor said nothing as he cupped the rounded end of the stethoscope in his hands then placed it on Kyle's chest and back, listening intently. "Sounds good. You said he's not coughing?"

"That's right." Emma was standing beside her boss, aching to hold the baby but reluctant to overstep. Trying to figure out where she fit in here.

"I'll just have a look at his throat and ears."

Kyle wasn't the least bit happy at being manhandled this way and reached out to Emma, refusing to hold still. That did it. She didn't care if she was overstepping. No way would she stand by and watch when this baby was so upset and wanted her. She reached past Justin to pull the boy into her arms and he clung to her. In moments the hiccuping sobs started to subside.

"I'm sorry, Dr. Stone. But when he cries like that it breaks my heart. Would it be all right if I hold him while you do the examination?"

"Absolutely," he approved. "If he's calmer, I can get a better look at what's going on."

She cuddled the baby close and cooed to him reassuringly while the doctor listened to his back, then used a scope to check his ears. Kyle squirmed, but quieted when she whispered that everything was all right and just hold still a little longer. Dr. Stone actually managed to get a quick look in his throat, too.

"His nose is running from crying," he observed. "Any color to the secretions?"

"I don't think so." Justin looked blank for a moment then deferred to her. "Is there?"

"No. They've been clear." She rubbed her hand soothingly up and down Kyle's bare back as she swayed from side to side. "Is it okay if I get him dressed?"

"Sure." Adam had a wry expression on his face as he looked at his colleague. "You've got it bad, bud."

"What?"

"It's a syndrome a lot of doctors come down with when their kids get sick. The main symptom is forgetting everything you learned in med school."

Justin rubbed his neck. "So I'm overreacting?"

"Yeah. When the child is yours, you run on pure emotion. Logic and training go out the window. In a couple months when Jill has the baby, you can give me a hard time when my turn comes."

"I'm holding you to that," Justin promised. "So, Kyle is all right?"

"It looks like a virus and you know as well as I do that it just has to run its course. Antibiotics won't do anything unless he has a bacterial infection and prescribing them now runs the risk of him becoming resistant to them if he really needs one. Don't worry. He's going to be fine."

"That's what Emma said."

She was sliding denim overalls on Kyle but looked over her shoulder and smiled. "I didn't expect public acknowledgment."

Justin looked sheepish. "She told me it wasn't serious and hydration was the most important thing."

"She's right. Whatever you can get him to take. Clear liquids, even Popsicles."

"Ginger ale?" she asked sweetly.

"That's good." Adam nodded thoughtfully. "You probably already know this, but a slight fever isn't dangerous. It's the body's defenses kicking in to fight whatever is attacking. Keep an eye on it and use over-the-counter children's medication if necessary. If you're concerned about anything, call me."

"Thanks, Adam." Justin looked at her. "Consider this more public acknowledgment of your expertise. You were right about the ginger ale."

"He's a sturdy kid and has an excellent nanny," the other doctor said.

After he was dressed, Emma picked Kyle up from the exam table. "Thank you, Doctor."

"Anytime." He looked at Justin. "I'd like to talk to you about a patient. Do you have a minute?"

"Sure." He looked at her. "Would you mind waiting for me in the break room? You were also right about keeping him away from sick people."

"Not a problem," she told him.

Adam just grinned as she walked out and closed the door. She knew the room he wanted her to wait in was down the hall by the backdoor and walked there with the baby in her arms. A woman wearing pink scrubs was pouring herself a cup of coffee. Emma remembered nurse Ginny Irwin from Kyle's one-year checkup.

Her salt-and-pepper-colored hair was cut in a pixie style. Blue eyes snapped with intelligence and something that looked a lot like curiosity. "Hi, Emma."

"It's nice to see you again, Ginny." She smiled at the little boy, who shyly buried his face in her neck. "And you probably remember Kyle Flint."

"I do." She smiled, then stared at Emma as if she was trying to remember something. "You remind me of someone."

She'd heard that before; people said it all the time. But, right here, right now, it meant something different. She knew her father and mother had been in the clinic yesterday. And before that, Maggie Potter had commented about her resemblance to Michelle.

"You know what they say—" She struggled to be casual. "Everyone has a double."

"Maybe." Ginny blew on her steaming coffee. "But I'd swear I've seen your double recently."

"Maybe I just have one of those faces." Her heart pounded and she hoped it didn't show. Explaining wouldn't be easy.

"Could be." She smiled at Kyle. "And speaking of that, he sure looks like his dad. This little boy is a cutie."

"That he is." As was his father.

"Nice to see you again. I'd love to stay and chat, but I need to get back to work."

"Don't let us hold you up. Have a good day." Emma returned the smile as the other woman left the room.

When she was alone, she let out a long breath. If Ginny recognized that she had a look-alike when they weren't even standing together, the resemblance to her mother must really be strong.

She'd looked nothing like the people who raised her and had never questioned it. What if there'd been a medical emergency and the truth came out with no warning? The shock would have been horrible. Since coming to Blackwater Lake she'd made her decisions based on her wish to spare the family any upset. But what if more people noticed the resemblance when they were together? And they would be together at the party.

She had to say something; she knew that. Now she wondered whether it would be easier to hear the news before or after the birthday party.

"Thanksgiving isn't for a couple of weeks. I could have gone grocery shopping for everything on my own," Emma said for the tenth time. "You didn't have to give up a day off to help."

Justin would have known she was in the car even if he couldn't see or hear her. The fragrance of flowers drifted around him and he was pretty sure that even Kyle, who was safely strapped in the backseat, could smell it. The three of them were just leaving the store parking lot and Justin checked traffic on his left before turning onto Main Street.

"Helping you buy and carry all that stuff is the least I could do to make up for being a jerk when Kyle was sick."

"Thank goodness he's better now."

"So you *were* worried." Justin made the turn, then glanced at her.

"Of course. But my concern was handled in a sensible, I've-got-a-plan way."

He appreciated her leaving out the part where his concern had manifested in an almost complete breakdown-of-rational-thought way. Glancing in the rearview mirror, he smiled at the bright-eyed little boy looking out the window and chattering away in the backseat. Halloween had come and gone. It had been a week since Kyle had been sick, but Justin still felt bad for taking out his anxiety on Emma. What was that saying? *You always hurt the ones you love.....*

No, it wasn't that. He couldn't think of a label for this *thing* simmering between them, but no way he'd call it love.

"Next time he's under the weather, I promise to defer to your wisdom," he vowed.

"I'll believe that when I see it." Her tone was brimming with amusement.

"How can you say that?" he protested. "I'm guilty before the fact?"

"We hope Kyle will never be sick again, but that's probably not realistic. As you well know, Doctor, he has to take his immune system out for a spin every now and then to exercise it. And when that happens, there's every reason to believe you'll do the same thing."

"Which was?"

"You'll behave like any other loving father would."

"But I'm a trained physician. I know better."

"There's no way to be objective when your child is the patient. Under those circumstances, a little knowledge is a dangerous thing. Knowing the worst makes it harder to stay calm."

He heard the patient understanding in her voice that somehow was approval of how he'd acted. The words were like a pardon and made him feel closer to her somehow. Like they were partners. Like... Nope, couldn't go there either.

Keep it light. "So, helping with the shopping is my penance for going into freak-out mode."

"Apparently you're a steadfast believer in do the crime, do the time?"

"It's fair to say that, yes."

"I'm not sure about this. Lugging an eighteen-pound lump of frozen poultry, plus all the rest of the Thanksgiving dinner fixings, seems like an out-of-proportion penance for behavior that was completely human and understandable."

He glanced over and thought how ordinary and special it was to have her there. She was sweet, steady, sexy and stunning. If things were different, he could be thinking that he was the luckiest guy in the world that she was with him. They could be any teasing, laughing couple out with their son. But that wasn't the way it was. If he reminded himself enough, maybe he would stop wanting her so badly.

"Human," he said. "You're very diplomatic, Miss Robbins. Sylvia would have had some colorful things to say about my behavior."

"If that's a challenge, you should know that I can be colorful," she defended.

"Okay. Right here, right now, dispensation from professional. Go for it. Be colorful."

"Let's see." She tapped her lip. "All right. Here goes.

You were a little insufferable, maybe a tad condescending. Just a bit egotistical and dismissive."

"Really? That's all you've got?" He laughed. "Sounded more classy than colorful."

"I've got more, but…" She angled her head toward the baby in the backseat. "Little ears. Kids absorb a lot more than adults realize. And Kyle is starting to repeat the sounds he hears."

"Then thank goodness he hears you. What he learns will be refined. Not to mention the extensive vocabulary he'll pick up."

"Please tell me that's not you putting pressure on him. You're not going to be one of those demanding fathers who makes his son study every waking moment. You know the kind. The one who goes ballistic over a B+ in school because it's not an A."

He heard the teasing in her voice and quickly looked over at her. "Have you met me? Do you not see what a marshmallow I am with him?"

There was laughter in her eyes. "So, you're one of those permissive parents whose child can do no wrong?"

He braked at a stoplight and rested his forearm on the steering wheel, thinking that over. "I could probably get behind that philosophy."

"I see we need to have an in-service on the merits of balance in parenting."

"Are you mocking me? Is that sass?"

"Probably. But only because you gave me a dispensation from being professional."

"Remind me not to do that again, Emma."

From the backseat Kyle said, "Mama—"

She half turned and looked at him. "Hey, sweet pea. Did you say Em-ma?"

"Mama," he said again, distinctly pronouncing both syllables.

"He's trying to say Emma. You know that, right?"

"I know."

And yet, mothering came so naturally to her that it seemed right somehow to call her that. Anyone could see how much she loved this child. In a perfect world, she would be Kyle's mother, but the world was far from perfect. There were no legal ties binding her to them. She worked for him and could move on anytime. The thought of that bothered him so much more now than it had during her interview.

He met her gaze for a moment, then the light turned green and he drove on. "Would it bother you if that name stuck?"

"Would it bother you?" she countered.

"It's as close to giving him balance as possible," he finally said. "He doesn't have a mother and will never know what it would have been like to have her in his life."

"And that bothers you. Even though you mentioned her—flaws."

He nodded and turned the car right, driving around the lake. "He'll never have a two-parent home, something most kids take for granted."

"I think what you need to focus on is what he *does* have."

"And what's that?" he asked.

"You." Her full lips curved into a smile. "There are a lot of children who don't have mothers or fathers. They're being raised by grandparents or other relatives. Or in the foster-care system. Or on their own, not knowing where the next meal is coming from. Kyle has a father who loves him enough to be an insufferable jerk when he's worried, but his mother is gone. Will that make him different in school?" She shrugged. "Maybe. But it's his reality and he'll adjust to what is."

"So you don't think he'll turn to drugs and alcohol to fill the void?" he joked.

"Did I mention that you have a flair for the dramatic?" She laughed. "He'll learn his values from his environment and unless there's something I don't know about, his surroundings are pretty okay."

"You think he'll be all right?" That was a completely serious question, because it would always be a concern.

"He'll make friends who are drawn to the bright, funny boy he is. People will like him or not for himself. Not who you are or because his mother isn't around."

He turned into his driveway and pressed the automatic door opener, then drove into the garage. "Are you saying I should let it go?"

"Yes."

That was good advice and he'd take it. He opened his car door. "Okay, then. Let's take this stuff inside."

"I'll get Kyle. You take the groceries."

"How is that balance?" He met her gaze before she got out of the SUV.

"You're still doing penance." She grinned, then slid to the ground.

That wicked smile cracked open a nugget of need that most of the time he managed to shut down, but right now he couldn't do it. Fortunately, she was busy getting the baby out of the car seat and didn't notice the longing Justin knew was in his eyes.

"I'm going to give him lunch, then put him down for a nap."

He reached into the rear of the SUV and grabbed several grocery bags at once. "He doesn't look tired to me."

"Trust me," she said. "He is."

Just then the little boy rubbed his eyes and yawned. Justin supposed that's what they called a "mom thing." A woman didn't have to give birth to know a child. His wife had carried Kyle inside her and had never bothered to get to know him. She'd been more concerned about her post-baby body.

As he carried everything into the house, Emma put Kyle in the high chair and gave him finger food while she assembled his lunch. He got some of it in, but then turned crabby and threw his sippy cup on the floor.

"He's done." She lifted him out of the chair and hugged him close. "I'll take him upstairs and clean him up. Then little man is going down for a nap."

Justin nodded and put the turkey in the freezer. After starting to unpack the grocery bags, it instantly became clear that he didn't have a clue where anything went. In surgery he had a system and wanted scalpel, gauze and sutures placed exactly the same way every time. He wanted to be able to find them with his eyes closed. Obviously the kitchen wasn't an operating room, but Emma would want to be able to find things.

It wasn't long before she was back with the baby monitor. "He's out cold."

"Already?"

"It's that time of the day." She looked at the boxes and cans littering the kitchen island and started putting them away. Holding the boxed stuffing in her hand, a sad look slipped into her eyes. "It just occurred to me."

"What?"

"This is the first Thanksgiving without my mother."

She'd had the same feelings around Halloween and Justin knew she was still grieving. Every holiday without the woman she'd thought was her mother would be difficult. There was a reason that the mourning period in the olden days officially lasted a year. But the woman had stolen Emma's life.

"She wasn't your mother. The woman kidnapped you." He knew it was probably the wrong thing to say but couldn't stop the words.

"I know." There was confusion and frustration in those two words. "What she did was wrong. But she never gave me reason to question whether or not she was my mother. She loved me, raised me."

"I can see how much you care for Kyle. Like a mother. Like you were cared for, but she robbed your real mother of that." Justin hated seeing her so tortured, but he had to say this. "Your mother would want to know that you're alive, and well, and happy."

"What are you saying?"

"I would never tell you what to do," he said. "But put yourself in her place. What if someone took Kyle? How would you feel? Wouldn't you want to know that he was all right? I certainly would."

She stared at him for several moments, then turned away and covered her face with her hands. Her shoulders shook with sobs.

"Emma— Damn it."

Justin moved close and put his hands on her arms, then turned her against his chest. He wrapped his arms around her and pressed a kiss to her hair. "I'm sorry. That was uncalled for. I shouldn't have pushed. Please don't cry. You can add lout, oaf and boor to that list of colorful adjectives."

She let out a sound that was part sob, part laugh. "It's okay. You're right about this." She looked up at him, tears streaking her face. "I've already made up my mind to tell them who I am, but after the party. I don't want to do anything to spoil Michelle's day."

"That's good." He studied her face.

Her cheeks were blotchy and there was distress in her eyes. But he saw something else, too. Yearning. Desire. Longing—everything he was feeling. And suddenly the need to comfort wasn't nearly as strong as the need to kiss her. The wanting was so big it pushed out shouldn't, wouldn't, couldn't.

He could and did.

He kissed her.

Chapter Eleven

Emma sighed at the touch of Justin's lips. Her mind had barely absorbed the sudden shift in mood, when he was kissing the tears from her cheeks and her heart went all mushy. In truth, it wasn't completely unexpected. Promises to be scrupulously professional had not smothered the sparks flaring between them. Right this minute she couldn't remember and didn't care about anything but being as close to this man as possible.

She slid her arms around his waist and he deepened the kiss, then traced her lips until she opened to him. He stroked the roof of her mouth and fire exploded through her. In a heartbeat the sound of their labored breathing filled the kitchen.

Just as suddenly, he took a step back and pulled her arms away, then brought one of her palms to his lips and pressed a kiss there. "I'm sorry."

She blinked at him. "For kissing me?"

"I'll never regret that." Tenderly he grazed her cheek with his knuckles. "I didn't mean to make you cry. I'd never hurt you. It's just that the words were out before

I thought them through. It's none of my business. I'm sorry—"

She touched a finger to his lips to stop him. "It's all right."

His jaw and his eyes turned the color of clouds growing into a thunderstorm. "That's not all."

"What's wrong?" she asked.

"Emma—" He blew out a long breath. "I don't want to want you."

"I know." She couldn't look at him now because she knew what she had to do. "Everything will be much simpler if I just go upstairs."

"It would be simpler." He squeezed her hands and didn't let go. "But in my opinion, simple is highly overrated."

The meaning of his words sank in and her gaze jumped to his, where need burned in his eyes. "Give me complicated any day of the week."

"I was hoping you'd say that." Then he looked at the baby monitor on the counter. "Kyle—"

"He usually naps for an hour or so."

"Or so…"

Justin threaded his fingers through hers and they walked to his room. Bright sunshine shone through the window as if smiling on them. They stood by the bed, close enough to feel the body heat but not touching.

He leaned down and when his lips touched hers, every single cell in her body responded. Being here with Justin felt too darn good to regret anything. Suddenly heat accumulated beneath her clothes and she yanked them off as fast as possible. Justin did the same and she shamelessly looked at the lean, hard lines of his body.

To look and not touch was like dieting in a bakery. She rested her hand on his chest and savored the arousing texture of the coarse dusting of hair that tickled her palm.

TERESA SOUTHWICK   155

Dragging a fingertip over the contour of muscle, she marveled at the beauty of his male form.

As her fingers trailed over his stomach, Justin sucked in a breath and caught her hand. Rays of sunshine coming through the window made the tension in his eyes glitter as he drew her onto the bed. After sliding under the covers, he kissed her, a slow insatiable kiss that was edgy and exciting. He dragged his mouth over her cheek and jaw then took her earlobe between his teeth and gently tugged until tingles danced over her shoulders and down her breasts.

Shivering with need, she turned on her side to face him and met his hungry lips with her own, wanting more of the whole-mouthed kisses that rocked her soul. At the same time, his hand cupped her breast, tracing lazy erotic circles over the sensitive softness until her skin burned and heat gathered everywhere. He slid lower, cupping her as one finger entered her.

"I can't wait, Justin," she gasped. "I need you now."

"Yes—" His voice was ragged, his breathing labored.

He left her long enough to open the nightstand drawer and then she heard the effective rip of the foil packet he'd grabbed. When he'd covered himself, he rolled to her again and took her in his arms.

With a grin, he pulled her on top. "I want to see all the expressions on your face."

It was her nature to be shy, but she wasn't with Justin. She straddled his hips and lowered herself slowly until they were one. Pleasure roared through her as sensations rushed fierce and fast. Too soon shudders began spilling over her in waves that made her light-headed with pleasure. He gathered her to his chest and held her until it was over. Gently, he rolled her to her back and settled on top, then slowly moved inside her.

His face was taut with tension and concentration as

he rocked against her, his thrusts lengthening until he groaned. Emma wrapped her arms around him and kissed his shoulder until he was still and spent. They stayed locked together for a long time before he sighed and slid away, leaving the bed to go into the bathroom.

Though the last thing she wanted was to move, Emma forced herself to get up. She dressed quickly and went to the kitchen where some groceries still waited to be put away. Her mind was racing, mostly telling her one time in his bed was a fluke. Twice was a pattern.

Before she was ready to face him, Justin walked into the room fully dressed, carefully staying just inside the doorway to keep his distance.

"Emma, I—"

"Don't." She met his gaze and panic skipped over her raw nerves. "Please. Let's not talk about it."

He slid his fingers into his jeans pockets. "We're going to have to at some point."

She wanted to tell him if they both worked really hard, it would be possible to ignore what just happened. But that wouldn't make the problem disappear any more than doing nothing had resolved her family issues. She was through running away from it.

"You're right."

"It was a moment of weakness," he said.

That was an understatement. "What are we going to do about that?"

"Not be alone together."

There was a tone in his voice saying what she had already realized: How were they going to pull that off what with living in the same house? She knew the answer but couldn't bring herself to say it.

And then Emma heard a sleepy, waking-up sound come through the baby monitor. "This discussion needs to wait for a bit. I have a lot of thinking to do and when we talk, there probably shouldn't be distractions."

More echoey, little-boy chatter squawked from the nursery and Justin nodded. "I agree. Do you want me to get him?"

"That's okay." She felt the need to hold the baby while she could. "I'll go."

She hurried up the stairs and her thoughts seemed to move just as fast. Earlier, Justin had said that he shouldn't have brought up anything about telling her family the truth, that it was none of his business. But he was wrong. The fallout from her revelation would affect everything and she was tired of wondering what it would be.

She was ready to resolve her life. It was the reason that she'd stayed in Blackwater Lake, and the time had come to do it. She could easily fall in love with her boss and she needed to tell her family who she was and give Justin notice that she was leaving town before she couldn't leave him at all. He'd made it clear that he wasn't interested in anything serious. If she stayed, she'd never be more than the hired help and an occasional lover.

That would destroy her.

Emma had never been so fidgety and nervous in her life. She and Justin had just pulled to a stop at the curb just up the street from the Crawford house, where her parents were inside. A lot of other cars were parked up and down the street, so they weren't the first ones to arrive.

Justin turned off the ignition and opened his door, letting the car's overhead light turn on. "Are you ready?"

"Yes."

"That's a lie."

"Busted." When had he come to know her so well?

"But I'll never be ready for this, so at least I can be punctual for the party."

"That's the spirit."

"Do you think Kyle is all right with Maggie?" They had just dropped the little guy off at the Potters' house. She touched the handle but didn't pull it to open the car door.

"I'm sure he's fine. He has excellent taste in friends, by the way. Danielle is very cute."

"She takes after her mom."

At play group that week Emma had mentioned the upcoming party and Maggie had offered to take Kyle for a couple of hours so the two little ones could play together. She wasn't going to the party but knew about it because her mother was a friend of the Crawfords and would be there along with town business owners, professionals and longtime friends. The staff from Mercy Medical Clinic were all planning to attend.

"Don't worry, Emma. Maggie has both of our cellphone numbers. If she needs us, she'll call."

"I know. You're right. It's just that this is the first time I've left him."

"Now you know how I feel every day." The interior light revealed his wry expression. "And you, Miss Robbins, are procrastinating."

"I was kind of hoping you hadn't noticed."

"Nothing gets by me." He grinned. "Mostly. Come on. Whatever happens, I'm right there with you."

"Thanks."

"Don't mention it."

When he slid out and shut the door, the SUV interior went dark, letting the night back in. She suddenly felt cold, alone and anxious. A single word of gratitude seemed totally inadequate when the truth was that she wouldn't have gotten this far without Justin Flint. It wasn't only the job that had made it possible for her to stay, but also the favor of a shoulder to lean on and someone to talk to. The dark was a reminder of how alone she was going to be when she had to quit her job.

But that wasn't happening tonight.

She opened the car door and slid to the ground. Justin was there and rested his hand at the small of her back as they moved down the street toward the house, then stepped up on the curb and walked along the curved sidewalk to the Crawfords' front door. The path was lined with vividly colored fall flowers and there was grass on either side. Her parents lived in a neat, two-story white clapboard house with hunter-green trim and a matching front door. There was a wraparound front porch with white Adirondack chairs where they could sit and greet neighbors who walked by or watch their children playing on the lawn.

Emma realized she had no idea how the woman she'd thought was her mother had managed to abduct her and get away with it. Suddenly she wanted to know how it all went down, and these people had the answer.

The sound of voices drifted to the porch from inside the house. Quite a few guests were already here. Justin rang the bell and a few moments later the door was opened by Alan Crawford.

He grinned. "Glad you could make it, Justin."

"Me, too. Thanks for the invitation. You know Emma."

"Hi." When did her throat get so dry?

"I've seen you in the diner. Nice to finally meet you."

"Same here," she managed to say.

He closed the door, then looked at Justin. "You should know that Michelle wasn't surprised. She figured out what I was up to a couple days ago. Still don't know how I tipped her off. Fair warning, Justin. She said men aren't subtle. Whatever that means."

"When you figure it out, let me know."

"Take a number," he said ruefully.

Emma smiled at the banter as she nervously looked around the inside of the house where her parents lived. One thing she'd learned in her time as a nanny is that a person's surroundings contained clues about their character. Michelle and Alan Crawford had a warm and spotless environment, if the entryway was anything to go by. The two-story entry had a dark wood floor and brass coat rack by the front door where jackets, hats and scarves were hanging. A chandelier hung from the high ceiling and was shining on the dark maple banister and railing, Framed pictures of lakes and mountains hung on the expanse of wall that joined the two floors and there was a wooden bench at the bottom.

"Hang your coats on the rack," Alan said. "Or you can put them on the bench there."

"How's the arm?" Justin asked, taking off his jacket and holding his hand out for hers.

The other man made a fist and flexed his forearm. He was wearing a sweater over his checked cotton shirt and the bandage was hidden. "It's healing nicely. No pain anymore."

"Glad to hear it." He hung up their coats.

"The birthday girl is in the living room," he said. "What can I get you to drink?"

"Beer for me," Justin said. He looked at her and his expression said he was wondering how she was doing.

"Do you have a chardonnay?" she asked.

"It's Michelle's favorite. Coming right up. I'm pretty sure you know a lot of people here. Go on in and make yourselves at home." Alan moved down a hall that presumably led to the kitchen.

"You okay?" Concern darkened Justin's eyes.

"As well as can be expected." She glanced at the place where the man disappeared. It would take a while to think of him as her father, if she ever could. "He seems nice."

"He is. Shall we go say happy birthday?"

There was no getting out of it now. Again he put his hand on her lower back. It was touches like this that contributed to her "moments of weakness." but right this minute she was very grateful to have him there.

His fingers were warm, his smile encouraging. Her heart skipped a beat and she was almost certain that would never change. She could and would have taken this step alone, but his steady presence helped her put one foot in front of the other. And when it was all over, she knew he would be there with a shoulder to cry on or as someone simply to talk to.

They turned left into a large room where the wood floor continued. An area rug contained a grouping of furniture that included two hunter-green floral-covered love seats and a couple of club chairs. The conversation area had a coffee table in the center. Ben McKnight and Camille Halliday sat on one love seat with Adam Stone and his wife, Jill, on the other. All of them waved a greeting.

Emma recognized Mayor Goodson, an attractive brunette who could be anywhere from thirty to fifty. She was leading Blackwater Lake's robust development, a strategy that included a summer and winter resort that would break ground soon.

"Who's that man standing by the love seat with the attractive brunette? The couple talking to Ben?" Emma looked up at Justin.

"Ben's brother, Alex, and his fiancée, Ellie Hart."

"Looks like they're having fun." And she wasn't just referring to the fact that all three women had varying sizes of baby bump. Love? Or something in Blackwater Lake's water? She wouldn't put her money on magic. If it existed, Justin might have been tempted to take another chance on love.

"That looks like a couples area." His tone said it was a place he didn't want to go. "And we're on a mission. Remember? Mingle with your family."

"Right." Knowing them a little better might make it easier to tell them who she was after the party was over. In a day or two.

As they walked farther into the room, people greeted Justin. It seemed practically everyone had been to Mercy Medical Clinic. More impressive, he remembered all the names and introduced her. Unfortunately, the detour just fed the tension growing inside her. Eventually they made it to where Michelle was standing with another woman beside the large fireplace, which had an impressive oak mantel. A roaring fire was going there. The two were obviously friends and as they moved closer, she extended her good wishes to the birthday girl and moved away.

Michelle smiled warmly. "I'm so glad you both could come."

"Me, too," Justin said. "I believe you've met Emma."

"Yes. How are you?"

"Good," she lied. "Happy birthday."

"Thank you."

Emma hesitated a moment, trying to think of something to say. Then she recalled what Alan had told them.

"How did you find out about the surprise party?"

Michelle's eyes twinkled. "When you've known someone as long as I've known Alan, it's pretty tough to get away with anything."

"How long have you known each other?" she asked.

"We were high school sweethearts."

"That's a while—" Emma realized what she'd said and

stopped. "I mean—" She shook her head. "There's no recovery from that. Let me just say you look fantastic."

"For my age." The woman grinned good-naturedly.

"For *any* age," Emma said sincerely.

It wasn't like looking in the mirror. More a preview of how she might weather the years. Awfully darn well if she'd inherited this woman's DNA. The lovely skin was relatively unlined and her trim shape showed that she took good care of herself.

"Life does march on and leaves footprints on a face," she said honestly. "There's a reason it's called a time line."

And life had thrown her a major curve, Emma thought. She'd been knocked around but hadn't gone down. That was impressive.

"So, you met your husband in high school. When did you two get married?"

"Right after graduation," she said.

"Your parents didn't have a problem with both of you being so young?" Emma asked.

"They just knew we were determined to be together and bowed to the pressure. And I'm glad to say they never regretted supporting our decision." She smiled, remembering. "I had the first of three boys about a year later." She glanced at the mantel beside her with lots of framed photographs sitting there.

Emma followed her gaze and realized the pictures were all family, individual and group. Dead center of all the frames was a photograph of an infant dressed all in pink.

It was a baby picture, a child roughly six weeks old. That had to be Emma and it was the only one. She couldn't seem to stop looking at it. Had she been stolen shortly after the photo was taken? Or like the average family who thinks they have all the time in the world, did they just get too busy to take more?

"That's Sarah Elizabeth."

Emma's gaze snapped back to the woman and there were tears in her eyes. From newspaper articles about the kidnapping she'd known the name she was given at birth. But hearing it from her mother's lips... What was she supposed to say?

"I'm sure you heard that she was kidnapped. It was a long time ago, but people remember. We'll always be the couple who own the diner and lost their little girl."

Profound pain brimmed in her mother's eyes and broke Emma's heart. "You don't have to talk about it. This is a happy occasion. It's your birthday."

"Mostly I don't say anything, but sometimes I find myself thinking about her and the words just come out." She wiped a tear from her cheek. "I'm sorry."

Emma touched her arm, a gesture of comfort. "It's all right."

"I didn't mean to do that." The other woman's mouth trembled when she tried to smile. "It's just that every once in a while I can't hold back the thoughts. Where is my child? How is she? Is she happy? Is she all right?"

This was the moment Emma had come to Blackwater Lake for and instantly her uncertainty disappeared. There was no question in her mind about the right thing to do. Her parents were in conflict every single day because of not knowing what happened to their child.

To *her*.

If Kyle disappeared, the not knowing would be hell. Justin was right. She looked up at him now and he nodded slightly, encouraging her. It was way past time to end her family's nightmare. Party or not, she had to tell them and knew now how wrong she'd been to wait so long.

She was about to say something when Alan walked

over with drinks in his hand. He gave the beer to Justin. "Here you go. And I have a glass of white wine for you."

A cold drink would feel good on her dry throat, maybe dislodge the lump there, but Emma's hand was trembling too badly to take it.

She shook her head, then looked at each of her parents. After taking a deep breath, she said, "You might want to sit down because I have something to tell you both."

Chapter Twelve

Emma hadn't let herself have any expectations about her family, let alone prepare for this moment if it ever came. She usually didn't have trouble speaking her mind, but she was at a loss for words now. The sound of conversation around them disappeared as if some mysterious force had dropped a cone of silence.

Michelle's expression went from curious to just this side of anxious. "What is it, Emma?"

"Why do we have to sit down?" Alan asked.

Justin cleared his throat. "Is there somewhere we can go that's quiet? With no people around?"

"They're everywhere," Michelle answered. "Kitchen, family room, dining room. Even the backyard. I don't understand— Why do we have to go somewhere private? It's never a good thing when someone says that."

"No one's in the garage," her husband said.

"Let's go there," Justin quickly said before either of them could ask more questions. He put his hand on Emma's elbow, a small bit of contact that was both encouraging and reassuring. "Trust me, you're going to want privacy for this conversation."

"You know what this is about?" Michelle's expression was even more apprehensive when she looked at him. "Now you're starting to scare me. Please, just say it."

"Justin's right. Let's go in the garage," Emma said.

Again, not the setting she'd pictured, but there probably wasn't a chapter in any etiquette book to cover this situation. She looked at her father. "Lead the way."

He nodded grimly and offered the white wine he was still holding to his wife. When she shook her head, he set the glass on an end table then took her hand and led her through the house. They filed past the family room, where guests milled around, and finally turned down a hall. They walked through a door in the laundry room and into the cold, dark garage.

Alan flipped a switch on the wall and a dim bulb overhead flashed on. As garages went, it was average except for one thing. There was a place for everything and everything in its place. Overhead suspension storage held bins of what looked like Christmas decorations. Tall white cabinets lined the walls and there was a workbench with Peg-Board above it for tools. Two vehicles were parked side by side, one a truck, the other a compact car.

"There's nowhere to sit unless we pull out the folding chairs." Alan put his arm around his wife's shoulders. "So, whatever it is, just say it. We've had more than our share of bad and we're still standing."

Emma could see him bracing for something awful. "Well, I hope this isn't bad. I don't think it is after what you said about wanting to know where your daughter is."

"You know something about our little girl?" Michelle's voice broke.

Emma met her gaze and saw fear and hope in the other woman's eyes. No more dragging this out. It must be excruciating for them. "I *am* your daughter."

There was complete silence for several moments as they stared at her. Probably she should have taken her father up on the offer to get out folding chairs.

Emma felt compelled to fill the hushed quiet. "I found out because my—" She couldn't call the woman "mother." That woman had turned their lives upside down and let Emma grow up living a lie. She was looking at her mother, the one who'd brought her into this world, and saw tragedy and pain on her face. With all her heart she wanted to erase it.

"The woman who took me only confessed the truth when she was dying. She gave me your names and told me where to find you."

Then she stopped, letting them absorb the information and steeled herself for skepticism and anger. They'd probably want a DNA test.

"You look just like your mother did in high school." Alan's voice was soft and cracked with emotion. "I can't believe I didn't see it."

"You weren't looking," Justin said.

"Maggie Potter saw." Michelle reached up and clutched the hand her husband had put on her shoulder. "At lunch that day when she had Danielle and you brought Kyle in with you. She noticed our eyes were the same color and the shape of our faces is similar. But I never thought—"

"I remember."

The other woman stared at her as if she couldn't look hard enough. As if she might disappear. "Does Maggie know who you really are?"

"No."

"But Justin obviously does," the woman continued.

"I felt it was necessary to tell him. Whatever happened would affect him and his son. I hate lies and should have been completely honest at the initial interview, but I wasn't sure what to do if I didn't get the job." Instead of firing her, he'd been nothing but caring and sympathetic in letting her find her way.

"Let me get this straight." Michelle blinked as if everything was slowly sinking in. "You've been here in Blackwater Lake all this time? Right here in town and didn't tell us that you're alive and well?"

"Yes. I'm sorry." And she felt incredible guilt. "I just knew everything would change. It was such a shock to me, finding out. I can't explain—"

"You've grown into such a beautiful young woman."

Her mother didn't sound angry, but Emma wondered how she couldn't be. "I didn't want to cause you more pain, or upset you. It sounds so silly now, but—"

Michelle's eyes filled with tears, this time joyful ones. She smiled. "I'm the complete opposite of upset. There are no words to express what I'm feeling. This is a moment I'd given up hope of ever having. I think that's why it didn't sink in when Maggie pointed out the strong resemblance. After so many years without a word, you just give up. Come here, baby." She pulled Emma into her arms. "My daughter. My girl."

Emma had so many feelings rolling through her, but mostly she felt a sense of peace and rightness. And emotion. Tears filled her eyes as she held the other woman and they stayed like that for a long time. Finally she pulled back.

Her mother put a shaking hand on her cheek and with her thumb brushed the wetness away. "Can you believe this, Alan? She didn't want to upset us."

Her father shook his head and his eyes were moist when he gently tugged her into a quick, hard hug. "No, I can't believe this. We thought about you every single day and prayed. Both of us thought it but we couldn't say out loud that we believed you were never coming back. I never knew being wrong could feel so good."

When he let her go, Emma looked at them. "I'll take a DNA test." She met Justin's gaze and he nodded slightly, letting her know he'd make it happen. "Then there will be no doubt."

"All right. But I'm absolutely sure you're my child," her mom said. "The family resemblance is unmistakable. You'll see when you meet your brothers. They're here, you know."

"That's going to be weird," she said. "But I've always wanted a big brother."

"How about three?" Alan grinned.

"The more the merrier," she said.

"DNA." Michelle shook her head as if to say that was a foolish idea. "If looks aren't enough proof for you, the innate kindness you showed in not wanting to upset us is a giveaway. It's something your father would do."

"Not you?" Emma asked.

She shook her head. "I upset people on a fairly regular basis."

"Your mother is fibbing, big-time."

"Then there's her choice of career," the big fibber went on. "Only someone who loves children would work with them like you do."

"That's just like your mom," Alan explained. "She couldn't wait to have babies."

Emma didn't think this was the time to tell them that the woman who took her also loved children, but her way of showing it was self-centered and destructive. This wasn't the time for that conversation.

Instead, she said, "I always knew I wanted to work with children—" She glanced at Justin, quietly supportive through this whole surreal nightmare and silently heroic right now. He was just watching over all of them. "In so many ways Justin made this reunion possible. If not for him I might not be here now. He gave me a job so I could earn a living while I was conflicted about what to do. He never pushed, but the way he loves his son finally convinced me that telling you was the only thing to do."

Alan held out his hand. "Thanks, Doc. For taking care of our girl. We're grateful to you for that."

"My pleasure." He smiled at her and even in such dim light the heat in his eyes was evident.

Emma felt the effects of that look all the way to her toes and the reaction showed no sign of weakening any time soon. There were decisions to make but this wasn't the time or place to make them.

"Justin—" Michelle stopped and just gave him a big hug. "I don't have the words. But nothing says thank-you like free meals at the diner for life."

"It's not necessary but much appreciated," he said. "And I'm not noble. Emma is really something. She's terrific with Kyle and a great cook. My guess is that she takes after one or both of you in that department."

Words of praise had never bothered Emma before. Really, who didn't want to hear they were doing a good job? But that was the point. He was talking about her work performance, when the reason she put her heart and soul into everything she did for him was profoundly personal.

She cared very deeply about Justin Flint and his son. None of it felt like a job.

Her father sighed. "I can see why you wanted to tell us about this quietly, Justin. Thank you for that, too. And breaking up this reunion is the last thing I want." He cocked his thumb toward the door leading into the house. "But there's a birthday party going on and folks are going to notice that the guest of honor is missing."

"Right." Her mother looked uncertain. "My daughter coming home is the best gift I've ever had. It's going to be practically impossible to keep it to myself. Your brothers will want to meet you. Do you mind if we share the news now?"

"I'm okay with whatever you want," Emma said. "You're the birthday girl."

"All right, then. It's efficient to let half the town know now so that when the rumor spreads maybe it will be something close to the truth." She linked her arm with Emma's. "Let's go announce the best possible news, sweetie."

The endearment warmed Emma's heart more than she'd thought possible. It wasn't comfortable with them yet, but she had a mother, father and three brothers. A family who was happy to have her home. She wasn't alone any longer.

She glanced at Justin and felt her heart drop as a realization hit hard. Her past was finally settled; her future was anything but.

Justin pulled into the driveway and stopped the SUV next to the empty space where Emma's car was usually parked. But tonight it wasn't there. He'd had a surgery that went late and told her this morning not to expect him for dinner. In the afternoon he'd received a text from her letting him know she and Kyle might be at her parents' when he got home. They'd been invited for dinner.

She'd seen them every day since telling them her true identity over a week ago. And he was glad she was getting to know the family.

He got out of the car and walked up the steps. The windows were dark and that was different, not in a good way. The house hadn't been dark when he arrived home from the clinic ever. First, Sylvia had been there with Kyle, and now Emma. But not tonight. After unlocking and opening

the door, he flipped on the light switch in the entryway.
At least he could see his way now, even if the strangeness
didn't go away. His first stop was the office, where he left
the paperwork he'd brought home.

Then he went to the kitchen. Like the rest of the place,
this room was unwelcoming. There were no good smells or
happy baby sounds. Even unhappy ones. Especially there
was no cheerful female chatter. No laughter. It was as if
the house was missing its heart.

"And that weird, whimsical thought deserves a beer,"
he said to himself.

He opened the refrigerator and grabbed a longneck from
the shelf on the door. In front of him was a plate of pasta
covered with plastic wrap and beside it sat a salad. On the
wrap was a note.

Justin: In case I'm not back when you get home
there's balsamic vinaigrette dressing, your fave, for
the salad. Put the plate in the microwave and hit
the button that says—wait for it—plate. =) Emma.

For the first time since turning into the driveway, he
smiled. Each word written in her familiar, neat, artistic
handwriting was wrapped in her voice. It made him miss
her more.

After tossing the salad and warming the food, everything was on the table beside his half-empty beer bottle.
A place setting for one. The high chair was neatly tucked
away by the wall and there wasn't another plate out. Everything just felt wrong.

And then he heard the front door open. A few moments
later Emma appeared in the kitchen doorway with Kyle in
her arms. He was sound asleep with his head on her shoul-

der, so obviously she'd managed to get him out of the car seat without waking him.

She moved closer and whispered, "He went out like a light on the drive. I know you like to spend time with him in the evening and I can wake him—"

"No. He looks so peaceful." At least one of the Flint men was.

"Worn-out is more like it." For a quick moment she touched her cheek to the baby's, an automatic tender gesture that clearly showed how deep her feelings went. "I'm going to put him to bed."

"Okay."

The sight of her and Kyle lifted Justin's mood some. The house was just as quiet, but knowing she was there smoothed over a restlessness he'd never known before. Day in and day out he'd been so consumed with seeing her, wanting her and not having her that there was no room to wonder what it would feel like without her.

Now he had a clue.

It wasn't long before she was back. Justin knew he was going to hell, but couldn't stop the rush of thank-you-God that the baby was settled and they were alone.

She looked at the table. "I can see you found dinner. Do you want me to heat it up?"

"Already done. It's a big portion. We can share it."

"I couldn't eat another bite. Michelle and Alan fixed a great dinner."

Justin nodded. "Why don't you keep me company while I eat?"

She glanced around the kitchen, either looking for an excuse to avoid him or just making sure nothing needed her attention. Then she smiled.

"Okay."

They sat across from each other and he took a long drink from his bottle of beer. "So, how was your day?"

"Really good." The happy smile made her radiant and more beautiful than ever. "How was yours? The procedure went well?"

"Perfect. It's delicate work, transplanting skin to cover a wound that doesn't want to heal. But I think there will be a positive outcome now."

"I'm glad."

As always, she didn't ask who the patient was. She already knew that privacy concerns prevented him from saying anything and didn't push. There were rules, even in a town as small as Blackwater Lake.

"Pasta is really good," he said after taking a bite.

"I got the recipe from Michelle. She's an amazing cook. I can learn a lot from her."

"You're a pretty incredible cook yourself."

"Thank you." But she shook her head, an awed expression on her face. "But I'm nothing like her."

"So it sounds as if you're getting to know them."

"Yes." She folded her arms on the table. "I can't believe how silly it was not to tell them the truth right away."

If that had happened, Justin thought, she never would have applied for the nanny job and he wouldn't have gotten to know her. Now it was hard to remember a time when she hadn't been here, in his life.

"I'm glad it's going well." Justin chewed a bite of salad and couldn't miss her serene expression.

"They're wonderful people. We've been bonding over the smallest things. Like how we talk with our hands. Certain gestures. Facial expressions."

He finished off the salad in the bowl, then said, "Inherited traits."

"Exactly. It's amazing when you think about it. Things

I have in common with Michelle and Alan. My brothers. Even though we didn't grow up together."

That surprised him. "Are they still here?"

"Yes. Even though the three of them have high-powered jobs and careers and aren't local." She shrugged. "I thought they'd leave right after the party, but they decided to juggle appointments and work remotely. To get to know me." She grinned. "I can't believe it. One day I'm all alone and the next I have a father, mother and three brothers. A real family."

What was he? Chopped liver. All this time with him had she felt abandoned? He'd done everything possible to make her feel included. Hadn't he?

Justin was happy things were working out for her, but a nagging feeling of discontent settled over him. After eating half the pasta, he pushed the plate away.

"You're finished?" There was surprise in her voice.

"It was filling."

She stood. "I'll take care of the dishes."

"I've got it."

"Let me put the leftovers in a container for your lunch," she offered.

"Okay."

Justin did his thing and she did hers and the whole time she kept up constant chatter about her new family.

"I brought Kyle's pajamas along in case time slipped away. It seems to do that when I'm over there. Michelle helped me give him a bath."

"Oh?"

"Can you believe she still has tub toys from when my brothers were little?" She was at the island and glanced over her shoulder to look at him. "She's saving them for grandchildren."

"So I guess she's looking forward to that."

Emma nodded. "So far she says the boys aren't cooperating, but she continues to hope."

"Optimism is good."

"Can't argue with that." She snapped the lid on the container and walked over to the refrigerator with it. "Kyle is so busy at their house and they love playing with him. But it sure does wear him out."

Partly he was pleased that his son was able to experience yet another social outlet, but a darker part of him wasn't so thrilled. He finished rinsing his dishes then dried his hands. Emma was close enough that he could reach out and touch her, pull her into his arms.

Kiss her.

"They are amazing people," she said. "I'm glad I came here and so grateful for all you did for me."

She moved in front of him and stood on tiptoe to press her lips to his cheek. Quickly, before he could shift and capture her mouth with his the way he planned, she backed up out of reach. The distance she was deliberately putting between them bothered him. And the way she was using past tense—*glad I came here. All you did for me…*

Was she saying goodbye? Preparing to give her notice?

For a short time tonight Justin had seen a glimpse of life without her and it unsettled him. When he'd been married, most nights he was alone while Kristina was out being the toast of Beverly Hills. He'd known her a lot longer and missed her a lot less than he'd missed Emma tonight.

And then there was Kyle. If she disappeared from his life, he was old enough to notice. She'd be gone and he wouldn't understand why. That could leave scars on a kid. Justin had to do something to make sure that didn't happen.

And without thinking it through, he said, "There's something I need to say."

"All right. Shoot." She looked up at him expectantly.

"I think we should get married."

Chapter Thirteen

"I'm sorry?" Emma blinked. "You want to do what now?"

"Get married."

It was on the tip of her tongue to say this is so sudden, but that sounded like something from a bad movie. All she could do was stare.

"Say something, Emma."

"Okay. You asked for it. This is so sudden." She turned away and began to massage her temples. Her head was starting to throb.

"You're right. I'm doing this badly. I'll pour us a glass of wine and we'll talk it through."

"I'd like that." She turned and smiled as hope squeezed through the knot of confused tension coiling through her.

Justin opened the refrigerator and pulled out a bottle of chardonnay. He took a foil cutter and corkscrew from the kitchen drawer and muscled the cork out, making the whole process look like the sexiest thing ever. Then he poured some of the pale yellow liquid into two glasses and picked them up.

"Follow me," he said.

Emma didn't trust herself to speak and simply nodded. She walked behind him into the family room, where he set the wine down on the coffee table. The stemware were side by side, an indication the two of them should sit next to each other, too. She went first and he sat down, so close their thighs brushed. And she still didn't know what to say.

This was big.

She hadn't been at a loss for words since... Come to think of it, the same thing happened when she told her parents who she was. That was big, too. And that started her thinking.

Who was she?

She'd been raised by a woman who wasn't her mother, a woman who'd stolen her away from her family. She'd grown up in a lie. Then her fiancé, the man she'd thought loved her, turned out to be a lying, cheating jerk who slept with other women pretty much the whole time they'd dated.

And now, Justin had said she should marry him. The question had to be asked.

"Why?"

"Why what?" He rested his elbows on his knees.

She stared at the full wineglasses neither of them had touched. "You said we should get married. That came out of nowhere. What's going on?"

"It makes sense."

"Really? To whom?"

"Think about it." He looked at her. "Don't we get along well? We have fun."

"Yes."

That was too true. In and out of bed. Justin made her laugh, something that had gotten her through a really bad time. But what was he proposing? Shouldn't it be more?

"And then there's this. Tell me you don't love my son." An element of challenge crept into his voice.

She met his gaze then. "I can't imagine loving him more if he was mine."

Justin's eyes went from teasing to tormented. "His own mother was too selfish to give up her parties and shopping for her own child. He's lucky to have you."

And the light was beginning to come on. "What is this really about, Justin?"

"You. Me." His movements were a little stiff when he took her hand into his and rested them on his thigh. "It's all working. More than one person has said what a beautiful family we are. Kyle would have a mother and father. We could give him normal."

Something was off; too many steps had been skipped. From the beginning Justin had indicated his goal was to do anything necessary to make his son's life as normal as possible. Anything but fall in love. Marriage without it was how far he was willing to go for his son. That was too far for her.

"As much as I care about Kyle, that's not good enough."

A muscle jerked in his jaw. "We like each other. That's important and a hell of a lot more honest than what I had before. Or what you had."

"And that's the thing. You told me after we, you know…" Had sex was what she was trying to say. Her cheeks burned, but she had to soldier on. "You were very clear that I should understand there was no chance of anything serious between us. You didn't want to lead me on." She looked at their joined hands and pulled hers away. "So I have to ask, Justin. What's changed?"

"It just seems like a good time," he said, not really answering the question.

Emma studied him and didn't think he was deliberately lying, but this wasn't the complete truth. Everything he'd said described the relationship they had and it had been fine until she revealed her true identity to her family. She'd done what she came to Blackwater Lake to do. So...

And then she got it.

Her mission was accomplished and he believed she would go back to her life in California. His life here would be disrupted, and more important, Kyle would be upset. A legal commitment would trump an employment contract and keep her here in Blackwater Lake. But the plan was fundamentally flawed.

He looked down at his feet. "So, I've made my case. What do you say?"

Deep down she'd hoped very hard that he would come up with the right reason to propose marriage. It broke her heart that he hadn't. "There's a problem."

He shook his head. "I don't think so."

"Maybe it's just a problem for me." She straightened and took a deep breath. There would be no taking this back. "You used the wrong L-word."

"You're not making sense."

"It's perfectly clear to me. We *like* each other, that's true. But when I get married, it won't be for convenience. Love is the only reason to take that step."

"So you believe in it." He wasn't asking a question.

"Yes." She stood and moved away as the pain in her heart started to get bigger. "Without love, marriage is nothing but a pretense. My whole life has been a lie. I already had a fake family and I don't want another one."

"That's not what it would be like." He stood, too, and looked down at her.

"You're wrong. A little while ago you talked about doing a procedure to help a wound heal. The thing is, you have a wound inside that you simply refuse to treat. What you're suggesting isn't right for me."

"I'll make it right." He reached for her.

Emma backed away from his touch, not trusting herself to resist him and the offer that was so very wrong. And she suddenly knew without a doubt that she couldn't stay here with him.

Justin wasn't the sort of man who took no for an answer. He would continue to make his case. Where he was concerned, there'd been enough weak moments for her not to know that if one more mistake happened, it would be the biggest one of all.

"I have to go, Justin."

"Of course. You're tired. We'll talk in the morning—"

"No. I mean, I'm leaving. I can't stay here."

Shock darkened his eyes, followed quickly by something that looked a lot like a sense of betrayal. "What about our agreement?"

"I'm sorry for the short notice. We can work something out until you find someone to live in, but I can't stay here in the house with you. Goodbye, Justin."

A short time later, Emma knocked on the door where the Crawfords had said goodbye to her and Kyle just a little while ago. It was now about eight-thirty. Shifting nervously, she kicked herself for not calling ahead, but there'd been a lot on her mind after leaving Justin's. If anyone came to her door at this hour, she'd ask who it is before she opened it. Fortunately, this was Blackwater Lake and only moments passed before Michelle was standing there.

"Emma? What's wrong?"

"Is it all right if I come in?"

"Of course." Without another word the woman stepped back and held an arm out, welcoming her.

She toyed with her keys. "I have a favor to ask and it's completely all right if you want to say no. So be honest—"

"Anything you need. Tell me." She closed the door.

"Would it be all right if I spent the night here with you?" She held up her hand as Michelle opened her mouth. "Before you answer, it will probably be more than one night."

"You can stay with us as long as you want." Michelle looked concerned. "Where's the baby?"

It was a logical question. Every time Emma had been here since revealing the truth at the birthday party, Kyle had been with her. "At the house with his father."

That explained almost nothing, but she was afraid to say more, afraid she would burst into tears. Justin's marriage-of-convenience proposal was still too painful and raw. She'd left the house with her jacket, purse and a whole bunch of confusion.

"Can I make you some tea?"

"That would be nice." Hard liquor would be better, but she didn't share that. For now, she was grateful Michelle wasn't pushing for details.

They walked through the house's dim interior and Michelle flipped on the kitchen light as she entered the room. Emma sat on a barstool at the black granite island separating the food-preparation area from the family room. The sink was to her left with a window above it, and she faced the stove topped by a stainless-steel microwave. An eating nook was on her right.

It was a homey room with a white baker's rack holding cookbooks and knickknacks. There were pictures everywhere. Suspended from the ceiling was a copper rack where pots and pans hung. Behind her, a flat-screen TV was mounted on the wall with a sofa and chair grouped around it. The furniture was conspicuously empty.

"Where's Alan?" she asked.

"Out with the boys for some male bonding while they're in town. I'm quite certain that beer and a pool table will be involved."

"Sounds fun," Emma commented.

"I'm sure they think so." She took an orange teapot on top of the stove and filled it with water from the faucet at the sink. Then she set it on a front burner and turned on the gas. "Frankly, this house is way too quiet with them gone. It's really nice to have female company, and you're actually doing me a favor being here."

"I'm glad."

Emma had been so upset on her way out of Justin's house it had slipped her mind that her brothers were here. "Are you sure there's room for me to stay? I didn't think about the guys being here."

"Pierce and Zach are checked in at Blackwater Lake Lodge. Only Kane is here"

While she talked, Michelle took mugs from an upper cupboard, then opened a canister on the counter and pulled out two tea bags. She held them up so Emma could see what kind and she nodded her approval of Sleepytime. It was doubtful that would live up to its name, but maybe the warm drink would do something about the cold inside her.

"So," Michelle continued, "I don't want to hear another word about putting anyone out."

Emma was pretty sure the other woman *did* want to hear words about why she'd asked for asylum so suddenly at night. That was something she wasn't ready to discuss. At the same time, she had to admire Michelle for her restraint. Not many women could hold back the questions she must have. It was very much appreciated because Emma needed to get her emotions under control first.

For the past year she'd been trying to figure out who she really was. Since she'd become nanny to his son, Justin had been there for her and now she was reeling because he'd asked her to marry him when he clearly didn't love her.

Despite all that confusion, one thing was crystal clear.

From the moment Michelle opened the door to her, she'd felt safe. For now she'd rock that feeling. She was procrastinating again but decided to cut herself some slack.

The teakettle whistled and Michelle turned off the burner then poured water into two tall mugs. She pushed the green one over to Emma and wrapped her hands around the orange one before walking to the other side of the island and taking the tall stool next to Emma.

She blew on the steaming liquid then said, "So, Thanksgiving is this Thursday."

Obviously the woman had picked what should have been a neutral subject, but Emma's heart hurt thinking about the upcoming holiday. She'd been so looking forward to fixing dinner for Justin and Kyle, to spending the day with them. That wasn't happening now. Why couldn't he have left everything alone?

Michelle filled the silence. "Seems like thirty seconds ago it was summer and now it will be Christmas before you know it."

"I love this time of year," Emma felt obliged to comment, and truth was always best. "The tree. Lights everywhere. Santa Claus and shopping."

"Did you believe in Santa?" It was clear the other woman put a lot of effort into keeping her tone neutral, but her smile was strained around the edges.

"I still believe." The smile lost a little of the strain and made Emma glad her words were light. "No one told me he wasn't real, so I'm keeping the magic alive."

"Good for you. Kane is thirty-two years old and I think he still holds a grudge against Zach for spilling the beans. They were eight and four when that particular Christmas magic died a painful death."

Emma experienced a wave of profound sadness. A Christmas crisis that had turned into a warm family memory had been stolen from her. All she could do was hear about it. "Why would he do that?"

Michelle laughed. "Alan and I took the boys to see Santa on Christmas Eve. The three of them were just too excited to be still, and channeling the energy seemed like a good idea at the time. Then Zach sat on Santa's knee and told him something that he wanted and hadn't shared with us."

"What was it?"

Michelle shook her head. "I can't even remember. But it was too late to shop. Needless to say, the item wasn't under the tree the next morning. Also needless to say, he wasn't a happy camper, and to salvage the day, his father and I decided it was time to tell him the truth." She shrugged. "The next thing we knew, he'd decided to share the information with his younger brothers."

"Once it's out of the bag, there's no way to put it back inside."

"Isn't that the truth. We wanted to strangle him." She smiled fondly at the memory. "At least one of our children still believes."

The youngest of Emma's brothers was four years older than she was. She'd have been too young to have the secret spoiled. What she'd said about still believing in Santa Claus had been the right thing to say and she was pleased.

"I'm glad you're glad." Emma took a sip of her tea and holidays through the years flashed through her mind. All the memories and milestones a mother would have missed. She felt a responsibility to somehow make it up. "You know, I have an album of pictures you might like to see. It's a collection of photos of me that my mother—"

The other woman was just lifting the mug and her hand jerked, spilling the hot liquid. "Darn it. That was clumsy."

She set it down and slid off the stool then hurried to the sink and a roll of paper towels on a holder beside it. Emma didn't know what to do or say. She shouldn't have called the woman who'd kidnapped her "mother" in front of the one who'd given birth to her. It was a stupid mistake but habits were hard to break.

"I'm sorry."

Those two words probably didn't help, but what else could she say? The truth was out and tests had been done, proving she was who she claimed to be. They'd notified the police, who had closed the long-open missing child case. All should have been right, but it wasn't. The wounds were still open and raw.

Michelle finally looked at her. "It's all right."

"I hope you know that I'd never purposely say or do anything to upset you."

"I know. It's just..." She pressed her lips together and shook her head. "Never mind."

Emma slid off the stool. "Seriously, that was thoughtless and I—"

"Forget it." Michelle threw wet paper towels in the trash then looked at the digital clock on the microwave. "You must be tired. Are your things in the car?"

"No. I didn't pack a bag."

"I see." Clearly she didn't, because questions and concern swirled in her eyes. "Well, I'll find something for you to sleep in and we'll worry about the rest in the morning. How's that?"

"Thank you." Emma meant that in so many ways.

Michelle was being awfully gracious in spite of that distressing slip of the tongue. Emma wanted her words back in the worst way. It was ironic really. She'd barely finished saying, in reference to the Santa incident, that once something is out of the bag, there's no way to put it back. How she'd wished to be wrong.

Neither of them said anything as they walked upstairs. Michelle opened the door to a room with an adjoining bath.

"The sheets are clean. I always make up the beds right away after the boys are here because they have a habit of dropping in without warning."

"Since I dropped in unannounced tonight, it appears that's another inherited tendency."

"I guess so." The other woman smiled a little. "I'll just get you something to sleep in."

"Thanks."

Alone, Emma looked around the room. There was a queen-size bed covered with a floral comforter in shades of pink and green. Across from the bed was a dressing table with a needlepoint rose on the cushion of the chair in front of it. There were pictures on the walls and three of them were coordinating prints. One was a little girl eating an apple while reading a book. Underneath, it said Fairy Tales. The second was a girl with a paintbrush stuck in a top-of-the-head ponytail captioned Budding Genius. Last was a character that looked like Cinderella, complete with poofy blue dress and cameo choker. It said, Little Princess.

This room had not been decorated with one of her brothers in mind.

There was a quick knock on the door. "Emma?"

"Yes." She whirled around.

"Here you go." Michelle set a pair of black-and-white flannel pajamas and a fuzzy pink robe on the bed. "We're about the same height, so those should fit. They might be a little big."

"I'm sure they'll be fine. Thanks so much."

"You're welcome." She edged out the door. "If you need anything, just ask."

"I will. I really appreciate this."

"Sleep tight."

Then Emma was alone and felt like slime for what she'd said. She wished Michelle would talk about it. This felt wrong and awful just when she'd thought at least part of her life was falling into place.

In the bathroom she washed up as best she could without her own toiletries and changed into the borrowed sleepwear. She'd just climbed into bed when there was another knock.

Emma turned the switch on the lamp beside the bed, bathing the area in soft light. "Come in."

Michelle opened the door. "I forgot to tell you. If you get cold, there are extra blankets in the closet."

"Okay." She hesitated, then decided what the heck. "Can we talk?"

"Of course." The other woman walked over to the bed and sat down at the foot. "What's on your mind?"

"What I said before. In the kitchen..." She picked at the soft green blanket. "I didn't mean to hurt you. I hope you know I would never do that on purpose."

"I know."

"It's part of the reason I was so conflicted about whether or not to tell you who I am." She blew out a breath. "I know she took me. I get that, but—"

"I was shopping." Michelle had a look on her face as if she had gone back in time and was in that horrible moment. "You were in the stroller. Six weeks old. Just an infant. The beautiful little girl Alan and I had wished for after three boys. It's no excuse, but I was so tired. I stopped in an aisle that was very close to the exit door and picked up a jar. It slipped out of my hand and broke. Pickles and juice went everywhere. I was embarrassed and distracted, trying to let an employee know about the mess so no one would slip and get hurt. It seemed only a moment, but when I turned back, you and the stroller were gone."

The haunted expression had Emma sliding forward to grip her hand. "I can't even imagine how that felt."

"No one saw anything. You just disappeared. There was so much confusion, searching the store. By the time what really happened sank in, she was long gone with you."

"That must have been awful."

"An understatement." She looked around the room. "Eventually we had to put your baby things away, but your father and I always hoped you were alive and would come home someday."

"So this room was mine." It wasn't a question.

The other woman smiled. "Yes."

"It's beautiful." Emma bit her lip, trying to figure out how to say this right. "The thing is, she did a bad thing and intellectually I know that. But she wasn't mean or a bad person. She raised me, she was kind and loving. I thought she was my mother. That's how I think of her, although now I'm also angry and confused. It will take a while for all of this to sink in."

"Understandable."

"But if that hurts you or makes you uncomfortable, I can leave—"

"No. Don't even say that. The situation is bewildering and will take some getting used to, but we'll get through this." She smoothed the blanket more securely over Emma's legs, then patted her knee. "Happy doesn't even begin to describe how I feel at having you back. I'll never recover the memories and experiences that were stolen and, I have to be honest, I'm not sure I'll ever forgive her for robbing me of that."

"Her name was Ruth."

Michelle nodded. "Your father and I named you Sarah Elizabeth after both of your grandmothers."

"I'm not sure what to say, except it's a nice name, but for me it's surreal."

"I just wanted you to know. I hadn't even thought about the legal ramifications because there's a birth certificate, but obviously she, Ruth, managed to do what was necessary to enroll you in school and anything else you'd need legal documentation for."

"I don't remember any problem with it. Obviously it was forged."

"Well, we've hired an attorney to figure this all out. But, for now, I feel incredibly lucky to have you here."

Emma smiled. "Me, too. I thought I was all alone."

"Never." She nodded firmly. "You're stuck with us now."

"Speaking of that..." She met the other woman's gaze. "I don't even know what to call you and Alan."

"You can call me Michelle. Hey, you. Or anything else you'd like."

Emma smiled and slid forward to hug the other woman. "How about Mom?"

Maternal arms tightened around her. "That works for me."

"Me, too—" Her voice broke.

Her mother held on for several moments, then took Emma's face between her hands. "I'm glad we had this talk."

"I am, too."

"Now you need to get some rest."

"Good night, Mom."

"Sleep tight, daughter." She stood and smiled. "I finally will sleep well now that my baby girl is back home."

When Emma was alone, thoughts of Justin popped into her mind. And Kyle. She wouldn't be there in the morning and his careful routine would be completely messed up. He wouldn't understand what was happening and that made her feel horrible.

But Justin was there and he'd take care of the little guy until she could figure out what to do so that baby boy didn't feel abandoned.

So much for sleeping.

Chapter Fourteen

The next morning Emma had the vague, sleepy impression of being in an unfamiliar place and opening her eyes confirmed it. This pretty room was different and there was no baby chatter to greet her. Everything came back in a rush, including Justin's proposal. There was nothing vague and sleepy about the pain that squeezed her heart. She missed Kyle terribly and wondered if he missed her, too.

It was Saturday and Mercy Medical Clinic was closed, so Justin wouldn't need her today. But she couldn't leave him hanging and would call later. During a sleepless night she'd decided to make a proposal of her own. Child care without living in his house.

She'd arrive before he left for work and leave when he got home, but only until he found someone to replace her. If he had an emergency during the night, she would come over and stay with Kyle. That was the best she could do. What he'd suggested was unacceptable to her.

She smelled coffee and had the pitiful, pathetic thought that it was just what the doctor ordered. Spotting the borrowed pink fuzzy robe still on the end of the bed, she got up and put it on. When she opened the bedroom door voices drifted to her and she followed the sound to the kitchen. Her brother Kane was sitting on the stool where she'd had tea the night before.

He was very handsome, all of her brothers were, but his rumpled, early-morning scruffy look was incredibly appealing. His dark brown hair was cut conservatively short and his blue eyes were full of the devil.

Their mother poured a mug of coffee and set it on the island in front of him. She moved through the doorway and they both looked at her.

"Good morning," she said, taking the stool beside Kane's.

"Morning, sis. Want coffee?"

"More than you can imagine."

He slid his mug in front of her. "Cream and sugar?"

"Cream, and if there's any low-calorie sweetener that would be great."

"Of course there is," her mother said. "What kind of B and B do you think I run here?"

Emma smiled when all the coffee stuff magically appeared in front of her. "Careful. You'll spoil me."

"Good. I have a lot of years to make up for."

Kane's grin was all big-brother wickedness. "Does that mean I get a free pass to pick on her?"

"Not if you want breakfast, young man." She gave him a mom look designed to put a boy in his place. "Speaking of that, what sounds good? Pancakes? Omelets? Crepes?"

"I don't care. Whatever is easy. Please don't go to any trouble." Emma wasn't particularly hungry.

Her brother gave her a "what?" look. "You're missing an opportunity here. This is going to wear off and you've got to work it while you can." He leaned close and whispered loud enough for people in the next county to hear, "Say omelets."

"That's *your* favorite," his mother said. "I asked what Emma wants."

"Omelets would be wonderful. If it's not too much trouble," she added.

"It's not."

Michelle assembled the eggs, cheese, mushrooms, onions, tomatoes and cooking utensils. Her brother got off his stool and refilled all their cups with coffee.

Emma realized her father wasn't there. "Where's Alan? I mean Dad."

"At the diner." Kane had noticed the slip and for just a moment there was a sympathetic look in his eyes. "Saturday mornings are traditionally busy or he wouldn't have gone."

Her mother stopped stirring the eggs in the bowl. "I'm here and not at work because we agreed that this was where I should be this morning. He'll be home as soon as he can, so there's no need for you to feel guilty."

"Too late," she said. "You really don't need to fuss over me—"

"Yes, I do. For all these years I couldn't be with you when you needed me, but now I can. And something is definitely going on. We'll get to it. But first I'm going to cook for my two youngest kids."

"She makes really good omelets," her brother said.

"I hope so or that means you've got really bad taste, brother."

"Okay, you saw that, right Mom? She drew first blood. The gloves come off. Watch your back." He grinned, then glanced at what his mother was doing. "What about fried potatoes?"

"If you want them, get over here and help."

"What about me?" Emma asked. "I want to help, too."

"Why don't you set the table, sweetheart."

"I can do that."

When her mom pointed out where everything was, she did just that. Soon they were seated at the round oak table in the nook. White shutters covered the window, but they were open, and the towering Montana mountains were visible in the distance. Three mugs had been filled with coffee and each of them had a full plate of food.

"This smells wonderful," Emma said.

"Tastes even better." Kane shoveled in another bite.

She watched in awe as he seemed to inhale everything. "How can you eat so much?"

"It's a guy thing."

Emma managed to get down half the omelet and a few potatoes, but the knot in her stomach stopped her from eating it all. "That was delicious."

"You're finished?" Her brother looked doubtful.

"It's a girl thing." She grinned at him. "And you should know that."

"Why?"

"You're a nice-looking guy. Don't you date?"

"The better question," their mother chimed in, "is when does he find time to work."

"So, you have a flourishing social life." Emma wrapped her hands around her mug and met his gaze. "But you're not married. Why is that?"

"Good question." Michelle set her fork on the plate and joined Emma in staring at the token male. "I'd like to know the answer to that, too."

"No fair." Kane squirmed and scowled good-naturedly. "My long-lost sister is back and ganging up on me?"

"What are sisters for?" She grinned at him.

"How come *you're* not married?" His plate was clean and he pushed it away.

"Because I was engaged to a guy who I discovered had been cheating on me the whole time we were dating." Emma found that it didn't bother her at all. She could actually joke about the fiasco that was her fiancé.

"Weasel." Kane's blue eyes narrowed a little dangerously. "I'll beat him up for you."

"Okay." She rested her forearms on the table. "I always wanted a big brother to do stuff like that."

"Now you've got three," he promised.

"So, is there a guy here in Blackwater Lake who needs a visit from the Crawford brothers?" Her mother's brown eyes had a knowing glint.

"You want to know why I'm here." Emma knew it didn't take a mental giant to figure out her sudden appearance last night had something to do with a man.

Her mother squeezed her hand. "It's time to confess why you ran away from Justin."

"Do I have to?"

"You'll feel better." Kane looked at his mother when she laughed. "What? That's what you always tell me."

"For all the good it does." She sighed. "You never talk to me about anything. I'm hoping Emma will."

"Wow, the honeymoon is over," Emma joked. Then the humor faded. "I showed up on your doorstep last night and you didn't hesitate to take me in. More important, you didn't ask any questions. I appreciate that. And you have a right to know what's going on."

"I notice you didn't include me in that," her brother commented.

"You weren't here. The Crawford male-bonding ritual was more important."

"Mom told you." He shrugged. "I'm here now. And you

should know I'm not leaving. Just in case you change your mind and need some muscle."

"Good to know." She smiled. "The thing is, I can't live with Justin anymore."

"I knew it." Kane's expression was two parts gotcha and one part anger. "He made a move on you."

He'd done more than that, but she'd been an eager accomplice. "He asked me to marry him."

Kane stared at her for several moments then said, "I'm not sure what to say. Do you want me to take him out back and beat the crap out of him?"

"You don't understand—"

"Ignore your brother, sweetheart. Take your time."

"Thanks, Mom." Emma sighed, remembering that sinking sensation when that oh-wow-he-cares feeling changed because his real intentions became clear. "He was proposing a marriage of convenience."

"Why?" Kane's tone was full of bewilderment.

"He wants guaranteed child care for his son."

"But not an emotional connection," her mother finished.

"Exactly. The thing is, he was married before and it didn't go well." The details weren't Emma's to share. "But he won't let himself care because love let him down in a big way."

"Okay." Kane nodded. "So he has his reasons."

"Now whose side are you on?" Emma asked.

"Mine." He stood and picked up his empty plate. "This is where you guys get into the mushy stuff and there's nothing I can add. So, I'm out of here."

He put his plate in the sink before leaving the room.

"Men." Michelle sighed. "They're good for opening stubborn mayonnaise jars and changing a tire. But when it comes to touchy-feely issues they're not much help."

"So much for the male point of view," Emma agreed.

Her mother looked thoughtful. "Justin was serious about getting married?"

"I'm sure he was. And it's weird because at my first interview he made it clear that he wasn't looking for a wife." It was practically the first thing he'd said. "So it was a shock when he brought it up out of the blue. If he wasn't prepared to follow through, why would he have asked?"

"I think he's serious. I mean, serious feelings," her mother clarified.

"Not possible." In his bed he'd told her not to get the wrong idea, although that wasn't something she was prepared to reveal.

"He might not want to have them, but a man doesn't get to the point of asking what he asked without deep emotion to back it up." Her mother's expression turned tender. "But I'm more concerned about you. How do you feel about him?"

Surprisingly, Emma didn't hesitate. The truth had been in her heart for a while but she'd refused to acknowledge it. "I love him," she said simply.

She was certain of it. He was a good man, a good father. And he would be a good husband if he'd let himself. But he'd given no indication of changing his mind about that.

"Emma, you have to face this head-on. Hiding isn't the answer and running away won't help."

"You're right." As difficult and awful as it would be, she needed to explain to Justin the reason she'd left. "But I don't think you're right about his feelings for me."

"Maybe not. But you won't know unless you face him. And take it from me, knowing is better."

Emma knew she wasn't just talking about the situation with Justin. Her mother had lived in limbo for so many years and still had the courage to put one foot in front of the other. She was the best kind of role model.

"I need to get my clothes," she said.

"Your brother will go."

"Doesn't that make me a coward?" Emma asked.

"No. You need your own things before you have that conversation with Justin." Her mother smiled. "A girl needs to look her best."

"I'm so glad you get it." Emma stood, then leaned down to hug the other woman.

"My first mother-daughter talk." Brown eyes so like her own glistened and her mom sniffled. "How did I do?"

"Pretty terrific."

And her family was pretty awesome, too. On this journey of self-discovery Emma had worried about where she belonged. How ironic that she'd found her place and lost her heart at the same time.

And nowhere in the law of karma did it say that life would let you have it all.

Justin was relieved when Camille Halliday opened her door, even though he'd called to say he was coming over. She and Ben McKnight lived a couple miles from his house and he needed a friend to talk to. He also thought a woman's touch might help calm Kyle. The baby had been out of sorts since waking up that morning and seeing him instead of his nanny.

"Emma's gone."

"What do you mean, gone?"

"She left last night and Kyle's fussy. He's not taking it well. And you're a woman."

The little boy took one look at her and let out a wail, then buried his face in Justin's neck.

Cam rubbed a hand over her pregnant belly. "I'm definitely a woman, but not the one he wants."

"It was worth a try."

Justin didn't like this. He didn't like curveballs. His

approach to life was planning and execution. Normally it was a win-win. Not this time. He'd acted spontaneously, made his pitch and everything fell apart.

"Come inside, Justin. You look terrible."

"Thanks." He walked past her and she closed the door. "For letting me in, not the making-fun-of-me part."

Sleepless nights were nothing new. During med school, internship, residency and private practice, a doctor often didn't get eight straight hours and frequently pulled an all-nighter. But that was professional. An employee walking out should have been, too. If Ginny quit her job at Mercy Medical Clinic, it would be inconvenient, but manageable. Emma leaving felt damn personal *and* unmanageable.

"I'll put on some coffee."

"Where's Ben?"

"Shopping. I think he's bringing home a surprise for the baby." She smiled. "A glider chair. So actually it's for me. And not really a surprise."

Cam headed to the back of the house where the large kitchen and family room combination had an entire wall of windows. There was an incredible view of the mountains, and normally the beauty had a calming effect, but not today.

Carrying Kyle, Justin walked over to the black granite-covered island as big as an aircraft carrier. There were green glass jars with delicate lids and a statue of a skinny French chef. A napkin holder beside crystal salt-and-pepper shakers finished off the knickknack grouping. Everything was breakable and his son wanted it all. He let out a frustrated cry when Justin pushed the things out of reach.

"Sorry, pal. Those aren't toys."

Cam pressed the button on the coffeemaker and instantly a sizzling sound filled the room. "Did you bring anything for him to play with?"

"Not unless there's something in the diaper bag." He lifted a shoulder where it was hanging.

"So you didn't pack it."

"No. Emma always took care of that."

"I don't have any toys yet." Cam moved her palm over her baby bump while she thought for a moment. "But I've got an idea."

In the kitchen she grabbed wooden spoons out of a crockery jar on the counter, opened a drawer and pulled out plastic measuring cups, then gathered nonbreakable leftover containers and lids. She carried it all to the family room and put it on the floor.

"Set him down. This might be a distraction because everything is unfamiliar to him."

The boy watched her with interest then made a grunting sound and reached out for the new stuff. After he was settled on the plush carpet, the first thing he picked up was a spoon. The first thing he did was whack one of the bowls.

"Good idea, Cam. He can't make too much noise banging on plastic."

She poured coffee into a mug, got herself a glass of water then awkwardly settled herself on a high stool that faced the family room. "So, what happened with Emma? You said she was gone. Where did she go?"

"To her parents'." Everyone in town knew that the Crawfords had their daughter back. "She called earlier to say she would watch Kyle during the day until I can find a replacement for her."

And that ticked him off. How was he supposed to do that? A daunting prospect would be climbing Mount Everest, but replacing Emma would take a miracle.

"That doesn't sound like she's gone, as in really *gone*," Cam commented.

Justin sat on the edge of the floral-covered sofa, close to where Kyle was busily slapping a green-and-white measuring cup on the rug. "How about this, then? Her brother Kane came over for her clothes and things."

The guy hadn't said much but was clearly protective. He hadn't been at the house long, but when he left with her packed suitcase, Justin's anger melted, releasing something that felt a lot like pain. If a doctor knew anything, it was that pain was an indicator of something very wrong.

"Let me get this straight." She tapped a finger on the granite. "She didn't leave you high and dry as far as child care is concerned."

That's not how it felt. His son's routine had been thrown into chaos and that was unacceptable.

"Kyle really feels her absence."

Cam smiled tenderly at the little boy chattering away to all the things around him. Then she met Justin's gaze and there was a knowing look in her eyes. He wasn't particularly fond of the expression women wore when they became aware of something a man couldn't seem to comprehend on his own.

"Kyle isn't the only one not taking this well."

"If you're talking about me, that's just wrong. I'm doing fine, if you don't count the part where household routine is turned on its ass."

"No, you're not upset at all."

"A grown man isn't allowed to be fussy," he said.

"Just crabby," she retorted.

"I'm not—" The look she aimed at him said protesting was a waste of breath. "Okay. Maybe a little."

"So...cool, calm, collected Dr. Flint is hot under the collar. That's clear evidence this is more than your nanny giving notice. Emma *put* you on notice by leaving. Spill it, Justin. Confession is good for the soul. What really happened to send her packing?"

He blew out a breath and weighed the pros and cons of telling her, then realized he had nothing to lose. "I asked her to marry me."

Cam's expression went from surprised to pleased. Then she frowned. "If that had gone well, you wouldn't be here in a snit and she wouldn't be staying at her parents'. What did you say to her?"

"We like each other. We have fun together. Marriage makes sense."

"Obviously not to her." Cam's eyes narrowed. "What else did you say?"

"I reminded her that she loves Kyle. He's lucky to have her. If she agreed to marry me, he would have a mother and father. We could give him a normal life."

And that was when Emma had reminded him of his own warning that he wasn't looking for a wife. He'd said what he'd said because he wanted to be up front with her. Look how well that turned out. Being honest had blown up in his face.

And speaking of faces...Cam's disapproving look made him want to squirm, but he held it together. She didn't need to know that Emma had called him out on using the wrong L-word.

"You didn't tell her you love her." So much for Cam not knowing. "Look, Justin, you didn't come here because taking care of your son is a challenge for you. When he was an infant and his mother was off doing whatever it was she did, you handled that little guy like a pro."

"Thank you."

"I'm not finished." Cam slid off the stool. "Next to my fiancé, you're the most honorable man I know, so don't start lying to me now. You came here because I'm your friend and you needed someone to talk sense into you. This reaction of yours is more than just to an employee quitting."

The words struck a chord, but he didn't like the tone he got. "If you're saying what I think you are, that's not a place I'm prepared to go again."

"Sometimes our head goes in one direction," she said more gently, "and the heart goes somewhere else, whether or not we want it to."

"You're trying to say I have feelings for her?"

Cam nodded like a teacher proud of the star pupil. "Any idiot can see that you're head over heels in love with her."

Justin's mind was racing at the same time he carefully watched Kyle push to his feet and toddle around the family room. A leather ottoman doubled as a coffee table, so no sharp corners or breakable stuff there. On short, chubby legs the little boy checked things out, then tottered over to Cam. She smiled but stayed still and let him get used to her.

"Can I give him a cookie?" she asked. "Vanilla wafer. Ben likes them, but I think it should be age appropriate for Kyle. I've been reading up on all the stages."

"He'd like that."

She moved to the pantry and the little boy followed her. He was right there when she pulled out the box. After squatting to his level, she reached in and took out a cookie for him. He grinned and snatched it away then said two unintelligible syllables that sounded a little like "thank you."

Cam's expression turned soft and tender. "Good to know food is a bridge to détente."

"You're a terrific friend. And you'll be an even more terrific mom," Justin said.

"Like Emma." She met his gaze. "That woman has set a very high bar."

"She's awfully good with him. It's obvious he misses her." Justin heard the longing in his own voice.

"You know how I felt about Kristina. Your wife was a schemer, and I never minced words to you about that, right?"

"I remember."

"Obviously I'm willing to hit you with the truth on bad stuff, so my opinion should count for something." At his nod, she continued. "I'm telling you that Emma is the real deal. She's a keeper and you know it in your gut. Trust your instincts."

"Because they've never let me down," he said wryly.

Cam put her arm around the little boy who was digging his little hand in the box for another cookie. "I understand why you're feeling snarky right now, but get over it. If you don't fix this with Emma, you'll be in big trouble."

Again the words struck a chord and Justin realized she wasn't wrong about that. The question was *how* to fix it when he'd made such a mess of everything.

Chapter Fifteen

Justin liked having a plan.

He was a surgeon and before picking up a scalpel, he studied notes and photos, went through each step of the procedure in his mind. By the time he'd scrubbed in, he knew exactly where to make the incision and how much pressure to apply so that every cut was as shallow as possible. Do No Harm was the cornerstone of medical practice, but when intervention was necessary it was a doctor's responsibility to do the least amount of damage possible to the body.

So he had a plan in place when he pulled the SUV to a stop at the curb in front of the Crawfords' house. After turning off the ignition, he ticked off in his mind what he would say to Emma.

Apologize for being insensitive.

Be honest with her about his feelings. He didn't like labels and that's what had landed him in trouble. The primary message he had to convey was that he cared for her deeply. After everything that had happened to her, she would appreciate truthfulness and integrity.

Finally, he would ask her to come home because he and Kyle missed her. His son just wasn't his usual cheerful self and clearly felt the change. Fortunately, Cam and Ben had offered to keep him while Justin convinced Emma to come back.

The sun was just disappearing behind the mountains as he exited the car and walked up the path to the door. It was opened almost immediately after he rang the doorbell.

"Hello, Justin."

"Sir."

Wow, he hadn't planned to say that. He'd been on a first-name basis with Alan Crawford since they'd met. But that was before Emma had started work as his son's nanny. Now everyone in town knew that this man was her father. And Justin was here because he'd slept with the man's daughter. That was sort of what was on his mind. Mostly he wanted her back in whatever way she would have him.

His plan had only included talking to Emma, but her father was the one standing there, a big clue that he hadn't thought this through. And then her brothers appeared behind Alan in the doorway. Justin had met them at their mother's birthday party, the night Emma had revealed her identity.

Kane, the youngest and the guy who'd packed her suitcase, stood directly behind their father and was about an inch taller. Middle brother, Pierce, was to the left. His hair was a shade darker than the other two and his light blue eyes had a challenge in them. This wasn't the time to let him know there was a procedure that could minimize the scar on his chin.

Rounding out the foursome was Zach, the oldest. He had brown eyes like Emma and his mother, but there wasn't an ounce of warmth in them. He was taller and broader through the shoulders than the other three, a rugged man who obviously worked hard.

The family was running interference for Emma and that was not part of his plan.

"Nice to see you all again."

"What do you want, Justin?" Alan did the talking, but the other three listened intently.

"I'm here to talk to Emma."

"Why?" Zach wanted to know.

"It's between the two of us."

Alan shook his head. "She's not alone anymore. Whatever is on your mind, you can say it in front of her family."

"Isn't that for her to decide?" Justin was pretty sure she wouldn't want their personal details made public. He sure didn't, and this inquisition was starting to tick him off. "Will you tell her I'm here to speak with her? Please."

"I'm not sure she even wants to see you." It was strange, but Kane's expression had just a touch of empathy. His voice wasn't quite as dangerous as her father's and oldest brother's. "According to what she told me, she can't be your live-in nanny anymore."

"That sounds final to me," Zach commented.

Pierce moved slightly closer to his father, making the four men a solid, united front. "She knows her own mind."

"And you're aware of this how?" Justin said. "You've known her for what? Thirty seconds?"

Alan's mouth pulled tight for a moment. "She's my daughter. A father has an instinct about his child and she's a strong, resilient woman. No one is going to push her around."

Anger rolled through Justin at the thought of anyone doing that to Emma. He blew out a long breath and said, "I'm not a bully."

"She never said you were." Kane rubbed a big hand

across his neck. "You've got your reasons for not being all in for whatever it is between the two of you. All of us—Pierce, Zach and me—we've all been where you are. But when it's over, it's over."

"Did she say it was over?" Justin rejected that with everything he had. It couldn't be over. The idea of her not being in his life was what had pushed him into the stupid things he'd said.

"What part of 'she can't be your nanny anymore' did you not understand?" Zach didn't exactly move forward but seemed to block his way more aggressively. "Maybe it's time for you to move on, Doctor."

"When Emma said what she said, there were things she didn't know about." That was all he was prepared to say. He met Alan's gaze because the man was her father and deserved the respect.

"What are your intentions toward my daughter?"

This was starting to feel like the Old West and any second he expected them to pull six-guns. Justin was pretty sure not many fathers in Beverly Hills asked that question. She was an adult, a smart, beautiful woman who could take care of herself. The reality was that *he* wanted to take care of her. Those angry words were a nanosecond from coming out of his mouth, when thoughts of Kyle popped into his mind.

If anyone hurt his son, Justin would be acting like the Crawfords. He owed her father the courtesy of reassurance that there was no way he would hurt or dishonor Emma.

"I already asked her to marry me."

"That's true," Kane confirmed. "She told Mom and me this morning."

"But she obviously said no." Pierce looked at his brothers. "So, I don't get why he's here."

"Married once," Kane said. "Wasn't good."

Zach nodded. "So, he's got reasons. Understood. But the question was asked and answered, so it doesn't seem like there's more to say."

Justin wasn't sure what bugged him more—the fact they wouldn't let him pass or that they talked as if he wasn't even there. "Trust me. There's a lot more."

"What?" Alan demanded.

"Look—" His reserves of patience were nearly gone. He was ready to break through this defensive line, but common sense stopped him. Alan was older, but his sons were in their prime. It was four to one, not good odds. "She obviously talked to you about what happened between us. When I've said my piece, if Emma wants you to know, she'll tell you."

Alan stared him down. "You hurt her once already in the last twenty-four hours. When she was stolen from me as a baby, the hardest thing was not being able to protect my little girl. I've got her back now and it's my intention to make sure no harm comes to her ever again and that includes you. Unless there's something you can say to convince me that she won't be hurt, you're not getting through us."

The other three men nodded and Justin knew they were determined. So was he. The need to see Emma was driving him crazy.

"All right." He looked from one man to the next then settled his gaze on Alan. "I think I love her."

"You think?" The other man stared at him for several moments, his eyes narrowing as the seconds ticked by. "Come back when you're sure."

Then the door slammed in his face.

Justin blinked at the solid wood. He wouldn't have been more shocked if Alan had punched him. Or pulled out a six-shooter.

Emma heard the door slam as she walked downstairs holding a magazine. An actual book would have required too much concentration. At least the magazine had pictures. Every time she tried to read a story with a plot, her mind wandered back to her last conversation with Justin. She wanted a do-over more than almost anything she could think of.

She reached the bottom of the stairs where her father and brothers were gathered just inside the door. All four of them were looking at her funny.

"I heard the doorbell a few minutes ago. Who was it?" she asked.

The four men exchanged what could only be described as guilty glances. Boys got bigger and became men, but they never outgrew the look they wore after doing something naughty.

She walked past each of them like a general inspecting the troops. "What's going on?"

"Nothing." Kane rocked back on his heels.

"Why don't I believe you?" She stood in front of Zach, a big, handsome man who would make any woman he cared for feel safe and protected. And she got the feeling that somehow he was protecting her. She appreciated the effort, but her curiosity was really humming now. "What about you? Want to tell me what's going on?"

"Why would you think anything is?" He shifted his feet on the wood floor and squirmed just a little. It was proof that the bigger they were, the harder they fell.

"Because you responded to a question with a question and didn't really answer what I asked. In nanny school I learned that's a classic avoidance technique."

"You went to nanny school?" Pierce asked. "Is that like Mary Poppins University?"

She moved in front of him and couldn't help thinking

she had the hunkiest brothers on the planet. They got even cuter when put on the spot. Why was it none of them were married, engaged or currently dating? That was a question for another day. Right now there was a conspiracy in progress and she would get to the bottom of it.

"The three of you are covering for each other."

"What makes you think that?" Kane did his level best to look innocent and failed completely.

"I know so because Pierce just created a diversion. And, for the record, it didn't work. But obviously someone was about to break and confess." She looked at her father. "You'll tell me the truth, right, Dad?"

"Honey—" One word in a tone that said, don't make me do that.

"I know parents walk a fine line in terms of telling the truth, what with the Tooth Fairy, Easter Bunny and Santa Claus. Technically, letting kids believe mythical characters are real is lying. But when that kid grows up, she can handle the truth. I'm all grown up. Now, who was at the door?"

Alan looked at his sons and shrugged. "She's just like her mother."

"I noticed," Zach said. "But you're stronger than this. Don't give in, Dad."

"I don't know how she knows something is up, but she does. And, like her mother, I suspect she won't let go of this until she gets what she wants."

"Dad, you're stalling," she said.

"Yes, I am," he admitted. Then his face softened. "Justin stopped by."

Emma didn't know why that surprised her. Maybe because he'd been so abrupt and distant on the phone earlier. "What did he say?"

"He wanted to talk to you."

"So, where is he?" She glanced around and could see

into the living room and dining room from this vantage point. She was about to go to the kitchen when it sank in that her father had used the past tense. Her gaze touched on each of her brothers. "No one let me know he was here."

"And there's a good reason for that." Kane looked at his oldest brother. "Tell her what it is, Zach."

His expression said he was very unhappy to have been put on the spot, but Zach squared his broad shoulders. "We wanted to make sure you weren't hurt."

"And just how do you propose to do that?"

"Dad asked him what his intentions are." Pierce obviously was aware that the front line had been breached and was singing like a canary.

Emma stared at her father. "Tell me you didn't really do that."

"I certainly did." He slid his fingertips into the pockets of his jeans. "And I'd do it again. For my sons, too, if it ever becomes necessary."

That was heartwarming and annoying in equal parts. She was going to hate herself, but had to ask. "What did he say?"

"At first nothing, but he could see we wouldn't back down." Zach looked extraordinarily pleased at standing their ground.

"At first? That means he said something eventually and I'd really like to know what it was." This mattered so much and her heart was pounding.

"I'll tell you, honey, but first I have a question." Her father's expression was half tender, half fiercely protective. "How do you feel about him?"

"Mom didn't tell you?" Obviously the female members of the Crawford family could keep things to themselves better than the men. But there was no reason to keep her feelings a secret. On some level they already knew. "I love him, Dad."

"You're sure?"

"Positive," she said.

"Then we screwed up, boys." He glanced at each of his sons.

"Dad was the one who shut the door in his face," Kane said when she looked at him.

"Why would you do that?" she demanded.

"I told him that he wasn't getting past us unless he could convince me that he wouldn't hurt my little girl."

"So he said nothing." Since he couldn't love her, there wasn't anything he could say. The hurt of it smacked her again.

"Not exactly." Her father rubbed his palm over the back of his neck. "He said that he thinks he loves you."

"Really?" Thinking he did was better than being positive he didn't.

"It was great, sis," Kane said. "Dad told him to come back when he was sure and shut the door in his face. You should have seen it."

She wished she had because she could have stopped it. If she had, her heart wouldn't be breaking now. Just to think he loved her was a giant step for Justin. They could have talked about this. Now...

Emma wasn't sure whether to be grateful for the family support or upset that they'd chased off the only man she would ever love. The choice was made when a single tear slid down her cheek.

"Oh, baby...don't cry."

Her father looked as if he would rather cut off his right arm than see her shedding tears. And her brothers were showing a similar tendency.

"He didn't leave that long ago," Zach said. "I'll go get him."

"I'm coming, too," Pierce chimed in.

"They might need help. Three is better than one. Don't worry, sis. We'll bring him back so you can talk to him," Kane assured her.

She shook her head. "If he discouraged so easily, there's not really anything to say—"

A sudden knock on the door beside them startled everyone and they froze. Emma recovered first because she had a pretty good idea who was there.

"I'll get it," she said.

"Let me handle this." Alan was closer and blocked the way as he opened the door.

Emma couldn't see over her father's shoulder but recognized Justin's voice.

"Alan— Mr. Crawford— Sir," he said. "I'm not leaving until you let me see her."

"Okay, son."

When her father stepped aside, she was face-to-face with Justin. She heard footsteps on the stairs and her mother's voice asking what was going on. All the Crawfords were present and accounted for.

Then Emma tuned them out and focused on Justin. "Hi."

He started to reach for her then let his hand fall to his side. "Emma—"

She studied his handsome face, the tired gray eyes and haggard expression. "You look terrible."

"That's what Camille said." One corner of his mouth curved up. "She and Ben are watching Kyle. Just so you know."

"How is he?"

"He misses you."

"I miss him, too." Moisture blurred her eyes again, but this time she battled it back, refusing to let him see. "Why are you here?"

Justin looked at the men behind her and pressed his lips tightly together. "To bring you home."

Nothing about loving her. "Why should I believe you're not just trying to keep your nanny?"

"I'm not a liar like the man who cheated on you." He moved close enough for her to feel the heat from his body. "But it was a lie of omission when I used the wrong L-word. The truth is that I don't just want you in my life, I want to make a life with you. I want more children with you. To spend holidays together."

"He looks sincere," Kane said behind her. Someone that sounded like her mother shushed him. "Just saying maybe you should cut him some slack."

"I don't deserve it," he said. "But if you do agree to come back, this probably won't be the last time we hit a speed bump. I don't understand why, but I want that, too. I want to laugh and fight and make up." He was looking at her father, his expression saying exactly how he planned on making up and didn't care what any of them thought about that.

"Pretend they aren't there," she told him.

"Kind of hard." His expression turned wry. "But I don't care who hears. I drew a line in the sand because I was afraid to cross it and get personal. It was a stupid stand to take. My only excuse is that I was attracted to you from the first time I saw you. And I started falling for you when I could see how much you cared about your family. You were more worried about what was best for them than you were for yourself. I've never met a more beautiful, self-less woman."

"Is anyone writing this stuff down?" Pierce asked and was shushed by his mother.

"I'm in love with you," Justin said, then nodded at her father. "I don't think it. I'm absolutely certain. Give me a chance to ask you to marry me. I swear it will be a proper proposal and I'll do it right this time."

"For goodness' sake, Emma—" That was her mother's voice. "Say yes and put the poor man out of his misery."

"Not unless you love me," he cautioned.

"I feel as if I've said it to everyone *except* the man who matters most." She threw herself into his arms. "I love you so much, Justin. More than anything, I want to marry you. There's no need to ask again because what you just said felt so incredibly right. It was truth straight from your heart. Being with you and Kyle feels right, too. I love that little boy as if he were my own. I want to be a mother to him."

"I know you do." He buried his face in her hair. "Thank God I didn't mess this up."

The sound of applause, shrill whistling and very loud cheering made her smile. "I think that means you don't have to ask my father for permission."

"That's a relief. He drives a hard bargain." There was laughter in his voice. "I might have to give up my first-born for his little girl."

"Take good care of her, son."

"Yes, sir. I plan to." Then he looked into her eyes. "I know you've just started to get used to the last name Craw-ford, but if it's okay with you and your family, I'd like to change it to Flint as soon as possible."

"That works for me." She glanced over her shoulder and saw her mother, father and three brothers alternately nod-ding and giving thumbs-up. She'd missed so much with them but was incredibly thankful that her family was there to see the beginning of the rest of her life with the man she loved. "Looks like it's unanimous."

Emma snuggled into Justin and smiled. She'd come to Blackwater Lake looking for her family, but it never crossed her mind that she would find the man of her dreams, too.

Now she had it all—family and forever.

* * * * *

A sneaky peek at next month...

Cherish™

ROMANCE TO MELT THE HEART EVERY TIME

My wish list for next month's titles...

In stores from 21st March 2014:

☐ Her Soldier Protector — Soraya Lane

& In a Cowboy's Arms — Rebecca Winters

☐ A House Full of Fortunes! — Judy Duarte

& Celebration's Baby — Nancy Robards Thompson

In stores from 4th April 2014:

☐ Behind the Film Star's Smile — Kate Hardy

& The Return of Mrs Jones — Jessica Gilmore

☐ Stolen Kiss From a Prince — Teresa Carpenter

& One Night with the Boss — Teresa Southwick

Available at WHSmith, Tesco, Asda, Eason, Amazon and Apple

Just can't wait?

Visit us Online

You can buy our books online a month before they hit the shops! **www.millsandboon.co.uk**

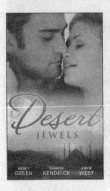
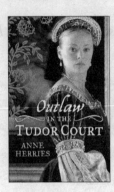

Bella Andre is back...

The US sensation Bella Andre is back with two brand-new
titles featuring the one and only Sullivan family.
Don't miss out on the latest from this
incredible author.

Now available from:

www.millsandboon.co.uk

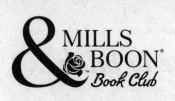 

Discover more romance at

www.millsandboon.co.uk

- ♥ WIN great prizes in our exclusive competitions

- ♥ BUY new titles before they hit the shops

- ♥ BROWSE new books and REVIEW your favourites

- ♥ SAVE on new books with the Mills & Boon® Bookclub™

- ♥ DISCOVER new authors

PLUS, to chat about your favourite reads, get the latest news and find special offers:

- Find us on facebook.com/millsandboon

- Follow us on twitter.com/millsandboonuk

- ♥ Sign up to our newsletter at millsandboon.co.uk